DANGEROUS ILLUSIONS

Books by Irene Hannon

Heroes of Quantico

Against All Odds
An Eye for an Eye
In Harm's Way

Guardians of Justice

Fatal Judgment
Deadly Pursuit
Lethal Legacy

Private Justice

Vanished
Trapped
Deceived

Men of Valor

Buried Secrets
Thin Ice
Tangled Webs

Code of Honor

Dangerous Illusions

That Certain Summer
One Perfect Spring
Hope Harbor
Sea Rose Lane
Sandpiper Cove

DANGEROUS ILLUSIONS

IRENE HANNON

Revell

a division of Baker Publishing Group
Grand Rapids, Michigan

© 2017 by Irene Hannon

Published by Revell
a division of Baker Publishing Group
P.O. Box 6287, Grand Rapids, MI 49516-6287
www.revellbooks.com

Printed in the United States of America

Library of Congress Cataloging-in-Publication Data
Names: Hannon, Irene, author.
Title: Dangerous illusions / Irene Hannon.
Description: Grand Rapids, MI : Published by Revell, a division of Baker Publishing Group, [2017] | Series: Code of honor ; #1
Identifiers: LCCN 2017020778| ISBN 9780800727673 (paper) | ISBN 9780800727765 (print on demand)
Subjects: | GSAFD: Mystery fiction. | Christian fiction.
Classification: LCC PS3558.A4793 D36 2017 | DDC 813/.54—dc23
LC record available at https://lccn.loc.gov/2017020778

This book is a work of fiction. Names, characters, places, and incidents are the product of the author's imagination or are used fictitiously.

17 18 19 20 21 22 23   7 6 5 4 3 2 1

To my husband Tom—
With deepest gratitude for all you take on
so I have the time and energy to write.
Three dot.
Always.

PROLOGUE

"Hello, Matt. Long time no see."

As the words slithered through the clammy night air, a jagged shaft of lightning illuminated the speaker's face for one brief instant.

But Matt Parker didn't need a visual cue to identify the man on the other side of his front door.

The glib voice was all too familiar.

Fingers clutching the doorknob, he stared at the shadowy figure as shock thrummed through his nerve endings. In the background, another eruption of electricity slashed across the inky sky. A sharp crack of thunder shook the walls of the house. Rain pummeled the tulips rimming the porch, beating their heads into submission.

Hollywood couldn't have staged a more dramatic—or ominous—reunion.

"Aren't you going to ask me in?"

When the man he loathed flashed the same smug smile he'd worn during their last conversation five years ago, Matt attempted to slam the door.

"Not so fast." A foot shot between the door and the jamb. "I've come a long way to see you."

"You wasted your time." The anger he thought he'd tamed churned anew in his gut.

"I never waste my time."

"Get your foot out of my door." He ground out the words through clenched teeth, knuckles whitening on the doorframe.

"We need to talk."

"I have nothing to say to you."

"I have some things to say to you."

"I'm not interested in hearing them. I told you five years ago—stay out of my life."

"I intended to. But I have a problem."

"Tough." A pair of headlights swung onto the long driveway that led to the house he'd called home for the past three years. "My pizza's here. Don't expect me to share." He kicked the foot away from the jamb.

Before he could shove the door closed, however, the interloper shouldered through. "I didn't come for pizza."

"Get out of my house." Fury nipped at every syllable as he grabbed the other man's arm.

"I don't plan to complicate your life for long, so back off and deal with the pizza guy." He yanked free and strolled toward the kitchen.

As the car lights swept across the front of the house, Matt muttered an obscenity—but remained by the door. Finding a pizza place willing to deliver to his wooded property on the outskirts of St. Louis had been tough, and he wasn't about to jeopardize their arrangement by ignoring a delivery on a night like this.

But once he took possession of the dinner he no longer wanted, the man in his kitchen was getting a swift kick out the door.

Literally, if that's what it took.

An older-model Sentra stopped in the drive, engine idling. The lanky kid who often delivered on Saturday nights bounded up the stone walkway through the driving rain and leaped onto the porch, juggling an insulated container.

"Hey, Mr. Parker." He cringed as a shaft of lightning pierced the sky, followed by another bone-jarring crack of thunder. "I thought April was supposed to bring showers, not monsoons."

Matt tried to conjure up a smile for the high schooler with the happy-go-lucky grin.

Failed.

"Thanks for coming out on a night like this." The charge for the pizza was already on his credit card, but he fished out a generous tip.

"It beats doing homework." The teen's eyes widened as he pulled the pizza out of the carrier and gaped at the bill Matt extended. "Are you sure about this? I mean . . . that's a lot of money."

"Put it toward your college fund. And be careful driving tonight."

"I will. Thanks a lot—and enjoy the pizza."

Not likely.

He waited until the kid was back behind the wheel, then closed the door and stalked to the kitchen.

His visitor had tossed his slicker over a chair and was sipping a can of pilfered soda when he entered. Water pooled on the tile below the garment, the puddle widening with every drip.

"I told you once to leave." He slammed the pizza onto the counter. "You have thirty seconds to clear out."

"And if I don't?" With infuriating nonchalance, the man settled on a stool at the island. "Is 911 in your plans?"

Matt clamped his jaw shut, silently cursing the obnoxious piece of scum across from him.

"I didn't think so. I've been watching you, Matt. You lead a quiet, off-the-grid life. I doubt you'd want to call attention to yourself by filing a police report . . . or dredging up our past."

The very thought of all that garbage seeing the light of day sent a cold shiver snaking down his spine.

But the man's first comment scared him more.

"What do you mean, you've been watching me?" Although Matt tried to contain his alarm, tension nipped at his words.

"I mean exactly what I said. I've been watching you. Observing. Studying." He started to lift the lid on the pizza. "Trish is pretty. I commend you on your excellent taste."

Matt shoved the box out of his visitor's reach, his blood chilling. "Leave Trish out of this."

"Hey . . . can't a man notice a pretty woman? You did. The two of you seemed very cozy at lunch last week."

Matt's stomach heaved. "Why have you been watching me?"

"I need your help."

"You expect me to help you?" Matt barked out a harsh laugh. "What a joke."

"I'm dead serious."

"You're also delusional. I wouldn't lift a finger on your behalf if my life depended on it."

A muscle twitched in the other man's cheek. "Too bad. Refusing isn't an option. But once you give me the help I need, you'll never see me again. Guaranteed."

"Forgive me if I have trust issues." He made no attempt to hide his sarcasm. "As for that option crack—you can't force me to help you. I want no part of your problems. If you've dug yourself into another hole, you can dig yourself out."

"That's what I'm doing. It's why I'm here." He finished off his soda and set the can on the counter. "To tell you the truth, I'd rather not involve you. It's too messy. But there's no other way."

"You *are* delusional." Matt planted his palms on the counter and leaned toward the man who was fouling the air in his house. "Read my lips. I said forget it. Now get out of here."

As a shudder of thunder rumbled through the walls, the lights flickered. Steadied.

His visitor regarded him, an odd mixture of emotions in his eyes. At last he stood. "Sorry, Matt. You *are* going to help me. Here's how."

With the pizza cooling between them and the aroma of spicy tomato sauce turning his stomach, Matt's heart stalled as the man he'd never wanted to see revealed his plan.

And as the seconds ticked by . . . as Matt stared across the counter at this specter from his past . . . as the rain pounded against the roof and the wind howled . . . one thing became terrifyingly clear.

The new life he'd created was over.

1

At the peal of the doorbell, Trish Bailey looked up from the lesson plan she was preparing.

"Matt's here." Her mother adjusted the afghan thrown over her legs.

"Punctual, as usual."

"One of his many virtues."

Here we go again.

Expelling a breath, Trish set her paperwork on the sofa beside her and stood. "Do you want to meet with him in the kitchen?"

"Yes. He's handsome too."

Best to ignore that as well.

She moved toward the door, stopping to rest a hand on her mom's shoulder as she passed the wheelchair. "Can I get you anything while I'm up?"

"No. I'm fine."

Hardly. But Eileen Coulter had never been a complainer—before the car accident two years ago, or since.

She gave her mother's arm a gentle squeeze. "I'll be right back."

"After we finish, nap for me. Matt might stay for cake."

13

Although the words were stroke-garbled, the meaning was clear. Her mom wanted her to stop mourning and start living again—a message the older woman had been communicating with increasing frequency over the past few weeks.

"We'll see."

"Means no."

"It means maybe." Without giving her mother an opportunity to press the issue, she crossed the living room to the foyer. Her parents' accountant *was* nice . . . and she'd enjoyed the lunch he'd suggested a couple of weeks ago . . . but she was in no hurry to dip her toes back into romance.

Besides, much as she liked Matt, there was zero zing. Not like there'd been with John from the first moment they'd met.

But perhaps that kind of instant attraction, that immediate feeling of simpatico, only came along once in a lifetime.

The bell rang again, and she picked up her pace—and propped up her spirits. She wasn't going to sink back into the morass of self-pity she'd languished in for the first few months after the accident. If her mother, who'd suffered far more, could carry on with a cheery spirit, she would too.

Trish straightened her shoulders, tugged the hem of her tunic down over her leggings, and summoned up a smile of welcome.

But as she pulled open the door, her mouth flattened.

Mercy!

The tall, sandy-haired man on the other side had a stitched gash on his temple, a purple-hued bruise on his forehead, and one wrist encased in a removable brace.

"Matt! What on earth happened?"

He grimaced. "Car accident. I skidded on wet pavement last Sunday going around a curve and had a close encounter with a tree. That's why I emailed your mom and asked if we could postpone our meeting until today. Sorry to infringe on your Saturday."

"We didn't have anything else planned. Come in." She ushered him into the foyer. "Are you certain you're up to this?"

"Yes. The cut and sprained wrist are healing, and despite some memory lapses and headaches from the concussion, my ability to count beans is unaffected." He gave her a smile that seemed strained. "To be honest, you look more tired than I do. Everything okay?"

"Fine. Busy."

"You take on too much."

"I have obligations."

"More of them could be delegated. You need some downtime. You've been dealing with a lot of heavy stuff for two years, and long-term stress can take a toll."

No kidding.

But her stress level was private territory, even if their lunch date had introduced a more personal element to their relationship.

"I want to be here for Mom as much as I can." Her reply came out sharper than intended, and she moderated her tone. "Give me a sec to fill her in on your accident. Otherwise it might be too much of a shock. Why don't you meet us in the kitchen?"

To her relief, he let the personal subject matter drop.

After rejoining her mother in the living room and sharing the news, she pushed the chair toward the back of the house.

"Matt." Her mother held out her functional left hand as Trish wheeled her into the kitchen. "So sorry."

He grasped her fingers. "I'll survive. You're looking well."

"Doing fine."

"Glad to hear it. Are you ready to review some numbers?"

"Yes. I read the reports you emailed."

"Any questions?" He pulled his laptop out of the case and booted it up.

"No. Very thorough."

"Then this shouldn't take long. Trish . . . are you going to sit in?"

"Yes." Her mother spoke for her. "Like always."

"Right." He touched his forehead gingerly. "This is causing a few memory glitches. I'll ask your pardon in advance if I have any other lapses."

"No worries." Her mother patted his arm.

Resigned, Trish scooted a chair down to the end of the table so she could see the screen. Since the charitable foundation her parents had set up six years ago would be hers to oversee someday, she did need to stay up to speed on the workings.

However . . . despite her attempt to pay close attention, ten minutes in, she lost interest as Matt explained the tax implications of a donation to a charity her mother favored. Her mind drifted back to the lesson plan for Monday's fifth-grade art class, the supplies she needed to pick up for Tuesday's mixed media class, the field trip she wanted to arrange to the exhibit at . . .

"I think we lost Trish a while back."

She zoned back in, her cheeks warming at Matt's amused comment. "Sorry."

"Numbers and Trish." Her mother shook her head, one side of her mouth curving up indulgently. "No interest. But superb teacher—and daughter."

"Well, you have me to deal with the numbers." Matt winked and closed his computer.

"Providential." Mom slid her a glance and yawned. "Nap time."

When Trish rose, Matt did too.

"I can see myself out." He slid the laptop into its case.

"No. Cake." Her mother motioned toward the two-layer chocolate confection on the counter.

"Um . . . I still have to count your medicine for the week, Mom—and finish my lesson plans."

"Cake won't take long."

She waited, hoping Matt would pick up on her lack of enthusiasm and decline to stay.

He didn't.

Drat.

All she could do was wolf down her cake and hustle him out the door fast.

"If you can spare a few minutes, you're welcome to stay and have a piece." The invitation came out more grudging than gracious, and one of her mother's eyebrows rose.

Matt didn't seem to notice.

"Thank you. I'd like that." He retook his seat.

"Coffee." Her mother gestured toward the pot on the counter, ignoring the disgruntled look Trish shot her.

"I'll put some on. It can brew while I take you to your room."

She moved to the counter, paying more attention to the conversation behind her than the rote task. Only once did her mom edge into personal territory, suggesting that if Matt wasn't up to cooking yet after his accident, he might want to join them for one of her daughter's delicious meals some night this week.

Trish rolled her eyes and swung around. She and her mom needed to have a long talk. Soon. "We'll have to see if we can find a night that works. I've got some meetings after school this week, so we'll be having more takeout than usual. Ready, Mom?"

Without waiting for a reply, she pulled her mother's chair back from the table and wheeled her down the hall.

Once in the bedroom, her mom waved away Trish's attempt to introduce the subject of matchmaking, claiming she was too tired for discussion.

Trish let it ride—for now. However, the delay tactic would buy her mother no more than a brief reprieve.

When Trish returned to the kitchen, Matt stood and picked

up his laptop. "I think I'll pass on the cake, if you don't mind. My head's beginning to throb."

Yes!

Perhaps her lukewarm response to her mom's suggestion had finally sunk in.

Whatever the reason for his quicker-than-expected departure, however, she wasn't going to argue. "It might not be a bad idea to go home and lie down for a while."

"I agree."

He followed her to the foyer, said a perfunctory good-bye, and strode down the front walk without turning around.

Not his usual, personable style.

But a concussion and bad headache could ruin anyone's disposition.

She wandered back to the kitchen to deal with the coffee they wouldn't need . . . and found a pot of hot water instead of fresh-brewed java. The filter basket with ground coffee was still beside the coffeemaker.

Frowning, she propped a hand on her hip. Had she been so distracted by the conversation between her mother and Matt that she'd forgotten to slide it into position?

Weird—but what other explanation could there be?

She emptied the pot of water and flipped off the switch on the coffeemaker. Her lesson plans were waiting in the living room . . . but as long as she was in the kitchen, why not count her mom's pills?

As she picked up the weekly pill organizer and box holding all the bottles of medication from their usual place at the end of the counter, Matt's suggestion to delegate some of her obligations replayed through her mind. He did have a point. The aides who came during the week could count out pills . . . but she felt more comfortable handling the job herself until her mom regained full use of her right hand—if she ever did.

Sighing, she sat at the table and went through the routine of opening bottles, shaking out pills, splitting those that needed to be cut in half with the pill cutter, and dropping them in the correct time slots for each day of the week. Despite the diligent efforts of the physical therapist, her mother had shown little measurable progress in weeks. It was very possible Eileen Coulter would never again use her sewing machine or whip up a batch of her famous chocolate mint cakes or work in the gardens she loved.

Trish's vision misted, and she fumbled a capsule. It skidded across the glass-topped table, but she managed to snatch it before it disappeared over the edge.

Wayward pill in hand, she examined the subtle tremors running through her fingers. Sleepless nights, stress, and grief did take a toll, as Matt had noted.

Perhaps he was right about letting go of some of the more mundane tasks. After all, her mother could afford to bring in additional paid help. Had offered to on multiple occasions.

Yet being busy had its benefits. If you were occupied every minute of the day, you didn't have a chance to dwell on the past—or the future. Depressing thoughts could only worm their way in during the middle-of-the-night hours when sleep was elusive.

She deposited the pill in its slot and popped the lid of another prescription container. On the plus side, life was settling into a routine of sorts—and routine was healing. Bit by bit, day by day, the darkness was dissipating. A new normal was taking shape. Each week was better . . . easier . . . less bleak . . . than the one before.

And that trend would continue.

It had to.

Because how could things get any worse?

■ ■ ■ ■ ■

Craig Elliott took a sip of his Scotch and thumbed the remote, paying scant attention to the succession of images strobing across Matt's TV screen.

Today had been productive.

Matt had played his role well, done the necessary reconnaissance, laid the groundwork for what was to come—and neither Trish nor her mother were the wiser.

It was an ingenious plan.

He downed another gulp of liquor, wincing. The inexpensive brand wasn't as smooth as the high-end Johnnie Walker Blue Blended he preferred, but it would do until he had more funds. And if the plan he'd revised after getting the lay of the land here played out as he expected, the coffers would begin filling soon.

But timing—and patience—were everything. Rushing his scheme would raise suspicions and draw too much attention.

Not a smart move in his situation.

He opted for a show with supernatural overtones, tossed the remote onto the table beside his chair, and surveyed his surroundings. Hardly plush—but he could upgrade, once he had more cash flow. The money would come. It always did, if you knew how to work the system.

Not that his previous efforts had been flawless, of course. If they had been, he wouldn't be stuck in this Midwest town whose biggest claim to fame was a giant silver version of the McDonald's arch. He'd be living the good life in New York or LA. Maybe even Paris.

But greed and haste had brought him down.

At least he'd learned his lesson. This go-round, he was in for the long haul. That's why he'd spent weeks doing his homework. Preparing. Learning everything he could about Matt's life. It was why he'd laid low the past week, getting up to speed on intel he hadn't had access to prior to his visit with Matt.

Smirking, he downed the dregs of his drink. The man's

expression when he'd opened the door last Saturday had been priceless.

Too bad the rest of the evening hadn't been as amusing.

His lips curled in distaste. After he'd revealed his plan, the situation had become uncomfortable. Painful, even. But he'd pushed through, done what he had to do, gotten what he wanted.

And he'd continue to do what had to be done going forward. He'd charted his course, and there was no going back.

A sudden flash on the TV screen drew his attention. One of the characters had morphed from human to . . . who knew what? Someone—or something—with superhuman abilities and power.

Craig swirled the ice in his glass as the action on the screen unfolded. Entertaining, if unrealistic. Absent extraordinary powers, humans had to have a superior intellect and more ingenuity than their superhero counterparts to win in the real world.

Fortunately, he had both—as Matt had discovered last Saturday.

Craig smiled again and set the glass beside him. The audacity . . . and sheer brilliance . . . of the endeavor had stunned the other man.

But you couldn't win big if you didn't think big.

And now the stage was set. All he had to do was follow through. Trish and her mother would continue to trust Matt—and on the surface, he would continue to be their friend.

Until that illusion was no longer needed.

He tapped a finger on the arm of the chair. The timing of that depended on Trish, and she'd turned out to be a bit of a wild card. Apparently she wasn't as interested in Matt as he'd surmised. That might change with more aggressive wooing . . . but if it didn't, his contingency plan was solid.

Whichever direction he took, the end result would be the same: one day soon, all his troubles would be history.

Along with anyone who got in his way.

2

The long, awkward evening was finally over.

Exhaling, Trish felt around in her purse for her keys as Matt walked her to the door. The dinner he'd shared at the house last week—at her mother's invitation—had been tolerable, thanks to Mom's presence. Tonight's movie . . . different story. Agreeable as Matt was, hard as he'd tried to generate some heat, there wasn't a glimmer of spark. Whether that was due to lack of chemistry or to her lingering, heart-numbing grief, Trish had no idea.

But whatever the reason, there would be no more dates. She'd just have to convince her mother that any guilt she felt about usurping her daughter's time was misplaced. That Trish's social life was nonexistent by choice, not because she felt compelled to spend every free minute at her mom's beck and call.

"Are you as parched as I am from that popcorn?"

At Matt's not-so-subtle ploy to wrangle an invitation to come in, she muffled a groan. He must still be interested in her despite this dud of an evening she did *not* want to extend.

On the other hand, maybe she *should* ask him in—and set

him straight as diplomatically as she could before he got too carried away.

She sighed. It wouldn't be the most pleasant end to the evening, but putting off hard stuff never made dealing with it any easier.

"Would you like a soda or some coffee?"

"Either would be fine. Thanks." He flashed her a smile, reached for her hand, and gave it a squeeze.

Great.

She freed her fingers on the pretense of opening the door and led the way inside. "Have a seat in the living room while I check on Mom."

Without waiting for a response, Trish ditched her purse and sweater on a chair in the foyer and fled into the hall.

Once she was out of Matt's sight, she paused to psyche herself up for the letdown she was about to deliver . . . as well as the consequences. The comfortable, relaxed relationship the two of them had enjoyed over the past year would be hard, if not impossible, to recapture. That's what happened when romance entered the picture—particularly if one of the parties wasn't feeling the love.

In truth, though, Matt had been . . . different, somehow . . . since the accident. There was a new, subtle tension in him. A disconcerting undercurrent of nervous energy. And his eyes had changed too. The curious, lingering hurt that had always lurked in their depths was gone. Now they seemed sharper . . . cooler . . . more calculating.

Or was she just paying more attention to nuances now that he was taking a personal interest in her?

No matter. After tonight, their relationship would be strictly business. She'd be pleasant, courteous, professional—but nothing more.

If fate was kind, he'd take that news with grace.

Light peeked through her mom's cracked-open door as she approached, and Trish picked up her pace. Why was the lamp on? Her mother was always in bed by nine thirty, and it was almost eleven. Was she having a bad evening? And if so, why hadn't the aide called her before she'd left at ten, as instructed?

Quashing her annoyance, she eased the door open and slipped into the room. Outside help might be necessary on weekdays while she was teaching, but situations like this were one of the reasons she preferred taking care of her mother's needs herself at night and on weekends.

Soft light spilled onto the floral comforter covering the bed as Trish tiptoed over, feet silent on the plush carpet. Her mom was on her side, faced away from the door and the lamp, apparently asleep.

Her tension ebbed, and she let out an unsteady breath. She needed to get over her constant worry or she'd end up with high blood pressure and heart disease, like her mom.

At the bedside table, Trish leaned down to flip the lamp off. Paused as she spotted the cell phone lying on the comforter.

Why was it so close to her mother's fingers . . . as if she'd dropped it?

And why was her mom so . . . still?

Dread congealing in her belly, Trish laid her fingers over the motionless hand on the comforter.

It was cool.

Too cool.

Suffocating panic ballooned inside her.

"Mom." She touched her mother's thin shoulder as she choked out the word.

No response.

"Mom!" Panic spiked the pitch of her voice.

Still no response.

She tugged her gently, until she could see her face.

Her mother's eyes were open.

Sightless.

NO!

Trish scuttled back from the bed, chest heaving, as her mother rolled back onto her side.

NO! NO! NO! NO!

"Matt!" The desperate summons came out a mere whisper. As if her lungs had no air to support words.

She tried again. "Matt!"

This time anguish shrilled her call.

Footsteps pounded down the hall, and an instant later he was beside her.

"Trish—what's wrong?" He grasped her shoulders, searching her face.

She waved a hand toward the bed. Tried to speak. Resorted to another spastic flip of her hand.

Matt surveyed the motionless form, then released her and circled the bed.

After a brief hesitation on the other side, he leaned close and pressed his fingers against her mother's neck.

Several eternal beats ticked by. At last he straightened up, his troubled gaze meeting hers as he pulled out his own cell phone. While he punched in three numbers, he rejoined her and draped an arm around her shoulders.

Though he was inches away, Trish heard his side of the conversation as if it came from a great distance. His words sounded muffled while he explained the situation to the operator. Answered questions. Provided the requested information.

Only two phrases from the exchange registered clearly, echoing over and over in her brain.

She's not breathing. I couldn't find a pulse. She's not breathing. I couldn't find a pulse. She's not breathing. I couldn't find . . .

"Paramedics are on the way." Matt slid his phone back into his pocket.

She stared at the opaque button on the front of his dress shirt, trying to accept the truth.

It didn't matter when the paramedics arrived.

Her mom was gone.

She knew that even before the two-person crew swept into the bedroom a few minutes later with all their medical paraphernalia. Before the two police officers who'd arrived first had a quiet exchange with the technicians while they packed up the few items they'd taken from their kit. Before one of the officers joined them in the corner of the room where Matt had led her, out of the line of traffic.

"You're the daughter, correct?"

"Yes." Matt answered for her. "I told that to the 911 operator."

"I'm sorry, ma'am." The officer's demeanor was sympathetic. "The paramedics say she was gone before we arrived."

Trish choked back a sob at the heartbreaking finality of those words.

"I'd like to ask you a few questions. It might be more comfortable if we move to the living room."

"No." She crossed her arms in a rigid tuck against her chest. "I want to stay with m-my mom."

"Trish . . . the living room would be better." Matt touched her arm. "You need to sit down. You're shaking."

"I said I want to stay here."

At her back-off tone, a muscle in Matt's cheek clenched.

"Here is fine." The officer pulled out a notebook and pen, altering his position to block her view of the bed. "Why don't you both give me some basics? Name, address, contact information."

After they complied, he flipped a page and focused on her. "Tell me what happened tonight."

"Mom and I had dinner. Then Matt and I went to a m-movie."

"What time was that?"

"About seven thirty."

"Was your mother here alone for the rest of the evening?"

"Only after ten. There was a home-health aide with her most of the evening."

"I'll need her contact information."

Trish gave him the woman's name and the name of the service where she was employed.

"How old was your mother?"

Was.

Pressure built behind her eyes. "Sixty-f-five."

"Did she have health issues?"

"Yes." Trish told him about her heart condition, the injuries from the accident, the stroke. "But she was fine earlier. A little . . . cloudy . . . when she took her evening medication, but that can happen if she gets tired."

Matt touched her arm again, twin creases embedded in his brow. "Is there . . . do you think she could have taken the wrong dose of one of her medications?"

She frowned at the bizarre question. "No. I'm the one who counts the pills. She only takes what I give her."

"But she does take a lot of medicine, right? Ten, twelve different kinds every day?"

"Eleven."

"That's a lot of pills to juggle . . . and you *have* been kind of distracted lately."

Her breath hitched. "Do you . . . are you suggesting I made a mistake?"

"I only bring it up because you said she was kind of fuzzy. You've had a tough two years, Trish . . . and details can slip through the cracks if you're stressed. Like that burner you left on under the frying pan when I came to dinner last week."

At his gentle reminder, her heart stumbled. She couldn't deny that mistake. Nor the incident with the coffee filter the night he'd almost stayed for cake.

"And you thought we were supposed to go to the movie tonight at seven, not seven thirty."

A quiver of unease snaked through her as she grappled with his stomach-churning implication. "Even if I did miscount one of the pills, Mom would have caught it. You know how sharp she is."

"But didn't you tell me one of her doctors adjusted her medication a few days ago? Isn't it possible she might not have questioned a change? Especially if she was a little out of it tonight."

"Does anyone else live here, ma'am?" The officer appraised her, a glint of suspicion sparking in his irises.

"No." She tried to switch gears. To erase the dark doubts Matt had planted in her mind. "It's just been me and Mom for the past eighteen months, since she came home from rehab."

"Are there other family members you need to notify?"

"No."

"Anything you'd like to add, sir?"

Matt explained his connection to her mother.

"Got it." The officer closed his notebook. "If you folks will excuse me for a minute, I need to make a phone call."

Trish watched him walk across the room and confer in low tones with the other officer and the departing paramedics. Numbness was setting in, and she felt herself drifting away from the scene. Almost as if she was having an out-of-body experience.

The distance was welcome. Insulating. Comforting.

Until Matt intruded, pulling her back to the harsh reality.

"I'm sorry, Trish." He rested a hand on her shoulder.

Turning her back on the strangers in her mother's room,

she scrutinized him. "You don't really believe I miscounted the medicine, do you?"

If she was seeking reassurance, his carefully worded response gave her none.

"I know you always did your best to take care of your mother. And I know how much you loved her."

"She was all I had, Matt." Her voice broke, and she sucked in a ragged breath. "I did everything I could to be here for her, to help her recover. Losing her too is . . . unthinkable."

"I'm so sorry, Trish."

The trite platitude grated like chalk on an old-fashioned blackboard.

She hugged herself and backed away, gripping her arms tight. "You don't need to stay."

He did a double take. "I'm sorry, I—"

"Stop saying that!" At her hysteria-tinged rebuke, the low rumble of conversation across the room ceased. Out of the corner of her eye she saw the police officers and paramedics look toward her.

She lowered her volume. "Go home, Matt."

"I can't leave you alone in the middle of all this."

"Actually . . ." The police officer rejoined them. "I'm going to need both of you to leave. The medical examiner is on the way, along with a detective. The CSU won't be far behind."

"CSU." Trish knew the acronym from TV police shows. "Why is the Crime Scene Unit coming?"

"We call them for any sudden or suspicious death."

"Look . . . there's nothing suspicious here." Matt glared at the officer. "If anything did happen with the medication, it was a mistake. But her mom's been in poor health anyway, and she had a heart condition. This was probably due to natural causes."

"The medical examiner will determine that."

"You want me to leave the house?" Trish was still trying to absorb this latest curve.

"Until we release the scene. Sometime tomorrow morning, I imagine. If you'd like to pack a bag, one of us can accompany you while you do that."

"Why don't you stay at my place overnight? I have a spare bedroom." Matt edged closer.

She backed away. "No. I'll . . . I'll go to a hotel."

The officer pulled his phone off his belt and skimmed the screen. "I need to take this." He motioned to the uniformed woman across the room. "Officer Wilson will be happy to go with you while you pack a bag."

He walked away, speaking in low tones, and the woman took his place across from her.

They weren't letting her out of their sight.

They were treating this like it was a crime scene.

They were acting like she was a suspect.

This was surreal.

"Don't you think you're overreacting?" Matt echoed her thoughts, anger tightening his words. "This woman loved her mother. She's obviously in shock."

"We're following standard crime scene procedure, sir." The woman folded her arms.

"But this isn't a crime scene!"

The petite officer drew herself up to her full height. "You may be right—but until we're certain of that, we stick to protocol. Ma'am, I'd be happy to accompany you while you pack a bag."

"Isn't there somewhere in the house she could . . ."

"Let it go, Matt." Trish massaged her throbbing temple, her voice dull. "My room's across the hall."

She didn't look back toward her mom as the woman followed her out. Looking back wouldn't change a thing, as she'd learned over the past two years. All you could do was carry on and move forward.

Or shatter.

Until now, she'd managed to carry on.

But after tonight, option number two was a very real possibility.

3

Night shift stunk.

Smothering a yawn, Detective Colin Flynn hung a left and guided his Taurus down a street lined with high-end homes. You'd think after twelve years with the St. Louis County PD, a man would adjust to the rotating schedule.

Instead, night work got harder instead of easier—especially when you drew the shift that ended at four in the morning.

On the flip side, he wouldn't trade his gig with the Crimes Against Persons Bureau for any other job on earth. There were a lot of ways to make the world a better place, but this one fit him to a T.

Easing back on the gas pedal, he peered at the address of the house he was passing. He was getting close to the scene.

As he accelerated again, he did another sweep of his surroundings. Night and day from the seedy bar where he'd spent the past hour sorting through an assault and battery involving two drunks—one of whom had done some serious damage with a knife. For once, the witnesses had all told the same story. It had been a simple case for him, if not for the guys being hauled to the station. That stupid knife stunt had made one of them a felon and would haunt him for the rest of his life.

Some people sat on their brains.

Colin stopped in front of his destination—a gracious two-story colonial house with muted accent lighting. The kind of home designed to host black-tie cocktail parties and Norman Rockwell–type Thanksgiving dinners, with generations of a family gathered around a laden table.

Also the home of a suspicious death.

He set the brake, snagged his sport coat from the passenger seat, and strode toward the front door, passing a CSU van on the way. The neighborhood might be posh, but as he'd learned through the years, ugliness didn't have a zip code. Crime happened everywhere.

A young patrol officer met him at the door with the crime scene log, and he flashed his creds.

"Where's the action?" He scribbled his name and filled in the time.

"Make a left off the foyer. Last door on the right at the end of the hall."

"Is Meyers back there?" Talking to the responding officer was his first priority. Sarge had given him a topline briefing, but it was always better to hear directly from the person who'd been first on the scene.

"He's in the living room. On your right after you enter."

"Thanks."

Colin passed through an ornate wooden door, crossed a parquet floor, and stopped on the threshold of a great room that would hold his entire condo with space left over. On the far side, a sandy-haired, thirtysomething man perched on a side chair, elbows resting on the arms, hands clasped in front of him. One wrist was in a brace, and there was a healing gash on his forehead.

Meyers joined him.

"Sarge gave me the basics." Colin shifted away from the other occupant of the room and lowered his voice. "But I'd like to hear it from you. Is this the boyfriend?" He cocked his head toward the guy on the chair.

"Yeah. Matt Parker."

"What's with the injuries?"

"He said he was in a car accident three weeks ago. I checked. It's legit."

"Where's the daughter?"

"Packing a bag. Wilson is with her."

"What happened?"

He listened while Meyers repeated what Sarge had already told him. Straightforward, factual police report stuff minus conjecture or assumption.

"Okay. Now give me your take." Meyers had been on the street for two decades, and the people insights from that kind of experience were invaluable. "I want the stuff that wasn't in your report. Why did you think this might be a homicide?"

"I didn't, at the beginning." The officer rested one hand on his holster. "The deceased was in her midsixties and had a lot of health issues. There was no sign of forced entry or a struggle. At first glance, it appeared she died in her sleep. But the daughter dispenses her mother's pills—and apparently she's become forgetful."

"How do you know?"

"Parker mentioned it. That's when a little red flag started waving. I'm not suggesting it was murder, but I'm not certain the death was from natural causes, either. Since the daughter is the only heir, and this place"—he swept an arm around the house—"isn't too shabby, I'm assuming she stands to inherit a lot." He shrugged. "You get suspicious after you've been in this business a while."

"I hear you." Colin tipped his head toward Parker. "Keep

him here while I touch base with the crew in the bedroom and talk to the daughter."

"Will do."

Colin continued down the hall, stopping at the last door on the right. Lacey Stephens from the ME's office was conferring with Hank, the crime scene tech, as she stripped off a pair of latex gloves.

"You finished already?"

"Yep." Lacey brushed a tight, gray-streaked ebony curl off her forehead. "And before you ask . . . no, I didn't see anything suspicious. On the surface, it appears as if death could be due to natural causes. We'll have to wait for the autopsy and tox results for more definitive answers."

"What's your estimate on time of death?"

"Based on body temperature, absence of rigor, and state of lividity, I'm guessing two to three hours ago—pending lab results. Hank, let me know when you're done in here so we can remove the body."

The tech, who had gone back to taking photos, grunted.

Colin's lips quirked. With his gray flyaway hair and brusque manner, Hank definitely did *not* fit the media stereotype of a CSU technician.

Rolling her eyes in the direction of the cantankerous tech, Lacey edged past him. "See you around, Colin."

"Yeah." He strolled toward the bed.

"Keep your distance until I'm finished." Hank barked out the order without looking up. "And don't touch anything."

"I know the ropes." But he halted anyway.

"Never hurts to be reminded. I don't want any slipups on my crime scenes."

"You think that's what this is? A crime scene?"

"Not my call. That's your job. But if you're asking whether I see any obvious evidence of foul play, the answer is no."

Lacey was right; it appeared they'd have to wait for the autopsy and tox screen results to get any concrete answers.

"How long are you going to be here?"

"No idea. It's a big house. I called for some backup, but I expect it could be a long night."

A click sounded in the hall, and Colin backed toward the door. "I'm going to talk to the daughter and her friend. We'll stay out of your hair."

"Good."

Colin escaped into the hall—and came face-to-face with a pale, slender woman in her early thirties, about eight inches shorter than his six-foot-three height. Faint streaks below her lashes were all that remained of her mascara, and only a few flecks of color clung to her generous lips.

Deb Wilson emerged behind her from the room on the other side of the hall, carrying a small overnight bag.

"You must be Detective Flynn." The woman's voice was shaky, her shock-glazed eyes the color of a cloudless summer sky.

"Yes." The word came out a tad rough, and he cleared his throat.

"I'm Trish Bailey. The officer said you'd want to talk to me."

"That's right."

She appeared to be on the verge of folding, and a powerful urge to take her arm rolled through him.

Fighting back that unsettling impulse, he motioned down the hall. "Why don't we sit in the kitchen?"

Her irises began to shimmer. "Is she . . . is my mom still in the bedroom?"

"Yes."

Her throat worked, and she steadied herself with a hand against the wall.

Once again, he had to wrestle down the inappropriate inclination to offer her his arm.

He transferred his attention to the uniformed woman. "Why don't you join us, Officer Wilson?"

She nodded and fell in behind as he took the lead down the hall.

"Make a left."

He followed Trish's instruction, taking a quick inventory of the huge kitchen as he entered. Granite countertops. Restaurant-quality stainless-steel appliances. Slate floors. Ceiling-height wood cabinets that had to be custom.

Yeah, there was some serious money in this family.

And based on what Meyers had said, the sole heir was the woman behind him.

People had killed for a lot less.

Yet as he and Trish sat at the glass-topped table while Officer Wilson melted into the background, it was hard to believe the distraught daughter across from him could be a killer.

"I spoke with Officer Meyers, who took your statement." Colin pulled out a small notebook. "He gave me a quick briefing, but I'd appreciate hearing the events of the evening directly from you."

She tucked her shoulder-length, light-brown hair behind her ears, knitted her fingers together on the table, and recited the same story he'd heard from Meyers.

"I understand there was some concern about medication dosage."

Her complexion lost a few more shades of color. "I manage . . . managed . . . my mom's medication, and Matt thinks I might have miscounted."

"What do you think?"

Distress tightened her features. "I don't think I did—but I *have* made a few mistakes lately . . . and I've been under a lot of stress. I suppose it's possible." She choked on the last word.

"Tell me about the stress."

"It's a long story."

"I don't have anywhere else to go."

She caught her lower lip between her teeth as she regarded him. He met her gaze straight on, keeping his posture open and receptive. It was possible they were dealing with murder, but every instinct he'd honed during his years in police work told him this woman wasn't capable of killing a mouse, let alone her mother. And he wanted to convey through body language that he wasn't judging her at this point.

At last she looked down at her interlaced fingers. Swallowed.

"Two years ago, my husband, John, and I were in town for my mom's birthday. My dad had bought tickets to *Phantom of the Opera* at the Fox for all of us, but I came down with the flu hours after we arrived. My mom had been excited about the show for weeks, and I insisted they all go without me. It was snowing that night. Being from Minnesota, John never let bad weather stop him."

Her voice rasped, and Colin angled toward Deb. "Could you get her a glass of water?"

While the officer complied, Colin turned back to Trish. "There was an accident."

"Yes." She waited until Deb handed her the water, took a drink, and set the glass on the table with both hands when the liquid sloshed close to the rim. "A tractor trailer crossed the median. It was a head-on collision. John and my dad were in the front seat. They d-died at the scene. My mom was critically injured. She already had heart issues, and the doctors weren't certain she'd survive. But she came through surgery, began to recover . . . then had a stroke."

As Trish took another sip of water, Colin fisted one hand. His own history wasn't exactly the stuff of storybooks, but this woman had endured enough blows to fell Goliath. The word *stress* didn't begin to capture what she'd been through.

"You've had some tough challenges."

"Mom more than me." She regarded the half-empty glass. "She lost her husband of thirty-eight years, suffered terrible pain, spent six months in rehab, and ended up in a wheelchair."

"I understand you moved back in here after the accident."

"Yes. After I finished out the school year. My house felt empty without John, and Mom was all I had left. Moving home felt right."

"Where did you and your husband live?"

"Cincinnati. We met in college, married soon after, and moved there for his job. He was an engineer."

"Any money concerns after he died?"

"No."

"You're a teacher?"

"Yes. Art." She named a school in a risky part of town.

"Not the safest area."

"I'm careful."

"Why that school?"

"Why not that school?" Faint creases appeared on her brow.

"There are plenty of schools closer to home."

"That have plenty of qualified teachers waiting in the wings." She took another two-handed sip of water. "Schools like the one where I teach have more difficulty finding skilled staff—and those kids deserve a quality education too. Like the one I had."

A woman who believed in giving back.

Nice.

"How does . . ."—he consulted his notebook—"Matt Parker fit into the picture?"

"He's my parents' accountant. He does their taxes and handles the day-to-day financial oversight of their charitable foundation."

Charitable foundation?

Another indication of wealth.

It also meant Trish wasn't going to inherit her parents' entire estate.

"Tell me about the foundation."

"Mom and Dad set it up six years ago. He was a senior executive, and during his career he made a lot of money—salary, stock options, bonuses."

She named the Fortune 500 company, and Colin jotted it down. Apparently the stories he'd heard about the handsome benefits and perks offered by that firm were accurate.

"Were you upset that they didn't leave their entire estate to you?"

"Of course not." No hesitation. "It was their money. And it's not like they intended to leave me penniless. They set aside more than enough for me to have a comfortable life. But my parents believed that if you've been blessed, you have an obligation to make a positive impact on the world."

Altruism must run in the family.

"Has Parker always been their accountant?"

"No. Only for the past year. Their previous finance guy died of a heart attack, and our pastor recommended Matt. He does a lot of pro bono work for the church and came with impeccable credentials."

"And now you're dating him?"

She traced the circle of condensation on the table with an unsteady finger. "We've gone out twice. My mom liked him a lot, and he *is* a great guy, but there's no . . . he doesn't . . ." She exhaled as a touch of color crept back into her cheeks. "Things aren't clicking."

"Yet you went out with him tonight."

"For the last time."

For some reason, Colin found that news pleasing.

"Does he know that?"

"I was going to tell him before he left. And then . . ." She bit down hard on her lower lip.

He assessed the woman across from him. In view of tonight's trauma, she'd held up well. But her composure was beginning to fray—and unless his intuition was failing, a meltdown was imminent. He needed to cut this off now.

"Where are you planning to stay tonight?"

"I . . . I don't know. Somewhere close. The Hilton, I guess."

"Give me a few minutes to talk with Parker and you'll both be free to leave."

"Could I . . . do I have to wait? Are you finished with me?" She wrapped her fingers around the glass. Tight.

It didn't take a genius to realize she didn't want to deal with the soon-to-be ex-boyfriend tonight on top of everything else that had happened.

But she was in no condition to drive, either. Even from across the table, he could see the tremors running through her body. And if she increased the pressure on that glass a hair, they were going to be dealing with cuts from the broken fragments.

"We're finished for now. But if Parker's willing to drop you at the hotel, you might want to accept." He flicked a glance toward her white-knuckled grip on the water. "It would be safer."

She looked down. Loosened her grasp. Examined her trembling hands. "I'll get a cab."

A smart suggestion. It was a safe option, and the lady could afford it.

Nevertheless, it didn't sit well.

"I'll tell you what. I have to pass by the Hilton on my way back to headquarters. If you're willing to wait another ten minutes, I can drop you there."

He could feel Deb Wilson's speculative gaze, and his neck warmed. Giving a potential suspect a ride might not be standard operating procedure—but it wasn't against the rules, either.

Yet Trish didn't jump at the offer. Not surprising. Considering how law enforcement had invaded her home tonight, she might want to get as far away from all of them as fast as she could.

And perhaps that was a wiser choice—for him *and* for her. Because he should *not* be noticing her sky-blue eyes . . . or the willowy figure that curved in all the appropriate places . . . or those soft-looking lips.

"If you wouldn't mind, I'd appreciate it." Tears once more dewed on her lower lashes. "I don't think I could handle it if I got a chatty cab driver."

So much for wise choices.

Yet despite his reservations, he wasn't backing out on his offer.

"This won't take long." He stood. "Officer Wilson will wait here with you. I'll talk to Parker in the living room and see him to the door after we're finished."

"Thank you. I'm not up to dealing with him tonight."

"That's what I figured. Sit tight and I'll be back in a few minutes."

Notebook in hand, he left the kitchen. It was doubtful Parker would have anything of substance to add to the story, and based on Trish Bailey's obvious anguish and sound financial footing, there was no apparent motive for foul play. If she *had* played a role in her mother's demise, it was likely a tragic mistake.

But he wasn't rushing to conclusions, either. He'd been in this business long enough to know that things weren't always what they seemed. Evil intent often lurked beneath a veneer of respectability.

And if the pieces didn't fit together the way he expected . . . if Trish Bailey wasn't as innocent and grief-stricken as she seemed . . . he'd make sure justice was served.

Yet as he entered the living room, he couldn't help hoping the ME would determine that Eileen Coulter's death was due to natural causes. That ruling would not only clear Trish's name and help assuage her guilt, it would free her to go on with her life—minus Parker.

A pleasant thought on this eventful night . . . for reasons he'd analyze another day.

4

She should have taken a cab.

Trish tucked her hair behind her ear, rested her elbows on the kitchen table, and dropped her face into her hands.

It had been kind of Detective Flynn to offer her a lift, but it was an imposition—and likely against the rules.

Yet the thought of climbing into a cab with a garrulous stranger was almost as unpleasant as the notion of being stuck in a car with a man whose romantic inclinations she didn't share.

Colin Flynn was the safest alternative.

But he's a stranger too, Trish.

True.

Yet for some odd reason, he didn't feel like one. From the moment she'd emerged from her bedroom to find him waiting in the hall, there'd been a . . . connection. It was as if they'd met before—or perhaps had been destined to meet. He'd felt like a friend. An ally.

And she needed one of those tonight, even if that notion was more fantasy than reality. Because the truth was, Detective Flynn wasn't in *anyone's* corner. The man struck her as a pro, whose only loyalty was to justice.

But for tonight, rational or not, she'd cling to the sense of kindred-spiritedness that made her feel less alone.

Without it, she might shatter before this night ended.

Voices spoke in the foyer, and she lifted her head. The words were too muted to distinguish, but she could identify Matt's annoyed tone and Flynn's more measured response.

In less than a minute, the front door opened and closed. Seconds later, the detective entered the kitchen.

"Everything okay?" The female officer picked up the overnight bag.

"Yes." He stopped at the table. "Your friend wasn't keen on leaving without speaking to you, but I convinced him you weren't up to another conversation tonight. I didn't tell him where you were staying . . . but I did promise to pass on the message that he'd call you tomorrow."

"Thanks." She pushed herself to her feet. "Do you think . . . would it be all right if I saw my mom once more before we leave?"

After an infinitesimal hesitation, he backed toward the hall. "Let me talk to the CSU tech."

She watched him turn and disappear, bracing herself on the tabletop, fingers splayed to add some stability.

"You might want to sit down while you wait." The female officer gave her a worried once-over.

She must look as ready to keel over as she felt.

"I'm fine."

But as the minutes ticked by and her legs began to quiver, she was less and less certain of that.

Just as she was about to sink back into the chair, the dark-haired detective reappeared.

"The tech is finishing up in the room. We can go in as long as we don't touch anything."

He let her take the lead and followed her down the hall.

As the door of her mom's room drew closer, however, her courage wavered.

"You can change your mind if you want to." The soft, empathetic reassurance came from behind her.

"No. I . . . I want to see her again."

He waited in silence while she summoned up the fortitude to say her last good-bye, here in the loving home her parents had created and filled with beautiful memories for her. Not in some morgue, or at the memorial service her mother had specified, where all that remained of her would be ashes in an urn.

But it was hard.

So hard.

Clenching her fingers, she forced her legs to move again. Down the remainder of the narrow corridor. Through the door. Across the room to the bed.

A gray-haired man was off to the side, near but not intrusive. She felt the detective's presence close behind her.

Yet all that mattered was Mom.

She was lying on her back now, her eyes closed, hands folded on top of the comforter—at the detective's direction, perhaps? To give her a more natural, peaceful appearance?

But nothing about her was natural anymore. Already death had left its mark. Her eyes were sunken, her skin waxy, her lips colorless.

The woman she'd loved was gone.

Forever.

Tears leaked down her cheeks, and she choked back a sob as the room shifted beneath her.

A steadying hand took her arm. Rock solid. Strong. Comforting.

The world settled back on its axis.

Exhaling, she took one more look at her mother. Commended her to God. Prayed for strength.

Then she turned away and walked out the door.

The female officer met them in the foyer and passed the over-night bag to the detective. He took it in one hand, keeping a grip on her arm with the other. As if he was afraid she was going to crumple into a heap at his feet.

A very real possibility.

In silence, they walked through the post-midnight darkness to his car. A few lights were on in the surrounding houses, the neighbors no doubt aroused from their slumber by the flashing lights and sirens. Wondering what was going on in the Coulter household.

In fact, Stan Hawkins was on his front porch, watching the proceedings from across the street. The instant he spotted her, the older man hurried down the steps toward them, passing under one of the muted streetlights. What was left of his white hair was tousled, and he'd shoved his arms into the ratty button-up cardigan he'd worn for as long as she could remember.

Once again, Trish faltered.

"Wait here." The detective released her arm and strode toward the man, meeting him on the sidewalk.

He was running interference for her.

One small blessing to be thankful for on this awful night.

A cool wind whipped past, and she shivered. Colin Flynn darted her a glance from a distance—as if he'd sensed her chill.

Fifteen seconds later, he hastened back to her while Stan crossed the street to his house.

"He's a n-nice man. He used to give me h-hydrangeas from his garden when I was a little g-girl." She couldn't stop her teeth from chattering.

"Is there a jacket in here?" Her escort hefted the overnight bag.

"No—but I left a sweater in the f-foyer."

"Hang tight." With one more glace at her neighbor's retreating figure, he jogged back to the front door. The officer on duty there slipped inside and retrieved it.

"Sorry. I should have thought to b-bring this." She snuggled into it as the detective rejoined her and draped it over her shoulders.

"You had a few other things on your mind." He guided her down the walk to a newer-model Taurus, holding the door as she slid inside. After stowing her bag, he circled the car and took his place behind the wheel.

"Thank you again for the ride . . . and for diverting Stan. I have a feeling neither is one of your duties."

"Some parameters of the job are written in stone"—he checked his rearview mirror and pulled away from the curb—"but we have a fair amount of discretion during an investigation."

Investigation.

Her stomach bottomed out at the ugly word, and she stared into the darkness on the other side of the window as he pointed the car toward the Hilton.

"I don't think I miscounted my mom's medicine . . . but what happens if I did?" She might as well ask the hard questions while she had this man's ear in the quiet, private confines of his car.

When only the thrum of tires on pavement broke the silence, she peeked over at him. It was too dark to see much, but in the headlights of oncoming cars, she could discern a strong jaw, furrowed brow, and serious demeanor.

"Why don't we wait and see what the autopsy and—"

"No. I'd rather know what to expect than spend sleepless nights wondering about the what-ifs."

He shot her a quick, assessing glance. Refocused on the road. "If an inappropriate dose of medication is found to be the cause of death, we'll want to talk with you at more length."

She let her grief-muddled brain digest that for a few moments—and came to the logical . . . and sickening . . . conclusion.

Since she managed her mother's medicines, if a wrong dose was the cause of death, the police would need to determine if it was an accident.

Or murder.

All at once, she started to shake again. "What would happen next?"

"Why don't we cross that bridge if we come to it?"

"If . . . or when?"

"For the record, I haven't drawn any conclusions, Ms. Bailey." His tone was straightforward. Nonjudgmental. Firm. "I'm waiting for evidence. My 'if' stands."

"I'd still like to know what happens next *if* medication is involved."

He turned right and accelerated on Clayton Road. In five minutes, they'd be at the hotel.

"If there was an accidental overdose, we'll make a report to the prosecuting attorney. You'd be free to resume your normal life while we wait for a decision. But assuming there's no reason to suspect foul play, it's doubtful any charges would be filed."

The coil of tension in her stomach loosened a tiny bit. Of course there wouldn't be any charges filed. How could there be, when every scrap of evidence to be found would prove she loved her mother?

Except . . .

"I'd still have to live with the guilt, though." Somehow she managed to choke out the words.

He didn't respond.

She didn't expect him to.

What was there to say, other than "I'm sorry." And she'd had her fill of "I'm sorrys" tonight from Matt.

They completed the drive in silence, and as he slowed under

the portico in front of the hotel entrance, she fumbled for the handle of the door.

"Sit tight. I'll get that for you."

On top of everything else, he was a gentleman.

That would be a plus if things happened to get dicey. She wouldn't have to worry about being treated with a lack of respect—by this man, anyway.

He retrieved her overnight bag from the backseat before pulling her door open.

"Thank you again for the ride." She reached for the bag, her fingers brushing his as she took it. Steady against shaky. Warm against cold.

The parallel lines were back on his forehead. "Are you certain you wouldn't rather call a friend? Hotels are very . . . impersonal."

"I wouldn't bother anyone at this hour. In any case, I was gone from St. Louis for years. I lost touch with most of my childhood friends—and I haven't had much chance to make new ones since I've been back. I'll be fine here."

That was a lie . . . but what other choice was there? Spending the night in Matt's guestroom wasn't an option.

Besides, she wouldn't be fine no matter where she spent the next few hours.

Another cool breeze whipped past, too chilly for the first day in May. No . . . it was May 2 now. A new day had begun almost two hours ago.

A limo pulled up behind the detective's car.

"I better move." He fished a card out of his pocket. "I'll be in touch tomorrow morning, as soon as the scene is released. In the meantime, don't hesitate to call me if you have any questions."

"Thanks." She fingered the card as the limo driver opened the passenger door. A tuxedo-clad man climbed out and extended a hand back for the glowing bride who emerged behind him.

Endings.

Beginnings.

All chaotically woven together in a tapestry only God could understand.

She watched the happy couple dash up the steps to the front door, high on champagne and hope and love, looking forward to the life they would spend together.

The crush of loneliness pressed harder against her chest.

"Ms. Bailey."

She angled back toward the detective, forcing air into her lungs.

"You're not alone in this."

The man also had excellent intuitive skills—a definite plus in his work.

But he was wrong.

She was as alone as a person could be.

"Thanks." Her fingers tightened on the overnight bag as she struggled to hold on to her composure. In ten minutes, she'd be in a room. Then she could cry. Not now. Not here. Not with this man, who was trying to be kind but who owed her nothing. She was a stranger to him. Just one more potential suspect in one of his many cases.

"I mean it, Trish." His gaze locked onto hers.

Once more, her lungs faltered. His use of her first name . . . the intensity in his deep brown eyes . . . the empathy radiating from him . . . all of those were a heaven-sent lifeline on this dark, dark night.

Detective Colin Flynn might not be a friend or ally, but he would do his best to get to the truth. She knew that as surely as she knew the days ahead would test her as she'd never before been tested.

And as she offered him a final, heartfelt thank-you and climbed the steps to the hotel, she had a feeling that if he was in her corner, she might just make it through the ordeal to come.

▪ ▪ ▪ ▪ ▪

Things had progressed faster than he'd expected.

Craig sat on the bed, swirling the ice in his glass.

Who knew the mother would die so soon? His research hadn't provided a definitive timeframe, nor an absolute guarantee the first attempt would be successful. It could have taken several tries.

But her quick demise could actually work to Matt's advantage. A grieving, bereft daughter with no close friends might think twice about pushing back from a man who liked her and wanted to be part of her life. A man who could help her through the difficulties ahead and offer a shoulder to cry on.

It was an ideal scenario.

Maybe she wasn't cooperating with that plan yet, but Matt had a golden opportunity now to worm his way into her good graces. To become an invaluable ally. A trusted friend who could relieve her of all the financial burdens she was about to inherit. As a woman who disliked numbers, she ought to welcome that kind of help—especially if it came from a man who enjoyed her loyalty and affection.

Matt needed to work on earning both of those.

He set the glass on the nightstand and leaned back against the headboard, lacing his fingers behind his head.

Early tomorrow morning, Matt should call her. Find out which hotel the police detective had taken her to and pick her up. Buy her breakfast. Offer to help her sort through whatever details needed to be attended to immediately. Be there for her. Stay close.

He also needed to keep his other clients happy. Maintain the status quo. It was important not to do anything out of pattern that might call attention to himself—but that wouldn't be difficult to manage. Compared to the kind of work he'd done in the past, Matt's current job was child's play. Anyone with a finance background could whip through the payrolls and tax returns for the small businesses he served, leaving plenty of time to devote to his most important client. To ease the yoke on her shoulders.

And the more Trish came to rely on Matt, the better for his plan.

Craig yawned and twisted his wrist. Three in the morning wasn't late by his former standards, but he needed to be at the top of his game right now—awake and fully functioning during daylight hours. Better get some shut-eye. He had a busy day tomorrow.

He picked up the glass of Scotch and finished it off in one gulp. With the way things were going, he might not have to wait as long as he'd expected to upgrade his libations.

A welcome possibility on which to end the day.

Even if it didn't bode well for a certain art teacher should she happen to get in his way.

5

"He's either got a hot new case or he's met a hot new woman."

As the mirth-tinged comment registered in his subconscious, Colin tuned back in to the conversation between his every-other-Saturday breakfast companions.

Now that Rick Jordan had voiced his opinion, he was hiding his grin behind an oversized coffee mug. The woman beside him, however, was making no attempt to disguise her amusement . . . and didn't hesitate to add her two cents.

"My money's on the latter." Kristin Dane bit into the huge cinnamon roll she'd ordered as a side to her over-easy eggs and sausage. "He never zones out like this about a case."

Colin took a sip of his coffee, scrambling to formulate a response. It better be credible, or the two people who knew him best were going to give him a boatload of grief.

"Maybe I'm just tired." He tried for a casual tone. "I did work the late shift last night, you know. Plus, I interrupted my shut-eye to meet you two so-called friends."

"Yep. It's a woman." Kristin scooped up some hash browns.

"Keep eating like that, you'll lose your girlish figure." Colin broke off a bite of omelet with his fork.

"Deflection." She swiped some icing off the roll. "More evidence to support my case, Mr. Detective." She grinned at him and sucked the powdered-sugar goo off her finger.

"I think she's got you, Colin." Rick doused his fries with more ketchup. "Better spill it or she'll pester you for the rest of the meal."

Kristin elbowed him. "Don't make it sound like I'm the only one interested. *You* started this."

"True." Rick chomped on a fry. "You're on, Colin."

"What's with the burger for breakfast?" He stabbed a mushroom that had escaped his omelet.

"I've been up since six. Ten o'clock is lunchtime for me. Quit stalling. We're waiting with bated breath to hear about this woman."

"You guys are nuts."

Neither of them spoke—but their smirks said volumes.

He was hosed. The more he tried to blow off his childhood friends, the more he'd dig himself into a hole. Because the truth was, he *had* been thinking about a hot new woman.

Trish Bailey.

And not just in the context of last night's events.

Safer to start with the case, though—and hope that satisfied them.

"Rick had it pegged at the beginning. I have a hot new case."

"What kind of case?" Kristin narrowed her eyes, skepticism sparking in their depth.

"Suspicious death."

"What's hot about it?"

The victim's daughter.

True—but not a tidbit he intended to share.

"It has some . . . interesting . . . nuances."

"Such as?" Kristin leaned forward, cinnamon roll in hand, gaze sharp and probing.

"I can't discuss an in-progress case."

"Hmph." With a disgruntled snort, she went back to eating.

"You may have a new case—but I think you met a woman too." Rick continued chowing down on fries.

"What is this, a tag-team event?" Colin scowled at the two of them.

"Touchy, touchy." Rick raised an eyebrow.

"No. Tired." He faked a yawn. "If you keep hassling me, this is the last time I cut my z's short to meet you two on a Saturday."

"Now he's resorting to threats." Kristin studied him. "No way you'd ever back out of the standing Saturday date with your two best friends in the world—unless a woman was involved. Romance can mess with your head." She turned to Rick. "Maybe this has been going on a while and he's been holding out on us."

"There is nothing going on, and I haven't been holding out on you." He wadded his paper napkin into a tight ball. "I only met her last . . ." A word unfit for polite company sizzled on his tongue before he clamped his lips together.

Talk about a dumb slip.

Kristin aimed her fork at him. "Aha. Now the truth comes out."

"I knew something was up." Rick shoved a red onion back onto his burger. "He has that goofy, distracted expression guys get when some woman catches their eye."

Colin took a sip of juice. Offense might be a better defense. "Since when have you become such an expert on male-female relationships? Last I heard, you were spending all your free time communing with nature at that camp you run—unless you've been holding out on *us*?"

Kristin gave Rick a speculative perusal and dismissed that notion with a flip of her hand. "Nah. If there was romance in the picture, we'd have sniffed it out. He's easy to read."

"Hey!" Rick shot her an indignant look.

"Chill." She gave him an affectionate nudge. "You're transparent only to us—and it's endearing. Right, Colin?"

"What is this? Psychoanalyze your friends day? I thought we were here to eat." He pierced another stray mushroom with the tines of his fork.

"We come here to feed the bond, not our stomachs." Kristin gathered some potato fragments into a neat pile on her plate, all levity gone. "I could eat a bagel in my condo. You could sleep in after a full night chasing down criminals. Rick could forgo the long trek in from the country. But every other Saturday for years we've shown up here. I'd hate for that to change."

"Why should it change?" Rick stopped eating his fries.

"Life . . . and love . . . can alter things." Worry was etched on her face.

Colin couldn't argue with her concern. He'd had the same thought through the years. No doubt they all had. They might joke with each other about being late bloomers, but someday—perhaps in the not-too-distant future—one of them would marry, changing the dynamic of the relationship that had sustained the three of them for more than two decades.

Kristin seemed to think it might be him.

But while he'd noticed Trish Bailey . . . while he'd felt a buzz in her presence no other woman had ever generated . . . while he was open to romance if the right woman came along . . . Kristin's concern was premature.

For all he knew, the woman he'd met last night would end up being a murder suspect.

And if she *was* innocent . . . if that buzz intensified . . . romance wouldn't fray the link he had with Rick and Kristin. They'd been through too much together, shared too many heartaches. The friendship they'd forged wasn't going to falter.

Colin put his hand in the center of the table. "We vowed

a long time ago to stick together and be there for each other. Nothing's changed for me. Nor will it. I'm still in."

Some of the trepidation faded from Kristin's demeanor, and she laid her hand on top of his. "Me too."

"Make that three." Rick added his hand. "Now let's eat or the food will get cold."

"I'm with you." Colin went back to his omelet. "But if it will ease your minds, I promise you'll be the first to know if I ever have anything to report on the romance front."

"Thanks." Kristin cut into her second egg. "Although we'll probably figure it out first."

Given how they'd both pegged the cause of his distraction today with mind-blowing accuracy, her prediction was likely sound.

Meaning he'd have to keep his guard up around them in the future.

And while he'd honor his promise to let them know if he ever met a woman with potential, he was nowhere near that point.

Even if Trish Bailey walked away from this experience blameless, she had a lot on her plate—including a hefty helping of grief. There wasn't much chance she'd be in the market for a new relationship in the foreseeable future.

For the remainder of the meal, the conversation ranged far and wide, as usual. There was laughter and discussion and teasing and sharing. All the things that made the Treehouse Gang important to him.

But as they said their good-byes forty-five minutes later and went their separate ways, his thoughts drifted back to Trish Bailey. He might not have any strong family connections, but he did have Rick and Kristin.

Trish was battling trauma and grief alone in a hotel room.

Car keys in one hand, he pulled out his cell phone with the

other. The CSU owed him an update on the situation at Eileen Coulter's house. Hopefully they could release the scene soon.

Giving him an excuse to call the woman who seemed so in need of a friend.

■ ■ ■ ■ ■

Matt was punctual, as usual.

At ten thirty on the dot, he pushed through the revolving door into the lobby of the Hilton.

Trish stayed in her seat off to the side, overnight bag at her feet, buying herself another few seconds. Accepting his offer of breakfast and a lift home during their phone conversation an hour and a half ago hadn't been the smartest choice. Except they did need to talk . . . and having a friend by her side when she returned home was appealing.

Unless Matt decided to ditch that friendship after she told him romance was a no-go.

At last he spotted her, lifted a hand in greeting, and crossed the lobby toward the chair she'd claimed.

Gripping the handle of her bag, she rose.

"Trish." He grasped her upper arms and searched her face, furrowing his brow. "You look exhausted. Did you get any sleep?"

"Some." An overstatement. The few minutes she'd clocked here and there added up to less than an hour of shut-eye.

He pulled her close, into a hug she didn't return, the overnight bag bumping her leg.

If he noticed her unenthusiastic greeting, he didn't comment on it as he released her. "Have you heard from the police yet?"

"No. The detective said he'd let me know when I could get back into the house. Sometime this morning, he thought."

"Have you checked out of the hotel already?"

"Yes."

"Then let's get some breakfast. How does Schneithorst's sound?"

"Fine." Better than fine. It was half a block away, making for a short drive, and the breakfast horde tended to be on the boisterous side. Letting him down in the midst of a high-spirited Saturday crowd would be far less difficult than if they were alone, in a more intimate setting.

Ten minutes later, after being shown to the corner table Matt requested, Trish gave the menu a quick skim and set it aside.

"That was fast." He continued to peruse the offerings.

"I'm not very hungry."

"You need to eat." He set his own menu down.

"I'll have some eggs and toast." More than she wanted, but she did need to put some food in her stomach.

A waitress appeared, filled their coffee cups, took their orders, and hustled off.

"I know there are a lot of details that need to be addressed. Tell me what I can do to help." Matt covered her hand with his.

She gently tugged it free and picked up her mug. "I've already called the home health service. That was the most immediate need. And I spoke with Reverend Howard about the arrangements for the memorial service." She took a sip of the coffee. "I can handle this on my own, Matt."

"But you don't have to." His eyes warmed, and he leaned close. "I'm here for you."

Just tell him, Trish.

The coffee in the mug began to ripple, and she set it back on the table, wrapping her cold fingers around the soothing warmth. "I need to talk with you about that."

"Okay."

"I was going to bring this up last night, and then . . ." Her voice choked. *Don't go there. Stay in the moment. Concentrate on what you need to say to him.* "The thing is, I like you a lot.

Mom thought the world of you, as I'm sure you know. That's why she was trying to push us together these past few weeks, in case you hadn't noticed."

"I noticed." One side of his mouth rose a fraction. "But let the record show the gentleman was willing to be pushed."

He wasn't making this easy.

"I appreciate that. But I don't think dating is the best idea. There's not any . . . we don't have a . . . I'm not ready to go there again. Especially now."

Coward.

The scold from her conscience echoed in her mind as she gripped the mug. She hadn't lied . . . but neither had she told the full truth. Dating wasn't the best idea because there was no zing, and she needed to be honest about that instead of leaving the door open.

"I can understand that. A lot's happened in the past twelve hours—not to mention all the stress you've been under with your job and your mom's health issues and the tragic accident." Matt touched her hand again. "I like you a lot too, Trish . . . and I think, once your life settles down, there might be potential. I'm willing to wait."

He was forcing her hand.

She'd have to lay it on the line—ready or not.

"I wish I could say I felt the same, but the truth is . . ." Her phone began to trill from deep within her purse. "Sorry. Let me get this. It might be the police."

She groped for the cell, scanning the screen as she pulled it out.

"It's the detective. Give me a minute." She pressed the talk button.

After returning her greeting, Colin Flynn wasted no time on chitchat. "I wanted to let you know you're free to return to your house. Our people have cleared out. Are you at the hotel?"

"No." She slid a glance toward her companion, who was

stirring some cream into the refill the waitress had poured for him. "I checked out about half an hour ago."

"Do you need a ride to the house?"

She blinked. "Are you still on duty?"

"No, but I'm . . . not far away."

"Thank you." The warmth of his kindness chased some of the chill from her heart. "But I already have a ride."

A couple of silent beats ticked by. "Parker?"

"Yes." Of course he'd assume that. She'd told him last night she didn't have any close friends here, and Matt had said he'd be in touch this morning.

"It's probably best if you have someone with you when you return."

"That's what I thought too." But she'd rather it be the man on the other end of the line.

"I'll be in touch as soon as we have results from the medical examiner's office. In the meantime, if you have any questions or concerns, don't hesitate to call. I have my cell with me 24/7."

"I appreciate that."

Another brief hesitation.

Could he be as reluctant as she to hang up?

Trish squeezed the cell, as if holding on tight could keep him from breaking the connection.

It didn't work.

"I'll let you go. Take care."

The line went dead.

Slowly she slid the phone back into her purse.

"All clear at the house?" Matt moved his mug aside as the waitress set his food in front of him.

"Yes." She stared at the plate of eggs the woman deposited in front of her, trying not to gag.

"I don't have anything urgent on my schedule today, so I can stay as long as you need me to once we get there."

"You don't have to do that." She tore off a corner of her toast. She needed to finish the conversation Colin had interrupted, since Matt had apparently been hearing her words but not her intent.

"I don't mind." He set an empty creamer on the table. "And in case you're thinking I have a thick skull, I understand where you were heading before the call interrupted us. I get that romance isn't high on your agenda at the moment. Maybe it won't ever be—with me. All I ask is that you don't jump to a hasty conclusion. Nothing in your life has been normal for two years. You might change your mind down the road. In the interim, I'll settle for your friendship."

So he *had* been listening.

Best of all, he was taking this better than she'd expected.

However . . . waiting wasn't going to change how she felt, and it wasn't fair to give him false hopes.

"I appreciate the offer of friendship. It would be comforting to know I have someone to call on if I get overwhelmed. But that's all it will ever be, Matt. I know that—and I don't want to string you along."

Some emotion—anger, perhaps?—flashed in his eyes, replaced so fast by acceptance and resignation she wondered if she'd imagined it. "Message received. I won't push."

A weight lifted from her shoulders. "Thanks for understanding."

"Hey . . . that's what friends are for, right?" He managed a smile and motioned toward her plate. "Now eat some breakfast."

She picked up her fork and tackled the eggs. With Matt's situation resolved, she might be able to choke down a few bites. And she did need the energy. The next few hours would be hard—as would the days ahead.

Especially if the autopsy report showed her mother's death was, indeed, due to a mistake with medication.

6

Writing reports was about as exciting as cleaning toilets . . . or doing taxes . . . or grocery shopping.

As Colin's eyes glazed over and the words on the computer screen blurred, he heaved a sigh. He needed a break from the boring task. Any excuse would do. A new case to work on . . . a suspect to interview . . . a lead to track down.

Too bad none of those were imminent.

He'd have to settle for checking email.

Straightening up from his slouch, he clicked on the icon and scanned his new messages. The one from the ME's office, with "Coulter Tox" in the subject line, jumped out at him.

Wow.

Two weeks for toxicology results had to be a record.

Either there had been nothing in the initial tests to indicate the cardiac arrest listed as cause of death in the autopsy was suspicious—or a red flag had gone up fast.

For Trish Bailey's sake, he hoped it was the former.

Leaning forward, he clicked on the email and skimmed through it.

Full report attached. Bottom line: E. Coulter was taking di-goxin, a drug often used to treat abnormal heart rhythms. Too much can cause ventricular tachycardia . . . which can lead to ventricular fibrillation . . . which can cause sudden death. The deceased had almost triple the amount that should have been in her system based on her prescription and the half-life of the drug—more than a therapeutic dose, but not necessarily lethal. However, it was in the potentially toxic range, given her medical issues and age. Call with questions.

Colin muttered a word he seldom used.

"Must be bad news if you're resorting to that kind of lan-guage." Mac McGregor arched an eyebrow at him from the adjacent desk.

Lack of privacy was a definite negative in the shared-office setup County had deemed adequate for detectives.

"Not how I wanted to start the week, that's for sure." He opened the attached report. "I was hoping for different findings from the ME."

"On which case?"

"Eileen Coulter. The suspicious death in West County."

"I take it the suspicions were valid?"

"That's what the tox report suggests. Sounds like too much of one of her medications could have triggered the cardiac arrest."

"Murder . . . or mistake?"

"The sixty-four-thousand-dollar question. You have some time this afternoon?"

"I could spare an hour."

"Can you give me two? I need to talk to the daughter again. She managed her mother's medication."

"You planning a long interview?"

"No. I'm building in travel to her house. She's already

dealing with a lot of trauma. I'd rather not put her through a trip to headquarters."

Mac leaned back in his chair and laced his fingers over his stomach. "Very considerate."

At the speculative gleam in his colleague's eyes, he busied himself straightening a stack of papers on his desk. "Just trying to bolster our good-guy image."

"Hmm."

"So are you coming or not?" Colin dropped the stack into one of his desk drawers.

"Yeah. I'd like to meet this suspect."

"She isn't a suspect."

"Then why are we questioning her?"

"Fine." He slammed the drawer shut. "She's a marginal suspect. I need to do a little more digging, talk to some references, verify she's a loving daughter who made a tragic error rather than a greedy offspring on the fast track to an inheritance. But based on my initial interview with her, my instincts tell me we're looking at a mistake, not a murder."

"Instincts are good. Intel is better."

"What's that supposed to mean?" He squinted at the other man.

"Just sharing some wisdom from my special forces days. What time do you want to go?"

Colin opened his mouth to tell him what he could do with his wisdom. Shut it as logic kicked in. Mac was as solid as they came, and while he might have less experience in law enforcement than a lot of the County detectives, the skills he'd honed during his SEAL days had come in handy in plenty of dicey situations. His opinions were always reasoned—and sound.

"I need to finish some reports this morning. I'll contact Trish Bailey and let you know what I set up."

"Works for me." Mac rose. Stretched. "It's great to be back on days."

"Tell me about it."

"Text me with an update. I need to follow up on a few robbery leads."

Colin gave him a thumbs-up.

Once Mac left, he rocked back in his chair in the empty room, eyeing the cell on the edge of the desk. He hadn't talked to Trish since his call to let her know the autopsy was finished and she could claim her mother's body. That had not been an easy conversation.

This one, however, would be harder. They were now crossing the bridge to the scenario she'd queried him about on their late-night ride to the Hilton.

But while he might not be happy about the direction this had taken, he'd maintain his neutrality during the investigation. Mac's diplomatic reminder had been unnecessary. He was a pro, and he'd do what needed to be done. If there was nefarious intent, he'd root it out.

More likely, though, he'd discover that Eileen Coulter's death had been due to a tragic mistake and there would be no legal culpability.

Emotional culpability—different story.

And as he picked up the phone to arrange a meeting with Trish, he suddenly wished that the only item on his agenda for this Monday morning was a stack of boring reports.

• • • • •

At four thirty on the dot, the front doorbell chimed.

Trish sucked in a breath . . . wiped her palms down the black fabric of her slacks . . . and prepared to face bad news.

If Colin Flynn was paying her a call with another detective in tow, this was a serious-business visit.

Trying to stay calm, she crossed the foyer and pulled the door open as Colin was leaning forward to press the bell again. "Sorry to keep you waiting. Come in."

The two tall detectives stepped inside.

"Ms. Bailey, this is Mac McGregor, one of my colleagues."

He was back to the formal Ms. again.

Not the best sign.

She took the hand the other man extended and returned his firm shake. "Would you like to sit at the kitchen table or in the living room?"

"Wherever you're more comfortable." Colin's tone was pleasant, and there was warmth in his eyes.

Or was she reading too much into his demeanor?

"The kitchen's fine. It will be easier for you to take notes at the table. I assume you'll be doing that?"

"Yes."

Stomach twisting, she led them to the back of the house. So much for any faint, lingering hope they might be here to pass on information rather than gather it.

Which could mean only one thing.

The tox results were back—and the ME had found irregularities.

Pressure building in her throat, she sat and forced herself to accept the truth. These men were here because her mother had died as a result of a mistake she'd made with the medication.

"My mom's heart attack wasn't from natural causes, was it?" No sense putting off the hard stuff.

"No." Colin didn't try to sugarcoat his answer. "The tox screen found an elevated level of digoxin. According to the ME, it wasn't a lethal dose, but given your mother's heart issues, it could be considered toxic. His report suggests the high level of that drug led to ventricular fibrillation—a deadly arrhythmia and a leading cause of sudden cardiac death."

"So it was my fault." She closed her eyes, struggling to accept the harsh truth. When a tear trickled down her cheek, she groped in her pocket for a tissue.

"Let me get you some water." Colin's quiet baritone filled the silent void in the kitchen.

Apparently he realized she needed a couple of minutes to compose herself, because he didn't hurry. And by the time his chair scraped again and he set the water in front of her with a soft clink of glass against glass, she had her emotions under control. Or as close to control as she was going to get.

"Thank you." She dabbed at the moisture on her lashes and took a sip. "I know you have questions. Go ahead and ask."

After scrutinizing her, Colin flipped open a small notebook. "It would be helpful if you gave us the names of a few people who are familiar with your relationship with your mother."

As his implication sank in, another jolt rocked her.

These two homicide detectives hadn't come to her childhood home just to deliver bad news. They were here because the police weren't certain the extra medication her mother had taken was due to an accident.

And if foul play was on their radar, she would be the prime suspect.

The room tipped.

"Ms. Bailey?"

At Colin's prompt, she wove her fingers together. "You don't actually think I would do anything to hurt my mother, do you?"

"We're still in the evidence-gathering phase. That's why a few names would be helpful."

"You want character references?"

He shifted in his chair. "That would be one way to look at it."

She crimped her fingers together, trying not to resent the men seated on either side of her. They were only doing their job. Colin Flynn might have been kind the night her mother died, but that didn't mean he was going to cut her any slack now. He'd become the lead detective in a potential homicide, and he didn't seem like the type who would let personal feelings or opinions influence his handling of a case—or a suspect.

"You could contact my minister, our neighbors, my mother's physicians, the home-healthcare workers who came here every day while I was at school, my mother's friends, one of my co-workers whom I socialize with on occasion . . . do you need more?"

"No. That's plenty."

She gave him the contact information for a dozen people.

"You already have Matt Parker's phone number and address, but you could talk with him too. He's been part of our life for the past year."

While Colin scribbled in his notebook, the other detective spoke.

"Other than the home-healthcare workers, who had access to your mother's medications?"

"Anyone who was in the house. I always left them on the counter." She gestured to the spot reserved for her mother's medications, empty since the CSU tech had carted it all off. "But except for an occasional repair person, very few people came inside. We didn't entertain. Mom's friends stopped by once in a while, and our pastor was a regular visitor. That's about it."

"Who was here the week or two before she died?"

"Our pastor dropped in once. And Matt, mom's accountant. He comes every month. More often in the past few weeks."

"Why?"

"He and I . . . we went on a couple of dates. But that's over."

"Because . . . ?"

She slid Colin a quick look. "I could tell he had serious intentions, and I didn't see any future with him."

"Did you end it before or after your mother died?"

"After."

"Is there anyone you can think of who would benefit from your mother's death?" Colin rejoined the conversation.

"No. I'm her sole beneficiary, but as we've discussed, the bulk of her estate is in the charitable foundation."

"Did your mother have any enemies?"

"No. Everyone loved Mom—including me." Her voice broke, and she fished out another tissue.

"I think we're done for today." Colin closed his notebook. "I'll contact some of the people on the list you provided and be back in touch."

He stood, and McGregor followed his lead.

Trish pushed her chair back and rose. After steadying herself with the table for a moment, she led them to the door.

In the foyer, Colin paused beside the satchel filled with art supplies she'd dropped there when she'd arrived home from school.

"Have you gone back to work?"

"Yes. A few days after Mom died. Sitting around here was depressing—and finding decent subs at my school is difficult. Plus, I didn't want to disappoint the kids. We're having an art show as part of our end-of-year party, and if I drop the ball, it won't happen."

"When does the term end?"

"Middle of next week. But I'm also doing a summer art program."

"Busy schedule."

"Busy is good right now." She swiped at another tear and pivoted away to open the front door. "Let me know if you need anything else."

"Thanks for your cooperation." McGregor extended his hand and gave her a quick handshake.

When it was Colin's turn to say good-bye, his warm fingers held hers a second longer than necessary.

Or was that only wishful thinking?

Before she could decide, he released her hand and followed his colleague down the front walk.

She waited by the door until they reached the Taurus parked at the sidewalk, then shut it with a quiet click and wandered back to the kitchen table. Picking up her glass, she eyed the contents as she walked to the counter. Half empty—or half full?

These days, half empty described her life far better . . . especially with the news Colin Flynn had brought about her culpability in her mother's death.

How was she supposed to live with that for the rest of her life?

Gripping the edge of the sink, she bowed her head.

God, please help me through this. You know how much I loved Mom, how I did everything I could for her. You know I was always careful with her medicine. I can't believe I made such a terrible mistake. But I have been distracted lately. Please give me solace, and fill me with the healing power of your love so I can face tomorrow with hope instead of despair.

As she finished the silent prayer, Trish unclenched her fingers from around the sink and straightened up. She might never understand why the Almighty had allowed so much tragedy to befall her during the past two years, but she wasn't going to turn away from him as many people did when life got tough. She was going to cling tight to his promise that he would be with her always. And she was going to trust that one day soon, life would be bright again.

Because if she didn't, the shadows hovering over her soul could swoop in and shroud her in darkness forever.

. . . . .

"I think you're right to give Trish Bailey the benefit of the doubt."

As Colin pulled away from the curb, he spared Mac a quick glance. "What happened to intel trumping instinct?"

"I stand by that—but I see where you're coming from with her. She doesn't strike me as a killer."

Reassuring to have his opinion seconded.

"Plus, there's no obvious motive." Colin accelerated toward the exit of the classy subdivision where Trish had grown up.

"There's that too. You going to contact everyone on the list she gave you?"

"Most of them."

"You want me to tackle a few of the names?"

"Do you have the time?"

"I can squeeze in two or three interviews. Now that you've brought me up to speed on the case and I've met the daughter, I'd like to see this resolved too."

"Another body on the case is always welcome. No pun intended."

"Glad to hear it, because that was lame." Mac stretched out his long legs as much as he could in the Taurus. "So . . . Trish Bailey is a very pretty woman."

Colin flexed his fingers on the wheel. Where had *that* come from?

Best to play this cool.

"Yes, she is."

"The water was a nice touch, by the way. Very considerate."

Colin kept his eyes pointed straight ahead. "She needed a minute to pull herself together."

"True."

When the silence between them lengthened, he checked on Mac. The other man was watching him with an amused expression.

Great.

"You know . . . I've been thinking." His colleague's words were steeped in mirth.

He wasn't touching that comment with the proverbial ten-foot pole.

Didn't matter. Mac didn't wait for an invitation to continue.

"Assuming Trish Bailey is as innocent as we both suspect, you could always stay in touch on a more personal basis after this wraps up."

"Why would I want to do that?"

"Because you like her."

He held on tight to the wheel and tried for a neutral tone. "How did you jump to that conclusion?"

"No jump needed. The evidence spoke for itself."

"What evidence?"

"The location of the interview. The water. Plus, you're unsettled by this discussion."

"I'm not unsettled."

"Watch the light." Mac motioned toward the traffic signal ahead.

Colin jammed on his brakes as the signal changed from yellow to red. Even with his foot mashed to the floor, the car crept a few feet over the line before it stopped.

"My mind's on the case, not the woman." A stretch.

"Too bad. She likes you too."

"What are you, a mind reader?"

"Nope. I just watched how she watched you."

"You're off your rocker."

"Nope. She looked at you a whole different way than she looked at me. Did you catch the glance she sent you while she was talking about breaking it off with Parker?"

"No."

"Too bad. It was significant."

Colin tried to replay the scene in his mind, but nothing jumped out at him.

"I think you're reaching. And since when have you become an expert on this kind of stuff, anyway?"

"Since I met Lisa." He grinned. "She was a first-class detective before she became a police chief, and she reads people better than anyone I've ever met. Thanks to my lovely wife, I'm a lot more tuned in to interpersonal nuances. Trish likes you. Trust me." He inclined his head toward the signal as a horn beeped behind them. "Light's green."

Turning his attention back to the road, Colin accelerated.

For the remainder of the drive back to headquarters, the conversation revolved around work topics—but part of his brain continued to process Mac's comments.

Did Trish like him—and might she be interested in getting to know him better once this whole mess was cleared up?

Perhaps.

But before he got too enthused about that possibility, he had some interviews to conduct. There was still a chance she might be involved in her mother's death. Slim, but possible.

So until this was sorted out, he'd concentrate on doing his job and keep his distance from a certain appealing teacher, except for professional reasons.

On the plus side . . . unless his instincts were way off base, the interviews would exonerate her—opening the door to a whole different kind of relationship. And the process shouldn't take long. All he had to do was talk to a few people, compare notes with Mac, and file a report.

Wrapping this up should be a piece of cake.

7

"Are you certain you're up to this, Trish? Your mom liked these monthly meetings, but they're not necessary. For the most part, the foundation runs itself, and other than a few checks that need to be signed, there's not much to discuss."

Trish set a glass of soda in front of Matt and joined him at the kitchen table.

"I'd like to keep up the tradition for a while. Even though I sat in on the meetings after I moved back, I never paid much attention. I have a lot to learn. Mom and Dad were passionate about the foundation, and now that they're both gone . . ." The word wavered, and she took a sip of her soda. "I'd like to carry on as Mom did until I feel up to speed."

"Of course. And we do have one order of business to attend to. By state law, the foundation needs to have three trustees. As you know, your mother asked Reverend Howard to take your father's place after the accident. You'll need to appoint a new trustee to join you and him."

"I haven't given a thought to filling Mom's spot." The very notion turned her stomach.

"That's understandable." He folded his hands on the table.

"If you'd like me to step in on an interim basis, I'd be happy to do that. It would satisfy the legal requirement and give you some breathing space until you're ready to name a permanent trustee. Since Reverend Howard has never played an active role in the foundation and you aren't familiar with all its ins and outs, it would be helpful to have someone in an official capacity who's thoroughly briefed on the structure and operation, as well as on your mother's wishes."

Trish played with the edge of her napkin. Matt's suggestion was practical, logical, and efficient—yet somehow it didn't feel right.

Telling him that, however, would be awkward.

"I appreciate the offer. Let me think about it for a few days, okay?"

"That's fine." His reply was smooth, but a muscle twitched in his jaw. "Is there someone else you're considering?"

"No. I'd just rather skip the interim step and appoint someone on a permanent basis. But I'm not familiar enough with the workings of the foundation to have a clear sense of who I should bring on board."

"The workings are straightforward. The amount your parents set aside for the foundation six years ago is invested in dividend-paying securities. Each year, they donated a certain percentage to various charities. The legal annual minimum is 5 percent of the fair market value of the foundation's assets, but they often gave more."

"So the value has decreased?"

"A bit. They never intended the foundation to go on forever."

She knew that much, at least.

"I know I have the discretion to either donate all the funds and terminate the foundation or maintain it through my lifetime, with the balance going to specified charities after I die."

"Correct. So unless you're planning to follow the first course, you need to think about another trustee."

"To be honest, terminating it is appealing . . . but I don't think that's what Mom would have wanted me to do. Not this soon, at any rate."

"I agree."

Trish rubbed her forehead. Trying to deal with her parents' charitable endeavor on top of everything else was overwhelming.

"Hey." Matt touched her hand—a comforting rather than romantic gesture, thank goodness. "You don't have to carry this burden alone. I may not be able to alleviate all your stress, but I can keep this ball in the air for as long as you need me to. Other than appointing a new trustee, there's nothing you need to do in the immediate future. I'll continue to see to the day-to-day details, as I did for your mom."

"Thank you."

"My pleasure. All I need from you today is your signature on checks for donations to a few charities your mother designated at our last meeting." He slid several in front of her. "They're all fairly modest amounts."

Trish scanned the names on the checks. Most she recognized. A few she didn't.

"What is WingHaven?"

"An organization that provides assistance to women from abusive backgrounds who are trying to build a new life."

That sounded like Mom.

"And Providence House Ministries?"

"They fund a variety of organizations that provide foster children with enriching experiences they wouldn't otherwise have access to."

Definitely Mom.

She signed the checks.

"Those are both new ones, aren't they?"

"Yes. Your mom called me about them after our last meeting."

That made sense. Mom had always handled foundation

business—even while recovering from the accident—and she'd been quite competent at it. There'd been little need for input from the other trustees.

But this was on her shoulders now.

"I feel like I'm way behind the curve on this." She combed her fingers through her hair.

"It's not rocket science. I can answer any questions you have."

"I don't want to waste your time. Why don't you email me the last three annual returns? I know they're in Mom's computer somewhere, but I'd rather not have to dig for them."

A glint of surprise sparked in his irises. "Are you certain you want to bother with that boring stuff? The 990 forms are mind-numbing. Think your IRS tax return—but worse." He gathered up the checks and slid them into his portfolio.

"Yes. I may not like numbers, but I understand them. That's why my math teacher in high school tried to convince me to major in finance in college."

He stopped zipping up his case midway. "Seriously?"

"Uh-huh. I mentioned that when you first took on the foundation work."

"Sorry." He touched the scar on his forehead, twin creases denting his brow. "This has messed with my memory."

"No worries. It was just a passing comment. Back in high school, the thought of working with numbers all day made my head ache. It still does. No offense intended."

"None taken." He finished zipping up the portfolio and stood as her phone began to ring. "Go ahead and answer. I can see myself out."

She crossed to the charger on the counter and plucked out the phone once she saw the name on the screen. "Yeah, I should take this. It's the father of one of my students. I've been trying to get in touch with him for days, but we keep missing each other. Would you send me a list of all the charities that have received grants from the foundation too?"

After a millisecond hesitation, he nodded. "Watch for everything in your email."

"I will. Thanks." She pushed the talk button, put the phone to her ear, and greeted the caller as she waved good-bye to Matt.

Ten minutes later, after a productive conversation with a father who was engaged and involved in his son's education—a rarity in the school where she taught—Trish returned the cell to the charger. The man's appreciation for all she'd done to encourage his son and help him apply for a scholarship for a summer art course was why she taught where she did. Making a difference mattered.

The very reason her parents had created the foundation.

And now it was her baby . . . ready or not.

She kneaded her forehead. The foundation might not be her top priority, but she'd do her best to carry on in her parents' footsteps . . . beginning with the financial info Matt was going to send. Boring or not, she'd plow through it and . . .

At the ring of the doorbell, she frowned. Who would be stopping by on a Wednesday evening at dinnertime?

She hurried to the foyer, peered through the peephole—and found Matt standing on the other side.

After unlocking the deadbolt, she opened the door. "I thought you left."

"That was the plan. But I stopped to check messages, and while I was on a call I found this in the grass at the edge of the driveway." He held up her keychain.

"That's weird." She took it.

"Did you lock your door while you went down the driveway to get the mail?"

"No."

"Maybe it fell out of your pocket."

"I don't keep my keys in my pocket. I keep them in my purse." She waved a hand toward the shoulder tote she'd dropped in the foyer. "Although I was juggling some grocery sacks while I unlocked the door from the garage. It's possible I slipped them in the pocket of my jacket. I've done that on occasion if my hands are full . . . but I didn't think I had today."

Another lapse. Like the coffee . . . and the frying pan on the stove . . . and forgetting what time Matt was going to pick her up for their movie date.

And Mom's medicine.

A wave of nausea swept over her.

The past two stressful years must have taken a bigger toll than she'd realized.

"Hey . . . it's no big deal. I'm just glad I spotted them. Now I really am leaving. The reports will be in your inbox later tonight or tomorrow."

"No rush. Whenever you get a chance."

After watching him follow the curving walk to the driveway, she shut the door, keys clenched in her fingers.

How could she have made so many mistakes over the past few weeks—one of them fatal?

Was it possible she could be losing it?

A shiver rippled through her.

What a scary thought.

Very deliberately, she tucked the keys into her purse . . . where they belonged. Then she double-checked that the front door and the door from the kitchen to the garage were locked. Verified she hadn't left any perishable items from the grocery store lying on the counter. Riffled again through the ads that had come in the mail to confirm no important letters or bills were tucked among them.

Other than the keys, everything appeared to be in order—but

if this kept up, she'd be second-guessing everything she did from now on.

And living in fear she'd make another mistake that could have dangerous repercussions.

· · · · ·

So Trish was good with numbers—and she wanted to step into her mother's shoes with the foundation.

That news was about as appetizing as the three-day-old pizza staring back at him from the shelf of Matt's refrigerator.

Spewing out a curse, Craig slammed the door shut. None of his surveillance or background research had revealed Trish's financial aptitude. Apparently she'd mentioned it to Matt at some point in the past, but the head injury had given him a convenient excuse to forget that important tidbit.

Craig paced from one side of the living room to the other. He needed to stay calm. Examine the facts. Yes, she'd asked for the 990s—but so what? They were in perfect order—all the i's dotted and t's crossed. Matt was meticulous about that. Every number, every decimal point was accurate and legit. Reviewing old returns wasn't a concern.

And it shouldn't be an issue in the future, either. All charitable donations would be recorded. The contributions would be made. Trish would sign the checks. Everything should flow smoothly—unless she continued asking questions like the ones today about the two new charities . . . or got too involved in the day-to-day operation of the foundation instead of letting her accountant run it, as her mother had . . . or gave the list of grant recipients more than a perfunctory scan.

He blew out a breath. The way things were progressing, it could take longer than he'd expected to get his own funds flowing. If Matt couldn't woo her into letting him take the leadership role in the foundation, he'd have to dazzle her with his managerial skills until she was confident enough to not only appoint him as the third trustee but give him check-signing and oversight authority. Once he had that, once she was content to step back and give his simplified monthly financial reports no more than a cursory review, the money could begin rolling in.

But getting to that stage would take time—and test his patience.

On the other hand, if she dragged her feet for too long, perhaps Matt could convince her to terminate the foundation after a few months. That might not be a bad alternative. He'd get the money in one fell swoop and could disappear before anyone was the wiser to live the good life under another new identity in some warm tropical locale.

In the meantime, he was stuck in this dull Midwestern city— and going stir-crazy.

Jingling his keys in his pocket, he wandered into the bedroom and pulled his second set of IDs from the dresser drawer where he'd stashed them. Weighed them in his hand. Surely he could find an off-the-beaten-path bar and enjoy a few drinks in anonymity, maybe round up some female companionship for a few hours.

Laying low was getting old—and lonely.

With sudden decision, he changed out his IDs. Why not give it a shot? The odds of pulling this off without a hitch were in his favor by very substantial margins. After weeks of clandestine surveillance, he was well-versed in simple appearance-altering tricks. Fake glasses, a baseball cap, jeans, and work boots, some gel to alter his hairstyle, tinted contacts—it was amazing how a few simple alterations could transform a person's looks.

A spurt of adrenaline pumped through his veins, elevating his heart rate as he pulled out the various props he'd need to create a new persona.

This was going to be fun. And given the low risk, he could

enjoy himself without worrying about jeopardizing the plan he'd implemented with such methodical care.

Operation Double Cross was rolling . . . and nothing was going to stop it.

. . . . .

"Here. Have some real coffee to start the day."

As a Starbucks cup slid into view, Colin looked up at Mac. "I owe you." He shoved the half-empty Styrofoam cup of department brew to the far side of his desk and picked up Mac's offering, lifting it in a toast.

"I got the feeling you were going to be here late last night when I left. Long days make for sluggish mornings." He sat at his own desk and took a sip of coffee. "What time did you leave?"

"About eight."

"You finish the report on the Coulter death?"

"Yes. Done and submitted. Based on our interviews with the references the daughter provided, I'm not expecting any charges to be filed."

"I agree. I didn't hear one negative. Just the opposite. Everyone sang her praises."

"Same here."

"She sounds like quite a woman." Mac leaned back in his chair, posture relaxed, eyes assessing. "So what happens next?"

"We wait for the prosecuting attorney to rule."

"I was talking about after that."

"The lady goes on with her life."

"You planning to be part of it?"

Man, Mac could be as persistent as a mosquito on a summer night in St. Louis.

Nosy too.

"I haven't given it a lot of thought."

"Right."

Colin sipped his java, eyeing the other man's grin over the rim. "Why do you care, anyway?"

"Because finding the right woman is life-changing. Lisa taught me that. So sparks are worth exploring."

"Who said there are sparks?"

Mac snorted. "With all the electricity zipping around in her kitchen the day we interviewed her, I was worried about getting electrocuted."

"Let's not get carried away . . ." His phone began to vibrate, and he pulled it off his belt. Trish's name flashed on the screen.

He swiveled away from Mac and put the cell to his ear. "Flynn."

"Detective Flynn, it's Trish Bailey. I was teaching a class when you called earlier and didn't check messages until now."

"I wanted to let you know we've finished our interviews of the references you provided and have submitted our report to the prosecuting attorney. Based on their input, I'm optimistic we're nearing the end of this process."

"None too soon for me. It will be a relief to have any legal issues resolved. As for the guilt . . ." Her sigh came over the line. "I'll have to try to find a way to live with it."

"People do make mistakes."

"Not often with fatal consequences." Her voice hitched, and she cleared her throat. "I, uh, need to run to the ladies room before my next class. Thank you for the update."

Based on the shakiness of her words, what she needed to do was lock herself in a stall for a few minutes and try to regain her composure.

Colin sized up Mac. He appeared to be focused on his computer screen, but the man had super-sharp hearing. No matter how low he spoke, Mac would hear every word.

Meaning he'd have to ignore the potent impulse to offer the

woman on the other end of the line some words of comfort and keep this impersonal instead.

"As soon as I get the all clear from the prosecuting attorney, I'll let you know."

"Thank you. I know how busy you must be, and I appreciate your personal follow-up. It means a lot."

After her tear-laced, heartfelt expression of gratitude, he couldn't hang up without saying *something* encouraging.

Cupping his hand around the cell, he dropped his volume almost to a whisper. "Hang in, Trish. Things will get better."

"I hope so."

"If you have any questions before I get back in touch, don't hesitate to call."

"I will. And thanks for being so . . . for your kindness." A bell sounded in the background. "I need to run. Talk to you soon."

The line went dead.

After a few seconds, Colin slid his phone back onto his belt and rotated toward his computer.

"I bet *Trish* was happy to get a positive report." Mac didn't take his gaze off the screen in front of him, but his inflection spoke volumes.

"Wouldn't you be, in her shoes?"

"Yep. But I expect she's still going to need some hand holding—and based on the evidence we've already discussed, I have a feeling she wouldn't object if the hand belonged to you."

"Maybe I'm not in the market for a relationship."

"You should be. You're not getting any younger—and Trish Bailey is worth further investigation."

He ignored that.

"Ah. The silent treatment. Telling."

"Look . . . if it makes you happy, I'll admit I find her attractive. And I might call her after this is over, test the waters. But in light of everything that's been going on, she may not have any interest in getting involved in a new relationship."

"Can't hurt to find out, though."

Colin narrowed his eyes. "I'm not sure I like you in matchmaking mode."

"I'm not sure I do, either." One side of his mouth quirked up. "It's a new role for me."

"How did I get lucky enough to be your test case?"

"You want the truth?"

At the man's sober question, a caution flag began to wave in Colin's mind. "I don't know."

"I'll give it to you anyway. I've known you two years, and we've worked together on several cases. Most of the other detectives talk about their families—spouses, children, parents, siblings. You've never mentioned anyone but your two friends, Rick and Kristin. That leads me to believe you either don't have any family or you don't stay in touch with them. None of my business. But whatever the reason for your lack of family connections, it seems to me if God sends someone your way who has partner-for-life potential, you'd be crazy not to follow up. I was happily single into my thirties, but believe me—marriage has much to recommend it."

"I'll keep that in mind."

"You do that. And now I have a new case to tackle." He rose, picked up his Starbucks cup, and disappeared out the door.

Colin leaned back in his chair. He didn't need a pep talk from Mac about marriage. He was more than ready to tie the knot if the right woman came along. Unlike his colleague, who was close to his brothers and parents and had grown up in a loving home, his own childhood had been fraught with angst and anger and soul-shredding grief. If it hadn't been for Rick and Kristin, he wasn't certain he'd have survived it. So the notion of creating a loving home of his own, of finding a woman who would fill his empty nights and share his daily joys and sorrows, was appealing.

He wasn't as certain as Mac was that Trish might be that woman. But he couldn't deny the electricity on his end—and according to Mac, it sizzled on her side as well.

So he'd make a few subtle overtures once the prosecuting attorney ruled, see if she was receptive to getting together socially.

And pray that if God had orchestrated their meeting, as Mac seemed to think, he'd smooth the road ahead rather than put more obstacles in their path.

8

She was here, just as she'd promised.

Craig melted into the shadows inside the door of the bar and gave the woman wearing the short skirt, spike-heeled boots, and figure-molding top an appreciative once-over.

Nice.

Better yet, she was friendly.

Very friendly.

His lips curved up as she tossed her mane of blonde hair and batted her fake lashes at the dude in a cowboy hat who was standing next to her stool. She knew exactly how to catch a guy's eye—his included.

In fact, thanks to her, he'd broken his rule and come back to the same dive twice.

His smile faded. Anonymity was crucial to these nocturnal excursions, and the best way to maintain it was to move from place to place. Becoming a familiar face that patrons—or the bartender—would remember wasn't smart.

But one slip shouldn't cause any problems. On a Saturday night, with the lights low, music blaring, and a shoulder-to-shoulder crowd wedged into every spare inch, there wasn't much chance he'd be noticed.

He didn't plan to hang around the bar long, anyway. He'd buy her a drink or two, then wrangle an invitation to her apartment. It hadn't taken much persuasion on Wednesday to convince her to skip out for some privacy. It never did with her type, if you knew how to turn on the charm.

All at once, she caught sight of him. He smiled again and lifted a hand in greeting.

Five seconds later, after blowing off the loser who'd been hitting on her, she wove through the crowd toward him.

"Hi, handsome." She sidled up close and linked her arm with his.

"Hi, yourself. Can I buy you a drink?"

"Sure. I've been watching for you. I put my stuff on a table in the back corner to save us a cozy spot."

He let her lead him around the dance floor filled with writhing bodies and sat beside her at the small table for two. A waitress materialized, staying only long enough to take their orders.

"So . . . did you have a good week, Joe?"

He took a few pieces of popcorn from the bowl on the table. He'd given her no more than a first name—and a fake one at that. But she hadn't been any more forthcoming . . . and Natalie might not be her real name, either.

Didn't matter.

No one who came to this kind of place was interested in a long-term relationship.

"Better since I walked in the door. You look great."

"You aren't too bad yourself."

"I like your boots."

She stuck her leg out from under the table and wiggled her foot. "They're new. A gift from a friend."

If that was a hint, she was out of luck. He had no intention of becoming more than a passing acquaintance.

"So how was your week?"

"Fine. Lots of customers at the salon. This is the season for manicures, apparently."

That's right. She worked at some hair place.

All at once, the band goosed the volume, and he winced. The sooner they got out of here, the better. He hadn't driven to this dive to listen to bad music.

The waitress delivered their drinks, and Craig took a sip. Watered down and overpriced, like last time—although Natalie appeared to be enjoying hers. And knocking it back at warp speed as she chowed down on the popcorn. The tab was going to rise fast at this rate.

Too fast.

"You want to dance?" He stood.

"But . . . you just got here. Don't you want to visit a little?"

"After the dance. We can't waste this song." Whatever it was.

"Okay." With a shrug, she grabbed some more popcorn and rose, twining her fingers with his. "But let's order another round first. The drinks'll be waiting for us after the dance."

"Fine." He signaled the waitress and doubled his tab.

One dance, another drink, he'd make his move.

The blaring song seemed to last forever, hurting his head. It was only endurable because of the way Natalie was gyrating against him. Like she couldn't wait to ditch this place either.

Good. They were on the same page.

When the so-called music ended, she took his hand, guided him back to the table, and picked up the empty popcorn bowl. "Would you mind getting a refill, sugar?" She gave him a coy nudge with her shoulder.

More popcorn would make her thirstier . . . but he had a

bottle in the car again, as he had Wednesday. They could continue the party at her apartment.

"I'll be back in a minute." He took the bowl.

"I'll be waiting." She dropped into her chair and picked up the drink the waitress had delivered.

By the time he shouldered through the crowd, got the refill, and returned, her drink was almost gone. Again.

"You're getting behind." She tapped a finger next to his glass and took another handful of popcorn.

Maybe if he downed his quickly, he could get them out of here before she wanted to order another one.

While she dived into the popcorn, he finished his Scotch in several swigs.

"The dancing must have made you thirsty." She swirled the ice in her glass.

"Yeah." He scooted his chair closer. "It's kind of noisy in here, isn't it?"

"Uh-huh. Crowded too." She stroked a polished nail down the back of his hand. "It's a lot quieter—and more private—at my apartment."

"You're reading my mind."

"Except I'm still thirsty and I don't keep a lot of booze in the place." She ran a fingertip around the rim of her glass.

Subtlety wasn't her strong suit.

"I've got us covered."

"I like a man who's prepared." She smiled and stood. "I'll wait by the door while you settle up."

After slinging her purse over her shoulder and picking up her jacket, she sashayed toward the exit.

Five minutes later, he rejoined her. "Sorry. I had to track down our waitress. This place is a zoo."

"Saturday nights are like that here." She linked her arm with his. "But my place will be a lot more . . . intimate."

Exactly what he was counting on.

"I'll meet you there, like last time."

"Won't work tonight. My car's in the shop. I got a ride here with a girlfriend."

His mouth tightened. He did *not* want her in his car.

But he did want what she had to offer.

He'd just have to clean the car in the morning, remove any traces of her . . . just in case. And he knew how to do that. He'd had plenty of practice.

"Fine. I'll take you."

He let her chatter during the short drive, tuning out most of what she said, thinking instead of the fun ahead. After that . . . he had a few tasks to finish before he called it a night. But he should be out of here in an hour, hour and a half, tops. Like the last visit.

She edged closer to him, straining against the seat belt, stroking his arm. Too bad he couldn't hook up with her again. She might not be the sharpest tack, but she had a body that didn't quit.

Not worth the risk, though. There were plenty of bars in town when he needed another diversion—and plenty of other women happy to indulge in a no-strings evening of entertainment.

"Home sweet home." She pulled the keys out of her purse and dangled them from a finger as he parked and set the brake.

"I'll get the bottle from the trunk."

"I'll wait for you to open my door."

He rolled his eyes as he slid from behind the wheel. You opened doors for ladies like Trish Bailey. Natalie—or whatever her real name was—didn't come close to qualifying for that title.

But he'd humor her—at least for the next hour.

She swung her legs out of the car after he pulled her door open, letting her skirt hike up her thigh. After lingering a moment to give him an unhurried view, she stood and took his arm while they crossed the parking lot to her apartment. He kept his head down in case anyone was wandering around, but the lot was deserted, as it had been on Wednesday.

Once they were inside the three rooms she called home, he waited impatiently while she moseyed into the kitchen for glasses. If it was up to him, he'd skip the drinking—but he doubted his companion would go for that. She liked her liquor.

"I have pretzels. I'll put some in a bowl and . . ." She frowned as she dropped her purse on the table. "Huh. I must have left my jacket in your car."

Another delay.

"You pour the drinks. I'll go get it." He set the bottle on the counter and retraced his steps to the car, once again watching for lurkers. Not that he was recognizable in this getup . . . nor would anyone be able to decipher his mud-smeared license plates . . . but he'd rather not have any witnesses to his late-night sojourns.

After retrieving the jacket from the floor of the passenger seat, he jogged back to the apartment, wiping the inside and outside doorknobs with his handkerchief before entering. Natalie had put on some soft music, lighted a few candles, and set their drinks on the coffee table along with a bunch of high-carb pretzels he didn't want.

"Thanks, sweetie." She took the jacket and gave him a kiss.

Now they were getting somewhere.

He grasped her arm as she turned away. "Let's try that again."

She didn't resist.

But when he took her hand and tried to tug her down the hall, she balked. "Let's have our drinks first. I made the living room real romantic."

He tamped down his annoyance. If he ticked her off, the night was over.

"Okay." He changed direction, tucked her close as they sat, and picked up his drink. "To us."

She clinked her glass with his. "I like that toast."

While he guzzled his Scotch, she took dainty sips.

Too bad she hadn't nursed the drinks in the bar like that. It might have saved him a few bucks.

"Why don't you have another?" She fluttered her fingers toward the bottle on the coffee table.

He inspected her half-empty glass. Why not? At the rate she was drinking, he had a few minutes to kill. Two drinks here, plus the diluted ones at the bar, wouldn't put him over the legal limit for the drive home.

As she finally drained the last drop from her first glass, he was finishing his second. And beginning to feel mellow.

Instead of waiting for him to make the next move, she rose, picked up the bottle, and held out her free hand.

He didn't need a second invitation.

And what followed was as enjoyable as the first time. So enjoyable that he let himself drift off to sleep afterward. What could a few minutes of shut-eye hurt before he drove home?

Except when he opened his eyes, sun was streaming through the window.

What the . . . ?

He bolted upright, only to have the room tilt.

"Morning, sweetie." Natalie entered, fully dressed, hair brushed, makeup perfect. She held out a glass of OJ. "I'd give you tomato juice if I had some. It's better for a hangover."

"I never get hangovers." But this sure felt like one.

"Uh-huh." She gave him a condescending smile. "This might help."

He waved the glass aside. Man, he must have drunk a lot more than he remembered. Or else the stuff he'd had at that bar had been more potent than he'd thought.

"What time is it?"

"Nine."

He spat out an oath and swung his legs to the floor. He had places to go on Sunday morning.

"Are you leaving already?" Her face contorted into a pout.

"Yeah. I never intended to stay the night."

"You weren't in any condition to drive."

"I am now."

She watched him tie his shoes. "When will I see you again?"

"Depends on how busy the week is." No reason to tell her the truth. It was easier to just disappear.

"I'll be at the bar again on Wednesday. Or sooner, if you can get away."

"I've got a lot on my plate for the next few days." He stood and pulled out his keys. "You want to give me your phone number? I could call you after I have a better handle on my schedule." Could . . . but wouldn't.

"Sure." She picked up a pen off the nightstand and scribbled some numbers on a scrap of paper while he took in the rows of shoes through the open closet door behind her. This woman gave Imelda Marcos some serious competition. "I'm pretty flexible." She held out the paper.

"I'll keep that in mind." He shoved it in his pocket, grabbed his glass and the bottle of Scotch from the nightstand, and strode toward the kitchen.

Nudging the faucet on with his elbow, he rinsed his glass and wiped it clean with a dish towel.

Natalie watched him from the dining nook. "Aren't you the neatnik."

"I told you on my first visit—I don't like germs."

"No problem. I like men who clean up after themselves."

He ignored that and headed for the front door.

"Hey!"

At her indignant summons, he turned.

"Aren't you going to say good-bye?"

"At the door." He waved a hand in that direction and kept walking.

She followed.

"So . . . thanks for a nice evening." He leaned down and kissed her.

She wrapped her arms around his neck and kissed him back—making it clear she was ready for more if he was.

For a fleeting instant, he was tempted.

But in the end, he eased back. He'd already broken a cardinal rule by seeing her twice. He needed to get out before she got any ideas.

"I'll be waiting to hear from you." She fiddled with a button on his shirt as she scrutinized him.

"I've got your number." He tapped his pocket.

"Be sure to use it." She opened the door.

"Yeah. Well . . . see you around." He slipped around her and jogged across the parking lot.

Not until his car was in gear and rolling away did he look back. Natalie was standing on the landing of her unit. She lifted a hand. He didn't respond. The hours with her had been a pleasant interlude—but it was over.

As he accelerated back to his own place, fighting the aftermath of too much liquor, the woman from the sleazy bar vanished from sight . . . and mind. He had other, more important matters to focus on.

Like figuring out ways Matt could ratchet up his strategy to convince Trish she should leave her parents' foundation in her accommodating accountant's very capable hands. His coffers were emptying, and Matt's income wasn't sufficient to refill them without a boost from a certain client's charitable fund. For a CPA who'd been in international banking, the man had settled for a sadly ordinary life.

What a waste of talent.

But he wasn't going to squander *his* abilities. That's why he'd embellished his original plan during his weeks of surveillance. Thanks to Trish and her mother, it was going to end up being an immensely profitable endeavor that solved two problems at once.

And one of these days soon, he'd be on easy street . . . with or without Trish's cooperation.

．．．．．

"Trish!"

At the summons, Trish stopped in the vestibule of the church, moving out of the line of congregants waiting to greet Reverend Howard as Matt closed the distance between them.

"Good morning. I didn't see you come in. Did you sit in the back today?" He'd been joining her in her pew every Sunday since Mom died, but perhaps he'd finally accepted that she had no romantic interest in him and had decided to keep a discreet distance.

That would be the answer to at least one of her prayers.

"Yes. The last shall be first and all that." He grinned.

"I see you're rid of the brace."

He flexed his fingers, grin fading. "Right. As of Friday. The wrist is healing well."

"I'm glad to hear that. Also, thank you for sending over the 990s. I haven't had a chance to review them yet, but it's on my list for this afternoon."

"Happy to be of service. And by the way, thanks for the heads-up about a possible call from that detective. He did contact me. I still can't believe the police harbor any suspicions about you. That's the most ridiculous thing I've ever heard."

"I think they've put their suspicions to rest. Detective Flynn called the other day to let me know they expect a favorable ruling from the prosecuting attorney."

"I should hope so. Everyone they spoke with would have told them how much you loved your mother."

"I made a mistake, though."

"Mistakes happen."

It was the same thing Colin had said—but coming from Matt, it did nothing to comfort her.

When she didn't respond, he motioned toward the diminishing line of congregants. "Shall we tag on to the end and say hello to Reverend Howard?"

"Sure."

He fell in behind her as she walked over. "School's winding down, isn't it?"

"Yes. Three more class days. The end-of-year party and art show are Wednesday evening. After that, I'll clean out my classroom and gear up for the summer session."

"You don't hang around down there at night, do you?"

"Not usually. I'll be leaving late Wednesday, but I expect a few of the other staff members will be too."

"I hope you're careful. That's a dicey neighborhood in the *day*time."

"I'm always alert—and I've never had any trouble."

"Trish . . . Matt . . . how wonderful to see you both." Reverend Howard took her hand and clasped Matt's shoulder, but directed his next comment to her. "How are you holding up?"

"Hanging in. I'm taking it a day at a time."

"A wise plan. You know I'm always available if you'd like to chat."

"I appreciate that. So far, prayer is helping me keep it together. God's a great listener."

"The best."

"I can't argue with that, but she's still too stressed," Matt interjected. "On top of everything that's happened, she's trying to bone up on the charitable foundation."

The minister wrinkled his brow. "I wish I could be more help to you with that, but my role was more of an honorary one. Your parents had a clear philanthropic vision, and your mother was very capable of carrying it out without my assistance."

"I'll work it out, Reverend." Trish shot Matt a disgruntled look, but he seemed oblivious to her displeasure. There was no need to put a guilt trip on this virtuous man who already worked sixty-hour weeks seeing to the needs of his flock. Her mother had never expected him to play an active role in the foundation. "Once school is out, I can give the foundation more attention. I'll be fine."

"But you need that third trustee," Matt said. "And my offer to step in on an interim basis stands. I'm more familiar than anyone with the inner workings, and it would buy you some breathing space."

"That sounds like an excellent suggestion." Reverend Howard's demeanor brightened. "Matt has impeccable credentials, and your mother trusted him implicitly. Letting him handle the foundation could relieve some of the pressure. It might be worth considering."

Trish looked from one man to the other. Had the two of them cooked this up, hoping a joint effort would sway her?

No.

Reverend Howard was the most aboveboard man she'd ever met. If there'd been a plan to enlist his support and gang up on her, it was all Matt's doing.

Yet Matt had never been pushy. Low-key and passive were more his style—or they used to be. But he *was* meticulous. Perhaps he was harping on this out of concern over the legal ramifications of being one trustee short.

Whatever the reason for his fixation on the issue—and despite the minister's endorsement—she was less inclined than ever to put him in an interim slot.

"I appreciate your concern for me." She encompassed them both with her comment. "And I'll think about the offer. But for now, I want to leave things as they are. You gave a wonderful sermon today, Reverend."

"Thank you." The man took the hint and let the subject of the foundation drop. "I hope to see you both next week."

"I'll be here."

"Me too." Matt echoed her sentiment—but with far less enthusiasm.

She stole a glance at him. His face was taut, and faint shadows hung beneath his lower lashes.

A wave of guilt washed over her. He'd had his own rough patch over the past few weeks, with the accident and injuries. Yet in spite of that, he was trying to relieve some of *her* burden. Her mother had thought highly of him. Reverend Howard had endorsed him. She ought to be grateful, take him up on his generous proposal instead of dragging her feet.

But as she opened her mouth to tell him how much she appreciated his willingness to help . . . and that she'd give it some serious consideration over the next few days . . . he looked down at her.

And her heart stumbled.

His eyes were almost . . . scary. Whatever emotion lay in their depths, it sent a chill through her despite the warmth of the late May day. He wasn't just hurt or angry because she'd rebuffed him. His reaction went deeper and darker than that.

Why?

All at once, as if he'd realized she was studying him, the tension in his features faded . . . his eyes softened . . . and the corners of his lips tipped up. "Can I walk you to your car?"

"Thanks, but I'm going to, uh, detour back inside." She exhaled, willing her pounding pulse to subside. "I could use a few minutes of quiet prayer."

"Take as long as you need." Reverend Howard cocooned her hand between his. "I'm not a substitute for the Lord, but call if you need to hear a human voice."

"I will. Thank you. Matt, I'll talk to you soon."

Without waiting for a response, she turned and reentered the sanctuary. Aptly named, since today it provided escape and refuge from reactions—both Matt's and her own—that had left her off balance and uneasy.

She walked halfway down the aisle and sank into a pew. What was going on with Matt? Where had the quiet, pensive man with the sad eyes, who'd taken on the foundation work with diligence and dedication, gone? The accident had changed him . . . and not for the better.

Or was she overreacting? Could she be letting the stress he kept mentioning skew her judgment, as it had undermined her memory and concentration? Was it possible the ominous feeling that had swept over her a few minutes ago was due to fatigue and an overactive imagination rather than to any true menace?

Trish took a deep breath. Let it out slowly. Repeated the exercise.

Too bad she couldn't bounce her concerns off a certain handsome detective who was trained to separate fact from fiction and dig for the truth.

Oh for pity's sake, Trish. Get real. For all you know, the man is married. Not every guy wears a ring. You're being foolish.

Clamping her jaws together, she straightened up and fixed her gaze on the cross that was front and center. Better to seek guidance and insight from a much more steadfast and accessible source.

And pray the days to come would hold answers rather than more troubling questions.

9

This was weird.

Trish tapped a finger against the keyboard and did a second, more careful scan of the hits for Providence House Ministries that had popped up in her browser.

Three screens in, she leaned back and frowned. No, she hadn't missed anything on her first pass. None of the hits were an exact match in name or mission for the organization Matt had described during his last visit.

Why wouldn't a charity like that have a website? Or at the very least, why hadn't it shown up somewhere in an article or news story?

She reopened the spreadsheet of grant recipients Matt had provided. Most were names she'd heard. The few unfamiliar ones she'd googled all had websites—except Providence House Ministries.

How had her mother found out about such an obscure organization?

But it must be legit. Matt always investigated new charities, as had his predecessor—and he was very conscientious about his work. The 990s he'd sent over for her parents' foundation had been impeccable . . . and far less painful to pore through than she'd expected.

Providence House was the only anomaly.

Rather than stew about it all day, why not give Matt a call? Answering a couple of questions wouldn't be a huge imposition on his Sunday. He could probably give her the scoop in two minutes.

Phone in hand, she tapped in his number and pulled a soda from the fridge.

After two rings, he answered.

"Trish? I didn't expect to hear from you again this soon. What's up?"

He sounded like the old Matt—friendly, gracious, obliging.

"I'm sorry to bother you on Sunday, but I was going over the information you sent on the foundation and I had several questions, if you have a few minutes."

"Of course. Didn't my numbers add up?"

At his teasing inflection, she smiled. "You get an A in math. As far as I can tell, the forms are thorough and accurate. My questions are about one of the grant recipients on the list you sent. Providence House Ministries."

She popped the tab on the soda, the carbonation hissing as she waited for his response.

When the silence lengthened, she wrinkled her brow. "Matt? Are you there?"

"Yeah. I was getting a bottle of water from the fridge. What questions did you have?"

"I googled some of the organizations I didn't recognize, including Providence House. I found websites for all the others. I know you always vetted new charities, and I wondered what the story was on this one."

"It's a little different than most. Hang on while I find the remote and mute the TV." If there was background noise, she couldn't hear it, but she waited while fifteen silent seconds ticked by. "Okay. I'm back. The bulk of their donations come from private foundations, like your mom's. She heard about it through a friend and asked me to check it out. I was leery of their low profile at first too, so I reviewed their fact sheet, recent 990s, and Form 1023—that's the application for tax-exempt status. Bottom line, they're legit."

"Where are they located?"

"Atlanta."

Trish took a sip of her soda. "I wonder why Mom chose an out-of-state charity when there are great needs here in our own town?"

"That's not the only out-of-state charity on the list."

"I know. I saw Angel Flight on there, and Patriot Paws."

"Right. She always sought out organizations that did unique humanitarian work and relied on private donations rather than government assistance. What she liked about Providence House was that it supported a number of groups around the country dedicated to providing foster kids with experiences they might not otherwise have. Educational trips, summer camps, Outward Bound programs . . . those kinds of activities. It's an under-the-radar kind of group."

"Why the low profile? It sounds like they do admirable work. Wouldn't they want to spread the word, increase donations?"

"It's a fairly small-scale operation run by an older couple who took in a lot of foster kids in their younger years and have a passion for the cause. They want to keep it to a manageable size."

That made sense.

"I can see why Mom would support an organization like that. She and Dad always believed small, grassroots efforts were most effective. Did you keep the background material on it?"

"I think so. I'll look around for it."

"Thanks. I wouldn't mind skimming through it. I can read up on the other organizations I'm unfamiliar with on the web."

"Shall I mail whatever I find or give it to you at church next week?"

"Next Sunday is fine. I won't have a chance to review it this week, with school ending and the art show to coordinate. Sorry again to intrude on your weekend."

"Don't worry about it. I was just doing some maintenance stuff around the place. Enjoy the rest of your day."

As the line went dead, Trish took another swig of her soda and powered down the laptop. As far as she could see from the documents Matt had provided, the foundation was in excellent shape. He'd done a stellar job, transitioning seamlessly from where the previous accountant had left off.

Maybe she ought to appoint him as the third trustee, after all. He was knowledgeable and willing—and she didn't need any more on her plate. As long as she reviewed the monthly financials, the grants, and the annual 990s, everything should run as smooth as when Mom was in charge. Plus, letting Matt carry the burden of the foundation would take the day-to-day responsibility off her shoulders.

If it hadn't been for that unsettling experience at church, the decision would be a no-brainer.

She wandered over to the back window. As always, the view of her mother's rose garden was a balm to her battered soul.

But it couldn't chase away the lingering unease from this morning.

Matt had sounded like his usual professional, buttoned-up, pleasant self on the phone, though. Perhaps she ought to cut him some slack. He might have had a headache at church, been out of sorts. He *had* looked tired and wan. It was also possible he wasn't sleeping well, given his injuries. And hadn't she read once that a concussion could cause personality changes for a few weeks?

Tipping up the can, she finished the soda. Why not sleep on it . . . pray about it . . . and make her decision in a day or two?

Besides, she could always change her mind. This wasn't as life and death as the mistake she'd made with her mother's medication.

Nobody would die as a result of her choices about the foundation.

· · · · ·

Colin rolled to a stop in front of Trish's house, set the brake on the Taurus, and straightened his tie. This might be an official visit, but now that the prosecuting attorney had concurred with their assessment that Eileen Coulter's death was the result of a tragic accident, he intended to lay some groundwork for further, less professional, contact.

God willing, the lady would be receptive.

After hefting the plastic bag of seized evidence from the trunk, he followed the stone path to the porch and rang the bell.

She answered at once.

"I've been watching for you. Come in." She pulled the door wide.

He moved past her, stopping in the foyer to lift the bag of no-longer-needed evidence. "Where do you want this?"

"You can set it there." She indicated a chair beside a small table.

"Everything's in there except your mother's medications. We generally destroy controlled substances and prescription drugs."

"That's fine. I never want to see them again." She shut the door. "Thank you for calling me with the good news from the prosecuting attorney—and for delivering Mom's things. Is this part of your standard service?"

He set the bag on the chair and turned to face her. "No."

Her eyes widened slightly. "Oh." She clasped her hands in

front of her. "Um . . . I appreciate the special treatment. Would you like a soda . . . or are you still on duty?"

"My day's over, unless something big breaks. A soda would be great. Thanks."

"Come on into the kitchen."

He followed her to the back of the house, taking a quick inventory while she busied herself retrieving a glass, asking his preference on soft drink brands, arranging a few Oreos on a plate. She'd lost weight in the past three weeks, and the shadows under her lower lashes spoke of sleepless nights. Worry and grief had also scored faint parallel lines above her nose, and her posture was taut.

The lady was pushing her emotional limits.

But Trish Bailey was strong. A lesser woman would have caved long ago under all the heartbreak that had been her lot. If she'd survived this long, she wasn't likely to fold—assuming the worst blows were behind her.

And how could they not be, given the magnitude of the tragedies she'd already endured?

"Why don't we sit on the terrace?" She motioned toward the back door. "It overlooks Mom's rose garden . . . a very peaceful spot."

"Peaceful works for me, after the day I've had."

"I can't imagine dealing with the kind of stuff that must cross your desk in the course of a week." She handed him a glass and picked up her own, along with the plate of cookies.

"Not every day is eventful." He opened the back door and held it for her.

"By your standards, maybe."

As she passed by, a faint sweet scent tickled his nose. Her perfume . . . or the heady aroma of the roses rimming the terrace?

"Doesn't it smell heavenly out here?" She sat at a wrought-iron table and drew in a lungful of the fragrant air.

Question answered.

"Yeah, it does." He surveyed the well-tended bed. "This rivals the botanical garden."

"Mom took a lot of pride in her roses." She wrapped her fingers around her glass. "This time of year, when they're in their first burst of bloom, was her favorite season. She used to spend hours working in the beds out here before . . ." Her voice choked, and she took a sip of soda. "Sorry."

"No need to apologize. You're dealing with a lot—and have been for two long years. I think you're holding up admirably."

"Thanks for the vote of confidence."

"I mean it, Trish." He set his soda down, rested his elbows on the table, and linked his fingers. "I also meant what I said on the phone a few days ago. Things will get better."

"I hope so. It's what I pray for every day."

Colin debated how to respond. In his interview with her pastor, the man had commented on Trish's strong faith. Told him how she lived a life based on biblical morality and had a strong relationship with God. Every scrap of evidence he'd seen supported the man's assessment.

Unfortunately, that could be a sticking point between them. Despite frequent prodding from Rick and Kristin, he'd never embraced the notion of a loving God. There was nothing in his experience, personal or professional, to suggest the Almighty cared much for the everyday woes and sufferings of the fallen race he'd created.

Now wasn't the time to bring that up, however. No sense introducing what could be a deal breaker before he had a chance to test the waters.

"I hope your prayers are answered soon. In the meantime . . . if you need to hear a friendly voice, I hope you'll give me a call. Even though the situation with your mom has been resolved, I'd like to stay in touch."

A faint tinge of pink crept over her cheeks. "A professional courtesy?"

"No." He wanted there to be no doubt about his interest. "This is personal."

She took a sip of soda, watching him over the rim of her glass. "That's direct."

"I'm too old to play games."

"I can appreciate that."

"I also believe in being up-front and honest—and I hope you'll reciprocate."

She squeezed the edge of a cookie, watching the crumbs fall. "It's funny. When Matt Parker asked me out, Mom pushed me to accept. She thought I needed to move on, leave the past behind. But our dates were duds. I assumed it was because I wasn't yet ready to dive back into romance." She lifted her gaze and met his. "As I'm discovering, however, lack of interest in romance wasn't the reason those dates flopped. It was lack of interest in the man."

Not quite as direct as his expression of intent . . . but her message was clear: she was open to getting to know him better.

His mood took a decided uptick.

"That's good news—for me."

"A word of warning, though . . . the timing's not great. With all that's happened, I feel like I'm in the Twilight Zone."

"I wasn't planning to rush you."

"I had a feeling you weren't. You strike me as an insightful man." She played with the pile of cookie crumbs. "You know what's strange about this? I feel like I know you better than Matt, despite the fact that we only met a few weeks ago and you've never shared any personal information."

"The latter issue can be rectified. What would you like to know?"

"Well . . . to be honest, I'm surprised a man with your many attributes isn't married. Or is there a divorce in your past?"

"No marriage. No divorce. The truth is, I've never met a woman with partner-for-life potential—and short-term hookups don't interest me."

She took a dainty bite of her mangled cookie. "Tell me about your family."

Uh-oh.

That wasn't a topic he'd planned to tackle today.

Leaning forward, he took as long as he could picking up an Oreo for himself while he tried to figure out how best to respond.

"Is that a sore subject?"

Trish Bailey might have had a few memory lapses in recent weeks, but her perception and empathy were razor-sharp.

"You might say that." He took a bite of the cookie and chewed.

It tasted like cardboard.

"I'm sorry. I didn't mean to pry." She set her glass down on the wrought-iron table, keeping a tight hold until she found a flat spot where it could sit without danger of tipping over and spilling its contents. "Given the shaky family situations of the majority of my students, you'd think I'd have learned to tread cautiously around that subject."

Colin washed his cookie down with a swallow of soda. If he wanted to develop a relationship with this woman, he'd have to share his history eventually. Why not give her a topline tonight? Perhaps if he opened up a bit, she'd realize his intentions were serious.

"You aren't prying. It's a fair question when two people are getting to know each other. I just don't talk about my family very often." Like not at all, as Mac had pointed out the other day. "But I can give you the basics."

"You don't have to."

"Yeah. I do. You might as well hear about the skeletons in my closet now. No sense putting it off."

"That sounds ominous."

"Not ominous. But not pleasant, either." He set his glass down and breathed deeply of the perfumed air. Maybe the sweet scent would mitigate some of the bitter memories. "When I was nine, my six-year-old brother and I were playing in the back-yard. I was supposed to be watching him, but I got engrossed in a comic book, he got bored—and the next thing I remember is hearing the screech of tires. He'd wandered out of the yard and was killed by a hit-and-run driver."

"Oh." The word was hushed, and shock flattened her fea-tures as she reached out and rested her fingers on the back of his hand, her touch warm. Comforting. Caring. "I'm so sorry."

"Me too." His voice rasped, and he swallowed. A swig of soda would help his parched throat, but he didn't want to break the contact she'd established. "The tragedy tore our family apart. My father blamed my mother. He said if she'd been paying more attention instead of drinking, it would never have happened. She countered that if he came home at a reasonable hour instead of working late at the office every day, she wouldn't drink so much—and he would have been around, keeping tabs on us when the accident happened."

"Did they . . . they didn't blame you, did they?" The pressure of her fingers increased with the intensity of her tone.

"Not in words. But I knew in their hearts they did. And they were right. I should have been watching him."

"No." She shook her head, her deep blue irises glinting with passion. "A nine-year-old isn't supposed to be his brother's keeper. You were a child yourself."

"I was old enough to take care of him in the backyard." Trish might be willing to cut him some undeserved slack, but he couldn't forgive himself as easily. "Anyway, an acrimonious divorce followed. We'd never been a model family. My mom always did drink too much, and my dad was a chronic worka-holic. Both vices worsened after Neal was killed. For the rest of my growing-up years, I shuttled back and forth between the two of them. I couldn't wait to go away to college and escape the constant tension."

"Do you stay in touch now?" She retracted her hand to take a sip of her own soda.

He missed the warmth of her fingers at once.

"I talk to my mom every few months. She lives on the West Coast now, is on her third husband, has a myriad of health issues—and still drinks too much. Dad died five years ago of a heart attack."

Trish let out a slow breath. "That's almost as bad as some of the family situations I encounter at school."

"I'm sure you've heard much worse."

"Bad is bad—different degrees of badness, yes, but similar ramifications. What kept you on the straight and narrow?"

"Nothing . . . for a while. I was one angry, hurting kid. I did some stuff that could have gotten me into a lot of trouble if I'd been caught, beginning with petty vandalism. I was heading for worse when my life took a turn for the better."

"What happened?"

"I met a foster kid in middle school by the name of Rick Jordan, who came from a much rougher background than I did. I tried to pull him into some of the stuff I was doing, but he wanted no part of it. Instead, he kept pushing me to go with him to his Sunday school. I resisted until he found the perfect bait—a weekend camping trip for the kids in his class. One of the volunteer chaperones was a cop from his church. He picked up on my attitude fast and talked a lot with me that weekend. And he stayed in touch afterward."

"Is he the reason you became a cop?"

"One of them." The rest he'd keep for another day. He'd

already spilled far more about his background than he'd planned. "He retired and moved to Florida, but I call him a few times a year."

"Sounds like God sent him your way when you most needed guidance. Without a strong support system, it's tough to change direction once you start down the wrong path."

He focused on her second comment, ignoring the first. "I had a strong support system in Rick and another friend too." But he'd told her plenty for this session. The story of the Treehouse Gang could wait.

As if sensing he'd reached his download limit, Trish leaned back. "Thanks for sharing all that."

"It seems only fair, since I already know a lot about you."

"That's true. You even checked my references."

"And all of them were complimentary."

"I'm glad to hear that." She motioned to his empty glass. "Would you like a refill?"

He inspected it. When had he downed all that soda?

"No, thanks." Much as he'd like to stay . . . perhaps spend the whole evening here among the roses with this appealing woman . . . he'd promised not to rush her. Better to take this in small increments at the beginning or he might scare her off. "I need to be going."

Was that a flash of disappointment in her eyes or just a trick of the early evening sun?

Impossible to tell.

"I'll walk you to the door." She rose, leaving behind her half crumbled, nibbled-at Oreo.

He followed her past the plastic bag he'd delivered, moving to the threshold as she pulled the door wide and stepped aside.

"I know you're swamped finishing up at school this week, but I'll call you Friday or Saturday."

"I'd like that."

"If you need anything before then, you have my number. Feel free to use it."

"I appreciate that."

He hesitated. She seemed so alone, standing in the doorway of this big, empty house that was a constant reminder of all she'd lost—husband, father, mother . . . not to mention the future she'd planned. The temptation to hug her was strong. Too strong to resist. He leaned toward her and . . .

Stop right there, Flynn! You've laid the groundwork. Don't overstep.

Check.

He jerked back. "I'll talk to you soon."

It took every ounce of his willpower to force himself to turn away. Stride down the winding stone path that led to the driveway. Get behind the wheel of his car. Back down the concrete to the street.

When he looked back, she was still standing in the doorway, a slender figure bathed in the warmth of the dipping sun.

Of its own accord, his foot eased back on the accelerator.

Man.

He'd never had this much difficulty leaving a woman behind.

Gripping the wheel, he pressed on the gas pedal and drove away.

But as soon as a semblance of normalcy returned to Trish's life, getting to know her a whole lot better was going to be his top priority.

Because now that the prosecuting attorney had decided there was no need for further investigation of Eileen Coulter's death, there should be smooth sailing ahead.

10

It was amazing what fifty bucks could buy you from a junkie desperate for a fix—especially when you dropped a hint there might be future jobs if he pulled off the first one.

Craig tugged his baseball cap lower, kept his chin down, and slipped out of the sleazy bar into the late-night darkness. Finding a suitable candidate hadn't been difficult. Addicts weren't hard to spot.

But this little adventure hadn't been in his Monday night plans.

He picked up his pace as he strode through the seedy neighborhood, peering over his shoulder, skirting dark alleys. He'd chosen this area for its close proximity to Trish's school, but that didn't mean he had to like being here. At least in his bar-hopping getup, no one had paid much attention to him—and if someone *had* noticed him, he looked nothing like he did in real life.

Nevertheless, this strategy was a bit of a gamble. Despite the promise of more cash in the future, the guy might decide it wasn't worth taking a chance after all and pocket the money.

Since the job could be done in less than a minute and there

was minimal risk, however, Craig was as certain as he could be his mark would come through for him.

Truth be told, there was more risk on *his* end—though that too was negligible.

Still, the inconvenience was annoying. If Trish had handed over the reins of the foundation to Matt, none of this would have been necessary. Who could have predicted that an art teacher prone to zoning out during numbers discussions between Matt and her mother would turn out to be a financial whiz who would dig into 990s and surf the web for info on the charities?

He muttered an oath and kicked an empty beer can out of his path. Lucky he'd had the foresight during his weeks of surveillance to create the documents he needed for Providence House. Once she reviewed them, she ought to be satisfied.

But it would be much, much safer if she left the administration of the foundation in Matt's hands. And if enough distractions—like the one he'd arranged tonight—kept her occupied, she might see the value of adding her trusted accountant as the third trustee, with full power to execute her wishes . . . and Craig's.

Mostly Craig's.

His lips curved up at the thought of all that cash wending its way toward the offshore account he'd established years ago. Trish might not be interested in Matt's romantic overtures, but she liked him. It was just a matter of nudging her to the point where she accepted the logic of putting him in charge. She could continue to designate the charities, and he'd write the checks. Better yet, he'd convince her to authorize electronic transfer of funds. Falsifying the books to suggest her wishes had been carried out would be child's play.

A car with rap music blaring through the windows decelerated as it approached him, and his momentary good humor vanished. Slowing cars were never a positive sign in a neighborhood like this.

He kept walking, but slipped his hand inside the pocket of his jacket and wrapped his fingers around the compact Beretta he'd tucked there.

The car and its occupants continued to roll past him—but he kept the gun in hand and picked up his pace.

After fifteen more minutes of fast and uneventful walking, the area began to improve. Fifteen minutes after that, he was sliding behind the wheel of the car he'd parked in a secure lot on the edge of downtown St. Louis.

Done.

Now he could make the long drive back to Matt's place and get some shut-eye.

Except he wasn't at all tired. His adrenaline was pinging like crazy from his walk on the wild side. In fact, he was pumped enough to pay Natalie another visit. Wouldn't she be surprised if he showed up at her door at this hour?

No doubt she'd welcome him with a smile—at the very least.

As he accelerated west on I-44, he toyed with that temptation for a few minutes. Dismissed it. He needed to be smart, and seeing any woman on a regular basis would be stupid.

But if everything went well on Wednesday, come Saturday night he'd find himself another bar . . . and another woman.

· · · · ·

"You about ready to call it a night?"

Trish looked over her shoulder at the school principal as she took another student drawing down from the wall of the classroom-lined hall.

"Close. I'd like to finish this first so all I have to do tomorrow is clean out the art room."

"That's fine. And great job on the exhibit. I had half a dozen parents tell me how much their son or daughter enjoyed your class."

She gave the middle-aged man a melancholy smile. "That's gratifying to hear. But I wish there'd been more intact families here tonight. I know some of the students were disappointed only one of their parents came."

"Hey . . . I'm grateful for what we can get. I worry more about the kids who didn't come at all because neither parent bothered to bring them."

"I hear you." Trish worked the tape off the edge of a drawing. "Are you waiting around for me to finish before you close up shop?"

"No. Chuck will do a final pass to turn off stray lights and lock doors. I was going to offer to walk you to your car."

"I appreciate that, but I'm parked close to the door. I'll ask Chuck to watch until I'm behind the wheel."

"Are you sure? Chuck's a fixture around here, but his arthritis is starting to impact his speed and agility."

"I'll be fine. We've never had any trouble on the property, and Chuck's vocal chords are in excellent shape. That booming voice of his has kept more than a few unruly students in line."

"No arguments there. I'll be around for a while tomorrow too, tying up loose ends. See you then."

After waving him off, Trish spent another fifteen minutes dismantling the exhibit she'd created on the walls. At last she packed up her bag, flipped off the lights in the art room, and went in search of the janitor.

She traipsed through the halls, peeked into classrooms, and called his name to no avail, pausing at last by the exit. Where could he be? The men's room? Having a smoke outside? On a phone call?

Wherever he was, she was *not* taking another tour of the school. She'd been on her feet for fourteen hours straight; her next destination was home.

From the depths of her shoulder tote she extracted tape, a

pad of paper, and pen. She scribbled a note to Chuck, ripped off the sheet, and stuck it to the door. He'd see it when he was ready to lock up and know she'd left.

Once outside, Trish inspected the schoolyard. The lighting was adequate, if not great, and her car was only fifty feet from the building. Other than the typical loud rap music coming from the open window of a nearby house and the revving of car engines in the distance, all was quiet on this Wednesday night. Matt's warning to be careful in this area was sound, but she'd had no issues during the past nine months—and the lot was empty except for her car and Chuck's.

Keys in hand, tote bag tucked against her side, she hurried toward her Civic, continuing to scan the schoolyard.

All clear.

But as she rounded the back of her car, everything changed.

Out of nowhere, a shadowy form leapt at her. Yanked her tote bag. Shoved her hard.

The attack was so sudden, so unexpected, that for a moment she was too shocked to do anything but clutch her bag and try to keep her balance.

The person jerked harder on the tote and shoved her again.

"Back off!" She yelled the command as loud as she could, inches from his face.

For an instant the guy—and it was a guy, no question about it despite the ski mask he was wearing—reared backward.

This was her window to run.

But he recovered too fast. As she began to swivel, preparing to dash back toward the building, he came at her again.

Letting her reflexes take over, she kneed him in the groin.

He grunted, doubled over, and spit out a string of words that scorched her ears.

But his fingers remained locked around her wrist, digging into the flesh like a vise.

The guy wasn't giving up.

As he once more stood upright, she countered with a wrist sweep to break his grip . . . poked him in the face with her key, aiming for his eyes . . . and punched him in the throat with her fist.

He yowled and released her.

She bolted for the building, screaming at the top of her lungs, praying her counterattack had deterred him.

It hadn't.

His steps pounded behind her . . . and the door was too far away.

Better to face him than let him grab her from behind.

She swung around, prepared to kick and punch again.

That's when she saw the knife.

Oh, God, help me!

She might be able to defend herself against a physical attack, thanks to the rudimentary tips she'd learned in that self-defense class she'd taken last summer, but she was no match for a sharp blade.

"Just take my money if that's what you're after." She threw her tote bag at him.

He batted it aside, eyes glittering with a wild rage.

The kind that could be drug-induced.

Her lungs locked.

Drugs would double or triple the danger.

"You hurt me, lady." The accusation came out in a guttural growl. "Nobody does that and walks away."

He lunged at her, knife blade glinting in the overhead lights.

She dodged him and screamed louder.

"Shut up!"

He sprang at her again, the point of the knife aimed at her heart.

Fear cycloned through her as she tried to sidestep him. If only she could buy herself a few precious seconds to get to the door, flip the inside lock, and call 911.

But that wasn't going to happen.

Because even though she managed to twist away from his grasp, the blade of the knife sliced through the flesh of her left forearm, leaving a long slash that immediately filled with blood. In seconds, rivers of crimson were running down to her hand, coating her palm, her fingers.

As shock rippled through her, the sudden wail of a police siren shattered the night air. It was close—and moving in fast.

After a minuscule hesitation, the guy turned, picked up her tote bag, and sprinted in the opposite direction of the siren, disappearing into the darkness.

Flashing police lights came into view, and the car swung into the school parking lot, the headlights blinding her.

Help had arrived.

She was safe.

As Trish raised a hand to shield her eyes from the harsh light, her shaky legs gave way and she sank to the blood-spattered pavement.

But there could have been much more blood. *Would* have been, if someone in one of the nearby houses hadn't heard her screams and called for help. If the police hadn't arrived precisely when they did. If the guy hadn't decided to run for it instead of making one more thrust that could have connected with a vital organ or artery.

As all of those ifs cascaded in her mind, the truth slammed home.

She'd almost been killed.

And with that stomach-churning realization, she lost her dinner.

. . . . .

"I think that covers most of the topics on our agenda. Any questions?" Kristin folded her hands on the papers in front of her and surveyed the small group gathered at the table in the church meeting room.

Rick slid some drawings in front of her and the two of them began hashing out scenery issues. Then the costumer wanted her to weigh in on a handful of fabric samples.

Colin leaned back and peeked at his watch. How the female member of the Treehouse Gang had managed to rope him in to do lights and sound for another one of her annual kids' shows was beyond him. Every year, he vowed it would be his last—and every year she guilt-tripped him into signing on again.

How could he say no to a few meetings and a one-week commitment during tech week, when she devoted months of planning and preparation to a project that built kids' self-esteem? He had the easiest job on the production crew.

Meaning he'd caved, as usual.

"What about you, Colin? Any questions?"

Rick, the costumer, and the publicity person were all looking at him, as was Kristin.

"Uh . . . no. It's the same physical setup as last summer. I'll use the same equipment suppliers. We should be good."

"How are you going to mike the Beast?"

"I'll figure that out once I see the costume." That would be the only challenge with the nonmusical version of *Beauty and the Beast* Kristin had chosen to direct for the church's youth theater production this summer. The rest of the stuff he could work out during tech week.

Kristin narrowed her eyes . . . but said nothing more. After all the kids' shows she'd directed, and all the years she'd conned him and Rick into helping with the technical stuff, she knew he'd come through.

"Okay. One more item before we break." Kristin riffled through her papers again.

As Colin stifled a groan, his phone began to vibrate.

Yes!

He'd take any excuse he could get to escape for a few minutes.

But as he pulled the cell off his belt and glanced at the screen, he frowned.

Why would Mac McGregor be calling him at nine thirty on a Wednesday night? It wasn't as if they socialized during off-duty hours. Now that he had a gorgeous wife waiting for him at home, Mac preferred spending his free time with her.

Go figure.

Colin managed to corral his grin as he stood and lifted the phone. "I need to take this. Someone from work."

He pressed the talk button, put the phone to his ear, and moved toward the corner of the room. "What's up, Mac?"

"A BOLO alert came in on the radio a few minutes ago. I thought you might be interested."

"Why are you tuned in to work stuff at this hour?" Colin squinted at the blank wall. "Aren't you on days this week?"

"Yeah. But Simmons had a family emergency and asked me to switch shifts with him today. The case in question is a first-degree robbery—and the victim was Trish Bailey."

Colin sucked in a breath and groped for the edge of the bookcase beside him. "Is she all right?"

"Yes—other than a mild case of shock and a bad laceration from the perp's knife."

Knife.

The word reverberated in his mind, his pulse ratcheting up with every echo.

Someone had attacked Trish with a knife.

"What happened?" He plunged his hand into his pocket, fumbling for his keys.

He listened as Mac filled him in on the statement Trish had provided to the city cop.

"Did they catch the guy?"

"Not yet. But officers are combing the area."

Bad news. If they didn't find this scumbag fast, they weren't likely to find him at all. That's how the odds worked, especially in that part of town.

"Where's Trish?"

"According to the cop at the scene, the paramedics bandaged her up and tried to convince her to let them take her to the hospital. She refused. She said she'd rather get stitched up at an urgent care center. The officer got the impression she doesn't like hospitals."

Understandable, based on recent family history.

"So what's the status?"

"She went to an urgent care center."

His grip tightened on the phone. "You mean she drove herself?"

"That's what I was told."

"The paramedics and the cop let her get in a car and drive after everything that happened?" Fury—and a healthy dose of alarm—nipped at his composure.

"Her injuries weren't life-threatening, and the blood loss wasn't severe. They couldn't force her to ride in the ambulance."

"One of the cops could have driven her."

"She refused that too. They also suggested she call someone to come and get her. She said she had no family and it was too late to bother any of her friends."

It wasn't too late to bother him. He'd told her to call, day or night. Why hadn't she taken him up on that offer?

A question he intended to ask her as soon as possible.

"Do you know which urgent care center she was going to?"

"Yeah." Mac passed on the name and address. "She picked one close to her house."

"Most of those places aren't open past eight o'clock."

"This one's open until ten. The officer checked for her and

alerted them she was coming. He also had one of the paramedics brief them on her condition."

"How long ago did she leave?"

"Minutes. They kept her talking until they were comfortable she'd calmed down and was steady enough to drive."

If she'd just left, he could probably beat her there.

"Thanks for the heads-up."

"Any time. Watch that heavy foot of yours on the way."

"I'll do my best." No sense defending his driving habits. Most cops—and detectives—drove too fast . . . on or off duty. Including him. And tonight wasn't going to be an exception.

"Let me know if I can do anything."

"Thanks. Sorry you had to work nights—but it was a lucky break for me."

"I doubt luck had much to do with it. God works in mysterious ways."

Since he wasn't up to a discussion about the enigmatic ways of the Almighty, he said good-bye . . . and turned to find Kristin and Rick hovering behind him.

"Are you okay?" Kristin laid a hand on his arm, the concern in her voice almost palpable.

He surveyed the room. It had emptied except for her and Rick, both of whom were regarding him with grave expressions.

"Yeah." The word croaked, and he cleared his throat. "Why?"

"You went white as a sheet." Kristin removed her hand but stayed close. "I thought you were going to pass out."

Colin jingled his keys. He needed to get out of here. Fast. But how to do it without tipping his hand about his feelings for Trish?

Rick saved him the trouble.

"This has something to do with that woman you met, doesn't it?"

Keeping secrets from these two was as futile as trying to control his heavy foot on the gas. Besides, since he hoped Trish would be playing a big role in his life going forward, why dodge the question?

Keys clenched in his fingers, Colin took a deep breath. "Yeah. She was mugged by a knife-wielding thug who sliced open her arm. One of my detective buddies called to tell me. She's on her way to an urgent care center. I'm hoping to get there first."

Kristin gave him a small push toward the door. "Go. Let us know how she is."

"I will." He started to walk away.

"Hey!"

He angled back.

Rick folded his arms. "What's her name?"

"Trish."

"Pretty." Kristin waved him toward the exit. "We'll want to meet her, you know."

The last part of her comment followed him outside as he pushed through the door.

Introducing her to Rick and Kristin was inevitable . . . but it wasn't a prospect he relished. She'd be in for an inquisition—and some ribbing, if they liked her. Which they would. How could anyone not like Trish—other than the mugger she'd tangled with tonight? From what Mac had said, she'd inflicted some damage of her own that would *not* endear her to him.

But she hadn't slashed the guy with a knife. Trish had taken the brunt of their scuffle.

Gritting his teeth, he slid behind the wheel, tore out of the parking lot, and ignored Mac's advice as he floored the Mazda. At this hour, and at this rate of speed, he should be able to make it to the urgent care center in ten minutes. Twelve, tops. Too bad he didn't have his work vehicle, though. With the Taurus's flashing lights and siren to clear his path, he could shave off a few more minutes.

As for Trish thinking it was too late to bother any of her friends—that might be true. But he was aiming to be much more than that.

And before this night was over, she'd know that beyond the shadow of a doubt.

11

She should have let the police officer drive her to urgent care.

As Trish guided the car down the final stretch, the dark splotch on the thick dressing the paramedics had applied to her injured arm continued to spread. To make matters worse, the cut throbbed and burned.

A lot.

A tear leaked out of the corner of her eye as she traveled the last half mile. There were acquaintances she could have tapped who would have come to her aid. Matt, for one. And Colin had told her to call at any time.

But she wanted no more personal encounters with Matt—and while Colin might have made it clear he'd like to get to know her better, thrusting him into the middle of a messy emergency wasn't the best way to start a relationship.

She could handle this herself.

Blinking back another tear, she slowed . . . executed a wide, careful swing into the urgent care parking lot . . . and angled into a spot near the front door.

She'd made it.

Barely.

Exhaling a shaky breath, she shut off the engine and rested her forehead against the steering wheel. The last hour had seriously sapped her stamina. The door might be only a short distance away, but she needed a minute to—

Tap. Tap. Tap.

At the gentle knock on her window, she jerked upright.

Colin's taut face stared back at her through the glass.

What in the world?

"Unlock the door." His muffled words seeped through the glass.

She reached across with her uninjured arm and groped for the automatic locks. The instant they clicked, he pulled open the door, hunkered down beside her, and gave her a fast but thorough sweep, his worried gaze lingering on the stained dressing before lifting to scrutinize her face.

"We need to get you inside. You're still bleeding."

"Not too much." A chill rippled through her despite the balmy late-May air. "The paramedics wouldn't let me leave until they were confident it was under c-control."

"It may have been then. It doesn't appear to be now." He stood and extended a hand.

She swung her legs out of the car and grasped his fingers. They were solid and strong and warm as he pulled her to her feet.

Good thing, because much to her disgust, she swayed.

"Whoa." He moved in close and grasped her shoulders.

"I'm f-fine. My legs are just . . . they're a little shaky. But I don't have far to go."

Instead of responding, he bent, slid an arm under her knees, and swept her into his arms.

"W-what are you doing?"

"Carrying you in." He shut her car door with his hip and

strode toward the entrance. "You look ready to fold, and you don't need a fall on top of a knife wound."

Since that made perfect sense, she decided not to object.

Besides . . . it felt like heaven to be held against his broad chest while his heart hammered a staccato rhythm against her ear.

"How did you know about this, anyway?" The cotton of his T-shirt was soft beneath her cheek, and she burrowed deeper, inhaling the rugged scent that was all male.

"The colleague who came with me to your house last week is on night shift and heard the report come in. He called me."

"Why?"

A muscle twitched in his jaw. "He assumed I'd want to know."

Before she could ask anything else, he pushed through the entrance of the building, into bright lights that made her squint.

"We've been waiting for you, Ms. Bailey." A thirtyish man in scrubs loomed in front of her.

"Where do you want her?" Colin tightened his grip. An endearing, protective gesture on his part . . . or wishful thinking on hers?

"First door on the left."

He continued down the hall to the room, where he gently sat her on an examining table, the scrubs-clad guy on his heels.

"You can stay if you like." The man directed the comment to Colin as he began unwrapping the dressing the paramedics had applied.

"Yes. Please." Trish touched his arm.

In response, he moved beside her, far enough back to give the guy room to work but close enough to touch her—and to see what was happening with her arm.

The nurse or technician or whomever the man was worked in silence until he'd removed the dressing.

When he took off the last strip of gauze, Trish's stomach heaved at the same moment she heard Colin's sharp intake of breath.

The oozing slice was six inches long, and it gaped open.

"That is one nasty cut." The scrubs guy deposited the soiled dressing in a waste disposal container, his tone conversational. "But the paramedics did a first-class job. Most of the bleeding has stopped. I'll clean it up, the doctor will suture it, and you'll be good to go."

His calm manner helped, as did the doctor's friendly demeanor once she entered. The woman introduced herself, donned some latex gloves, and examined the wound.

"You were very lucky. It looks worse than it is. If it was any deeper we'd be dealing with a more serious scenario. Go ahead and lie flat. This won't take long."

As she swung her legs up, Colin shifted his position and rested one comforting hand on her shoulder.

She winced while the woman administered the shots to numb her arm, and he gave her a gentle, reassuring squeeze.

The doctor went to work, explaining each step. The flush with a saline solution to remove any dirt. The application of antibacterial ointment. The types of sutures she was using. Once she began to stitch, she made small talk.

It wasn't a bad bedside manner, but Trish was too weary for conversation. Having Colin inches away was the only reason this night was bearable. That, and the numbing shots that had vanquished the pain.

After a while, the doctor got the hint and concentrated on stitching rather than speaking.

Once she finished and Trish was again sitting up, she handed her a list of complications to watch for, a sheet of instructions, and prescriptions for pain medication and an antibiotic to ward off infection.

"You can come back here in a week to ten days to have the stitches removed, or have your own physician take care of it. I saw in your file you were in for a tetanus booster six months ago, so you're covered on that score. We also have your medical insurance information from that visit. Unless there's been a change, all we need is a signature on a few forms."

"My insurance is the same."

"Then let's wrap this up so we can all go home. If you'd rather save yourself a trip to the pharmacy, we can fill the prescriptions for you here."

"That would be great." No way was she up to yet another stop tonight.

Five minutes later, prescription and paperwork in hand, Trish walked out the door, Colin close on her heels.

"I'm parked over there." He took her uninjured arm and motioned toward a Mazda, leading her that direction.

Her step faltered. "I can't leave my car here overnight."

"Yes, you can." He kept walking, urging her along. "I spoke with the doctor about it while you were signing papers. I also asked County to send a patrol through here a few times tonight. You can't drive with a numb arm."

Oh yeah. If she'd been thinking straight, she'd have realized that.

But she didn't want to ruin the rest of Colin's evening.

"Look . . . I can get a cab." She held back, forcing him to slow his determined pace. "You don't need to drive me home."

"Yes, I do. Assuming you have a key stashed somewhere on the property, that is." He urged her forward again.

That's right. Her keys were in the snatched tote bag.

But her mother had always kept one under the fairy statue in the rose garden. It would still be there.

"Yes. There's a spare in the garden." She continued to drag her feet. "But I've already intruded too much on your night. I bet you were in the middle of something when you got the call from your colleague."

With a resigned huff, he stopped and turned to her. "I was—

and itching for an excuse to leave. There's no need to feel guilty about pulling me away."

He seemed sincere, yet . . .

"Even so, it's late. You must be tired."

"Trish." He rested his hands on her shoulders again. Despite the shadows cast by the overhead lights, she could detect the worry etched in his features. "I'm not tired. And I'd have been a lot more upset if I hadn't found out about this until tomorrow. I want to drive you home. It's not an imposition. Okay?"

Her throat clogged. For two long years her own needs had taken second place to those of her mom and her students. Week after week, month after month, she'd shouldered all the duties and obligations and responsibilities alone. Only at night, when her time was at last her own and the busyness of the day was over, did she allow herself to yearn for the days when her life had been filled with love and laughter and companionship. When John had stood by her side as partner and friend and ally.

For this one evening, Colin had stepped into that role—and she didn't have the strength to refuse his generosity and kindness . . . even if it inconvenienced him.

"Okay. You can drive me home. Thank you."

Without a word, he linked his fingers with hers, guided her to the car, and helped her with her seat belt.

Once behind the wheel, he put the Mazda in gear and aimed it toward her house.

He drove without speaking—and after two silent miles, she gave him a surreptitious perusal. Although the car was dark, his brow appeared to be wrinkled. He was either worried about her . . . or he hadn't been as anxious for an excuse to get away from his earlier commitment as he'd implied and was regretting what he'd left behind.

Could that commitment have been . . . a woman?

She played with her seat belt. Wednesday wasn't a typical date night, and he'd been very clear about wanting to get to know her better—but that didn't mean his social life was lacking. With those sable eyes, that dark brown hair, and a pair of shoulders broad enough to be the envy of a Hollywood heartthrob, Colin Flynn was the epitome of tall, dark, and handsome.

If he sat home on Saturday nights—or Wednesday nights—it was by choice.

But he hadn't been sitting home tonight.

So where had he been?

If she wanted to dig, this was her chance. In five minutes, she'd be home.

"You, uh, said you were busy when your coworker called you about me but were looking for an excuse to escape." She played with the edge of the dressing covering her arm. "That's how I feel at some of our staff meetings."

A marginal opening . . . but the best she could come up with in her present state.

"Close." He hung a left. "A friend of mine directs a church-sponsored children's show every summer. I do the sound and lights. We were having a production meeting."

Not what she'd expected.

But impressive.

"That sounds like a commendable volunteer activity."

"I'll concede it's a worthwhile program. However, I don't have an ounce of greasepaint in my blood. To be honest, I'd rather coach a soccer team or take the kids on a camping trip. But this means a lot to Kristin."

Her stomach dropped.

The friend he'd mentioned was a woman—and he was doing a job he obviously disliked to please her.

That did *not* bode well. If he'd signed on for an activity in which he had no interest to stay in this woman's good graces, they had to be more than mere friends. Right?

Except . . . hadn't he told her just two nights ago he'd never met a woman he liked enough to consider a potential partner for life?

So who was this Kristin?

"I can't imagine tackling a project like that. Dealing with kids in art class is taxing, but putting on a stage show . . . wow. Your friend is braver than I am. She sounds amazing."

"She is. But don't sell yourself short. You've weathered some tough storms over the past couple of years. I also heard you put up quite a fight tonight. When did you take the self-defense class?"

He'd shifted the spotlight back to her.

So much for her interrogation techniques.

"After I was hired at the school. I took a one-day seminar, more to please my mom than anything else. The few instructions I remembered did slow the guy down, but if the police hadn't shown up when they did . . ." A shudder rolled through her.

He reached over and laid his hand on her knee. "You're safe now."

"I know." In fact, she had a feeling she'd always feel safe if Colin was beside her.

"Call coming in." He withdrew his hand, pulled out his phone, and scanned the screen before he put it to his ear. "What's up?"

For the most part, the conversation was one-sided—on the other end—but after Colin hung up, he gave her the gist.

"That was Mac, my colleague. The officers found your purse tossed in an alley. The wallet was inside, and your credit cards and driver's license were still there. The cash was gone."

She sighed and shook her head. "He took a lot of risk for a very small payoff. I never carry more than thirty dollars."

"A word of advice." Colin turned into the residential area

she called home and shot her a quick glance. "If this ever happens to you again—and I hope to God it doesn't—let go of the bag. A few bucks and potential credit card hassles aren't worth your life."

"I know. I can't believe I held on to it as long as I did. That was a huge m-mistake." She swallowed past the catch in her voice. "I seem to be making a lot of those recently."

"Hey." He touched her knee again. "I'm not trying to beat up on you. I should have waited for a better time to broach that subject."

"Don't apologize. You're right. They hammered that into us in the class, but it was like my brain froze even though my body responded on autopilot with defensive moves."

"Everyone reacts differently in a panic situation. You may have forgotten to let go of the bag, but you bought yourself precious seconds by doing the other stuff. And all's well that ends well. Plus, now that they've got the purse, they might be able to find some prints and nail this guy."

"Oh." She clapped her hand over her mouth. "I just remembered. The guy was wearing latex gloves. I should have told that to the officer."

Silence as he swung into her driveway and shut off the engine.

"That's not the best news I've had all day. Let me pass it on to Mac. He can let them know."

Once more, he pulled out his phone, punched in some numbers, and gave his colleague the update.

"Assuming the bag's clean, you'll have it back tomorrow." He pocketed the phone. "Sit tight. I'll get the door."

She didn't argue. Weariness, self-reproach, and worry over a woman named Kristin had depleted the last reserves of her energy.

A few second later, the door swung open and she got out, with a welcome assist from Colin.

"How's the arm feeling?"

"The numbness is starting to wear off."

"In other words, it's beginning to throb."

That was putting it mildly.

"I'll take a painkiller in a few minutes." She cradled her arm as she walked, his hand under her uninjured elbow. Steadying. Guiding. Supporting.

"Where's the spare key?"

"In the back." She described the location.

"Give me sixty seconds."

He left her on the front porch, easing her into one of the wicker chairs that had been there for as long as she could remember, their chintz cushions faded from the sun.

One minute passed. Two. Three.

At the four-minute mark, she pushed herself to her feet. Finding the fairy statue in the dark would be a challenge for someone unfamiliar with the backyard. She'd have to help him.

But as she walked across the porch, he jogged around the side of the house.

"Sorry." He took the steps two at a time. "Finding fairies isn't my forte." After flashing her a grin, he unwrapped the foil-encased key, slipped it in the lock, opened the door . . . and frowned. "Why isn't the security system beeping?"

So he'd noticed the keypad by the door in the kitchen during his previous visits.

She had a feeling not much got past this man.

"I didn't set it today." She edged past him, into the foyer.

"Why not?"

"There's never been any trouble in this neighborhood. But I always set it at night."

"You need to set it from now on whenever you leave the house."

"It's safe here, Colin."

"Nowhere is safe. And the thug who did that"—he laid his

fingers on her bandaged arm—"knows who you are and where you live."

Panic swept through her, followed by a wave of nausea.

"But . . . it was just a random mugging. Why would he come all the way out here to find me? He got what he wanted." Yet even as she asked the question, she recalled the fury in his eyes and his words after she fought back.

Nobody does that and walks away.

"I'm not saying he will. I'm saying always assume the worst and take precautions."

"So much for sleeping tonight, even with an armed security system."

"I could stay. You have plenty of couches in this place."

"Seriously?"

"If it would help you get some rest."

Of course it would help her get some rest!

But the man had his own life, and a job to go to tomorrow. It wouldn't be fair to impose any more than she already had.

"I appreciate that—more than I can say—but I'll be fine." She managed to infuse her tone with far more bravado than she felt. "The doors and windows have excellent locks, and the security system is top-notch. I tripped the alarm by mistake once not long after I moved back, and I couldn't remember the password when the alarm company called. The police were here in four minutes flat."

He studied her for a few moments. "If you want the truth, I think *I'd* sleep better if I stayed."

Warmth filled her heart at his revealing admission, and she touched his arm. "You'll sleep better in your own bed. I wouldn't mind if you called me once you got home, though. By then I'll have the alarm set for the night and everything should be safe and quiet."

A few beats ticked by. At last he covered her hand with his.

"Fine. But I also want you to promise you'll keep your phone within reaching distance, and that you'll call me if anything spooks you—day or night."

"I'm not in the habit of bothering people late at night."

"I'm used to being bothered at all hours. It goes with the job. Promise me."

With his intent brown eyes fixed on her, it was hard to think—and impossible to say no.

"I promise."

"And call me in the morning as soon as you wake up. I'll either drive you over to get your car or tap an officer to do it if I'm tied up."

"I can get a cab to—"

"Trish."

She fell silent.

"In case you haven't figured it out, I want to be part of your life. I wish you'd had the officer or paramedics call me tonight instead of trying to drive with a bleeding arm." His voice scraped, and his Adam's apple contracted. "I know you're a strong, independent woman who's used to handling things on your own, but there's nothing wrong with calling on friends when you need them. And I'd like to be one of those—at the very least."

"I'd like that too."

"Good." Before she realized his intent, he leaned down and brushed his lips over her forehead. "I like to back up my words with actions." The murmured statement was a gentle, oh-so-lovely puff of warmth against her skin.

When he eased away, it took every ounce of her willpower to remain motionless instead of throwing herself into his arms and begging him to stay.

He too seemed to be fighting the impulse to get close again.

Instead he turned and clutched the knob. "I'll call you in twenty minutes."

"Thank you for everything you did tonight."

With a lift of his hand, he exited, closing the door with a quiet click behind him.

Trish moved to the sidelight window. He was striding toward his car, as if he needed to put distance between them before he succumbed to temptation and did more than kiss her forehead.

And she'd have let him.

Colin Flynn might be new in her life, but already he was becoming an integral part of it.

She stayed by the sidelight until his red taillights disappeared, then methodically checked the doors and windows, set the alarm, and retreated to her bedroom, cell in hand, to await his call.

Once in bed, she adjusted the pillows behind her head and sent a silent thank you heavenward for the favorable outcome of this night.

As for the future . . . she prayed it would be calm and trauma free. And after all she'd been through, surely God would grant that request.

Wouldn't he?

. . . . .

Colin sat on the edge of his bed and set his phone on the nightstand. Trish might think he'd sleep better here, but he hadn't been exaggerating when he'd told her he'd get more shut-eye at her place.

Hearing her voice over the phone hadn't helped his peace of mind, either. Hard as she'd tried to hide them, subtle threads of apprehension had woven through her words as she'd assured him the house was secure and the alarm was set.

She was scared.

Plus, she had to be hurting.

How was he supposed to sleep, knowing both of those things?

His cell vibrated again, and he snatched it up. Could she have changed her mind, decided to take him up on his offer?

But the name on the screen dashed those hopes.

"Hi, Mac." He leaned back against the headboard.

"Did I wake you?"

Was he kidding?

"No. Did they catch the guy?" Why else would his colleague be calling back at—Colin peered at his bedside clock—eleven o'clock?

"Sorry. No. But I touched base with the city detective assigned to the case and asked him to keep us in the loop on any developments. He called to let me know he found something interesting during his walk around the schoolyard. You're not gonna like it."

He tensed. "What did he find?"

"A photo of Trish Bailey."

As the implication sank in, Colin bolted upright.

Tonight's mugging hadn't been a random act of violence.

Trish had been targeted.

He raked his fingers through his hair and stood. "Someone had her in their sights."

"That's how I read it. The guy must have dropped the photo while he was running away. It was partially folded, but there was enough visible to catch Delaney's eye on his walk-around. Candid shots of young Caucasian women aren't exactly common in that neighborhood. He showed it to the responding cop, who identified her. He agreed to take a picture of it and email it to both of us."

Colin began to pace, dissecting this latest development.

"I'm not liking what this suggests. If the mugger needed a photo to identify his victim, this had to be a paid job. Someone gave the guy Trish's photo and told him when and where to find her. The question is who would do that . . . and why?"

"Maybe the lady can provide some answers. She might have an enemy she neglected to mention."

"You've met her. Does she strike you as the type to have enemies?"

"No—but what other explanation could there be?"

He wished he knew.

"That's what I'll have to find out. Will you call me if anything else breaks tonight?"

"It's getting late."

"You won't be interrupting my sleep."

"Got it. But don't hold your breath. They're done processing the scene, and the guy wore gloves. Unless a witness comes forward, this case is over."

The chances of anyone in that area volunteering information were nil. It was a miracle someone had called the police in response to Trish's screams.

"I hear you. Thanks for being proactive on this."

"I don't like loose ends, either. Good night."

The line went dead, and Colin checked his email. No photo yet from the city detective.

Cell in hand, he headed to the kitchen for a soda. Going to bed would be futile. He wanted to see the picture the city detective had found first.

After that?

He might lie down. Tomorrow was going to be busy, and with his adrenaline-laced job, he needed to be at the top of his game every day. Sufficient sleep was imperative to that, and most nights he had no difficulty logging seven or eight hours.

But tonight wasn't going to be one of them.

12

Colin was early.

As the chiming doorbell echoed through the silent kitchen, Trish steadied her mug of coffee and glanced at the digital clock on the microwave. Nine twenty instead of the nine thirty they'd agreed on during their phone conversation an hour ago.

Not that his premature arrival mattered. She'd been up for three hours. What was the point of staying in bed, staring at the ceiling, once the sun came up? She hadn't logged more than three hours of restless sleep during the dark hours of the night, and there was less chance she'd catch any shut-eye with light spilling into the bedroom window.

Leaving her mug in the kitchen, she smoothed a hand over her hair, crossed to the foyer, and peered through the peephole.

Frowned.

Why had Matt Parker shown up unannounced?

She flipped the deadbolt and pulled the door open. "Good morning. This is a surprise." Stepping back, she ushered him in.

"Sorry to intrude without warning, but I was in the area and thought I'd drop off the material you wanted on Providence . . ." As he eased past her into the foyer, he gaped at the edge of the bulky dressing, visible below the three-quarter-length sleeve of her shirt. "What happened?"

"I was mugged." She shut the door and gave him a quick recap of her eventful evening.

"I can't believe someone attacked you with a knife." Faint red splotches mottled his complexion, and an undercurrent of anger tightened his voice. "Did they catch the guy?"

"Not that I've heard. Would you like a cup of coffee?"

"I could use one, after that news."

"Why don't I bring it out to the front porch? It's relaxing there in the morning sun."

"All right." He lifted the folder of material in his hand. "Where do you want this?"

"On the chair is fine." She transferred the bulky bag resting on the seat to the floor.

"Would you like me to carry that somewhere for you? It's not part of your standard foyer décor—and you shouldn't be straining that arm."

"That's okay. It's all the stuff the CSU team collected, but I'm not ready to deal with it yet. I'll meet you in front in a minute."

She left him in the foyer, already regretting her offer of coffee. No way did she want him hanging around, with Colin scheduled to arrive in mere minutes.

But her mother had trained her well, and rudeness was a no-no. If the man had made a special trip to drop off the material she'd requested, the least she could do was offer him a beverage.

Halfway across the kitchen, though, she paused. Did he take cream and sugar? For the life of her, she couldn't recall.

Better ask.

She retraced her steps, the rubber soles of her flats noiseless on the tile floor.

As she started to turn the corner of the hall into the foyer, however, she pulled up short. Matt was angled away from her, but she had a clear view of him—and he was rummaging around in the CSU bag.

What on earth . . . ?

Melting back into the shadows, she watched him poke through the contents for another few seconds. Then he picked up the Providence House folder from the chair and slid it inside. After securing the top, he slipped quietly out the front door, closing it with a soft click behind him.

Trish stared into the empty foyer, trying to make sense of what she'd seen.

Failed.

There was no reason for him to paw through the CSU bag. Those were personal effects—and none of his business.

As for taking the folder inside . . . what was that all about? She'd never think to look there for it after watching him put it on the chair. Instead, she'd scour the house, wondering if she'd picked it up and set it somewhere else—all the while fearing she'd had another memory lapse. Like leaving the burner on under the frying pan. Forgetting to put the filter basket in the coffeemaker. Mistaking the time of their movie date. Miscounting her mother's . . .

She gasped.

Groped for the doorframe.

Tried to breathe as a staggering possibility took shape in her mind.

Was it conceivable she hadn't miscounted the medicine?

What if . . . what if her so-called mistakes hadn't been lapses but setups? An attempt to make it seem as if she was losing it?

Her head began to pound in rhythm with the throbbing in her arm, and she rubbed her temple.

No.

This was crazy thinking. She was jumping to ridiculous conclusions.

Matt could have a logical explanation for rifling through the CSU bag—and there might be a reason he'd put the Providence House folder in there.

Before she got too carried away, why not give him his coffee . . . and a chance to explain?

Pulse racing, she returned to the kitchen, filled a mug, and joined him on the front porch.

"You were right. This is a perfect spot in the morning." He rose from one of the wicker chairs as she came through the door. "Aren't you joining me?" He took the mug she handed him.

"I had mine already." She rubbed the damp palm of her un-injured hand down her jeans, trying for a casual, conversational tone. "Do you need cream or sugar?"

"Black is fine. Shall we?" He motioned to a cushioned seat. She dropped into it and perched on the edge.

"You seem tense." He sat beside her.

"I didn't sleep well."

"I'm not surprised, after everything that happened last night." The blotchiness in his complexion had evened out, and his voice was calmer now. "I can't believe you got mugged. It's shocking. But that isn't the best part of town—especially at night."

"I've never had any trouble there in the past." She needed to redirect the conversation. Give him an opening to talk about his strange behavior in the foyer. "Um . . . thanks again for dropping off the Providence House material."

"Happy to do it."

"You put the file on the chair in the foyer, right?"

"Yes. You saw me do it." His eyes thinned. "Did you forget?"

Not a word about moving the folder.

She squeezed the arms of her chair. "No. Just double-checking."

He took a sip of his coffee, watching her. "I worry about you. I think all the strain you've been under is taking a serious toll."

"I'm hoping life will be calmer going forward—but there are still difficult tasks ahead. Like going through the CSU bag."

"There's no hurry on that. Whatever is in there can wait, can't it?"

He would know, after poking through it minutes ago. Yet no mention of that, either.

This was freaking her out.

"Trish?"

She blinked at him. What had he asked? Oh . . . about waiting to sort through the CSU bag.

"Yes. There's nothing in there I need. I'll get to it next week."

A familiar Taurus pulled up in front of the house, parking on the street instead of the driveway since Matt's car occupied that spot.

"Are you expecting company?" Twin creases appeared on Matt's forehead.

"Yes. Detective Flynn offered to bring my tote bag by this morning and drive me over to pick up my car at urgent care."

"I would have been happy to do that." The grooves above his nose deepened.

"I appreciate that." She tried to smile, but her stiff lips refused to cooperate. "It's a moot point, though. My neighbor ran me over earlier."

As Colin strode up the driveway, her bag in hand, Matt drained his mug and stood. "I need to be going."

"Thanks again for stopping by." She rose too.

Colin ascended the steps to the broad front porch, gave Matt a quick scan, and shifted his attention to her. "I hope I'm not interrupting anything."

"No. Matt was leaving. You remember Matt Parker, my mom's accountant."

"Of course."

After the two men exchanged a quick handshake, Matt set

his mug on a side table, said good-bye, and retreated down the stone walkway to his car.

"Everything okay?" Colin lowered his voice, narrowing his eyes as he scrutinized her.

"I'm not sure. Why don't you come inside for a minute?"

He didn't ask any questions, just followed her in as Matt pulled out of the driveway and drove away.

Once the door closed behind them, he set her tote bag on the floor and twined his fingers with hers. "What's wrong?"

She wanted to lean into him, let him wrap his strong arms around her, ask him to solve this new, disturbing puzzle.

But she wasn't the leaning-in type. Nor was she the type to foist her concerns on someone else.

A helping hand and a fresh perspective, however, would be welcome.

"Just when I think life is beginning to calm down, I get hit with another curveball."

"Like last night?" He touched the edge of the dressing on her arm.

"No. This morning."

One of his eyebrows rose. "What happened?"

"See that bag?" She pointed to it.

"Yes. It's the one I brought you from the CSU."

"It's been there since the night you delivered it. I haven't opened it—but Matt did, while I went to get his coffee." She told him the story, including how he tucked the Providence House folder inside. "I offered him a chance to explain before you got here, but he didn't take it. Instead, he reiterated he'd left the folder on the chair. Why would he do that?"

Colin pondered that for a moment, brow furrowed, then shook his head. "I have no idea."

"Neither have I—but I do have kind of a . . . bizarre . . . theory."

"I want to hear it. But first . . ." He stroked a finger down her cheek. "Tell me how you are. Did you get much sleep?"

"Some."

"Have you eaten anything yet this morning?"

"No. I wasn't hungry."

"Do you have any eggs in the house?"

"Yes."

He took her arm. "I'll make you an omelet. After that, we'll talk."

"You don't have to cook for me."

"I'll make one for myself too. I think better on a full stomach."

She had a feeling his offer was more about ensuring she ate than enhancing his thinking ability, but she didn't argue. No one had prepared a homemade meal for her in years.

After settling her at the table with a fresh cup of coffee and some juice, he went to work . . . and in less than five minutes there were two cheese and mushroom omelets on the table.

"These smell delicious." She inhaled the savory aroma.

"I don't cook much, but the few dishes in my repertoire aren't bad. Better yet, they're fast and easy. Eat up."

He picked up his fork, but when she bowed her head to say a brief, silent blessing, he froze. Only after she finished did he dig into his omelet.

"Did that make you uncomfortable?" Better to get a handle on his faith now, find out if that was going to cause a snag in their relationship.

His fork stilled for a minute, and then he cut off a piece of the egg dish with the edge of the tines. "I don't pray much."

"Because you don't believe?"

"I believe in God. Prayer, not so much. I was raised in a Christian home—in name, at any rate—but I've never seen much evidence the Almighty has any interest in his creation. I prayed like crazy after Neal was hit by that reckless driver, and he still died. Nor do I see many examples of his goodness and kindness and mercy in my job."

She propped her chin in the palm of her hand. "Yet you're still in law enforcement. Despite all the shortcomings you see in your fellow man, you haven't given up. You continue to seek justice and try to protect people."

He shot her a wary look. "And your point is . . ."

"That's sort of how God operates. This is a flawed world, no question about it—but he saved it anyway . . . and he's never given up on us."

"How can you say that after all the bad stuff you've had to deal with in the past two years?"

"It hasn't all been bad. And in the midst of the bad stuff, there's been good too."

"Like what?"

"I met you."

He squinted at her, a hint of warmth—and amusement—springing to life in his eyes. "Were you on the debate team in high school or college?"

"No."

"Their loss. Go ahead and eat." He dived back in.

The conversation about God was over.

But he believed. That was a plus. And they could continue this discussion another day, when bizarre theories weren't whirling through her brain.

Trish followed his example, her appetite returning as she scarfed down his offering.

He kept the conversation on impersonal topics until she finished her meal, then refilled her coffee, removed her plate, and sat across from her.

"Now tell me your theory."

"It's more a suspicion than a theory—and it's going to sound nuts."

"I hear crazy stuff every day in my job. Coming from you, I doubt it's going to sound nuts."

"You better reserve judgment on that." She wrapped her fingers around her mug. "I'm beginning to wonder if all those mistakes I've supposedly been making these past few weeks aren't mistakes after all."

If he was taken aback by that startling announcement, he gave no visible sign of it. Maybe all detectives had the inscrutable demeanor down pat.

"Tell me more." He took a sip of his coffee.

"There isn't much. I haven't had a chance to think through this yet. But when I line up all my apparent memory lapses, Matt was always involved."

"What about your mom's medication?"

He'd homed in on the very question that was nipping at the edges of her composure.

"On at least two occasions he was in the kitchen alone, and the medicine was very accessible."

"Are you suggesting he might have meddled with it?"

She exhaled and combed her fingers through her hair. "That's where all the speculation falls apart. Matt is a solid Christian guy with excellent credentials. Why would he want to hurt my mom?"

"Why did he put the folder in the CSU bag?"

Another question with no answer.

Colin tapped a finger on the glass-topped table. "What do you know about his background?"

"You mean personal stuff?"

"Yes."

"Not much. He never mentions his family or what he does in his free time, other than taking care of his property. He has a small house on twenty or thirty acres outside of St. Louis, so I imagine maintenance takes a lot of hours—especially if he's as meticulous about that as he is about his accounting work."

"What did the two of you talk about on your dates?"

"Our lunch lasted less than an hour, and all we did was chitchat. The movie wasn't conducive to conversation. The only new information I learned that night was that he was born in Boston." She rested her sore arm on the table. "I may not know a lot about his history, but he has excellent professional credentials, and everything I've observed over the past year suggests he's conscientious and hardworking. That's why the notion he might be involved in anything . . . nefarious . . . is off the wall."

"I've heard—and seen—stranger things, believe me. I've also learned that the lack of an apparent motive doesn't mean there isn't one." He pulled out his cell phone. "As a matter of fact, I have one new piece of information that gives your theory more credence. I was going to show you this after we ate breakfast."

He tapped a few buttons, then shifted the phone so she could see the screen.

Her own image stared back at her from an unfamiliar photo.

"Where did you get that?"

"The city detective investigating the mugging found it in the schoolyard. It's a computer printout. We're assuming your attacker dropped it."

"You mean he was carrying a photo of me?" She tried to wrap her mind around that. "Why would some random mugger have a . . . oh!" Her stomach bottomed out as the implication slammed home. "It wasn't random, was it? He was after me specifically."

Colin rested his hand on hers. "That's our theory."

"But why would some junkie want to mug *me*, and not someone else?" She tried to swallow past the sudden, acrid taste of fear on her tongue. "Why not rob the first person he came across? Their money is as good as mine."

"Unless he wasn't after money." Colin stroked his fingers back and forth over her knuckles, never breaking eye contact. "Someone may have paid him to mug you. Any cash he got from your purse was a bonus."

"But . . . why would anyone pay to have me mugged?"

"I don't have an answer to that. Nor do I have an answer to why Matt Parker might have been trying to set you up to seem forgetful. Or why he might have fiddled with your mother's medication. But if this is all some sort of grand plan, the stakes are deadly. You could have been killed last night . . . and your mother did die."

As his quiet words hung in the air between them, she began to shake. It had been hard enough to accept her own culpability in her mother's death, but now he was talking premeditated murder.

The situation was becoming more surreal by the minute.

"What's going on here?" Her words came out in a hollow whisper.

"There are a lot of questions floating around this room, none of which I can answer. But I can promise you this. Over the next couple of days, I'm going to do some digging on your friend Matt. It's possible he's the key to all of this."

"That makes no sense. He does pro bono work for the church, and he never misses a Sunday service. Our pastor holds him in high regard, and my mother thought the world of him."

"How long has he lived in St. Louis?"

"I think he moved here three years ago from somewhere on the East Coast. I know he also lived in London for a while too."

"What did he do there?"

"He mentioned investment banking once. I assume his job took him there."

"And now he's a small-time accountant in St. Louis. A curious career downshift. Any idea what prompted it?"

"No. He never said."

"I'll see what I can find out about that—and a lot of other things." He finished his coffee, rose, and began stacking their dishes in the dishwasher.

"I can do that."

"It will only take a minute. Then I'll drive you over to the urgent care center."

"No need. My neighbor saw me on the porch earlier while he was working in his garden, and after he heard my story he offered to take me. I thought I'd save you a trip. I don't want to become a nuisance."

"Trust me, you don't have to worry about that." He paused to lock gazes with her for a moment, then resumed stacking. "What are your plans for the day?"

"I was going to clean my classroom, but I already called the principal and told him I won't be down until next week. For the next two days I'm going to hang around here and be lazy."

"Sounds like a smart move."

"Will you let me know if you unearth anything helpful?"

"Yes. In fact . . ." He finished slotting their plates and turned to her. "I was hoping you might have dinner with me tomorrow night. Something casual. Do you like Mexican?"

Warmth bubbled up in her heart, chasing away a tiny bit of the chill that had taken up residence there over the past forty-five minutes. "Love it."

"How does Hacienda sound?"

"Perfect. They have a great patio."

"I know. Let's try for six thirty. Barring an emergency, that will give me a chance to go home and change into jeans. If some big case breaks and I get delayed, I'll call you."

"I'm flexible. Whenever you come will be fine."

"Walk me to the door?" He held out his hand.

She stood and linked her fingers with his as they strolled to the foyer.

At the door, he leaned down and brushed his lips over her forehead again. "Take a nap this afternoon—and arm the security system while you're sleeping."

"You don't think that guy is going to come after me again, do you?"

"I don't know what to think. My gut says no. If seriously hurting you was the goal, he'd have pulled the knife the instant you came around the car. Based on what you told the city cop, he only did that after you fought back. I'm thinking the attack might have been a scare tactic."

"Who would want to scare me? And why?"

"That's what I'm hoping to discover." He leaned a shoulder against the doorframe, his expression speculative. "Did you tell Parker what happened?"

"Yes."

"What was his reaction?"

"He seemed shocked . . . and a tad angry. I might not have wanted to date him, but he's a nice man, with a kind heart. He may be a little different since his accident, but . . ."

"Wait." Colin straightened up. "Define different."

"I'm not certain I can. He comes across as kind of . . . tense. On edge. And his eyes . . . I don't know." She lifted a shoulder as she struggled to capture her impressions. "They feel different somehow. But he did have a head injury, and that can affect personality. My instincts might be off."

"I doubt it. And never discount instincts. They've saved my hide on more than one occasion. Let me see what I can find, and I'll fill you in tomorrow night. Lock up after me."

"Believe me, locking up is my top priority."

"Keep it that way." He squeezed her fingers, then slipped out.

She bolted the door behind him, yawning while she watched through the window until he pulled away. She needed another cup of coffee.

Skirting the CSU bag, she suppressed a shiver. She might not want to believe Matt was capable of doing anything to undermine—or hurt—her, but the baffling behavior she'd witnessed less than an hour ago suggested there was a furtive side to the man.

What was going on with him?

Who was Matt Parker, really?

Had he played a role in the mugging . . . and in her mother's death?

Once in the kitchen, she pulled out her laptop and booted it up. Colin could find information on Matt she didn't have access to, but the internet was a great tool. Who knew what she might discover?

And between the two of them, perhaps they'd turn up a few answers to the list of troubling questions about an accountant whose mild manner was beginning to look like a dangerously deceptive façade.

- - - - -

He'd paid for a mugging, not a knife attack.

If he could get his hands on the jerk who'd slashed Trish, he'd kill him.

Craig shoved aside the sliding door at the back of Matt's house and stomped out onto the deck. He couldn't care less about Trish's injuries . . . but a knife assault got a lot more police attention than a mugging.

And now that detective was hanging around her.

Hovering cops were never a good thing.

And Colin Flynn was as sharp as they came, based on the research he'd done on the man.

He slammed his beer onto the patio table next to the turkey sandwich he'd made for lunch and glared into the backyard. Three squirrels played a game of tag through the uncut grass. A cardinal swooped down to the empty bird feeder and left disappointed. Two deer picked their way through the shadows of the woods that abutted the lawn, skirting the tall weeds that separated grass from forest.

His lips curled in distaste.

What could have attracted Matt to this solitary game preserve, where the only lights at night were provided by the moon and stars and the closest decent restaurant was twenty miles away?

But he wouldn't be here forever—and it was better than the dives he'd called home in the weeks preceding his grand entrance on that stormy night.

He dropped into the chair and released the tab on the beer can, the pent-up carbon dioxide hissing in the quiet air.

It was also a safe retreat. A secluded place where he could hang out without fear of being discovered. The perfect cover for a man in his position.

Unless that detective got nosy, thanks to the botched mugging that had been intended to distract Trish, not attract undue police attention.

He swigged the beer, waved a hungry fly away from his sandwich, and inhaled a lungful of the pollen-laced air. He was probably getting worked up for no reason. There was nothing to connect him to that mugging. If they happened to catch the junkie—an unlikely prospect in that part of town—the guy didn't know who he was, and he'd been careful not to leave any prints on the money or photo he'd tucked into the envelope. So what if the detective hung around Trish? There was no evidence to implicate him or Matt in her attack . . . or in anything else.

The latter was the one piece of positive news to come out of

Matt's visit to Trish's house this morning. None of her mother's medicine had been in the CSU bag. The cops must have followed standard protocol and destroyed it.

It wouldn't have mattered much in any case, though. Even if a few of the vitamin capsules that had been emptied and refilled with powdered digoxin were still around, who'd think to look inside them? And the only prints on the bottles would be Trish's. Caution had been the key word in this operation. That's why there was always a pair of latex gloves tucked into his pocket—and Matt's.

He picked up his sandwich and took a healthy bite, feeling better by the minute. There was no need to worry. All the bases had been covered. The mugging might have taken a different turn than he'd expected, but it had accomplished its main goal of distracting Trish—hopefully enough to convince her to let Matt worry about the foundation.

If it didn't . . . there were other persuasions in his bag of tricks.

Leaning back in his chair, he lifted his face to the sun and let his tension seep out. Why not enjoy this perfect day? He was past the hardest part. The pieces were falling into place. His goal was in sight. All he had to do was bide his time and keep his eye on the prize.

The road ahead should be smooth and straight.

13

"How's your friend Trish doing?"

Colin was focused so intently on his computer screen that it took a second for Mac's question to register.

He glanced over as the other man dropped into his chair at the adjacent desk. "Last I heard, she was okay."

"When might that have been?" Lips twitching, Mac linked his hands behind his head.

He would ask that.

"We had a brief conversation at lunchtime."

"In other words, you have a recent update."

"Yeah. You have an issue with that?"

"Nope. I'd be disappointed if you weren't pursuing her. She strikes me as a class act. Hot too."

"I wonder how Lisa would feel about that comment?"

"Hey—I'm married, not blind." He straightened up and rolled closer to his desk. "What're you working on? Your nose was glued to the screen when I came in."

Colin tapped a finger against his keyboard. Why not get his colleague's take on the latest developments? Mac's instincts were strong, and he could use some additional brainpower on this puzzle.

"Are you going to be here for a few minutes, or is this a quick in and out?"

"I'm here for the duration . . . unless Sarge assigns me to a breaking case. But at three o'clock on a Friday afternoon, I'm hoping that doesn't happen. Lisa and I have plans for the evening. Why?"

"Trish shared an odd experience with me yesterday. I've been doing some digging and I wouldn't mind a fresh perspective on the situation."

"Lay it on me."

Colin recapped the behavior Trish had witnessed yesterday in the foyer, ending with her theory about the alleged lapses. By the time he finished, Mac was frowning.

"That's raising some red flags."

"No kidding . . . especially in light of the photo found in the schoolyard, which implies the mugging was a setup. Given all that's happened, I decided to dig into Matt Parker's background."

"Find anything suspicious?"

"Not yet. According to his LinkedIn page, he has an MBA from Wharton and worked in international finance for . . ." He consulted his notes and read off the name of the firm. "That's a prominent banking syndicate. He started out in New York, was based in London for two years, finished up in Atlanta."

"Why did he leave a plum job like that?"

"Unknown. Based on the progressively more complex job descriptions on LinkedIn, he was on an upward career path. But five years ago, he quit. He next surfaces here, three years ago."

"What was he doing during the two years in between?"

Colin lifted his shoulders. "No idea. It's a black hole."

"You look anywhere besides LinkedIn?"

"I did a basic background check. He appears to be clean. No criminal record or financial red flags popped up in a preliminary search, and his past addresses follow his career moves. I did discover he was in Boston—his hometown—during the black-hole years."

"Any news from the city detective on the mugging?"

"Nothing positive. I talked to him earlier this afternoon. They're still putting out feelers, but the guy appears to have vanished."

Mac rolled a pen between his fingers. "So we have a death that was ruled an accident—but may have been homicide. A mugging that seemed random—but may have been a targeted attack. An accountant with excellent credentials and the image of a respectable, law-abiding citizen—but who may have a darker side. A stressed-out woman who appears to have made some mistakes—but who may be the victim of a setup. Am I missing anything?"

"No."

"That's a lot of maybes—with no proof any of them are legit."

"Thanks for pointing that out."

"There's a little problem of motive too."

"Yeah." Laid out like that, the theory that Parker might somehow be involved in an evil plot sounded highly speculative—at best. "But Sarge is on board with further investigation."

"You must have done some fast talking."

"It worked."

"You going to chat with Parker again?" Mac pulled out his phone and glanced at the screen.

"I might—depending on what I find after I do some more digging."

"If you need any help, let me know. This is intriguing."

"I might take you up on that if the case heats up. Have fun tonight with Lisa."

"Always." He grinned and put the phone to his ear.

As Colin went back to googling, Mac's comment lingered in his mind. The case *was* intriguing . . . but it was more than that.

It was also unnerving.

Because if his and Trish's instincts were right, the odd occurrences over the past five weeks were somehow related—and Matt Parker could be the link.

But whoever was behind them, one thing was clear.

He or she had a motive powerful enough to trigger murder.

. . . . .

Oh. My. Word.

As Trish peeked through the peephole at six thirty sharp, her heart skipped a beat.

Colin Flynn would turn any woman's head in his work attire of dress slacks, dress shirt, tie, and jacket . . . but in tonight's casual jeans and a rolled-to-the-elbows shirt, he was one handsome hunk of masculinity.

He leaned over to reach for the doorbell again, and she jerked away from the peephole.

Good grief. She'd been gawking at him like a love-struck adolescent.

Doing her best to rein in her galloping pulse, she pulled the door open and smiled. "Hi."

"Hi back." His lips curved up too, and a tingle ran through her as he gave her casual, shoulder-baring sundress a swift but appreciative scan. "You look very nice."

"Thanks."

"How's the arm?"

"It doesn't hurt anymore. And as you can see, I downsized the bulky dressing." She lifted her arm to display the narrow strip of gauze she'd taped over the stitch line. "Would you like to come in?"

"If you're ready, why don't we head for the restaurant? I don't know about you, but I'm starving."

"Me too." Which was a welcome change. Since her mom's death, her appetite had vanished—until Colin had restored it with his omelet . . . and his presence in her life. "Let me set the alarm and I'll join you on the porch."

Less than a minute later, she slipped out, locking the door behind her.

He took her arm as they walked down the stepping-stones to his Mazda. The courteous gesture felt good—as did the easy conversation that flowed between them during the drive to the restaurant. He didn't bring up his promised research, and neither did she. There would be time for that later. For now, she wanted to pretend this was a simple date unencumbered by death and knife attacks and malice.

Colin seemed to be similarly inclined. During dinner under the muted outdoor lights, he kept their exchange focused on pleasant topics, telling stories that made her laugh and asking her opinion about movies and books and sports.

Only after he reached over to wipe some stray salsa off the corner of her mouth with his napkin, then ordered dessert, did he introduce more serious subjects.

"I've been doing some digging on your friendly accountant."

"So have I." At his raised eyebrow, she shrugged. "Since I didn't have anything important on my agenda for the past two days, I thought I'd see what I could unearth. I don't have access to all your resources, but the internet can be a gold mine if you persevere."

"Does that mean you came across some useful stuff?"

"Curious might be a better word—but I'd rather hear what you found first."

She listened in silence until he finished filling her in on where he'd searched and what he'd discovered.

"Well, at least he isn't a criminal."

"I didn't say that. The National Crime Information Center database culls from local, state, and federal files . . . but it's not a perfect system. For example, misdemeanors often aren't in there. They have to be sent from the county to the state and from the state to the FBI, and breakdowns can happen. However, I think it's safe to conclude he's not a felon. What did you find?"

"My search wasn't as official as yours. I tapped LinkedIn too, and googled a lot of the information that was on there. I found news releases about his promotions, some blurbs in alumnae magazines, an article about his volunteer work in Atlanta with Big Brothers . . . all positive stuff that verified the information on LinkedIn and my own impressions of him. There wasn't one negative."

"I thought you said you found something curious."

"Yes." She waited while the waitress set an order of sizzling hot apple pie à la mode in front of each of them and moved off. "Knowing Boston was his hometown, I tried googling his name in connection with that city. I stumbled onto this." She pulled a folded sheet of paper out of her purse and handed it to him. "It's a death notice for a man named Lawrence Adams, from three years ago. Look a few lines down."

He gave it a quick read as she dipped a spoon into her melting ice cream, homing in on the part that had caught her eye. "'Faithful husband of the late Margaret, loving father of Matt Parker, cherished friend to many.'"

"Yes. Isn't it curious that a father and son would have two different last names?"

"He could be a stepson."

"Or he changed his last name for some reason. The birth

certificate you mentioned you're waiting for should shed some light on that. To be honest, I doubt I'd have given it a second thought if we weren't dealing with a bunch of other baffling stuff."

He set the sheet down and tackled his own pie. "At this point, anything out of the ordinary is worth investigating."

"I do have one other piece of information that could be relevant. I googled Lawrence Adams's name and got a lot of hits. He was a lifelong resident of Boston, ran a small construction company that did residential developments, won a number of industry awards, and was known for his honesty and integrity. However . . . there were rumors he had financial difficulties near the end of his life."

One side of Colin's mouth quirked up. "If you ever want to change careers, we could use your investigative skills on the force."

"No, thanks. My teaching job provides plenty of adrenaline."

"Eat your pie." He waved his spoon toward her dessert. "And tell me about these rumors."

She scooped up a hearty bite of apple and pastry. "There were a couple of stories in the community newspaper and in the local construction industry newsletter about delays in his last development. A few vendors said bills were being paid late. Some home buyers weren't happy about how long it was taking to build their houses. He also sold his own house, moved into a small condo, and relocated his office to less expensive real estate. I can forward you the links."

"That would be helpful. Was Parker mentioned in any of those stories?"

"No."

"Did the residential development get finished?"

"Yes—three weeks before Adams died. The company was subsequently closed."

"Closed, not sold." He set his spoon down. "There had to be some blue-sky value if he was in business for a lot of years."

"Maybe not much after the rumors of financial instability." Trish scraped the bottom of her dish, gathering up the last of the pie.

"Less if all the physical assets had to be sold to keep it in the black."

"Right. But interesting as all this is, I don't see how it could have anything to do with what's going on here, three years later."

"I don't either . . . although my gut tells me there's a connection." He leaned back in his chair. "I may need to have another talk with Parker."

"Won't he be upset about you digging into his background based on nothing but instinct?"

"What you witnessed in your foyer is fact."

Her stomach tightened. "Are you going to bring that up to him?"

"I don't know yet. I may just tell him we're continuing to investigate your mother's death—unless I can think of another excuse to talk to him."

She shifted in her seat. "I'm not comfortable with lying."

"It's not a lie."

"What does that mean?"

He scooted around the small round table and leaned in close, lowering his voice. "I talked with my boss today. He's given me the green light to dig back into the case, based on what's been going on. I also called to see if your mother's prescription medication might still be in the evidence locker. It is—and they're going to hang on to it."

"Why?"

"It may prove helpful."

"How?"

"I don't know—but I want it to be available if we need it."

She pushed her empty dish aside and folded her hands on the table. "You really think foul play might have been involved in my mom's death? That someone actually wanted her to die?"

"I think it's a possibility. That's why my boss also let the prosecuting attorney know we're continuing to investigate. I expect he'll issue a taken-under-advisement ruling, which would change the case status to open-ended and allow for the possibility that further evidence might be presented." He covered her clenched fingers with his. "The difference is, this time you're not the prime suspect."

Prime suspect.

The qualifier sent a shock wave through her.

Did he consider her *one* of the suspects?

Apparently so, based on his next comment.

"Now that the case is open again, I'm going to need to keep a professional distance until it's resolved. But I want you to know my long-term goal is the same . . . and I'll continue to be a phone call away, day or night. Okay?"

Okay?

Was he kidding?

She dropped her chin and regarded his strong fingers covering hers. His warmth and caring and kindness had been her lifeline through this torrent of crises.

Now she'd have to soldier on alone.

"Hey." He squeezed her fingers. When she looked up, his intent gaze locked on hers. "In case you're wondering, my feelings about you . . . and us . . . haven't changed. I intend to do my best to wrap this up and get us back on track ASAP—but I can't date a woman who's involved in an active case. I wanted us to have this evening together so you'd know what my intentions are once this is over, but for now I need to concentrate on finding out the truth behind your mother's death . . . and your mugging."

Of course he did. That was his job.

And she wanted to uncover the truth as much as he did.

The waitress came by with their check, and as soon as he paid the bill, they left.

Colin didn't talk any more about the case on the drive back to her house or as he walked her to the door—but there was no good-night kiss . . . even on the forehead. Nor would there be until this wrapped up.

He touched her cheek, reminded her to arm the security system, then turned and walked down the path to his car.

Leaning against the doorframe, she watched him drive away—and prayed God would lead them to answers soon.

Because they could use all the help they could get figuring out the motive behind the evil things that had already happened . . . and those that might be looming in the days ahead.

14

An arc of headlights swept across the front of the house, and Craig tossed the TV remote onto the table beside him. Finally. Waiting forty-five minutes for a pizza was ridiculous.

But he was lucky anyone was willing to deliver to this godforsaken place.

After extracting three singles from his wallet, he gave the TV an annoyed glance and crossed to the front door as the bell rang. Pizza and the idiot box—talk about a boring Saturday night. Still, he'd had his fun yesterday at that new bar he'd tried. Trixie had given his pleasure her top priority.

The corners of his mouth tipped up as he pictured the curvaceous—and friendly—redhead.

Very friendly.

Smiling, he reached for the knob. He might have to give that place a second go too. He'd visited the first bar twice without any repercussions, and . . .

"Hi, there."

His lips flatlined. What the . . .

"Aren't you going to ask me in? I drove a long way to see you."

He gaped at the familiar blonde on his doorstep. What was

her name again? Natasha? Naomi? Natalie. Yeah, that was it. Natalie.

But what was she doing here?

And how had she found him?

The beams from another set of headlights swept through the trees, and a surge of adrenaline goosed his pulse.

He grabbed her arm, yanked her inside, and slammed the door shut.

"Hey! Not so rough, big boy. I'm glad you're happy to see me, but I have all evening. There's no rush."

Her words only half registered as he tried to wrestle his panic into submission. To think. Her car was in the driveway; the pizza kid would see it. Did that matter?

He surveyed his unexpected visitor. It might, if the kid got an eyeful of her micro skirt, low-cut blouse, dramatic makeup, and mane of blonde hair.

"Wait in the kitchen." He tightened his grip and propelled her toward the back of the house.

She stumbled along beside him in her four-inch heels. "Take it easy. These shoes weren't designed for running."

The doorbell chimed.

He pushed her through the door, closed it, and jogged back toward the front of the house. He'd have to wing it if the kid mentioned the car.

Fate was on his side, though. The teen on the porch was a new face, and he was jiving to some tune coming through his earbuds. His conversation was limited to a quick thank-you for the tip.

Perfect.

Craig watched until he returned to his car and drove away, then pivoted back toward the kitchen—and the big problem waiting there. He had a dozen questions . . . and he needed answers before he could decide how to handle this complication.

Better play along with her until he had more information, however. Otherwise, she might clam up.

Pizza in hand, he walked to the back of the house and pushed through the door.

Natalie was sitting on one of the stools at the island, legs crossed, one foot dangling, crimson nails peeking out of the open toe of a dramatic spiked heel shoe that was more eye candy than practical. Like the dozens of other pairs he'd spied in her closet during his second visit.

"This is a surprise." He slid the pizza onto the counter, trying for a pleasant tone.

"A happy one, I hope." She gave him a provocative smile. "I'm not interrupting anything, am I? You said you were unattached."

"I was just spending a quiet night in front of the TV."

"Oh, I think we can do better than that." She tapped the pizza box. "Are you going to share?"

"Sure. You want some beer?"

She wrinkled her nose. "Don't you have anything with a little more kick?"

"There's some Scotch left."

"Sold."

He filled a tumbler with ice, poured her a drink, and took a beer for himself. No hard stuff for him. He needed a clear head tonight.

She helped herself to a piece of pizza as he leaned a hip against the island. "This is a deluxe, isn't it? My favorite kind. It was almost like you knew I was coming."

"How could I know that? I never gave you my address." He took a pull from his beer, watching her.

"Oh, I have ways of finding addresses." She gave a throaty laugh.

"Want to let me in on the secret?"

"Hmm. I suppose it couldn't hurt . . . Matt."

He choked on his beer.

She thought he was Matt?

Wait.

How did she even *know* about Matt?

Craig took a shallow breath, trying to mask his shock.

"My name's Joe."

"Funny. That's not how your car is registered." She scooped up some wayward cheese and piled it on her pizza.

His stomach clenched. "How do you know that?"

"Now don't get upset, honey. A girl has to make sure she's not being taken advantage of, you know? I needed contact information in case you didn't call or show up at the bar again. I know how guys operate. You tend to forget promises. I couldn't find your driver's license or any credit cards in your wallet, so I checked the plates."

Craig bought himself a minute by taking another slow drink of his beer. Stashing his plastic and ID in the car while he'd retrieved her jacket had paid off. But when had she gone out to get the number on his plates? They were mud-smeared . . . and he was a light sleeper. If she'd left the room, he'd have heard her.

Except . . . he'd been dead to the world for hours that night. And he didn't remember much of what had happened after that second drink.

It was almost as if he'd been drugged.

The truth body-slammed him.

"You put something in my drink, didn't you?"

The slice of pizza paused halfway between the counter and her mouth . . . then continued to its destination.

"You had a lot to drink." She took a big bite.

"Not that much."

"You might have drunk more than you remember. We had other things on our mind." She gave him the seductive smile she'd used in the bar.

It had zero effect tonight.

"I know my limits. I didn't drink too much."

"Like I said, you were distracted."

He ran through the events of the night in his mind as she ate his pizza. When had she doctored his drink? It had to have happened at her place or he wouldn't have been able to drive them back to her apartment. But they'd been together the whole . . .

The light dawned.

"You spiked my drink while I went out to get your jacket, didn't you?"

After a brief hesitation, she shrugged. "Like I said, a girl has to take care of herself."

He fought back the anger churning in his gut.

Stay cool, Elliott. You need information, and you won't get it if you yell at her.

Somehow he managed a pleasant tone. "You're very clever."

She chewed for a moment, studying him. "Are you mad?"

"Do I look mad?"

"No—but some guys are put out after I track them down."

Another shock wave rippled through him.

She'd done this before. He wasn't her first victim.

The question now was . . . what was her game? What did she want?

"I admire smart people." He slid onto a stool beside her. "What did you use to knock me out?"

"GHB."

Gamma-hydroxybutyrate. The date-rape drug—typically a male weapon.

How ironic.

"Like I said . . . clever." He took a piece of pizza. "So who ran my plates for you?"

"I have connections."

A cop in her debt, maybe—or a friend who happened to be

a PI. It wouldn't be that hard for someone with her assets to curry favors from a man.

"You know . . ." She tilted her head. "You look a lot different here than you did at the bar. More . . . refined. When you opened the door, I'm not certain I would have recognized you if I didn't know you lived here." She leaned closer and squinted at him. "Your eyes are even a different color. Hazel, not green."

Natalie was too observant—and too clever—for her own good.

"I like to be incognito when I barhop."

"Yeah." She gave him a leisurely head-to-toe. "You're a lot higher class than you let on at the bar. I bet you don't want anyone to recognize you at a dump like Arnold's." She swung her foot back and forth. "Is Craig high-class too?"

His lungs locked, and black spots exploded in front of his eyes.

"Are you okay, sweetie?" She touched his arm.

He gripped the edge of the island. "How do you know about Craig?"

"From his credit card." She waved a hand toward the far counter. "I noticed it while you were talking to the pizza guy. I figured he must be a friend who was visiting—unless you have a roommate."

He bit back an oath as he scowled at the plastic card. He must have left it there after he'd gone through his IDs earlier, trying to decide what to keep and what to destroy. He should have ditched it months ago when—for all practical purposes—Craig Elliott had ceased to exist.

"No. No roommate. He's just passing through."

"Will he be around later?"

"No. He had . . . other plans for tonight."

"Kind of like us, huh? My timing was spot on." She winked

at him and held out the glass for a refill. "You have a comfortable place. I'm gonna enjoy hanging out here."

Like that was going to happen.

He topped off her drink and sat back on the stool beside her while she sipped it, his brain reeling. She knew about Matt. She knew about Craig. What else did she know—and what had prompted her to home in on him?

"You went to a lot of effort to find me. Why?"

"I like you."

Too simple.

"Come on, Natalie. Be honest. What are you after?"

"You. I like you. We were good together. I want more of that."

No mention of money. No threats. No hint of blackmail. And her eyes were guileless.

Could this be on the level? Did she really just want to hang with him?

"Why me?"

"You're different than any of the guys I've met for a while. I only track down the ones who are special. You stood out."

If that was supposed to be a compliment, she'd missed the mark.

But he had to play along.

"I appreciate that—as long as our relationship stays between you and me."

"Of course! I respect your privacy."

What a joke. She'd already trampled all over it.

But as long as no one else knew about him, it didn't matter.

"You mean you haven't told anyone about me?"

"I mentioned to one of my friends at the shop that I'd met someone new, but I didn't give her any details. I know how to be discreet."

"What about your family?"

She snorted. "My parents threw me out the day I turned

seventeen. Said I was nothing but trouble. So I got on a bus and rode till my money ran out. I never planned to stay in St. Louis, but it worked out fine here. There was no reason to leave."

"Where do they live?"

"My folks? Phoenix, last I heard. But that was ten years ago. They could be dead for all I know—or care."

She had no contact with her family and hadn't told anyone his name.

That was the best news he'd had all night. Taking care of this problem would be a cinch.

The issue was when. Tonight was best, in case her lips got loose and she decided to tell one of her salon friends more than she claimed she already had. But her car was here—and he didn't want to get within touching distance of it. Too much risk of leaving trace evidence he might not have a chance to get rid of.

Tonight was out.

He'd have to put off dealing with the dicey situation for a day or two and convince her to keep her mouth shut in the meantime.

Pasting on a smile, he picked up a piece of pizza he didn't want. "I have to admit, this is a lot more fun than eating alone."

"I'm glad you're happy to see me. To us." She lifted her glass toward him in a toast.

He clinked his beer can with it. "You know . . . we ought to celebrate finding each other. Are you free on Tuesday night?"

"No. I work at the salon until nine. Thursdays too. What did you have in mind?"

"Dinner at an upscale restaurant."

"Yeah?" Her eyes lit up. "I'd like that. I could go Wednesday."

He played with his beer can. Too far away. Every delay increased the risk she'd spill some dangerous piece of information.

"I don't want to wait that long to see you again. Why don't we go on Monday?"

"Works for me."

"I'll pick you up at eight thirty."

She frowned. "Isn't that kind of late for dinner?"

"Not in Europe. In Spain they don't eat until nine or ten—and I want to take you to a fancy, European-style restaurant." He also wanted it dark when he picked her up—and dark during his detour back here to retrieve his conveniently forgotten wallet.

"Where?"

"It's a surprise."

"I love surprises!"

Good.

Because she was in for a big one.

And she wasn't going to love it.

"You want some more pizza?" He motioned to the grease-stained cardboard circle.

"I wouldn't mind having another piece or two . . . unless you're in a hurry."

"No rush. We have all night."

While she demolished two more generous pieces, he leaned back against the island, nursing his beer. As long as she was here and he was bored, no reason not to take advantage of whatever she was willing to offer.

Especially since she wouldn't be offering it again.

▪ ▪ ▪ ▪ ▪

"Sorry I had to bail yesterday. I appreciate you guys being flexible."

As Kristin slipped into the booth at the popular Sunday brunch spot, Rick handed her a menu. "To tell you the truth, the delay worked out better for me. We're in high gear at the camp, with the summer session about to start. Ducking out for a couple of hours yesterday would have put a serious crimp in my schedule."

"Glad to hear it wasn't an inconvenience. And I'm betting

our friend here didn't mind sleeping in yesterday, after his hot date with Trish Friday night."

Colin choked on his coffee.

"Take a deep breath." Kristin patted him on the back.

He bought himself a few seconds to think by taking a slow sip of water. There was no way Kristin could have known about his dinner with Trish unless she'd been at Hacienda.

"I take it you were in the mood for Mexican on Friday too?"

"Uh-huh." She skimmed the brunch menu and set it aside. "She's very pretty."

"For the record, it wasn't a hot date."

"No? It seemed awfully cozy to me." She leaned toward Rick and spoke in a stage whisper. "They were holding hands."

"We weren't holding hands. I was trying to . . . reassure her."

Kristin sniggered. "Talk about a lame spin."

"Why didn't you call and give me the scoop?" Rick shot the female member of their gang a disgruntled look.

"Because there wasn't any scoop to give." Colin fisted his hands in his lap and turned his attention to Kristin. "And how do you know it was Trish, anyway? Were you eavesdropping?"

"Not necessary. The bandage on the arm was a dead giveaway."

Oh yeah. There was that.

"We were discussing the mugging . . . among other things." He pretended to read the menu.

"I'll bet." Kristin grinned.

"It was all very professional."

"Right." Rick chuckled.

"What's that supposed to mean?"

"If it was professional, you wouldn't be flustered."

"I'm not flustered."

"Then why did you just add a bunch of cream to your coffee when you always take it black?"

Colin peered into his mug. Diluted brew stared back at him.

He was hosed.

"Is everyone ready?" A waitress stopped beside their table, pen poised over order pad.

Yes! Perfect timing. After this diversion, he might be able to redirect the conversation.

But Rick didn't give him a chance. The instant the woman walked away, he pounced again.

"Cream in coffee. Want to talk about it?"

No—but based on their determined expressions, he was going to have to give them a few crumbs.

"Fine. I like her."

"You're smitten." Kristin added a heaping spoon of sugar to her java.

"Let's not get carried away."

"We're not the ones getting carried away." She leaned toward him. "And it's okay. She looks like a very nice woman. If you want to date her, you have our approval."

"Gee, thanks."

"Speak for yourself. I haven't met her yet." Rick elbowed Kristin.

"Neither have I. But we will . . . soon. Right, Colin? You could invite her to our next Saturday breakfast."

"I don't think so."

"What? You don't trust us to be couth?" Rick tucked his napkin in the top of his dress shirt and fluffed it.

"Very funny." Colin yanked out the square cloth and tossed it at his friend. "I won't be bringing her because it would be unprofessional."

"What does that mean?" Rick tucked his napkin back onto his lap, where it belonged.

"It means County is digging into the case again."

Kristin exchanged a look with Rick. "The case of her mother's death? I thought that was closed."

"Not anymore. Some . . . peculiar . . . new developments have raised our suspicions."

"About Trish?" Rick rested his elbows on the table and steepled his fingers, all levity gone.

"No. But I need to keep a professional distance until we get some answers."

"Based on what I saw Friday night, that's not going to be easy." Kristin played with her fork.

Colin sighed. Why deny what was apparently obvious? To his two childhood buddies, at any rate.

"No, it's not. But it will be harder on her. She's alone. Totally. I have you guys." His voice scratched, and he took a sip of water.

"You want me to call her? Invite her to lunch?" Kristin gentled her voice and touched his hand.

"You haven't even met her yet."

"If she's important to you, she's important to us. Right, Rick?"

"Right."

Colin toyed with that notion for a few seconds. Trish had told him she'd had little time to nurture friendships over the past two traumatic years. Perhaps she'd welcome an outreach from Kristin. Friends didn't come any finer than these two— and if everything played out as he hoped, she'd be part of their lives, anyway.

"Let me mention it to her. And thanks for the offer."

"My pleasure."

The waitress delivered their food, and though he knew his friends were dying to ask some questions about the new case developments he'd referenced, the conversation moved on to other topics. They'd learned long ago he didn't discuss active investigations.

But as they said their good-byes and went their separate ways, Colin thought back to Trish's comment in her kitchen while they'd eaten his omelets. About how good often came out of bad—like meeting him after the death of her mother.

Despite his less-than-idyllic childhood, he had to admit her point was applicable to this situation. God might not have saved Neal . . . and he might not have healed their fractured family . . . but he'd brought Kristin and Rick into the circle of a lonely little boy when he'd most needed friends. Without that lifeline, Colin wasn't certain he'd have survived those tough years.

Maybe, as Trish had suggested, God had been at work even during the dark days when he'd felt no divine presence.

Maybe God was *still* at work, bringing a lovely woman into his world just when he'd begun to think love might have passed him by.

And maybe God would give them a future by bringing closure and resolution to a situation that grew more puzzling with every passing day.

In light of all the strange . . . and sinister . . . new developments in this case, that was a prayer worth offering.

15

"You haven't mentioned Trish all week. What's up with that?" Mac hung a right at the corner in the rundown business district.

Colin surveyed the storefront addresses as the car rolled along the main street of the small municipality in unincorporated St. Louis County. "We're getting close to our address."

"End of the block, I'm guessing. You gonna answer my question?"

His colleague's tenacity was a definite plus on the job. Not so much when it came to personal topics.

"Nothing's up. We're on hold until the investigation is over."

"No mixing business and pleasure, huh?"

"Something like that."

"Been there, done that—with Lisa. Tough spot to be in."

Tough didn't begin to capture it.

"At least I had a reason to see her, since we were working a case together." Mac jumped back into the silence. "Maybe you can come up with an excuse to drop by or call."

"Yeah."

Except he'd already caved and tried the call tactic. Trish hadn't answered, and he hadn't left a message.

Why not try again after they wrapped up here, though? Their Mexican dinner six nights ago seemed like ancient history.

He motioned to a shop with photos of hairstyles plastered to the windows. "We've arrived."

Mac pulled into the curb with a practiced twist of his wrist, set the brake, and surveyed the faded sign. "Polly's Beauty Boutique could use some beautifying."

"That's an understatement. You ready?"

"Yeah. Investigating a missing person report should be a breeze after the double homicide that hit our plates this week. Assuming this woman is even missing."

"I hear you." Colin gave the past-its-prime shop another sweep and opened his door. A fair number of missing adults disappeared by choice, and there was nothing the police could do in those situations except try to confirm there'd been no foul play. "Let's see what we can find out."

Mac circled the car and met him at the entrance. "You want to take the lead while I observe?"

"Sure."

After stepping through the door, he gave the interior a quick scan. Hair dryers on one side, sinks on the other, a row of chairs in front of mirrors, a table containing a rack of nail polish. Every person in the shop was female . . . and every head swiveled their direction.

He stepped forward. "We're looking for the owner."

A fiftyish buxom brunette with streaks of purple in her black hair and a doughy face painted with too much makeup murmured a few words to her customer and walked over. "I'm Polly."

Colin introduced himself and Mac. "Is there a private place where we could talk?"

"My office in back is about as private as it gets. And I don't have a lot of time. We're busy today." Annoyance scored her words as she swept a hand over the interior. "Give me a minute to finish up with my customer."

Without waiting for a response, she returned to the gray-haired woman in the chair and put a few more rollers in her hair.

Colin leaned closer to Mac and spoke under his breath. "Not the warmest welcome I've ever received."

"I'm wondering why she bothered to call in the report."

"Ditto."

While they waited, Colin surveyed the middle-aged-and-older clientele. Some were openly ogling the male visitors; others were more discreet, peeking over the tops of their Hollywood gossip magazines. He wasn't silver-screen handsome, but you'd never know it based on the admiring looks these women were giving him and Mac. Tall, youngish males in jackets and ties must be a novelty in a place like this.

His gaze paused on a young woman cutting hair in the far corner. She was surreptitiously watching them too—but her expression wasn't flirty or curious.

It was nervous.

Why?

He angled toward Mac and tipped his head toward her station.

The other man gave a slight nod. He'd noticed her edgy behavior too.

"All right. Let's go into the back." Polly brushed past them, leading the way through the shop and into the tiny office. After circling behind a desk cluttered with product samples, piles of paper, curlers, and a wig stand sporting a mass of frizzy hair, she motioned to two molded plastic chairs.

Colin folded his long frame into one, grunting as his knees hit the front of the desk. Mac closed the door, scooted the other chair back until it hit the wall, then sat and wedged his legs between the desk and the seat.

"We're here to follow up on the missing person report you

filed on Natalie James." Colin shifted his weight, trying without success to find a more comfortable position. "I understand she's an employee here. Are you also related to her?"

"No. Far as I know, she doesn't have any family. That's one of the reasons I called the cops."

"What were the other reasons?"

"She's my best manicurist—and I've got customers with appointments. Canceling is bad for business."

"When did you realize she was missing?"

"I told all this to the cop who showed up this morning." She glared at him.

"If you don't mind, we'd like to hear it again."

The woman huffed out a breath. "She was supposed to work Tuesday afternoon and evening. She didn't show. She was also on the schedule yesterday. Again, she didn't show. And she isn't here today, either. Her shift was two to nine. I've lost a chunk of change, thanks to her. Now I'm scrambling to find a replacement."

"How long has she been employed here?"

"Four years."

"Has she been reliable in the past?"

"Yes. Never missed a day except last year, when she had the flu. She actually came in, but I told her to go home. I didn't want the rest of my girls or the customers to get sick."

"Have you tried to contact her?"

"Yes. Cell phone, home phone, email, texting. I even drove by her place and knocked on the door at lunch today. No answer—but her car was in the lot. That's when I called the cops."

They already knew she wasn't at her apartment . . . and that her car was. That had been their first stop. Trying to trace her cell phone had been a dead end too. No signal.

"Does she have a boyfriend?"

The woman sniffed. "I don't gossip with my employees or ask about their personal business. As long as they show up and do their job, I don't pry."

"But you may have overheard her talking on the phone or to one of your other staff members." Mac stepped in, his tone easy. Conversational. Empathetic. "That's not prying—and this *is* your shop. I imagine you hear a lot of tidbits in this business that require discretion."

"You've got that right." She eyed Mac, her demeanor softening under his megawatt smile.

"If there's anything at all you could tell us that would assist in our investigation, we'd be grateful. We couldn't do our job without citizens like you who go out of their way to help people who might be in trouble."

Man, he was laying it on thick.

But it was working. The woman practically preened under his praise.

"Well . . . I don't know anything else myself, but you might want to talk to Maxine. She works here too."

"Is she the one at the corner chair?" Colin rejoined the conversation.

Polly did *not* seem pleased by his interruption. Her grudging demeanor immediately slipped back into place.

"Yes."

He passed the baton back to Mac with a look. His colleague was having a whole lot better luck getting cooperation from this woman.

"Are they friends?" Mac picked up the questioning.

"I don't know if they socialize outside of work, but they talk a lot here. It's possible she might know some useful information." Polly adjusted one of the springy, wayward curls on the wig stand. "To tell you the truth, Maxine is one of the reasons I called in the report. She was worried, but she didn't want to get involved with the police. A bad experience with a restraining order she got on an old boyfriend, I think. I heard he went ballistic and she ended up worse off than before. That's hearsay, you understand."

Colin glanced at Mac and read his own thoughts in the other man's face.

If this Maxine didn't like police, she might dodge their questions.

But it was worth a try.

"Would you mind if we talked to her for a few minutes? We won't keep her away from your clients for long." Mac gave her another warm smile.

"I suppose that would be okay." She pushed herself to her feet and smoothed the too-snug tunic top over her ample hips. "I'll send her back as soon as she's at a stopping place with her customer."

The instant she disappeared, Mac stood. "That is the most uncomfortable chair I've ever sat in."

"I think it's safe to say this office wasn't designed for comfort." Colin rose too. "Based on this Maxine's history, she might not have much to say."

"I know. I've seen more than a few restraining orders gone bad—and it's never pretty."

No, it wasn't.

"Why don't we . . ."

The young brunette from the corner chair appeared in the doorway, hovering on the threshold as she tucked a long strand of hair behind her ear. "Polly said you wanted to talk to me."

"Yes." Colin introduced them, giving the woman's hand a firm shake before signaling Mac to take the chair behind the desk. "Why don't you have a seat? We won't keep you long." He claimed the chair closest to the wall and tapped the one next to him.

She edged into the cramped space and perched on the edge of the rigid plastic.

"Polly said your name is Maxine. Could you give us a last name to go with that, and some contact information?" Colin tried to mimic the smile Mac had used to soften up the owner.

It didn't work with this woman. Her posture remained stiff, her features pinched.

"What I tell you isn't going to be public, is it?"

"No. It will stay in the case file."

She fiddled with a button on her shirt, uncertainty flashing in her eyes, but finally complied.

"Polly told us you and Natalie were friends." Colin finished writing and looked up. "She also said you were worried."

"I am." Maxine twisted her fingers together. "It's not like Natalie to miss work."

"When and where did you last talk to her?"

"Here, on Monday."

"What kind of mood was she in?"

"Happy. Upbeat. Excited. She had a hot date that night."

Colin didn't need to check with Mac to know the other man's antennas had gone up too.

A hot date one day, missing the next.

Suspicious.

"With a boyfriend?"

"No. She didn't have a boyfriend. Not a steady one, anyway. Natalie kind of . . . she sort of played the field."

In other words, she slept around.

Also a scenario more likely to lead to trouble.

"Do you know anything about the guy she saw Monday night?"

"Not much. She could be kind of close-mouthed about some stuff. Apparently he was a higher-class dude who didn't want it known he went slumming at one of the bars Natalie liked."

"How long has she known him?"

"He's a new one. They met a couple of weeks ago and hooked up a few times."

"Did she tell you this guy's name?"

"Like I said, she was kind of cagey about that. At first she said it was Joe—but she thought it might be a made-up name. On Monday, she said it was Matt."

"Did she give you a last name?"

"No. But she mentioned a Craig Elliott too. She said he was a friend of this guy's from out of town, but he wasn't there the night she dropped by to visit. First she called him Elliott, then backtracked and said it was Craig. I think she mixed up the first and last names. She was kind of flustered. She told me she saw the guy's credit card on the counter at Matt's house and used the number to buy some shoes for her date on Monday. I think she was worried Matt would figure it out when the guy got his bill and he'd be mad at her."

A logical assumption. Using someone else's credit card wasn't just unethical, it was illegal.

"Do you know anything else about this Joe or Matt?"

"Not much. She said he had kind of a germ phobia—and he lives in the country somewhere."

Colin stopped writing.

A higher-class guy named Matt who lived in the country.

Like Trish's accountant.

Bizarre coincidence—or was it?

"Did Natalie have other friends who might be able to offer us any more information?"

"I don't think so. She was kind of a loner, except for the guys she picked up. I was probably her closest friend, but we didn't hang out together outside of work."

"Can you give us the name of the bar where she met this guy, and any other bars she frequented?"

After jotting the names down as she recited them, he closed his notebook. "Mac . . . do you have anything else?"

"No. This was very helpful. Thanks for talking with us."

"You're welcome." The brunette stood. Twisted her fingers together. "Do you think she's okay? I mean, we weren't like sisters or anything, but she was always decent to me. I'd hate to think anything bad has happened to her."

"It's too soon to answer that question." Colin wrested himself free of the molded chair and stood too. "But I can promise you we'll do our best to find her."

With a dip of her chin, she backed toward the door and disappeared.

"Let's say our good-byes to the owner and talk in the car." Mac circled the desk. "The fumes from whatever concoctions they use in this place is making my eyes water."

"I'm with you."

Sixty seconds later, under the appreciative scrutiny of the female patrons, they bolted into the fresh air.

Mac drew in a lungful of air. "How could anyone stand to work in there all day?"

"You've got me. You'd think the EPA or OSHA would be all over places like this." He inhaled too, then took the passenger seat.

"So what do you think?" Mac slid behind the wheel and started the engine.

"I think I'm impressed by your charm. You had Polly eating out of your hand."

One side of Mac's mouth hitched up. "I seem to do better with the older ladies—Lisa being the exception. And that's not what I meant."

"I know." He adjusted his seat belt. "With Parker on our radar screen, it's an uncanny coincidence that Natalie's date was named Matt and lived in the country."

"Agreed—but it's a stretch to think they're connected."

"Stranger things have happened."

"True. But my top priority is Natalie. I'll get a search warrant rolling for her apartment and car. If she's got a computer, forensics might come up with some leads. I also want to check out this Craig Elliott and visit the bars where Natalie hung out. I'll pull a few other guys in to assist with the bar circuit."

"Sounds like a plan." Since Mac was the lead case detective, this was his show to run. "You want me to see what I can find out about Elliott while you get the search warrant going?"

"That would be helpful. Thanks." Mac pulled into traffic. "When are you going to fit in work on the Eileen Coulter case? You have a full plate already."

"I'll manage."

"I'm predicting a chunk of overtime in your future." Mac guided the car toward the interstate.

"Some."

"Anxious to see justice done . . . or to clear the slate so you can date Trish?"

"I'll take the fifth."

"Enough said." Mac shot him a grin. "Let's debrief some more on the two interviews we just did."

Colin forced himself to shift gears. Eileen Coulter's death was much older . . . and colder . . . than Natalie James's disappearance. It could wait a few hours.

But no more than that.

Sarge might think they could investigate this at their leisure, that it was a lower priority than other cases—but the strange urgency buzzing in his nerve endings . . . the feeling that danger was hovering in the shadows and could escalate at any moment . . . the disquieting sense that Trish could find herself once more in harm's way . . . were compelling motivations to push this. Hard.

And that included dissecting Matt Parker's background. The man's reputation and history might be stellar, but there were murky, turbulent waters beneath the placid surface he presented to the world.

So however much sleep he had to forfeit, he was going to find out why Parker had been going through that evidence bag in Trish's hallway—and why he appeared to be setting her up to look forgetful . . . and to take the rap for her mother's death.

. . . . .

"Good news, boss. We may have a lead on Elliott."

Dmitri Kozlov swiveled away from the panoramic view of the Miami oceanfront as Oleg Petrov spoke from his office doorway.

"Come in. Sit." He waved a hand across the expanse of burled walnut that formed his desktop, toward one of the plush, leather-upholstered chairs on the other side. "Tell me."

Oleg took the chair he'd indicated. "We had a hit on his credit card."

"Interesting." Dmitri leaned back, set his elbows on the cushioned arms of his chair, and pressed his fingertips together. Why would Elliott use that card at all . . . and why now, after so many weeks? "What did he buy—and where did he buy it?"

"Shoes . . . in St. Louis. For less than one hundred dollars."

That made no sense.

Dmitri tapped his fingertips together. Elliott knew how the operation worked, knew the connections they had, knew their tracking abilities. Why would he risk using a credit card they could easily trace for such a small purchase?

Whatever the reason, though, this was a welcome lead. To disappear for such a long stretch had been quite a feat. It was difficult to escape from this organization, as others had learned to their regret.

As Elliott would learn too, once they found him.

"You are certain it was his card?"

"Yes."

"Perhaps it has been stolen."

"That's possible. Or he might have used it by mistake."

Not likely. Elliott was impatient and greedy, but he was also meticulous. There was a story behind his sudden reppearance. But as long as it led them to him, that story was irrelevant.

"Touch base with our contacts who have access to law enforcement in St. Louis. See if his name is on police radar."

"As you wish."

A hint of reluctance underscored the man's words, and Dmitri studied him. "You have concerns?"

"Yes."

If anyone else had been sitting across from him, Dmitri would have dismissed such a reservation with a flip of his hand. But Oleg had been in his employ for more than three decades. He was smart, played by the rules of the organization, and had keen insights. Dmitri might run the show in southern Florida, but trusted lieutenants were worth their weight in gold—and Oleg's thoughtful analysis of situations had proven valuable in the past.

"Tell me." He leaned back and laced his fingers over his flat stomach.

"I do not think you will want to hear what I have to say."

"I would not ask if I did not want to hear. Speak."

"Very well." He smoothed a hand down the knife crease in his slacks, and when he continued, his words were careful and precise. "We have already expended great time and effort on this search. I am wondering if pursuing it further is the best use of our resources and contacts. This will require cashing in favors that could be reserved for larger matters."

"He stole from the organization, Oleg."

"Yes. Eighty-five thousand dollars over eighteen months. But that is small change for us."

"Small change adds up. Worse, if he gets away with this, others will try to do the same, with less fear of reprisal." He rocked back in his chair, weighed Oleg's input . . . but in the end stayed with his original choice. "I appreciate your honesty and your recommendation, but we must make an example of him. It is the betrayal more than the theft that must be punished."

"As you wish. I will begin to make inquiries." Oleg rose, all hesitation gone.

Dmitri smiled his approval. As always, Oleg understood his role in the organization, accepted the decisions of his superiors, and would carry out orders. A good man.

"Keep me informed."

"Of course." With a slight bow, Oleg retreated from the office.

Once the door closed behind him, Dmitri again rotated his chair toward the expanse of glass that offered a commanding view of the sparkling blue ocean. This lead was positive news, and they would exploit it until Elliott was found—and paid the price for his betrayal.

Too bad he'd turned rogue, though. The man had amazing talent with numbers. His ability to structure transactions to avoid bank reporting requirements had been of great value to the organization. Bigger rewards would have come his way, had his skills continued to contribute to their coffers.

But he'd lost patience and succumbed to the temptation of greed, using those very skills to his own advantage. His stellar financial talent and ability to juggle numbers were no doubt the reason his skimming had gone unnoticed for eighteen months, despite close oversight of his work.

That might also be the reason he'd taken a new identity when he'd moved to Miami five years ago. Perhaps he'd pulled a similar stunt somewhere else—though they'd never discovered his original name, despite diligent background checks. He'd done an excellent job erasing his past. But they'd watched him for months, monitored their police contacts to make certain his new identity wasn't on law enforcement radar, before "promoting" him from club manager to a more useful role in the organization.

Then he'd violated their trust.

The phone rang, and Dmitri turned his back on the stunning view to pick it up, putting Elliott out of his mind. There was no reason to waste worry on him now that he'd surfaced. He would be found.

And this time, there would be no escape.

16

What an odd start to her Friday.

Frowning, Trish watched Matt drive away from the meeting he'd requested. She couldn't fault the logic of his suggestion to change charitable foundation donations from physical checks to electronic funds transfers. Her mom might have preferred the old-fashioned method of making donations, even after the stroke had impaired the fine motor skills in her hand and left her signature almost illegible, but it made sense to move the process into the modern world.

Yet for reasons she couldn't explain, it didn't feel right.

And Matt had *not* been happy with her decision to maintain the status quo. His inflection and expression had remained agreeable, but anger had lurked in the depths of his eyes. It had flared again when she'd demurred after he'd pushed her to make him a trustee on at least an interim basis.

Was he displeased because she was hindering his efforts to do what he thought best for the trust . . . or was there a darker reason for his irritation?

Her phone trilled in the kitchen, and she jumped, her hand flying to her chest.

Goodness. She was way too jittery.

Squaring her shoulders, she closed the door, locked it, and marched toward the back of the house. She needed to get her nerves under control. So what if Matt was acting a bit out of character? His odd behavior and subtle personality changes could be related to his concussion and have nothing to do with her—despite the suspicions that were beginning to swirl around him.

And if those suspicions did have any basis in reality?

Colin would nail him.

The very man whose name had popped up on the screen of her cell.

She snatched up the phone from the counter and put it to her ear. "Good morning. I was just thinking about you."

"Pleasant thoughts, I hope."

"Very."

"Best news I've had this morning. I didn't wake you, did I?"

"At eight thirty?"

"School's out. I was afraid you might be sleeping in."

"No. My body clock wakes me every morning at six thirty. I've already had a meeting today. Matt stopped by."

"Why?" His tone sharpened.

"To discuss a few things about the foundation—and push me again to appoint him as a trustee. I know it's a legal requirement, and I know he's qualified, but with all that's been going on, I'm not comfortable putting him into that slot."

"Did you tell him that?"

"I was more diplomatic in my phrasing. But he wasn't happy about it—or the fact that I balked at his suggestion to get rid of physical checks and make contributions electronically."

"Why would he care about that one way or the other?"

"I guess he's trying to be diligent about doing his job. He said electronic contributions are protocol for foundations. They're cleaner and easier to track."

"You don't agree?"

"It's not that." She began to pace. "But I'm still getting unsettling vibes. When I mentioned I'd reviewed the material he left on his last visit and told him I found it in the CSU bag instead of on the chair in the foyer, he went into that you're-under-too-much-stress-and-it's-taking-a-toll routine again." A shiver rippled through her. "I don't want to believe he's involved in anything underhanded, but . . ."

"But it feels like you're being set up."

"Yeah. For the life of me, though, I can't figure out why. Matt's always been aboveboard and reliable. Why would he want to undermine my mental capacities?"

"If we knew that, I have a feeling a lot of pieces would fall into place. That's why I called—to assure you I'm working on getting answers to our questions. Other cases have required my attention, but I'll have a chance today to continue digging. I do have one question for you. Has Parker ever mentioned someone by the name of Craig Elliott?"

"Not that I recall. Why?"

"Elliott's name came up in another case and I wondered if there might be a connection. It's a long shot, but I'm going to see where the trail leads. What's on your agenda today?"

"I'm finally going down to school to clean out my classroom. The summer program starts in ten days."

Several beats ticked by. "Can you wait until tomorrow? I could loan you an extra pair of hands to speed up the job—and I take orders well."

Warmth bubbled up in her heart. "I hate to infringe on your Saturday."

"It's not an infringement. Given the mugging and safety

concerns, it's a legitimate opportunity to see you that doesn't qualify as a date. Think of me as your protection detail."

"When you put it that way . . . does nine o'clock work, or is Saturday *your* day to sleep in?"

"Sleeping in is a luxury I rarely have. Nine is fine. How's the arm?"

"It's not too pretty, but it doesn't hurt—and as far as I can tell, it appears to be healing well. I'm getting the stitches out this afternoon."

"In that case, plan on me doing any heavy lifting tomorrow. You need to give that another week or two of healing before you put any strain on it."

"Is that the voice of experience speaking?"

"I've had my share of stitches."

"Job related?"

"Some."

Silence.

He didn't want to talk about his own injuries.

Fine with her. Violence might be part of his job, but if he'd been shot or stabbed in the line of duty, she wasn't up to hearing about the ongoing risks of his career just yet.

"Well, I'll be glad to get rid of mine. I'll see you at nine tomorrow."

Once they said their good-byes, Trish picked up her cooling coffee and wandered out to the terrace. Weeds were beginning to invade the rose garden, withering blooms should be dead-headed, bushes needed to be fed. The past two summers, she'd handled those chores while her mom supervised from the terrace. They'd both cherished those calm interludes in a world turned upside down by death and tragedy.

Her throat tightened, and the colorful blossoms blurred as a fresh wave of grief swept over her. The welcome numbness that had insulated her for the first couple of weeks after her mother died was wearing off, the reality of this fresh loss setting in. The tears she'd been holding inside welled and spilled out while a vibrant red cardinal chirped nearby . . . a dog barked next door . . . the sweet aroma of the roses wafted past her on a gentle breeze. Life around her went on, the same as always.

Yet hers had changed forever.

Sinking onto the low stone wall at the edge of the terrace, she closed her eyes and let the consoling reminder from Ecclesiastes scroll through her mind.

To everything there is a season.

She wrapped her free hand around the rough stone, clinging fast to that promise. This might be her time to mourn and to weep, but one day soon her long season of grief would end, as every season did. Then, with God's help, she would again laugh . . . and love.

In the meantime, she would be grateful that during this dark, turbulent period, the Almighty had sent her a man like Colin Flynn to help her weather the storm.

■ ■ ■ ■ ■

Craig slammed the heel of his hand against the steering wheel as he barreled down the highway. Matt's visit with Trish today had been a total bust. Despite all the distractions he'd orchestrated, despite all the doubts Matt had planted in her mind about stress-induced forgetfulness, despite her grief over her mother's death, she wasn't letting go of the foundation's reins.

Meaning it wasn't yet safe to dip into the funds that were calling his name.

He spat out a word that singed the air. Yeah, he had enough in reserve to manage for a while. But his high-end standard of living in Miami had seriously eaten into his offshore account balance, and the money he'd skimmed from Dmitri's empire was long gone, spent on incidental luxuries. Matt had a small nest egg, and his clients paid him a modest, steady income . . . but that wasn't sufficient to fund the lifestyle he'd set his sights on once he'd gotten wind of the sweet deal the man had with the Coulter charitable foundation.

Funny how his priorities had changed over the past few months. He'd come here with a single goal: to save his life. To escape Dmitri by vanishing off the face of the earth.

Who could have known his surveillance and research would lead to an unexpected bonus—access to millions of dollars?

It had been too tempting to ignore.

So once his inspired escape plan had been implemented . . . once he was certain he'd eluded the long arm of Dmitri's organization . . . his focus had shifted to getting his hands on the Coulter Foundation money.

Except Trish wasn't cooperating.

Grinding his teeth, he tightened his grip on the wheel. He could get at the money without Matt running the foundation, but it would be simpler if she put that responsibility into her accountant's hands and contented herself with reviewing doctored updates.

If he was patient, it was possible she'd reach that point on her own. Or, better yet, she'd agree to terminate the foundation and he could accomplish his goal in one fell swoop. Not his original plan, but one that grew more appealing every day.

Either way, the ultimate blame—should the embezzlement be discovered—would fall on Matt, while he once again disappeared . . . just as he'd done in Boston, leaving Larry holding the bag.

Craig smirked. He was very proficient at setting up other people to take the rap for his misdeeds.

His fingers loosened on the wheel, and some of his tension ebbed. All he had to do was give this time. Enduring a more modest lifestyle for a while was a small sacrifice for the payoff that would come eventually.

In the interim, he should be glad he was alive—and grateful for the tip-off from the insider he'd bribed to let him know if Dmitri began to get suspicious. With that one warning phone call, the man had earned all the money he'd been paid to alert him if he needed to get out fast.

Without that heads-up, he'd be dead instead of sitting on a potential gold mine that would set him up for life.

Smiling, he flipped on his signal and moved into the exit lane. Things had worked out fine.

He was home free.

. . . . .

"You in the building?"

At Mac's abrupt greeting, Colin grinned and adjusted the cell against his ear as he jogged across the street. "Hello to you too."

"I have news related to the Coulter case."

Colin's smile evaporated. "I just left the courthouse. I can be there in five minutes."

"I grabbed the conference room. Meet me there."

The line went dead.

After a quick detour for two Americanos at Starbucks, he arrived on the threshold of the conference room six minutes later and held one out to Mac.

"Thanks." The other man took a sip. "After a night on the bar circuit for the missing person case, I needed this."

"What have you got?" Colin dropped into the adjacent chair.

"Once the search warrant came through yesterday, we dived into Natalie James's apartment. She did have a computer. One of our forensic guys reviewed her recent emails and gave me a list of senders, receivers, and names mentioned in the body of messages. Guess who popped up?"

His adrenaline spiked, boosting his heart rate. "Parker."

"Yep. His name was in a reply to a message she sent to a

less-than-stellar PI asking him to run a license plate. Given what Maxine said about the Matt that Natalie mentioned, I think we can assume our quiet, clean-as-a-whistle accountant has another side he tries to keep hidden."

"A darker side, if he had anything to do with Natalie's disappearance." Colin's fingers tightened on the coffee.

"Very dark."

"This also fits with what I found out about Craig Elliott. Or maybe I should say, what I didn't find out. I was going to track you down this afternoon to bring you up to speed. I was able to get a definite ID based on the recent credit card purchase here. Elliott's last address is in Miami—but deep as I dug, I couldn't find any record of him prior to five years ago. And he disappeared again in February."

"In other words, Craig Elliott is a fake ID."

"That's my assumption. He's not in the NCIC database, but I did talk with a Miami PD detective. Elliott was on their radar for a while for a possible insurance fraud scam, but they never got him on that. However, my contact put me in touch with the FBI's organized crime squad down there. Apparently Elliott was also in *their* sights in conjunction with an ongoing investigation into Russian Mafia activity."

Mac's eyebrows rose. "Big-time stuff."

"Uh-huh. Word on the street, according to my FBI source, is that Elliott was skimming money from the organization before he disappeared. The FBI thought Dmitri Kozlov, the head of the Miami organization, might have had him taken out."

"Instead, he shows up here—at his friend Matt's house. The plot thickens."

"And gets dangerous. We're not dealing with an amateur here. This guy's impressive. Eluding the Mafia is no small feat."

"But there's a high probability Natalie's shoe purchase blew his cover."

"Agreed." Organized crime had no qualms about illegally accessing private financial information. "But we have an advantage. They have no idea where he is in St. Louis. We do."

Mac gathered up the papers in front of him. "My afternoon agenda suddenly got more interesting."

"So did mine. We need to interview Parker and Elliott."

"You want to show up unannounced or give them a heads-up?"

"The element of surprise could work to our advantage. As far as we know, Parker has no idea we're digging into his background—and Elliott won't be expecting us, either."

"I'm with you. Give me ten minutes to return a few calls."

"I need to do the same." Colin pushed back his chair. "I'll meet you in the office."

He exited into the hall, grappling with the twist this case had taken. Mild-mannered accountant leading a secret life of women and booze, with a possible connection to murder and mugging and a friend on the lam from the Russian Mafia in Miami.

Bizarre didn't come close to capturing the situation.

As for how it would play out—Colin had no clue. But he did know one thing.

The link between the Natalie James and Eileen Coulter cases wasn't just unnerving; it was treacherous. One person had already died. Another was missing. And Trish, for whatever reason, was in the middle of everything.

Jaw hardening, he picked up his pace. They needed to get to the bottom of this. Pronto.

Before anyone else disappeared—or died.

* * * * *

Working on Matt's books for his other clients was b-o-r-i-n-g.

Craig yawned and moved the cursor to the accounts receivable column. Creative accounting was much more fun. Like the kind he'd done in Boston . . . and Miami . . . and would soon be doing here. *That* was a challenge.

And much more profitable.

But this mundane stuff covered expenses. If he was going to live in Matt's house, he had to do his part to ensure the bills got paid.

He leaned over to retrieve a file. Froze at the faint crunch of gravel and the barking of a dog in the distance.

Someone was coming up the driveway.

It wasn't the pizza guy. He hadn't decided on his Friday night dinner yet. Nor was it an invited guest. He wasn't entertaining at the moment. And it wasn't Natalie. She wouldn't come calling again.

So who could it be?

Leaving his laptop on the deck, he pushed through the sliding door, strode toward the front of the house, and peered through the sidelight glass.

A black Taurus was slowly approaching up the drive.

He squinted, but the tinted glass and glare from the afternoon sun hid the identity of the driver and anyone else inside.

Whoever it was, though, wasn't welcome. In his world, unexpected visitors were never a good sign.

He edged to the side of the window as the car slowed. Stopped. A stranger in a jacket and tie got out of the passenger side. Gave the house and grounds a quick, professional sweep.

A red alert began to beep in his brain at the man's practiced perusal.

This was not a casual visit.

The driver-side door opened—and his pulse skyrocketed.

Detective Colin Flynn had sought him out, with a colleague in tow.

The two men exchanged a few words and started toward the door.

Lungs locking, he fell back and tried to catch his breath. Why were the police nosing around? He hadn't made any mistakes. They couldn't be on to him.

Could they?

A tremor of fear rippled through him, and he steadied himself with a hand against the wall.

Don't panic! Stay calm. They don't know a thing. This might be part of a routine follow-up to Eileen Coulter's death. Trish is the prime suspect there. You made sure of that. Maybe they're just closing a loop.

Through the pounding in his ears, he heard footsteps on the porch.

What to do?

Think!

He couldn't flee. That would be stupid. Nor could he ignore them. Matt's car was clearly visible through the open door of the garage. They'd know someone was home.

Let Matt handle it.

Yes. The perfect solution. He was squeaky clean. Even after Trish's mother died, Flynn had asked him only a few perfunctory questions.

The doorbell rang—and he raced toward the bedroom at the back of the house. There was no time to prep. Matt would have to wing it, splash some water in his hair, claim he'd been in the shower. But he'd been convincing so far, pulling off every task without a hitch. There was no reason he couldn't handle a visit by the police.

And once they left, once the purpose of their visit was clear, Craig would decide on next steps for both him and Matt.

17

"Ready?" Colin leaned toward the doorbell of Parker's house.

At Mac's nod, he pressed the chime.

A muffled peal sounded from within.

Thirty silent seconds later, he tried again.

No response.

After exchanging a look with his colleague, he angled away from the door. "It's possible he's somewhere on the property. Trish says he has twenty or thirty acres and spends a lot of time maintaining the place."

"You wouldn't know that to look at his lawn."

"I noticed." Colin surveyed the overgrown front yard. "I expected the grounds to be as meticulous as the books I'm told he keeps. We could take a stroll around back and . . ."

The lock rattled, and he swiveled around as Parker pulled the door open.

"Sorry to keep you waiting. I was in the shower." He combed his fingers through his damp hair. "Detective Flynn . . . this is a surprise."

The first of many to come. It would be instructive to see how the accountant responded to their questions.

Colin introduced Mac, who shook hands with the other man.

"If you have a few minutes, we'd like to ask you some questions."

"Of course." He pulled the door wider and stepped back. "Come in."

Colin entered, giving the living room Matt led them to a quick sweep.

The space fit the quiet, unassuming, conservative image Parker projected to the world. An upholstered recliner, positioned in front of a flat-screen TV. A nondescript couch, flanked by matching ceramic lamps. Side chair. A neutral beige carpet, mini blinds rather than drapes, off-white walls bare of ornamentation.

He shifted his gaze to the mantel, where family photos were often displayed. There were none in this house. Only a pair of brass candlesticks and a small Celtic cross occupied the long expanse.

"Make yourselves comfortable. Would you like a soft drink or some water?" Parker claimed the recliner.

"No, thanks." Colin took the side chair, while Mac sat at the far end of the sofa. The separation would allow each of them to observe the man without being in his direct line of sight while he answered questions from the other.

"What brings you all the way out to my humble abode?"

"A missing person case, for one thing."

As Mac spoke, Matt's head swiveled his direction, a slight frown marring his forehead. "Missing person?"

"Yes." Mac pulled out his notebook. "A woman by the name of Natalie James."

For one fleeting moment, shock registered in Parker's eyes. But it was gone so fast Colin would have missed it had he not been homed in on the man's face.

"Why are you talking to me about her?" Puzzlement scored his words, but a hint of wariness lurked underneath.

"We found your name in her email."

Parker's breath hitched, and his fingers tightened on the arm of the chair. "That's bizarre. In what context?"

"She had a PI run your plates."

The furrows on his brow deepened, and a muscle flexed in his cheek. "Why would some stranger do that?"

"Was she a stranger?"

"Yes." Not one iota of hesitation. "I don't know a Natalie James."

Mac flipped to another page in his notebook. "Then why don't you tell us about someone you do know? Craig Elliott."

The shock wave that flattened his features was impossible to hide. "Is he involved in this missing person situation?"

"We were hoping you could answer that question."

"I have no idea." He rose. Rubbed the fading scar on his temple. Paced to the end of the room—and back. "So much for being a good Samaritan."

"So you do know him?"

"Yes. Well . . . I knew him before he was Craig Elliott. In college he was Jack Adler. We hung out together. Junior year, he disappeared with no explanation—there one day, gone the next. Everyone suspected foul play, but the police never found any evidence to support that theory. Ten days ago, out of the blue, he contacted me and said he needed a place to stay for a few days. Given his history, I should have expected trouble."

"Is he still here?"

"No. He left on Tuesday."

"Did he say where he was going?"

"No."

Mac flicked him a glance, and Colin picked up the questioning. "Where were you on Monday night?"

Matt stopped pacing and swung toward him, hands fisted at his sides, stance wide-legged. "Why?"

"That appears to be the night Natalie went missing."

"You think I had something to do with that?"

"A friend of hers said Natalie told her she had a date on Monday night with a high-class man named Matt who lived in the country. She said they'd hooked up after meeting in a bar. Your name popped up in her email. That's a powerful lead."

"This is absurd!" Matt's complexion grew ruddy, and his posture stiffened. "I'm not in the habit of frequenting bars. Nor do I pick up women."

"The evidence would suggest otherwise. I'll repeat my question. Where were you on Monday night?"

"Working on the property until after dark. Alone." He exhaled and retook his seat. "But Craig did borrow my car that night—and two or three other times. He said his own car had been stalling a lot and he didn't want to drive it much until a mechanic gave it a going-over." He massaged the bridge of his nose. "This . . . what was her name? Natalie? She must have assumed he was me after she had the plates run. What a nightmare."

Colin exchanged a look with Mac. The story was plausible . . . and he might be willing to give Parker the benefit of the doubt . . . except for the man's odd behavior at Trish's house, plus some of the background information he'd discovered.

They needed to keep pushing.

"Why don't you describe him for us?"

"I'm not good with descriptions. In my job I look at figures, not faces."

"Try."

He wiped a hand down his face. "He's about my height. Dark hair, a little on the long side. Green eyes. He looked to be in pretty good condition."

"Any distinguishing marks—scars, tattoos, that kind of thing?"

"Not that I noticed."

That was about as generic a description as you could get.

Colin stifled an annoyed sigh. "Let's shift gears for a minute. I'm curious about why you gave up a prestigious, fast-track career in international banking to practice small-time accounting."

Parker's features hardened. "You've been digging into my work history?"

"We leave few stones unturned in an investigation."

"Why I changed my career plans is a long and personal story that has no bearing on this woman's disappearance. Look . . . do I need to call a lawyer?"

"That's an option." But not one Colin wanted him to choose until they had more information. "At the moment, we're just asking some casual questions. You're not under any obligation to answer them—but we would appreciate your cooperation. A woman *is* missing."

"Right." Some of the tension in Parker's features eased. "I want to help if I can. But Craig would be the one to question."

"Did you ask why he needed a place to stay?"

"Yes. He didn't offer much. I got the impression he was trying to put some distance between himself and a sticky situation."

"So you welcomed a virtual stranger who you suspected might have issues into your home. Wasn't that risky?" Mac rejoined the conversation.

"He was a college buddy." Matt shrugged. "I didn't see how giving him a place to sleep for a few nights was a big deal. I didn't think he was involved in an illegal activity that would put me at risk."

"What was your relationship with Lawrence Adams?" Colin picked up the questioning.

At the non sequitur, Parker did a double take. "That's ancient history."

"It's also a simple question. He's listed as your loving father in his death notice—but the last names don't match."

Parker leaned forward, rested his forearms on his thighs, and clasped his hands together. A dozen mute seconds passed before he responded. "He was my foster father—but he treated me like a real son. His death was a terrible blow."

"I'm sorry for your loss." Colin tried for a compassionate tone, but Parker's grief wasn't ringing true. While his words were appropriate, his perfunctory inflection conveyed no sadness. "Our research indicates his business was in dire financial straits in the months preceding his death."

The other man assessed him. "You've done your homework."

"It's our job. Can you tell us what went wrong?"

"Yes—but I'd prefer not to. It was . . . messy."

"Were Adams's money woes the reason you abandoned your career and went home? To help out?"

"The short answer is yes. After he died, I didn't have the heart for the relentless pace or heavy travel of international finance anymore. And there was nothing left for me in Boston. I decided a fresh start in the Midwest would better suit me going forward."

So far, Parker had nimbly dodged every question, or come up with a glib answer.

Time to throw him another curve.

"I think we're about done here . . ." Colin slanted a look at Mac, who dipped his chin. "But I do have one last question. Why did you look in the CSU bag in Trish Bailey's foyer the day you brought some charitable material for her to review . . . and why did you move that material from the chair to the bag while she was in the kitchen?"

The man's expression went blank. "What?"

Colin repeated his question.

"I have no idea what you're talking about."

"She saw you do it."

Parker exhaled. Unclenched his fingers. "She's been under so much stress these past two years . . . I worry about her. For the past few weeks she's been making mistakes, forgetting things . . ." He shook his head. "All I can tell you is that whatever she thought she saw isn't reality. I do remember straightening the bag as I walked to the front door, but that was it."

This guy was a champion dodge-ball player.

"Okay. Thanks for your time." Mac stood, retrieved a card, and held it out. "We'll be back in touch if we have any additional questions—and if you hear from Elliott again, we'd appreciate a call."

"Of course." The man pocketed the card.

Colin rose, added his thanks, and followed Mac out the door.

Only after he put the car in gear and they were driving down the gravel road did he speak. "Either Parker is innocent, or that was a very smooth performance."

"I vote for the latter." Mac slipped on a pair of dark shades. "My gut tells me he was making a lot of that up on the fly as we tossed out questions."

"The factual parts are easy to verify. His relationship with Elliott, and what happened on the night in question, are going to be tougher to crack."

"What did you think of his response to your question about the CSU bag?"

"That he's lying. Trish *has* been under a lot of strain, and she *is* carrying an enormous load of grief, but her faculties are sharp. Besides, it's too coincidental that all of her so-called mental lapses have occurred in situations involving Parker."

"So where do we go from here?"

"I think you should continue to search for Elliott while I fact-check what Parker told us."

"I'm on board with that, since I think Elliott's got the answers I need about Natalie's disappearance."

"Good luck tracking him down."

Mac snorted. "Given that he eluded the Russian Mafia, I'll need it."

"Now that his credit card has been used, they may find him for you."

"If they do, I may never know it."

True. If the Mafia got to Elliott first, there might not be much left to find once they were finished.

"Do you think we should have mentioned to Parker that his friend was involved with organized crime?"

"We threw enough at him for one day—and I'm not sure what that would have accomplished. I'm more of a tell-them-only-what-they-need-to-know kind of guy."

"Okay. Let's go our separate ways once we get back and text each other if we find anything relevant." Colin swung out onto the main road, accelerating once he hit the paved surface.

"Works for me."

Mac pulled out his cell to scroll through messages, giving Colin a chance to run their meeting with Parker through his mind again. They'd taken the man by surprise with both their visit and their questions, no doubt about it. He'd played it as cool as he could, but based on a few subtle cues, they'd thrown him off balance. That, in itself, was a positive outcome.

People who were flustered often got nervous.

And a nervous person was more liable to make a mistake that could help them unravel the tangled knots of a case that kept getting more and more complicated.

. . . . .

Craig slammed down the lid of the laptop on the deck, startling a nearby robin into panicked flight.

What a mess.

All because he'd gone out looking for a night or two of much-deserved fun.

Now the police were nosing around.

He snatched up the laptop and stalked inside, shoving the sliding door shut behind him. Why had he believed Natalie's claim that she hadn't told anyone about their liaison? A woman who'd drug her date for the evening to get his ID was devious—and high risk.

Now what?

He ditched the laptop on the counter and went in search of the Scotch. After emptying the inch Natalie had left him into a glass, he took a long swallow, letting the alcohol burn down his throat as he transitioned to analytical mode.

He'd listened to every word the cops had said to Matt, his mind evaluating at warp speed. As far as he could see, there were no holes in the story he'd told them. Acting dumb had been the logical way to play this. It was credible—and if Trish hadn't witnessed that little maneuver in her foyer, the two detectives probably would have bought it and focused on finding Craig Elliott.

A lost cause that would have left them spinning their wheels.

Craig Elliott had dropped off the radar four months ago, never to reappear. They would find no trace of him since February. Their investigation would go nowhere.

Plus, given Natalie's estrangement from her family, there wouldn't be any relatives pushing for closure. The police would give her disappearance some initial attention, but with the caseload detectives carried these days, it would drop down the priority list fast if no new leads surfaced.

And they wouldn't. He'd touched nothing directly in Natalie's place other than her—and the glasses he'd used, which he'd washed. If they looked hard enough, there was a remote chance they might find a hair for DNA matching—but if that happened, he had another ace up his sleeve. While it wasn't a card he wanted to play, it was always helpful to have options.

He took a sip of his Scotch, his nerves quieting. There was nothing to worry about. If, by some remote chance, the situation started to go south, he had excellent new documents waiting in the bedroom for the person he'd become after he'd diverted sufficient foundation money to his offshore account and was ready to exchange this backwater dump for more lavish digs in a sunny tropical locale. He'd had plenty of time since moving in here to arrange for those. If he had to use them sooner than expected, he would.

But most likely that wouldn't be necessary. This glitch would blow over soon enough. The search for Natalie would grow cold, and the detectives would put it on the back burner to deal with newer cases.

He tipped the glass against his lips and finished off the Scotch.

Matt had done well this afternoon. Despite everything the cops had thrown at him, he'd kept his head, stayed the course, and done an excellent job deflecting suspicion.

Exhaling, he set his empty glass near the sink, wandered over to the window that offered a view into the woods, and rotated the kinks out of his shoulders.

He was safe.

If the cops came back, Craig Elliott would disappear again— and the only other people who had an interest in the man were far away in Miami. Dmitri and his crew had no idea where he'd gone. Matt's home in the middle of a forest might not be much to look at, but it had given him great cover.

And he'd continue to use it until he was ready to walk away a rich man . . . leaving no regrets behind.

18

"Is this the last one?" Colin tapped a corrugated box filled with holiday decorations and miscellaneous art supplies.

"Yes." Trish pushed a strand of hair back from her damp forehead and surveyed her classroom, cleaned and prepped for the summer session at record speed—thanks to her handsome helper. "Everything else is loaded in the car."

"Good. I'm ready for another cold drink."

"Me too. Sorry it's so warm in here. They keep the air set high when classes aren't in session." She started toward the small cooler she'd brought. "I have more soda."

"I was thinking colder—like a Frappuccino."

She halted. "Sold."

One corner of his mouth quirked up. "That wasn't hard."

"I'm hot."

He gave her a quick sweep, the banked fire in his eyes raising the air temperature another few degrees. "No arguments there."

She planted her hands on her hips as a tingle rippled through her. "Are you flirting?"

"No. Just stating the facts."

"Smooth line."

"It's not a line if it's the truth."

Hmm. Maybe he was finally loosening up. Since picking her up at nine o'clock sharp, he'd been pensive and quiet. All her attempts to engage him in conversation had fallen flat.

"I was beginning to worry about you." She slung her tote bag over her shoulder and dug out the keys for the classroom. "You haven't said much this morning."

"Sorry. I'm a little preoccupied. Plus, it was a long and busy week. I got pulled into a double murder and a missing person case."

Whoa.

That was a perspective restorer.

"And I thought my job was tough."

"It is. I couldn't do what you do with these kids every day." He hoisted the box. "I apologize for the lack of conversation. I've been thinking about Parker. My colleague and I had a talk with him yesterday."

"You waited until now to tell me that?"

"I've been in processing mode—but I'll fill you in while we drink our Frappuccinos. I'd like to get your take on what he had to say."

"Any hints?"

"No. Let's ditch this sweat box and head for cooler climates."

"I'm with you. I'll let the janitor know we're leaving."

Five minutes later they were in his car zipping west, the air conditioning cranked up to full blast. But he focused on chitchat until they settled into a quiet corner of the busy Starbucks near her house, Frappuccinos in hand.

"The perfect cure for heat exhaustion." Trish took a refreshing sip, then leaned toward him. "Okay, I've been more than patient. Tell me what happened with Matt."

Colin sipped his own drink before he spoke. "You remember

I asked you whether Parker had ever mentioned a Craig Elliott, who we were investigating in connection with another case?"

"Yes."

"Turns out he does know him. Get ready for some surprising twists."

As he relayed Elliott's connection with Matt, she listened with growing disbelief. When he got to the part about the Russian Mafia, her jaw dropped.

"Are you certain we're talking about the same Matt Parker?"

"Bear in mind he denies having anything to do with the missing woman . . . or the lifestyle suggested by the tale her coworker told. And as far as we know, he isn't aware of Elliott's connection to the Mafia."

She sank back in her chair and slowly exhaled. "You know, every time I think my life can't get any weirder, a new wrinkle blindsides me. But this one is . . . wow."

"I agree. What's your take on Parker's response to our questions?"

"That he's telling the truth. I know he's been acting kind of strange lately, but I can't believe the man I see at church every Sunday would be doing any of the things you describe. This Elliott must be the one who visited the bar and picked up the missing woman, like Matt said. What do *you* think?"

"I try to keep an open mind during an investigation."

"Not fair. I gave you my opinion."

"You're not being paid to remain impartial until all the facts are uncovered."

"Hmph."

"On a different subject—I told Parker you saw what he did in the foyer with that charitable material."

Her pulse picked up. "What did he say?"

"That you imagined it."

"What?" She stared at him.

"He didn't use those words, but that's the gist. He also reminded me again how stressed you've been."

"That's ridiculous!" Anger bubbled up inside her, warming her cheeks. "I know what I saw!"

"Why would he lie?"

Checkmate.

Stomach knotting, she studied him. Did Colin believe Matt's story rather than hers?

"Does that mean you're keeping an open mind about my mental competence too?" Despite her attempt to maintain a conversational tone, the words came out stiff.

He leaned closer and covered her clenched fingers with his hand. "No. I've seen plenty of evidence that you're intelligent, intuitive, and mentally sharp. I think Parker's lying about what happened in your foyer. That's why I spent last night and the early hours of this morning digging deeper into his background and trying to verify the other information he gave me."

"Did you find anything worthwhile?"

"The Jack Adler disappearance is legit, and he did attend the same college as Parker at the same time. I also have a call in to the Boston branch of the Massachusetts Department of Children and Families to see if the foster kid story is true."

"Did Matt offer you any details about the financial mess at his foster father's company?"

"No. And those are tough to find. Private companies don't have to make their data public. But I've left messages for a few construction industry people mentioned in the articles you found, and I'm hoping to get the name of someone who worked there and who might be able to offer more information than Parker provided."

"You *have* been busy."

"I want to get to the bottom of this."

"No more than I do." She took another sip of her Frappuccino, eyeing the man across from her. Should she tell him about the doubts that had been plaguing her during her recent restless nights when sleep had been elusive? Would he think they were crazy—or credible?

Only one way to find out—and she needed to share the disturbing notion with someone.

She cleared her throat and gripped the cool drink with both hands. "You know . . . in light of everything that's been happening, I've been toying with a theory that's kind of off the wall."

"Off the wall is par for this case. Tell me what you're thinking."

"Well . . ." She took a steadying breath and plunged in. "You know how Matt's been pushing me to appoint him as a trustee for the foundation? I started wondering if maybe . . ."

She stopped as a fresh set of qualms assailed her. Was it wrong to cast more aspersions on a man who'd served the foundation so well, to darken the cloud of suspicion already hovering over him?

"Hey." Colin touched her hand. "It's not disloyal to play with theories in view of what's been going on over the past six weeks. And if it puts your mind at ease, nothing you can say could make me distrust Parker any more than I already do. He's been a red alert on my radar screen for a while."

She cocked her head. "How do you do that?"

"What?"

"Read my mind."

A smile tugged at his lips. "I could say it's my detective training and experience—but the truth is I seem to be on your wavelength. I'm interpreting that as a positive omen for the future, by the way."

Nice to know.

And after that comforting reassurance, sharing her fears became a no-brainer.

"Okay . . . so I'm wondering if his attempts to plant doubts about my mental acuity might be part of a campaign to convince me to turn control of the foundation over to him. Since Mom would never have done that, I'm also wondering if he might have . . ." She swallowed past the bad taste on her tongue that even the lingering rich chocolate flavor couldn't banish.

"If he might have played a role in your mother's death."

At least he hadn't used the word *murder*.

"Yes." It sounded awful, put into words. "But Matt's never done one thing since I've known him to deserve that kind of suspicion."

"Until the past few weeks."

"Those minor incidents shouldn't be enough to justify the kind of suspicions polluting my mind. I mean, it's a leap from suspecting someone of undermining your capabilities to . . ." She couldn't say the *M* word either.

"Unless there's a stronger motive."

He was still on her wavelength.

"Are you thinking embezzlement?"

"It's a possibility. I'm assuming there's a fair amount of money in the foundation's coffers."

"But why would he do that?" It was the same question she'd been asking herself since the suspicion had taken root in her mind during the wee hours of the morning. "Do you think he needs money?"

"His credit report was clean."

"Then what would be his motive?"

"Greed comes to mind."

"That doesn't make sense. Why would he get greedy all of a sudden?" Frowning, she ran a fingertip around the lid of her drink. "Do you think his car accident could have caused some sort of odd mental shift?"

"I've never heard of anything like that—although the timing does seem more than coincidental." He tapped a finger against the tabletop. "Let's assume Parker does want money for some reason and is trying to get you to relinquish control so he can embezzle funds. Tell me how the foundation works."

"It's a simple setup. The money is invested in a variety of financial instruments, which Matt oversees. Mom and Dad wrote checks to charities they felt were worthwhile. Mom met with Matt every month to discuss those donations and review the financial statements. To be honest, she didn't need to see him that often—but she liked Matt and enjoyed the social interaction."

"How much control does Matt have over the organization?"

"A fair amount. After Dad died, Mom gave the previous accountant—and then Matt—a lot of oversight responsibility. Mom was a smart woman, but she didn't have a head for numbers. That was Dad's strength. Matt reviewed investments with the fund financial adviser and made recommendations to Mom. She also redirected fund mailings to him, and he prepared a simplified monthly report for her."

"Have you reviewed all the charities that receive donations from the foundation?"

"Yes—and the recent financial reports filed with the IRS."

"Spot anything suspicious?"

"No. The numbers were fine. There were a few charities I didn't recognize, but all the websites appear to be legit. The only one I questioned was Providence House Ministries." She told him what Matt had shared with her about the organization. "His explanation for their low profile made sense—and I read all the material he gave me. No red flags popped up."

"Do they have a mailing address?"

"A PO box. But that fits with how he described the organization's operating philosophy."

"I wouldn't mind digging deeper into the material he provided on that one. It shouldn't be difficult to do some due diligence. Our white-collar fraud people are very adept at that."

"I'll give it to you when we get back to the house." She played with her straw. "I know you want to keep a professional distance until this is over, but will you let me know if anything useful surfaces from all the contacts you made over the past twenty-four hours?"

"Yes. Case-related conversations are fine—and I'll find a reason to have those on a regular basis until we wrap this up." He smiled, the warmth in his brown irises seeping straight into her heart. "So what are your plans for the rest of the day?"

"I need to weed the rose garden."

"Not a chore you enjoy?" He gave her a keen look, apparently picking up the faint whisper of sadness in her voice.

"I don't mind the chore . . . but it reminds me Mom is gone."

Once more he reached over and covered her hand with his. "We may not talk about it much, Trish, but I haven't forgotten about your loss. I want you to know I've been praying for you every day."

That news was almost as startling as his case update.

"I thought you and God weren't communicating."

"I've reopened the dialogue."

"That's one positive result from all of this, then."

"More than one." He squeezed her fingers. "I just wish I could be around more for you."

"I understand why you need to keep your distance—and I respect your professionalism."

"I do have an offer for you, however. Remember I mentioned my friend Kristin?"

The woman he was helping with the summer show, even though he had zero interest in theater?

Of course she remembered.

"Yes. The one who's doing a children's production at her church."

"Right. She said she'd enjoy meeting you, and asked me to see if you'd be open to a call from her."

Interesting.

Did this Kristin want to size up the competition . . . or was there another reason for her offer?

"I'm always open to meeting new people." She took a sip of her drink, striving for a casual tone. "But why would she want to meet me?"

"To be honest, part of it is nosiness." He grinned. "She and Rick have picked up on my interest in you, and I think she wants to check you out. Plus, if we continue to click, you'll be part of our group."

"What group?"

He considered her for a long moment. "Do you have a few more minutes to spare?"

"Yes. The roses can wait."

After taking a long drink, he set his cup aside and folded his hands on the table. "You already know about what happened with my brother when I was nine, and how our family fell apart after that. Once my parents divorced, I lived with my mom and spent every other weekend with my dad. To be blunt, life stunk."

"Until you met Rick—and the cop from his church."

"Yeah." He seemed surprised she'd remembered those details. As if she would forget. "He and I bonded, to use current lingo. He grew up in foster care after his mother was killed in a domestic violence incident. Compared to his background, mine was a Disney story—and hearing his history helped restore my perspective. Anyway, the two of us were inseparable. It was a club of two . . . until we met Kristin."

"So you've known her since you were kids?" That was encouraging. If the two of them had been destined for romance, surely those sparks would have developed long ago.

"Yes. She was a year younger than us, and I doubt we'd have given her a second look if we hadn't noticed her sitting in the middle-school cafeteria alone every day at lunch. Her isolation bothered us, and we felt sorry for her."

Her heart melted.

How many boys that age would pay attention to a little girl's isolation . . . let alone care enough to step in and try to help?

Colin rose several more notches in her estimation—as did his friend Rick.

"You guys adopted her?"

The corners of his lips twitched, and he took a sip of his drink. "You're giving us too much credit. Sitting with her at lunch was as far as our benevolence went in the beginning."

"But . . ."

"But we ended up liking her. Once we got past her intense shyness, we discovered she was smart and funny and kind. We also found out she was as much in need of a friend as we'd been. Unlike us, she came from money—but her parents were gung-ho career people who had no time for their surprise child. They showered her with material things but were stingy with their attention."

"That's sad." Yet all too common.

"We thought so too. And we learned a lesson—even an intact family, with all the material possessions you could possibly want, wasn't always the happiest place to be. That was a revelation for both of us."

"So you felt sorry for her and invited her to join your club."

"Not at first. We weren't that altruistic. But once we found out she had an amazing two-level treehouse, it was a no-brainer." He grinned and finished off his drink. "We dubbed ourselves the Treehouse Gang, and the name has stuck."

"Did you have a secret password and handshake?"

"No." His demeanor grew more serious. "But we did have a code of honor—and a pact that as adults, we would do our part to make the world a better place."

A noble if lofty ambition for a bunch of preteens—except Colin had taken it to heart.

"You're honoring that agreement with your police work. Did Rick and Kristin follow through too?"

"Yes. Rick was in the service for a few years and now runs a camp for kids who are in the foster system. Kristin owns a shop that sells fair-trade goods."

A group of honorable high-achievers.

Impressive.

"And you've stayed tight."

"Very. We meet for breakfast every other Saturday. So . . . circling back to the beginning of this conversation . . . our close friendship is one of the reasons Kristin would like to meet you."

"Do I have to pass some kind of test to be an honorary member of your group?" Though she couched it as a joke, her question was more than half serious.

"You've already passed my test—and my vote has the most weight in this situation." He winked at her, allaying her concerns.

"Then by all means, give Kristin my number." If she couldn't hang out with Colin until this case was over, why not get to know one of the important people in his life? Plus, she might pick up a few more insights into the man she suspected was destined to play a key role in her future.

And it would be lovely to have a girlfriend again. As a young married couple, she and John had devoted all their free time to each other—and the past two years had been filled with grief and work and caring for her mother. Cultivating new friends had been a low priority.

"I'll do that. Ready to go?"

She swirled her drink. There was an inch left, but the ice had melted. Didn't matter. It had already done its job. She'd cooled off—even as her heart had warmed.

"Yes."

The drive to her house was short, and within ten minutes Colin was walking her to the door. "While you dig weeds, I'm going to dig for dirt on our mysterious accountant."

"I may do some googling myself once I finish with the roses."

"Have at it. The more hands on deck for this one, the better. I'll call Kristin on the drive to the office. Don't be surprised if she gets in touch later today. She's chomping at the bit."

"I'll look forward to meeting her. And thanks for your help at school."

"Anytime."

He gave her hand a squeeze and retreated down the walk to his car while Stan Hawkins watched the proceedings with unabashed interest from across the street, hedge clippers in hand.

After Colin pulled out and drove away, the older man broke off a hydrangea blossom and trotted over, arms shoved into his ratty, button-up cardigan despite the early June warmth.

"How're you doing, Trish?"

"Hanging in."

"I sure am sorry about everything that's happened."

It was the same well-meaning, earnest sentiment he expressed whenever their paths crossed.

"I appreciate that."

"Thought this might brighten your day. I remember how you liked them as a little girl." He passed over the vivid blue bloom. "Happy memories can be comforting."

Her throat tightened. "Yes, they can. Thank you. How's Mrs. Hawkins?"

"She has her good days and her bad days. Arthritis interferes with a lot of the activities she used to enjoy—but I suppose that's to be expected once you hit your eighties. Maybe it's the Lord's way of telling you to slow down and smell the roses. Or the hydrangeas." He touched a fragile petal, then motioned in the direction Colin had disappeared. "Pleasant young man. Polite too."

"Yes, he is."

"I like him better than that serious accountant fellow your mom set such store by. I've never seen the man smile."

Trish tried to hide her amusement. "I didn't realize you knew either of them very well."

"We haven't had long conversations, if that's what you mean. But you don't always have to talk a lot to know when it feels right in here." He tapped his chest. "Like with the missus. I knew the first time I saw her she was the one for me. It can happen like that, you know."

"I suppose so."

"I *know* so. You want my best piece of advice? Always listen to your heart. If you've put your trust in the man upstairs and lived a virtuous life, it won't steer you wrong."

"If it makes you feel better, I have no intention of getting serious about Matt Parker."

"What about the detective?"

"He has . . . possibilities." And wouldn't Colin get a kick out of this conversation?

"Glad to hear it—because he thinks *you* have possibilities."

What?!

"How do you know?"

"I've watched how he watches you. I may have creaky joints, but this old heart can still pick up sparks and hear the song of romance. Just ask the missus." He gave her a playful nudge with his elbow. "Now it's back to work for me. I have bushes to trim. You need anything, you give us a shout."

"I'll do that. Thanks."

He waggled his hedge clippers and traipsed back across the street.

What a sweetie.

And sharp too, if he'd picked up the vibes between her and Colin from a few casual encounters with the man.

As her neighbor tackled a shaggy bush, she turned to go inside, his advice replaying in her mind.

Always listen to your heart.

Not bad counsel. That's what she'd done when she'd met John, and though their marriage had been far too brief, it had been happy. The kind she wanted again if she ever took another chance on love.

The kind she had a feeling she might find with Colin down the road—for as she'd told Stan, the new man in her life did have serious possibilities. Ones she intended to pursue as soon as they got past the obstacles that kept cropping up.

Those detours, however, were temporary. They were on the verge of finding answers that would help them piece together the circumstances that had pulled her into an episode from the Twilight Zone. She could feel it.

Yet as she locked the front door behind her and her gaze fell on the CSU bag in the foyer, a shiver rippled through her.

Based on all Colin had told her today . . . based on the questionable circumstances of her mother's death . . . based on the mugging Colin seemed convinced was a setup . . . it was possible this situation could take another dangerous twist before it wound down.

Not the most comforting thought.

But all she could do was hope answers would be found and guilty parties apprehended without further incident.

And pray God would protect her through the shadowy unknown looming ahead.

19

"I've got an update on Elliott, boss, if you have a few minutes."

Dmitri motioned Oleg to join him in the conference room, where he was enjoying an excellent Monday dinner—no . . . lunch, here in America—of borscht, baked grouper, saffron rice, and the black bread of his homeland. Despite his French chef's disdain, Pierre had learned to make the staple rye loaf.

As well he should, given the ridiculous salary he was paid.

"Would you like some food? There is plenty."

"No, thank you. I have already eaten."

The appropriate response. Oleg knew his superior's invitation was no more than a rote courtesy.

"Sit and tell me what you have found."

The man chose a chair on the opposite side of the table and laid a folder in front of him. "Our sources tell us the police in St. Louis are also looking for Elliott."

That was a positive sign. If he'd caught the attention of law enforcement, he'd made a mistake.

And any mistake would make him easier to locate.

"Why are they searching for him?"

"He is a suspect in a missing person case."

Dmitri broke off a piece of bread. "Who is missing?"

"A woman."

He took a bite of the bread and chewed slowly, savoring the tangy rye flavor. "He never was one to deny himself the ladies . . . but I am not aware he ever harmed one. Who is this woman?"

"A manicurist he found at a bar."

"Ah." He gave a dismissive wave of his hand. "Someone who does not matter."

"She matters to the police—fortunately for us. But they have not found her . . . or Elliott . . . yet."

"Then how does this information help us?" Oleg wouldn't waste his time unless there was more concrete news to convey.

"Another person is also being investigated in conjunction with the missing woman. According to our sources, Elliott was staying with him."

Dmitri stopped eating. "What is his name?"

"Matthew Parker."

"You have found this man, I assume?"

"Yes—and we have prepared a dossier on him." He opened the folder and withdrew a single sheet of paper. "This is his photo. I think you will find it interesting."

As Oleg slid it toward him across the polished surface, Dmitri's breath hitched.

"*Nu i nu.*"

While the soft exclamation hung in the air between them, he picked up the image.

Well, well, indeed.

At last he lowered the photo back to the table, pushed aside his half-finished lunch, and folded his hands.

"Let us talk strategy."

▪ ▪ ▪ ▪ ▪

Yes!

As Colin glanced at the Massachusetts area code displayed on his vibrating cell, he rose, caught Sarge's attention, and held up his phone. Without waiting for an acknowledgment from his boss, he hustled toward the door of the conference room. The Monday morning department meeting about new email procedures was a snoozer. He could read the recap later.

This was a call he legitimately needed to take.

Once in the hall, he strode toward his office, cell to his ear. "Colin Flynn."

"Detective Flynn, this is Walt Hanover with Hanover Construction in Boston. You left a message late Friday. How can I help you?"

He gave the man a topline on the reason for his call, concluding with his request. "Since you were in the same industry, I thought you might be able to give me the name of someone who worked at Lawrence Adams's company during the last few months it was in business."

"I can do better than that. We hired one of his best sales reps, Zach Brennan. Sharp guy. He's in the office this morning. If you like, I can transfer you to him."

Finding an inside source had been much simpler than he'd dared hope.

"That would be great."

While he waited, Colin finished the walk to his office, sat, and pulled out a tablet and pen.

"Zach's on the line. Let me know if I can offer any further help."

"Thanks. I will." Colin scooted his chair into his desk as a click sounded. "Mr. Brennan?"

"Yes. Walt told me you wanted to speak with someone who worked for Larry."

"That's right. Were you there during the period he was having financial trouble?"

"Yes . . . until I was laid off after money got tight."

"I'm trying to dig up some background on the company's financial issues. As far as I can tell, the firm had always been profitable. I'm curious why it almost went belly up."

"I don't know if I can help you much." The man's tone was cautious. "I wasn't privy to the private conversations that took place on that subject. My knowledge is limited to hearsay."

"Duly noted. I'm just trying to get a handle on what *might* have gone wrong. Hearsay could be helpful."

"Well . . . I never saw the books, but from what I heard, bills weren't being paid. Most of our vendors were longtime suppliers, and they cut Larry a lot of slack in the beginning. They didn't even complain at first. By the time they began to grumble, I think the company was deep in a hole. Larry seemed blindsided by the whole mess."

"Had the business suffered a downturn?"

"No. We were working on a new residential development of single-family homes, and most of the lots had been sold when the financial problems came to light."

"Do you think the money was being mismanaged?"

"That was one theory—but there were more . . . shady . . . ones."

Colin squinted out the window at the dark clouds beginning to mass on the horizon. "Such as?"

"For years the chief financial officer was a college buddy of Larry's. As far as I know, there was never a hiccup in the books while he was in charge. But after he got cancer and retired, Larry brought in a guy named Michael Parker to take over."

"You mean Matt Parker?"

"No. Michael. He's Matt's brother."

Matt had a brother?

That was news.

He jotted the name on the tablet.

"Tell me what you know about the two brothers."

"Not a lot. Michael didn't mingle, and Matt didn't come back until after I'd been let go."

"Do you know anything about their history?"

"Bits and pieces. From what I gathered, Larry and his wife took the boys in as foster kids after the state yanked them out of a tough home environment. Rumor had it Michael was a handful, and after Larry's wife began having health issues, they couldn't deal with both boys anymore. So Michael got recycled into the system. I think Larry might have felt guilty about that, and that's why he helped Michael with college expenses and ended up bringing him on board at the company."

"So Michael was in charge of the books when the company began to tank."

"Yes."

"Was he incompetent?"

"Just the opposite. I think he was some kind of financial and computer genius. Larry was always bragging on him. He trusted him and gave him a lot of latitude. But apparently the money going out of the company wasn't being used to pay the bills—though I heard that wasn't reflected in the financial reports."

Zach Brennan didn't have to spell it out for Colin to catch his drift.

Matt's brother had siphoned off company funds, cooked the books, and sent his generous benefactor's firm reeling toward bankruptcy.

A real class act.

"What about Matt Parker?"

"He had some hot-shot job in Europe for a while—but I know he came back after everything hit the fan. I heard he sank most of his own savings into the company to try to shore it up. With his help, Larry weathered the storm and came out whole . . . but he died soon after. You probably knew that."

"Yeah."

Colin drew a series of intersecting circles on the sheet of paper as he mulled over the differences between the brothers. Matt had given up a promising career to go home and try to help his foster father save face . . . and rescue the company.

A legitimate class act.

Which made his present behavior all the more bizarre.

"This has been very helpful." Colin drew a line between the two brothers' names. "What happened to Michael Parker?"

"He disappeared."

"You mean Lawrence Adams let him get away with embezzlement?"

"If there was any truth in the grapevine, Michael had set the whole thing up to look as if Larry was at fault. I'm not sure he had a choice about how he handled it. I heard he poured every dollar he had—including his retirement account—into satisfying his creditors and giving the homeowners the houses they'd paid for. He might have let it ride to avoid a scandal. Or maybe he felt guilty, thinking if he'd done more for Michael while he was growing up, he might not have gone bad. Or he might have been afraid he'd go to jail himself."

All of those were possible motivations. It wasn't that uncommon for embezzlement in family businesses to go unpunished—for a myriad of reasons.

"You've been a tremendous help. Would you mind sharing your cell number in case any other questions arise?"

He jotted it down while the man recited it, skimming the screen as an incoming call alert beeped.

Cecilia West—the woman from the Massachusetts Department of Children and Families he'd talked with early this morning.

Yes!

Getting information out of the *local* social services folks could be a challenge, let alone an administrator with another state's foster program. If she was calling back, she'd followed up on his request and found some information she was able to share.

After saying a quick good-bye to Brennan, he took the woman's call, gave her a fast greeting, and got down to business. "I'm hoping you found some information you can pass along."

"It took some digging. These files are twenty years old, you know. But yes, I did. I do need to verify the name you asked about, though. I have two Parker brothers in the system for the dates you specified. You were looking for information on Matthew, correct?"

"That was my original intent—but I didn't know there was a brother until this morning. I'd appreciate whatever you have on both boys."

"Why don't I give you an overview and we can go from there?"

"Perfect."

"Based on the intake notes, the brothers were removed from their home after their mother was arrested for heroin possession. Their father was already serving time for drug dealing. A Lawrence Adams and his wife took the boys. The file indicates they stayed there together for two years. At that point, Michael returned to the system."

She didn't say why, but Zach Brennan had already provided a credible explanation.

"What happened to Michael?"

"It appears he was placed with a number of different foster families after that. I do see that he was in one bad home situation. Those foster parents were later charged with child abuse. Michael left that home before the charges were filed, however."

But that didn't mean he hadn't been mistreated—and abuse could have a lasting impact. Most foster kids had endured plenty of stress already before they entered the system. Additional trauma would exacerbate any existing psychological issues. In

Michael's case, it might have pushed him to do increasingly atrocious things.

Like embezzling money—or worse.

"Is there any indication why Lawrence Adams never adopted Matthew?" He wasn't likely to get much more out of the woman, but it was worth a try. "I understand they were very close."

The sound of paper shuffling came over the line.

"It doesn't appear his mother ever relinquished her parental rights. That's not unusual. Many children in foster care aren't available for adoption."

"Were the boys ever reunited with her or their father?"

More paper shuffling.

"The father died in prison while the boys were in foster care. The mother was living when they were released from the program at eighteen, but the files don't indicate if there was any further contact."

Colin rocked back in his chair. His conversation with Cecilia had provided some additional information, but few new insights.

One conclusion seemed clear, however.

Given Matt's heroic efforts to help Lawrence Adams in the wake of his sibling's betrayal, it was unlikely the brothers were close, if they communicated at all. Besides, Michael had disappeared five years ago, according to Zach Brennan.

The pieces weren't fitting.

He let out a slow, frustrated breath. "I appreciate all your help. Are there any other facts in the file that you think I might find of interest, or anything that strikes you as unusual?" As he asked the routine wrap-up question, he was already thinking ahead to possible next steps.

"The only thing that seems a little odd is that more effort wasn't made to keep the boys together while they were in the foster system."

"I expect it can be a challenge to find families willing to take multiple children."

"Yes—but I would have thought they'd have tried harder in this situation."

"Why?" He yawned. All the extra hours he'd spent digging into this case over the weekend were taking a toll. The minute this call ended, he was going to make an emergency run to Starbucks for a venti Americano with three shots of espresso. That might help him get through the—

". . . identical twins."

As the tail end of Cecilia's response registered, he jerked upright in his chair. "What did you say?"

"That it's always best not to split up identical twins."

What?!

A few seconds ticked by as he tried to absorb the startling news.

"Detective Flynn? Are you still there?"

"Yes. Are you saying Michael and Matthew are identical twins?"

"That's correct. I thought you already knew that."

"I only knew they were brothers." He did his best to sound coherent, his mind racing. "Thank you again for your assistance. I'll be in touch if I have any other questions."

He pushed the end button and stared at the screen, his pulse accelerating as a wild—and deeply disturbing—possibility began to take shape in his mind. One that seemed too far-fetched to be credible.

Yet it explained a lot.

Like . . . everything.

"I can't believe you pulled the old urgent-call-coming-in phone trick to get out of that meeting. In case you didn't notice, Sarge gave you the evil eye as you—" Mac came to an abrupt halt in front of his adjacent desk, twin furrows denting his brow. "What's wrong?"

Slowly Colin swiveled toward him. "I just had two very enlightening conversations."

"Wanna tell me about them?" Mac rested a hip on his desk and crossed his arms.

"Yeah. I need your take before I go too far down a very crazy road."

He gave his colleague a fast but thorough briefing, focusing on the key suppositions Zach had shared and the most pertinent facts Cecilia had passed on.

By the time he finished, a gleam of speculation had begun to glimmer in Mac's eyes.

"The twin twist suggests some intriguing possibilities."

Colin scrutinized him. "Are you thinking what I'm thinking?"

"I don't know—but a lot of the pieces are suddenly falling into place if what I'm thinking has any basis in reality."

"I have a feeling we're on the same page."

"Lay your theory on me."

"It sounds nuts."

"So does mine."

"Okay . . . but bear with me while I try to put this together. I'm still working through all the moving parts." He rested his elbows on the arms of his chair and pressed his fingertips together, assembling the pieces as he went. "After Michael disappeared from Boston, he relocated to Miami and took a new identity."

"Craig Elliott."

"That's my guess. I'm thinking he crossed paths with the Russian Mafia, and they recruited him after someone in the hierarchy recognized his genius with finance."

"So far, we're tracking down the same path. Keep going."

"At some point, he decided he could use his genius to skim off funds. They eventually caught on to him. He managed to get out . . . but he knew they had a long arm and excellent contacts everywhere. Where could he hide?"

"Inside his brother's skin."

"Bingo. Even if the Mafia knew his real name—and it's possible they didn't, if his Craig Elliott cover was solid—they may not have realized he had a brother, let alone an identical twin. Let's suppose they did, though. Do you think they'd expect him to pull such an audacious stunt?"

"*We're* considering it." The creases reappeared on Mac's brow. "But if he did change places with his brother, it could be very hard to prove. Identical twins have virtually the same DNA. It takes some very sophisticated—and expensive—testing to distinguish between them. That's only been done in a handful of cases."

"DNA may not work, but identical twins don't have the same fingerprints."

"Are Matt Parker's on file anywhere?"

Good question.

"Not that I know of." Colin rose and began to prowl around the small office. He needed some outlet for the restless energy that had kicked in without a trace of caffeine to jump-start it. "Man. What a brilliant—if evil—plan."

"Given that Eileen Coulter is dead, Natalie James is missing, and Matt Parker may also be AWOL, I'd say that's an apt word."

"Don't forget about Trish's mugging. I'm convinced they're all related." Colin shared the suspicions Trish had voiced on Saturday about her mother and the foundation. "Her concerns are getting more credible by the minute."

"You think the idea of embezzling foundation money was part of the initial plan . . . or a lucky bonus?"

"I'm betting it's the latter. He probably found out about the existence of the foundation while he was scoping out Matt's life, and the opportunity was too enticing to pass up."

"He must have been watching his brother for weeks to be able to step into his shoes so seamlessly." Mac folded his arms.

"Yeah. I bet he hacked into his computer too. Maybe even planted some bugs in the house, or put a GPS device on his car to track his movements."

"And he had the concussion to hide behind if he had any lapses. The man didn't miss a detail."

"Wait a minute." Colin frowned. "The concussion was legit. There's a police report on the accident, a record of the call in the paramedic log, and the hospital verified he'd been treated."

"It's not that hard to fake a concussion. A mild head injury doesn't always show up on an MRI or CT scan. If you can spew out the symptoms, you can get the diagnosis."

"What about the cut on his forehead? You think he did that to himself?"

"If it's a matter of slicing open your forehead or being killed by the Russian Mafia, which would you pick?"

As usual, his colleague had cut straight to the heart of the matter.

"When you put it that way . . ." Colin stopped pacing. "You know . . . if our hypothesis is accurate, this has almost diabolical vibes."

"Agreed—minus the almost. Unfortunately, it's not going to be easy to prove our theory. But as long as we're wandering down this shadowy road, let's speculate a little more. Assuming Michael eliminated Matt Parker and Natalie James, where do you suppose the remains might be?"

"I haven't gotten that far yet . . . but now that you mention it, those twenty or thirty secluded, wooded acres he lives on would be an excellent place to dispose of a body or two."

Mac nodded. "That's what I'm thinking."

"I'd love to get a search warrant for the place, take in a cadaver dog or two."

"Since most of what we're dealing with is coincidence and conjecture rather than facts and evidence—and the man in question is unlikely to admit he's not Matt Parker—I'd say the odds of getting one are zero to none."

"Then we'll have to round up some evidence."

"How do you propose we do that?"

"I have a few ideas. But first, I think we should talk to Sarge and get him on board. Assuming Craig Elliott and Michael Parker are one and the same, our two cases have merged."

Mac stood. "Let's do it. Sarge has been around a lot longer than either of us. He might have some creative ideas."

"That's what I'm hoping."

He strode toward the door, Mac on his heels. At the very least, once they were finished briefing Sarge, he intended to pay Parker another visit. Keeping the man off balance, reminding him he was on their radar, could only work to their advantage.

Lighting a fire under the white-collar crime investigator he'd touched base with this weekend was also high on his agenda. If the information Parker had provided to Trish on Providence House Ministries turned out to be bogus, that might give them the ammunition they needed to get a search warrant for the house and grounds.

If it didn't . . . he'd find another way to put pressure on the suspicious accountant. Make him sweat. Rattle him enough that he started making mistakes.

And he needed to do it fast.

Before the Russian Mafia figured out where he was and dispensed their own brand of justice to his prime suspect.

And before the woman who was fast laying claim to his heart was exposed to any more danger.

20

Was that the doorbell?

Trish leaned her ear toward the French doors that led from the screened porch to the house.

Yes. The chime was faint, but someone had definitely come calling.

She wiped her hands on a rag and stood. It must be Stan, with the homemade ice cream he'd promised after hailing her while she collected her mail from the box on the street earlier.

Nice man.

Smiling, she hurried toward the door and pulled it open—only to find another nice man standing on her threshold in the early afternoon sun.

Better than nice, actually.

Colin gave her snug shorts, cropped T-shirt, and bare toes an appreciative sweep. "I like the outfit."

She tugged at the hem of the worn shirt. "I'm not dressed for company."

"You look fine to me. In fact, you're sparkling. Here." He grinned and touched her cheek, then her nose. "And here."

"Oh." She lifted a hand to her face, where the warmth from

his finger lingered. "I've been in the screen porch prepping for my summer art class. I was dividing glitter into containers for each work table."

"Sparkle suits you." Amusement tickled his voice.

"Ha-ha." Who cared if she was wearing her supplies? Colin was here . . . and after three days of no communication other than a cryptic text yesterday about Matt, this was a treat. "Would you like to come in?"

"Yes. I have some news I want to—"

"Afternoon, folks." Stan huffed up the walk carrying a plastic container. "Welcome back, young man." He beamed at Colin.

"Thanks."

"As for you, young woman . . . you're sparkling."

Trish rubbed her nose again. "I was working with some glitter for my summer art program."

"That wasn't what I meant." He winked and passed her the container. "Here's your ice cream, as promised. I made strawberry today, with berries from my garden. You can't get a fresher—or more natural—product than that. And it's a lot cheaper than that froufrou organic stuff they sell in the grocery stores nowadays."

"Thank you. I've been looking forward to this for the past two hours. Your ice cream is the best."

"It *is* tasty." After patting her arm, he directed his attention to Colin. "You'll have to let me know if you agree, young man. I saw you through the kitchen window while I was dishing this up, so I added some for you too."

"I appreciate that. Ice cream has always been my favorite dessert."

"I knew it. I sized you up as an ice cream man the first time I saw you." He slapped the tall detective on the back. "I won't keep the two of you standing out here jabbering or you'll be drinking your treat. Enjoy." He lifted his hand and ambled back down the walk.

"Homemade ice cream. That's an unexpected bonus." Colin eyed the container. "And it will be a sweet way to wrap up our visit after you hear my less-than-sweet news."

Her heart skipped a beat. "Is your news related to the text you sent yesterday, about calling you if Matt contacted me?"

"Yes."

She ushered him into the foyer. "Let me put this in the freezer while we talk."

She led him to the kitchen, stowed the ice cream, and motioned toward the screen porch. "If you ditch the jacket and tie, it's not too hot to sit outside. The porch is a comforting spot, with the flowers and birds and fountain. I've been spending most of my days out there since the incident in the parking lot."

"Comforting sounds perfect." Even as he spoke, he was shrugging out of his jacket and loosening his tie.

"Would you like a cold drink? Or if you haven't eaten lunch yet, I have some chicken salad in the fridge."

"Thanks. I hit a drive-through on the way over." He tugged his tie free and hung it over the jacket he'd draped on the back of one of her dinette chairs. "Ready whenever you are."

She crossed to the adjacent family room and opened one of the French doors. From here, the terrace off the living room was out of sight, and there was only a limited view of the rose garden, with its melancholy memories. The faint splash of water from the small fountain in the shade garden was soothing, and wind chimes were a gentle accompaniment to the song of the birds.

Colin gave an approving nod. "I see why you like this spot. It's peaceful."

"Very. Let me move some of this stuff out of the way." She started to clear the table.

"Not necessary." He stopped her with a touch on her arm. "I don't need table space, and you've got everything organized for sorting." He surveyed the containers of glitter, tiny shells, buttons, feathers, beads, yarn, small pieces of ribbon, colored paper, twigs, and sundry other items. He picked up a nail from a pile of assorted bolts, screws, and washers and hiked up an eyebrow.

She smiled. "It's a mixed media class for fourth and fifth graders. We'll be creating collages, greeting cards, sculptures—among other things—based on different themes."

"I can't say I've ever thought of a nail as art."

"Most people don't—but you can make amazing pieces with everyday items. Have you ever heard of Brother Mel Meyer?"

"No."

"He had a gallery here in St. Louis and sold his work all over the world. I have a bowl he made out of stainless steel cutlery. It's beautiful."

"If you say so." He set the nail down and took a seat across the table from her. "I do know this. If I'd had a teacher who let me work with this kind of stuff as a kid, I might have tried a little harder to develop whatever limited artistic talent I have."

She sat too. "It's not just about becoming an artist. Few people are born with that gift—but everyone can learn to appreciate art. That's my goal with the students I teach."

"Like I said . . . I wish I'd had a teacher like you."

"It's never too late to learn."

"I'll keep that in mind once we get past the present issues. Maybe we could arrange some private tutoring."

"I'll pencil you in."

"Write it in ink." After flashing her a smile, he grew more serious. "In the meantime . . . there have been some surprising new developments."

"I think I'm past being surprised."

"You may change your mind after you hear what we've discovered."

Colin gave her a topline in the concise, thorough-but-no-frills style she'd come to associate with his on-duty persona.

Normally, she appreciated his cut-to-the-chase manner. But her brain was struggling to keep up with the startling developments he was lobbing at her.

When he paused at last, she rubbed her temple. "Wow."

"That was our reaction. And there's more."

"I'm still grappling with the fact that Matt has an identical twin who you suspect is also Elliott—and who could be impersonating Matt."

"It makes sense though, if he's trying to hide from the Mafia. Ready for the next piece of news?"

She gripped the arms of her chair. "No . . . but tell me anyway."

"Our white-collar fraud group has done some research on Providence House Ministries. It appears to be bogus."

Her stomach flipped. "You mean . . . it doesn't exist?"

"It exists. On paper. It files all the appropriate government forms—and has for the past seven years."

"Two years before the Boston situation came to light. Interesting timing."

"And more than coincidence, I'm guessing."

"But if the paperwork is in order, why do they think it's bogus?"

"They haven't gotten in too deep yet, but they did give a couple of the charities Providence House supports a quick review. Again, they appear legit on the surface—but my white-collar guy thinks the groups may be shell organizations. He suspects money is being transferred from them to an offshore account."

"Wow again."

"They're continuing to dig, but it may take time to sort this out."

"In light of the twins' background, isn't it ironic that Providence

House was supposed to be funding organizations that benefit foster children?"

"Ironic . . . or sweet revenge, given Michael's shuffle through the system. Maybe he figures if no one helped him as a kid, he'll help himself as an adult."

"Only a sick mind would think like that."

"I'm not going to dispute that."

She picked up a button and squeezed it between her fingers as she asked the obvious . . . and scary . . . question. "So if this is all some sort of elaborate setup to provide Michael with a safe refuge from the Mafia and to steal from the foundation, where is Matt?"

Even before he responded, his grim expression confirmed he shared her suspicions.

"We think he may have met the same fate as the missing woman, Natalie James."

Meaning he thought they were both dead.

Murdered.

Like Mom?

She set the button down and fought back a swell of nausea. "You don't think my mother's death was an accident, do you?"

The quiet question hung between them for a few moments.

When Colin finally answered, his voice was gentle. "In view of what we've discovered about Michael Parker and the foundation, as well as what's been happening with you the past few weeks . . . no. The only consolation, if there is any, is that it wasn't your fault."

"I wish that made me feel better." The last word scratched past her tight throat.

He covered her hand with his. "We'll get him, Trish. Whatever it takes."

"How? From what you've said, none of your suspicions will be easy to prove."

His forehead puckered. "Some documentable fingerprints for Matt would do the trick."

"They could be tough to find. I think he preferred to work paperless. Everything he sent Mom was electronic, and I assume he followed the same procedure with other clients."

"Too bad. But we'll find a way to nail Parker. I'm not letting him win."

"I appreciate your tenacity."

"That's how I'm wired." He removed his hand and twisted his wrist to see his watch. "I need to get going."

"Can you spare five more minutes for the ice cream?"

"I never pass up ice cream."

"Good. I could use a taste of sweetness about now." And since his lips weren't available, Stan's offering would have to suffice. "Give me three minutes."

Colin stood when she reappeared at the French doors faster than she'd promised, pulled one open, and took the dish she held out.

"Let's sit over there." He motioned toward two wicker chairs away from her work area.

"So what happens next?" She dipped her spoon into the creamy confection and sank onto the cushioned seat.

"Since Parker is sticking to his story, we'll continue to shake the bushes for leads—and hope we get answers before the Russian Mafia does."

"Will you put him under surveillance?"

"That would be ideal." Colin jabbed at a strawberry, frustration etched on his features. "Unfortunately, we don't have the resources for that. The department's stretched too thin dealing with breaking cases and following hot leads to be able to spare personnel for the kind of round-the-clock surveillance this sort of situation needs. I know that's not what TV cop shows suggest, but it's the reality."

She drew swirls in her ice cream with the tip of her spoon, toying with an idea. "What do you think about private investigators?"

"We don't use them."

"I assumed you didn't. What I meant was, what do you think about them in general? Are there any competent ones out there, and would they be helpful in a case like this?"

"Why?"

"I want this wrapped up as much as you do. Maybe more. Mom and Dad left me a generous inheritance. I can't think of a better use for some of that money than putting the man likely responsible for multiple deaths—perhaps even my mugging—behind bars."

He finished off his ice cream and set his bowl on the side table. "I can't make an official recommendation. We've had our share of run-ins with less-than-professional PIs. In general we steer clear of them and approach with caution if they do happen to cross our path."

"I understand. But there *is* someone you feel comfortable with, isn't there?" She could see it in his speculative gaze.

"Off the record . . . yes. There's a group called Phoenix Inc. that does excellent work. The PIs are all former law-enforcement operatives—County homicide detective, undercover ATF agent, and Secret Service agent."

"A distinguished group."

"Yeah. They've tackled—and solved—some tough cases. I'd feel comfortable with them doing the surveillance piece of this. However, they don't come cheap."

"A conversation to put out some feelers and get an estimate won't cost much. Who should I contact?"

"Cal Burke. They're all equal partners, but the company was his brainchild and he's the unofficial leader. I know him from his years in the department, and he's a sharp, meticulous guy."

"I'll give him a call this afternoon. Can I tell him you referred me?"

"Sure. He'll handle that information discreetly."

"Is there anything he should know that you haven't told me?"

"No. All we need them to do is tail our subject and watch his place. We'll want a log of Parker's movements and a report of any activity at the house. But get a bid first. You may be shocked at the cost."

"Like I said, it's money well spent if it gets us the answers we need. How long do you think we might have to watch Parker?"

"Let's not commit to more than a week. At that point, if there's been no suspicious activity, we may have to regroup."

"Do you think the Mafia's going to show up?"

"Sooner or later. If we found out Elliott's here—aka Michael Parker—they will too."

"Unless they've stopped searching for him."

"That's not their typical modus operandi. Betrayal in an organization like that isn't taken lightly." He tapped the edge of her dish. "Better finish that. It's too good to waste."

"You need to go, don't you?" She scooped up what was left of her melting ice cream.

"Yes."

"I appreciate you stopping by with the latest update."

"I thought the new information was better passed on in person than over the phone." He stood.

"Shall I give you an update after I talk with Cal Burke?"

"I'd appreciate that. And assuming you proceed, if they alert you to anything unusual they've seen or heard, call me night or day." He took her bowl. "Walk me out?"

"Of course." She rose and followed him to the kitchen. "By the way, Kristin called. I'm meeting her after my art class on Monday for dinner."

One corner of his mouth hitched up. "Strategic timing."

"How so?"

He deposited the empty bowls in the sink, slid his arms back into his jacket, and knotted his tie. "The gang's every-other-Saturday breakfast is this week. If she met you before that, she knows I'd grill her over her eggs. This way, she can dodge my calls." He continued to the foyer.

"Smart woman. I think I'm going to like her."

"I do too." He stopped by the door and grew more serious. "Until this is over, I'd like you to take extra precautions. Keep the doors locked while you're here, arm the security system at night, try to avoid going out in the dark, and watch your back even in daylight. Also—I meant what I said in my text about Matt. Let me know if he tries to contact you . . . and don't answer the door if he shows up here."

"Are you trying to scare me?" Her attempt at a teasing tone fell flat. A guy like Colin didn't give idle warnings. If he was concerned about her, there was reason to be.

"No. But I want you to be cautious. We're way past a few setups to suggest you're incompetent. If Parker's done what we suspect, he won't hesitate to get rid of anything—or anyone—who stands between him and the money he's after. And if the Russian Mafia enters the picture, the situation could get dangerous fast. I don't want you caught in the crossfire."

Not the most comforting thought.

"You don't really think there's much chance of that happening, do you?"

"No—but it's within the realm of remote possibilities. Parker's plans have to be in disarray now that his liaison with Natalie James has come back to haunt him. If he panics, who knows what he might do? He wants the money in the foundation's account, but until the past week there was no hurry to get it. If the Mafia appears, that could accelerate his plans—and force him to take some desperate actions."

"Like what?" She shoved her hands into the pockets of her shorts and curled her fingers until her nails dug into her palms. "The bank will only accept paper checks, and I have the checkbook. He can't force me to sign a check."

"Could he go around you and authorize electronic transfer of funds? Fill out the paperwork in your name?"

"Not without triggering a phone call to me. My parents were paranoid about that kind of stuff after someone stole Dad's identity a few years ago. They spent months unraveling the mess. After that, they put all kinds of security measures in place on every account they had, including the foundation. On top of that, donations over a certain dollar amount will prompt a phone call."

"Did Matt know about that?"

"Yes. In fact, it was his suggestion. But I doubt he'd share that kind of information with his brother."

"All of that will work to our advantage." Colin dug out his keys. "I almost hope he tries to tap into the money. That would give us grounds for a search warrant . . . which could lead to the discovery of a lot of other incriminating evidence."

"Don't you think he's being extra careful now that he knows he's on your radar?"

"Yes. But there could be evidence lying around—or buried— at his place that he doesn't want found and may try to dispose of elsewhere. Once the Phoenix team is in place, though, they'll spot that kind of activity."

"Then the faster I get them there, the better. I'll call as soon as you leave."

"My cue to exit."

He stepped outside, and she followed him to the edge of the porch. "I'll give you a ring after I talk with Cal Burke."

"Thanks." He took her hand and gripped her fingers. "Be careful."

"I will." She squeezed back and inclined her head slightly toward Stan, who was weeding the flower bed that rimmed his front walk and watching the proceedings across the street. "We have an audience—and I think he was hoping for more than a handshake. In case you haven't picked it up, he's a closet matchmaker."

"I'd love to oblige him." He moved in close, blocking the older man's view of Trish, and dipped his head until his lips were inches from hers. "But up close and personal will have to suffice for today."

She got lost for a moment in the warmth of brown irises flecked with gold. "Okay." The word came out in an adolescent squeak.

For one tiny, hopeful second, she thought he was going to forget about the parameters he'd set and make the illusion he'd created for Stan a reality.

But then he backed up . . . released her hand . . . and walked away.

She grabbed the porch rail to steady herself. Hard to imagine what a real kiss would be like if just being that close to the man turned her knees to putty.

As he approached his car, Colin gave the older man a thumbs-up and called out to him. "The ice cream was great."

Stan acknowledged his comment with a jaunty salute.

And once Colin backed out and drove away, Stan smiled and gave *her* a thumbs-up.

She responded with a flutter of fingers and escaped into the house.

Locking the door behind her, she gave her lungs a few seconds to regain their rhythm, then returned to the screened porch. She had a class to prepare for—and a phone call to place to Cal Burke at Phoenix Inc.

Her breath hitched again . . . for a far less pleasant reason.

This wasn't the time to indulge in romantic fancies about Colin Flynn. Not with all the unanswered questions lurking in the shadows and the situation coming to a head. Her top priority had to be helping the police get the evidence they needed to nail the perpetrator.

Because as long as this was unresolved . . . as long as there was a probable murderer on the loose . . . she could be in danger. That risk might be remote, as Colin had suggested, but it was real.

And until the guilty party or parties were out of circulation, she'd do exactly what he'd suggested.

Take every precaution she could and watch her back.

21

He was going stir crazy.

Craig aimed the remote at the TV and surfed through the channels, watching the images parade across the screen in Matt's living room. Man, afternoon programming sucked.

Mashing the off button, he checked his watch. Four ten—and the long, endless evening stretched ahead.

Now what?

Barhopping was out—for a while, anyway. The cops might be watching him . . . and he wasn't about to risk getting burned by another predatory woman.

He could work on books and payroll for Matt's clients—except there was nothing more to do. He'd whizzed through all the pending tasks for this week hours ago . . . and it was only Wednesday. If he had to do this mindless work much longer, his brain would turn to mush. Why Matt hadn't died of boredom was beyond him.

The grass needed attention—but manual labor? Not happening. One of these days he'd have to hire somebody to cut the front lawn before it became a full-fledged hayfield.

Yawning, he rose and wandered to the kitchen for a beer.

Maybe Matt ought to give Trish a call. She might have claimed she wasn't interested in romance, but that could have been grief speaking. After all, the two of them had seemed cozy at that lunch they'd shared a couple of months ago. Her every smile and gesture had suggested she was receptive to further overtures. Perhaps Matt would have better results if he cranked up the charm.

Beer in hand, he pulled the tab as he mulled over that idea. A solicitous phone call today. Another one later in the week that included a suggestion for coffee. Nothing too aggressive or threatening. Just one concerned friend touching base with another.

Even if she dug in her heels and refused to consider romance, it wouldn't hurt to build some rapport. A closer relationship might make the notion of appointing Matt a trustee—and giving him more power over foundation funds—more palatable.

Armed with that plan, he helped himself to a few pretzels from the bag on the counter and strolled back to the recliner in the living room as he chomped. There was no need to mention business during the chat. It would be best to confine the conversation to questions about her summer class, an inquiry about her arm, a funny story that would make her laugh. In other words, lay the groundwork for . . .

He froze as a flash of light bounced off the wall in the hall—like a reflection off a shiny object.

A car, perhaps?

The last pretzel crumbled in his fingers.

It had to be those detectives again. No one else came to Matt's house other than kids from the pizza place and an occasional courier dropping off client paperwork. During all his weeks of surveillance, those were the only vehicles that had ventured through the woods to the house.

And no one had ordered a pizza or called about a delivery today.

He brushed off his fingers and took another swig of beer to wash down the pretzels. What new questions could the cops have? They'd tossed plenty at him when they'd shown up unannounced again on Monday afternoon. All related to ancient history, running the gamut from foster care to Larry's business.

But they'd left unsatisfied. He'd seen the frustration in Flynn's face as the man had slapped his notebook shut, in the glance he'd exchanged with the McGregor guy. Although the two of them had tag-teamed their interrogation, he'd sidestepped every hardball they'd thrown.

He snorted and took a pull from the beer. They weren't dealing with an amateur here. No way was he giving them one speck of new information. They were on their own if they wanted to keep digging.

As well they might.

It was possible they'd even find out about the identical twin situation—or already had and were keeping that close to the vest for now.

No matter. Whatever suspicions that fact might generate, they wouldn't be able to prove anything.

He remained where he was as a faint crunch of gravel overlaid the hum of the air conditioner. He could ignore them today if he chose. The car was tucked away in the closed garage, there was nothing else to indicate anyone was home—and another round of bob and weave was *not* on this afternoon's agenda.

However . . . if the door went unanswered, he wouldn't know why they were continuing to snoop around. Sticking your head in the sand was an avoidance tactic, not a strategy. Better to know the reason for their visit—and use that information to plan next steps.

Besides, Craig Elliott was their man . . . and there was no

trace of him to be found. If Matt continued to cooperate with them, they'd eventually leave him alone.

He rose and crossed to the door, tucking himself into the shadows as he peeked out the sidelight.

Huh.

Instead of Colin Flynn's black Taurus, a silver Cadillac was sitting in the driveway.

Definitely not a law-enforcement-issue car.

Who could it be? In all his weeks of surveillance and hacking, no luxury-car driver had surfaced.

Staying out of sight, he wedged himself against the wall and watched the vehicle.

Sixty seconds ticked by.

He frowned. Why wasn't anyone emerging from behind the tinted windows? Had the driver taken a wrong turn and realized his or her mistake? Perhaps the car would back up, reverse direction, and . . .

The driver's door opened.

A large, muscular stranger unfolded his tall frame from behind the wheel and gave the area a thorough, practiced sweep . . . much like the detective had done.

A niggle of unease slithered along Craig's spine.

This was not a casual visit—and the furtive quality in the man's actions didn't bode well.

Decision made.

He was *not* answering the door.

In fact, he was going to retrieve his Beretta and keep it close at hand until his uninvited visitor left.

As he started to turn away from the window, muscleman moved to the back door and pulled it open.

After a brief pause, the passenger emerged. A man in his fifties, with wings of silver in his light brown hair and an all-too-familiar face.

The air whooshed out of his lungs.

Oleg Petrov was here?!

The floor tilted, and Craig splayed the fingers of one hand against the wall to steady himself as a riptide of panic swept over him.

No!

This was impossible!

Dmitri couldn't have found him!

Yet his eyes weren't lying.

But . . . but how could this be? He'd been careful. Months had passed since his escape from Miami. The break had been swift, clean, and successful. He'd left no clues for them to follow.

Unfortunately, the reality unfolding dozens of yards away said otherwise.

Sucking air into his stalled lungs, he recalibrated his strategy.

He couldn't ignore the bell. If Oleg had come all the way from Miami at Dmitri's direction, he wasn't going to leave without nosing around. The locks wouldn't stop him. He and his goon would get in.

So he had to *let* them in.

And maybe . . . just maybe . . . this wasn't the end of the world.

His brain began clicking again.

If someone in Dmitri's organization had discovered Craig Elliott's real identity, it wouldn't have been difficult to discover he had an identical twin—one who was easy to track down. He'd found Matt himself in less than five minutes on the net.

Oleg might be here to see if Matt knew anything about his brother's whereabouts.

Or he might harbor darker suspicions.

But so what?

Only one brother remained, and as far as the world was

concerned, that brother was Matt. There was nothing to prove otherwise.

Unless . . .

His heart stumbled.

Did Dmitri's people have his fingerprints, by chance? He'd never been asked to provide them, and it wasn't standard practice in the organization to collect prints—but he was an outsider. Might they have obtained his without his knowledge?

If so, he was in deep trouble.

Because if they got his prints now, his cover would be blown.

They'd know he wasn't Matt, but Michael.

Oleg started toward the front door, the bruiser falling in behind.

Sweat broke out on Michael's upper lip, and he dashed it away with the back of his hand.

Chill, Parker. You cannot *show any outward sign of fear. If they had your prints on file, they'd have dusted this house when you weren't here to verify your identity and taken you out already. They wouldn't be coming up your front walk like normal visitors. Oleg is here to fish. So play dumb, tell him a slightly amended version of the story you gave the cops—and hope he buys it.*

The two men stepped onto the porch, and Michael eased back into the shadows, forcing himself to take long, slow breaths.

He could pull this off. He'd been impersonating Matt for weeks, fooling everyone—including people who knew the man. He could surely dupe Oleg, who'd never met his brother.

The doorbell rang.

Hands clenched, legs stiff, he jerked forward and twisted the knob.

"Good afternoon." Oleg gave him a smooth smile that held

no warmth, his eyes sharp and probing. "Mr. Parker, I am Oleg Petrov. There is some business I would like to discuss. May I have a few words with you?"

He didn't bother to introduce the man hovering at his shoulder. Typical.

Bodyguards were invisible to the likes of Oleg and Dmitri. No more than soulless robots valued only for the service they performed.

"I have a full roster of accounting clients already, Mr. Petrov. And most prospective customers make initial contact by email or phone." His tone was perfect. Cordial, but curious.

"I do not have that kind of business to discuss. I am here to talk about Craig Elliott."

So they knew Elliott had been here. There was more to this visit than picking Matt's brain about his twin brother.

That meant Dmitri had called in favors from the organization's contacts in law enforcement.

He needed to play this just right.

Gripping the knob tighter, he pulled the door wide and backed up. "Come in."

Oleg entered, followed by his shadow, who remained in the doorway between the foyer and the living room. The Russian claimed the same chair Flynn had occupied.

Michael moved to the sofa, angled toward the man so he could keep both visitors in view . . . and waited. He'd let Oleg take the lead. Offering more than was asked for—or necessary—would be a tactical error.

The older man crossed his legs and adjusted the crease in his pinstripe suit. "Let us be honest, yes? You and I both know your brother and Elliott are the same man."

At least they still believed—or were pretending to believe—he was Matt.

Since it was unlikely this conversation would get back to the police, he could modify the story he'd told to law enforcement.

Letting out an exaggerated sigh, he raked his fingers through his hair and gave Oleg a look he hoped came across as pained and conflicted. "Yes."

"You have kept in touch—despite what happened in Boston?"

They'd done their homework. Dmitri knew . . . or had surmised . . . what had taken place five years ago.

He leaned back in his chair, buying himself a few seconds to think.

Remember, you're Matt. The police haven't mentioned the Mafia connection, and Matt would have no clue about it. He'd be surprised by this man's knowledge—and wary.

"You know about that?" He injected a healthy note of caution into his voice.

"We know many things. You have kept in touch all these years?"

"No. After the fiasco in Boston, I told Michael I never wanted to see him again."

"Embezzlement in a family business is never pretty."

"No."

"Stealing money from a person who trusted you should, of course, be punished."

At the man's less-than-subtle implication, fear coiled in his stomach.

"I couldn't turn him in. He's my brother."

"Ah yes. Loyalty. An admirable trait. And blood ties are strong. Is he here?"

"No. He stayed only a few nights."

"Why did you take him in?"

"He said he wanted to make amends for Boston." Michael shrugged. "I've become active in my church, and over the past three years I've heard a number of sermons on forgiveness. When he called, it seemed as if God was giving me an opportunity to turn the other cheek." The glib words sounded smooth and sincere even to *his* ears.

Amazing.

"A most virtuous sentiment." A speculative gleam flickered in Oleg's ice blue irises. "You have told this story to the police?"

"They know Elliott was here. They don't know he's my brother."

"And if they find out?"

"I'm hoping they don't. But if they do, I'll have to backtrack."

"You would put yourself at risk for a man who caused you such trouble?"

"He *is* my brother—and I'm trying to let go of the past."

Oleg linked his fingers. "You know he is a person of interest, as they call it, in connection with a missing woman?"

"Yes."

"That is a serious charge."

"I realize that—but they've got the wrong man. He might have made some mistakes, but he's never physically hurt anyone."

"Perhaps he has changed."

"I don't think so." Michael stole a look at the muscled statue keeping silent vigil. The man's expression was impassive, but he was no doubt listening to every word. "You mentioned you had unfinished business with him?"

"Yes. Do you know where he is or how to reach him?"

"No. He didn't offer contact information, and I didn't ask for any. Forgiveness is one thing—but we're never going to be friends."

"Too bad. We will have to continue our search. But we *will* find him." Oleg's steely gaze bored into his.

Michael met it, trying not to flinch.

This was not a man who tossed out idle threats.

While he'd had no personal dealings with Dmitri's minion, he'd heard the stories. How, in his younger days, Oleg had been adept at killing with his bare hands . . . and had done so on several occasions.

He was older now, and perhaps no longer capable of such legendary feats—but the intimidating bodyguard he'd brought along could do his bidding if necessary.

Would do it if Oleg gave the word.

Michael suppressed a shudder.

When the silence lengthened, Oleg rose. "I've intruded enough for one day."

The caveat wasn't lost on Michael.

Their meeting might be over . . . but their business wasn't.

Either he hadn't been 100 percent convincing, or Oleg was under strict instructions not to return to Miami until he got what Dmitri wanted.

Namely, Russian Mafia justice.

The man walked toward the door, his bodyguard a few paces behind.

Michael followed, tamping down his panic. "It's been five years since my last contact with Michael—and when he left, I didn't get the impression I'd hear from him again anytime soon."

"That may be true." Oleg stopped at the door while the other man went outside and did another scan of the area. "But one can hope. As a matter of fact, I have a feeling he is nearby . . . and my instincts do not often fail me." He glanced at the guard, who gave a slight nod. "Have a nice day, Mr. Parker."

With that, he strolled down the walk to the Cadillac, his shadow close behind, and disappeared behind the tinted windows.

Michael closed the door, watching through the sidelight as the car executed a wide turn and rolled down the drive, followed by a cloud of dust.

Only after the luxury vehicle disappeared around a bend in the woods-rimmed lane and the air cleared did Michael twist the lock on the door and back away from the window.

This was a disaster.

And hard as the truth was to swallow, it was of his own making.

Messing with organized crime had been stupid.

He lurched toward the recliner and sank down. Stealing from Larry, siphoning funds from Trish's trust . . . those were low-risk operations compared to pilfering Mafia money. Smart as he'd been, carefully as he'd hidden his theft, he'd gotten caught—and Dmitri wasn't going to let him walk away, as Larry had, if he figured out his real identity.

But how could he?

How could anyone?

He'd covered his tracks. His fingerprints weren't on file anywhere. Neither were Matt's. His Boy Scout brother had probably never even gotten a parking ticket. And there weren't any of his prints here. Not after the thorough scouring he'd given this place—and the car—once he'd moved in. Nor would his clients have any, in light of his brother's penchant for paperless communication. Without comparison prints, no one could dispute his story that he was Matt.

Still . . . there could be issues if anyone started poking around on his land.

Fingers trembling, he brushed some stray pretzel salt off the arm of the chair. The graves were deep in the woods and well disguised, but if anyone did stumble across them, the situation could get messy.

Hopefully, it wouldn't come to that.

But if it did, he'd better be prepared with a credible explanation for the two dead bodies on his property.

He also needed to accelerate work on the escape plan he

hadn't expected to need for months—or even a year or two, if he drained the foundation funds more slowly while he hid out. Now he needed to be able to slip away fast . . . and undetected . . . if things got too hot.

On the plus side, his new ID was ready and waiting, far better than the crude one he'd cobbled together after he fled Florida. What else had he had to work on in his abundant free time over the past few weeks?

But he didn't yet have the funds to pay for the lifestyle he'd set his sights on. Thanks to his upscale preferences in Boston and Miami, less than a hundred grand remained in his offshore account.

Trish's foundation, however, had plenty of money to boost that balance.

He rose and began to pace, scrubbing at the few stray grains of salt that refused to relinquish their grip on his fingers.

Maybe he ought to accelerate the timetable on the funds transfer. Do it all at once. The system he'd set up while in Boston continued to work flawlessly. Trish's "donation" check to Providence House Ministries had gone through without a hitch, traveling first to Providence, which had parsed it out in smaller amounts to his shell-company charities. From there he'd channeled the funds to his offshore bank account in the Cayman Islands.

It was a brilliant scheme, easy to manage online . . . and almost untraceable if you were savvy with VPNs and remailers. Sure, if law enforcement dug deep enough, they might be able to link the transactions back to him—but in the past they'd never had a reason to do that. Larry hadn't pressed charges . . . and neither would Dmitri.

The local detectives, on the other hand, were a wild card. That Flynn guy and his colleague came across as the determined type.

But it took time to come up with the grounds necessary to get search warrants if they wanted to nose around his property. Longer than it would take for him to transfer the money and disappear.

The last grains of salt finally released their hold on his fingers . . . but they left a sticky residue behind.

Huffing out an annoyed breath, Michael headed toward the kitchen to rinse his hands, weighing his options.

It had seemed safer in the beginning to hide under cover of Matt's identity until the Miami situation cooled. Dmitri wouldn't have tracked him forever.

Now that they'd traced Craig here, however . . . and now that he was on the cops' radar too . . . it might be smart to alter his plans.

He twisted on the tap and let the cool water wash away the dregs of the salt as that notion took root.

Accelerating his plans was sounding more and more appealing. It wasn't as if he was loving the country life Matt had chosen. Having an excuse to ditch this low-key accountant gig sooner than planned wasn't such a bad thing.

The challenge was getting the money faster than anticipated.

He dried his hands and slapped the towel onto the counter. This would be so much simpler if Trish's parents hadn't specified only check donations in the foundation's bylaws. As it stood, the financial institution holding the funds wouldn't release money without that signed piece of paper.

Forging Trish's signature would be simple—but she kept the checkbook. You couldn't forge—or wash—checks you didn't have.

Unfortunately, even if he convinced her to amend the bylaws, the paperwork and implementation took time he might not have.

He needed to pay her another visit—and go prepared to suggest several donations that would appeal to her. Once he had a few signed checks in hand to wash, a well-funded escape would be a piece of cake.

If she didn't cooperate . . . well, there were other, more risky ways to get to those checks.

But for both their sakes, he hoped she gave him what he needed without any resistance.

22

"Quit hovering. I'll let you know when I'm finished." Hank shot a don't-mess-with-me glare over his shoulder.

Colin withdrew his head from the ransacked bedroom, where the cranky CSU tech was dusting for prints. "I'll be in the kitchen talking to the homeowner."

"A better use of your time."

Sheesh. The man had attitude with a capital A.

But his forensic skills were top-notch.

As Colin retreated down the hall of the high-end home where the owner had walked in on a burglary in progress, his cell began to vibrate.

He pulled it off his belt, scanned the screen . . . and ducked into a nearby bathroom. Trish could leave a message while he dealt with this crime scene—but he'd rather talk to her in person.

A smile tugged at his lips as he put the phone to his ear. Since he'd shared ice cream with her yesterday and talked to her hours later after she'd connected with Phoenix, you'd think the need to hear her voice again wouldn't be all that urgent.

Wrong.

Which was proof he had it bad.

And he didn't mind in the least.

"Hi." Still smiling, he propped a shoulder against the doorframe.

"Hi back. Do you have a minute?"

Not really. But he'd take one . . . or two . . . for her.

"Yes, but not much more. What's up?"

"I had a call from Cal Burke. There's been some activity at Matt's house."

He straightened up. "Tell me about it."

"Cal says he had two visitors about an hour ago." She passed on the details about the duo in the Cadillac.

"Did they get any photos?"

"Yes. Cal made it a point to tell me they weren't trespassing, though. He said one of their guys was watching from adjacent public land."

"That doesn't surprise me. They run a by-the-book kind of operation—for the most part." He knew of only a single instance when Phoenix had deviated from that rule, and if they hadn't, the woman one of Cal's partners later married would have died.

"He wanted to know whether they should try to identify the two guys or email me the photos to pass on to you. I got the impression they thought the visitors might be affiliated with the Mafia."

Cal and his guys wouldn't have jumped to that conclusion without sound reasons. They must have observed some behavior that had tipped them off.

The Florida mob had moved in faster than he'd expected.

"Go with the email. If these guys *are* Mafia, the contacts I made in Miami may recognize them. We should be able to get an ID through official channels quicker than Phoenix can—and save you a few bucks in the process."

"A resolution is more important to me than the money."

"Let us take a crack at it first. If we don't nail it within a few hours, you can turn it back over to Phoenix."

"Okay. Cal also said the Cadillac is a rental car. Do you want the license?"

"Yeah." He fished out his pen and notebook and jotted down the number. "If this is a Mafia rental, I suspect we'll find a John Smith name on the paperwork. But it's worth checking."

"Cal implied that too. I'll call him back and let him know you're going to handle the ID on the . . ." A beat of silence passed. "Huh."

"What's wrong?"

"I've got a call coming in from Matt's number."

Colin's pulse picked up.

The Mafia visits him, and soon after he calls Trish.

The timing had to be significant.

"Let it roll." He didn't want her anywhere close to whatever was going to go down between Matt and the Mafia and County. "You can play his message after we hang up."

"Do you think this call is related to his visitors?"

"Yeah." Better to be totally aboveboard with his suspicions so she'd remain on high alert. "I'm thinking the guys in the Cadillac spooked him and he's getting ready to make some kind of move."

"Like what?"

He wished he knew.

"His message may give us a clue." The officer who'd responded to the burglary appeared in the hall and beckoned to him. "Look . . . I need to go. Listen to the message and I'll call you back as soon as I can."

"Will do."

The line went dead.

"Sorry to interrupt." The officer rested one hand on his holster. "I think the homeowner is about to have a meltdown."

No surprise there. Having a gun pulled on you and being tied up by two armed robbers could do that to a person.

"Have the paramedics left?"

"On their way out. They didn't find any substantive injuries, and the victim refused to go to the hospital for further evaluation."

"Okay." He slid his phone back on his belt and psyched himself up for what could be a difficult conversation. Too bad her husband was out of town. His presence might help calm her. He'd have to do his best to settle her down on his own and get some answers.

Fifteen tense minutes later, however, he'd accomplished neither. The woman was no less freaked out, and despite careful, specific questions designed to elicit details, the best description she could provide was twentysomething, dark hair, and tall.

Like that would help a lot.

Maybe Hank would have better luck with fingerprints, shoe impressions, or trace evidence that could yield a DNA sample.

After thanking the woman, he retreated down the hall. The CSU tech was still at work, so he stepped out onto the patio to call Trish back.

She answered on the first ring. "You're at a crime scene, aren't you?"

"Yes, but I've got a few minutes. What did Parker want?"

"He invited me out for coffee."

"Social or business?"

"He didn't mention the foundation. I got the feeling it was social."

Not likely, with everything that was going on.

"There's more on his agenda than small talk."

"Such as?"

He paused as a cigarette butt wedged between two bricks caught his eye. Intact, despite last night's rain—meaning it was recent. If the owners didn't smoke, he'd alert Hank to this . . . even though the man would probably get huffy and tell him he would have found it on his own. Which was no doubt true.

"Colin?"

He refocused. "Good question. One we need to answer. Let me discuss approaches with my boss and a colleague. We'll also try to ID the two visitors. Until I get back to you, let your phone roll if he calls again. Do you have any commitments that require you to leave the house over the next couple of days?"

"Other than a grocery run, no."

"Stay put. If you need food, call me and I'll deliver."

"I could lie and say the cupboard is bare to give me an excuse to see you . . . but the truth is the freezer's full."

"Then stay there until we sort this out and come up with a plan. I'll call you later today or early tomorrow. If you hear from the Phoenix guys again, let me know."

"I will. And the photos Cal sent should be in your inbox."

"Thanks. I'll get right on them. Talk to you soon."

The instant the line went dead, he opened his email. The one with the photos was near the top.

Cal and his crew had provided several images of each of the guys—full face, profile, close up, whole body. They were strangers to him—but his contacts at the Miami PD or FBI office might recognize them.

And if they did . . . if the Mafia was on Parker's doorstep . . . they needed to wrap this up fast.

Before anyone else got hurt.

. . . . .

Phone pressed to his ear, Dmitri swirled his daily shot of Stolichnaya Gold in a crystal tumbler, rocked forward on his toes in front of the picture window, and watched a cruise ship glide toward the horizon forty-two floors below as Oleg finished his report.

"Excellent work. Now that you have given me the facts of your visit to St. Louis, tell me your impressions." He sipped the vodka.

"He was nervous—but he did not make any mistakes. All of his responses and reactions would be appropriate for Matthew Parker."

"Acting is a useful skill. Very convincing when well done." He held up the glass of clear liquid to the light. While it wasn't the most expensive vodka on the market, it was the best. Only fools paid disgraceful amounts of money for artsy bottles. What mattered was the contents. "But you have keen insights. That is why I sent you. What is your opinion about his identity?"

"It is difficult to know for certain . . . and much is at stake."

"We will get more proof before we act—but if you think there is little likelihood this man is Michael Parker, we will not waste our time there. Give me your odds."

The man's response was slow and measured. "I believe there is at least an 80 percent chance this is the man we knew as Elliott."

Dmitri tossed back the rest of his vodka, tracking a yacht as its bow cut through the water, churning foam in its wake. If Oleg said 80 percent, that meant the odds were closer to 90 percent. His trusted aid tended to err on the side of caution when offering probabilities.

"Then we will need to concentrate our efforts in this location. Pick those who you think will provide the skills you need and arrange for them to join you by tomorrow." He returned to his desk, sat, and set the empty tumbler aside. "Now let us talk about how we will proceed."

· · · · ·

"Oleg Petrov has quite a résumé." Sarge closed the file Colin had handed him and leaned back in his desk chair. "Who's the other guy?"

"My contact in the Miami PD didn't recognize him. Neither did the special agent I talked with down there from the FBI's Russian squad unit. He said he's probably a lower-level player. The Feds have their hands full watching the big guns."

"I bet they do." Sarge took off his glasses and rubbed his eyes. "Russian Mafia in our backyard. Just what I needed to make my week complete."

"I don't think they're here to stay."

"Let's hope not." He leaned forward again and looked from Colin to Mac. "I'm assuming you gentlemen want to propose a plan of action now that your cases have merged."

Colin exchanged a glance with his colleague. "Yes."

"I'm listening."

"At this point, short of a confession, we can't prove the man presenting himself as Matthew Parker is lying about his identity. The best we might be able to do is pin a murder rap . . . or two . . . on Parker—whichever brother he is."

Sarge arched an eyebrow, and Mac jumped in. "The easiest and least risky way for Parker to get rid of bodies is to bury them on his own property, away from prying eyes. We want to search his house and grounds."

"Do you have grounds for a warrant?"

"Not yet."

"But evidence of embezzlement would give us what we need." Colin jumped to the heart of their proposal, since Sarge was up to speed on their suspicions about the foundation. "Parker called Trish Bailey yesterday and asked her out for coffee. Coming so close on the heels of the Mafia visit, the invitation would suggest he's getting nervous and wants access to the funds in her parents' foundation faster than he'd planned. We think he wants to be ready to run if the situation gets any hotter."

"A reasonable assumption. How does that give you grounds for a warrant?"

"The foundation is set up to trigger an alert if a donation over a certain dollar limit comes through. To the best of our knowledge, Parker isn't aware of that. We think it makes sense for Trish . . . Ms. Bailey . . . to keep the date with Parker. We expect he'll bring up the foundation. But whether or not he does, she'll take a few modest checks for reputable charities to their meeting and ask him to handle the donations for her."

Sarge folded his arms. "You're thinking he might wash the checks, write in sizeable amounts, and send them through the bogus charity he set up."

"Yes—and once those checks arrive at the bank, they'll be flagged. We'll alert bank officers in advance that they could be coming and ask them to give us an immediate heads-up. Once we have that piece of evidence, we shouldn't have any trouble getting a search warrant."

"Is Ms. Bailey agreeable to your plan?"

"I haven't asked her yet, pending your approval, but she's as anxious to get to the bottom of this as we are. Her mother was one of Parker's casualties."

"I'm aware of that." At Sarge's dry comment, heat crept up Colin's neck. "Why not have Ms. Bailey send him the checks? Why risk a meeting?"

"That would be my preference." Colin rested his elbows on the chair and linked his fingers in his lap. The farther away she stayed from Parker, the happier he'd be. "But he's already asked her out, and it may be helpful to hear what he has to say."

"Any concerns about danger to her?"

"Not from Parker. We'll be close by. And even if the Mafia is keeping tabs on him, Trish would be of little interest to them.

She's a client—and she thinks he's Matt. She can't help them make a positive ID."

"Do you think she'll be able to pull off this meeting without clueing in Parker that we're on to him?"

"Yes." Colin didn't hesitate. Parker might have tried to undermine Trish's mental steadiness, but she was a lot tougher than she looked. If she thought this would give them the answers they needed, he had every confidence she'd be able to disguise any nervousness . . . along with her disgust.

Sarge squinted at them as several silent seconds ticked by. "Fine. I'll leave the details of their meeting to you two, but I'd suggest it take place in public, that she wear a wire, and that we have one or two of our undercover people on hand in the location. If Parker's done everything you both think he did, I wouldn't trust him for an inch."

Exactly what he and Mac had discussed. There was no reason a coffee date should be risky, not with Trish prepared to give Parker access to the account via washed checks, but he intended to put as many safeguards in place as possible.

Just in case.

"We agree." Mac closed his notebook. "We've already talked about a lot of that and are ready to move forward."

"When do you want the meeting to take place?"

"Tomorrow."

"Go for it. If Parker takes the bait and tries to get the money, you'll have your search warrant."

"Thanks." Colin stood. "We'll keep you updated."

"Do that."

Mac followed him out.

"Now that we have Sarge's buy-in, we need to get this plan in gear." Colin shifted aside in the hall to let another detective pass.

"I'm ahead of you. I've already put out some calls to line up a couple of cadaver dogs."

"We don't have the search warrant yet."

"We will. Parker won't be able to resist the bait, not with the Mafia lurking in the shadows."

"I hope you're right. You want to get some undercover people prepped?"

"Yeah. Where do you think the meeting should take place?"

"There's a Starbucks near Trish's house. It's one of the bigger ones. Our people should be able to keep their distance and watch the proceedings without drawing attention."

"The one at Lindbergh and Clayton?"

"Uh-huh."

"I've been there. It will work. You want to call Trish, make certain she's on board?"

"She will be . . . but yes, that's next on my agenda." He exhaled. "I wish there was a way to keep her out of this entirely."

"Once she gives him the checks, there's no reason for them to have any more contact. I don't see a whole lot of risk in terms of Parker."

"I don't, either—but there are a lot of moving parts to this. Just having the Russian Mafia in the picture escalates the danger."

"They're after Parker, not her. And as you told Sarge, she can't help them with a positive ID. My biggest concern is getting to him before they do."

"True." He pulled out his phone. "Let me fill Trish in. Assuming she's willing, she can make the date with Parker. I'm thinking midmorning. There's less activity then, so our people will have unobstructed views. Once she confirms that with him, we can get everything set from our end."

"Works for me. I'll be at my desk. Let me know when we're ready to roll. And take a deep breath. If those dents in your forehead get any deeper, they'll give the Grand Canyon some competition." With a grin and a slap on the shoulder, Mac strolled toward their office.

Colin slipped into a conference room down the hall, flipping the light switch as he entered the dark room. Mac was right; he was worrying too much. Given all the life-and-death situations the ex–Navy SEAL had seen, his danger meter had to be a lot more accurate than most people's. If he didn't think the meeting between Trish and Parker was risky, it probably wasn't.

Yet as Colin keyed in her number, he couldn't quite extinguish the flicker of fear licking at his nerve endings.

23

She was in over her head.

Trish sipped her latte and surreptitiously glanced around the Starbucks, busy but not frenetic at ten twenty on Friday morning. Was the woman paging through the *Wall Street Journal* on the far side one of County's undercover detectives? Or maybe the guy dressed like a construction worker who seemed glued to his cell a few tables away? Or that woman in yoga pants, tank top, and fanny pack who looked like a young mother dropping in for a cool one after exercise class?

Impossible to tell.

Which was the point.

If she could pick out an undercover detective, her date would be able to also.

She set the cup down and wrapped her shaky fingers around it, trying to ignore the microphone taped to her chest. There was no need to be anxious. Law enforcement people were inside, and Colin and his colleague would be listening in from the parking lot at the restaurant next door—close at hand in case anything went wrong.

But it wouldn't.

This was a public place, and she was going to give Parker exactly what he was after—a way to get the money. All she had to do was call up her rusty acting skills from her college theater days.

Her lips curved up as she thought back to Colin's warning when she'd mentioned that to him.

"Don't tell Kristin you were a thespian or she'll rope you into helping with her children's theater project before you can say, 'To be or not to be.'"

"You're in a happy mood today." Matt—or Michael—slid into the chair across from her.

Good grief. She hadn't even seen him come in.

So much for *her* surveillance skills.

Fortunately, that part of this operation was in the hands of experts.

"I'm enjoying my latte." She nodded toward her cup.

Keep smiling, Trish. Act normal. You can't let him think anything has changed or you'll blow this.

"I would have gotten that for you."

"I was early and thirsty. You can get me a blueberry scone if you like, though." Not that she'd be able to eat much of it.

"Save my seat." He rose and touched her hand.

She tried not to flinch.

In less than five minutes he was back, his drink and her pastry in hand. "Thanks for meeting me this morning—but I'd have been happy to come by the house."

"Like I told you, I was glad to have an excuse to get out. I've been spending too much time alone."

"You know I'm available if you want company."

"I appreciate that—but I'm not the most upbeat person to be around these days."

"You've had a lot to deal with." Sympathy radiated from him.

If this was the man responsible for her mother's death, he deserved an Oscar.

"Getting ready for the summer art class has helped distract me. And once it starts, dealing with the kids will keep me occupied."

"Tell me a little more about the class."

She complied, watching him as she spoke. He appeared to be interested, asking pertinent questions, making amusing comments.

Not a word about the foundation.

"Isn't the scone fresh?"

She looked down at her pastry. She'd only taken two tiny bites, and a fourth of it was crumbled on her plate.

"Yes. We've been so busy talking, I forgot about eating." She broke off a piece and stuck it in her mouth, chewing until it turned to mush. Easier to swallow that way.

"This reminds me of the lunch we shared." He took a leisurely sip of his coffee. "Our conversation flowed that day too."

Had it? She couldn't recall what they'd discussed. It had been a brief, pleasant interlude—nothing more. Definitely not memorable.

"So what have you been up to?" The instant she spoke, she regretted the words. She knew what he'd been up to . . . but he didn't know she knew—so best to stay cool. It was a logical question between acquaintances.

If he caught the sudden surge in her nerves, he gave no indication.

"The usual. Working on books for clients, maintaining the property, keeping the church's ledgers up to date. But I do build in some fun."

He proceeded to tell her a story about a recent rollerblading attempt that did *not* end well. The tale was funny—but she had to force herself to laugh, knowing what the man across from her was capable of if their suspicions were correct.

When his humorous account wound down, she peeked at her watch. They were twenty minutes in . . . the point at which Colin had suggested she force his hand.

After brushing the pastry crumbs off her fingers, she reached for her purse.

"Do you need to leave already?" Some of Parker's jovial demeanor faded, and a tiny flicker of alarm flared in his hazel eyes.

"Soon. I have a number of errands to run this morning. I appreciate your invitation, though. Did you have anything specific you wanted to discuss before I go?"

"Just one small piece of business." The words were casual, but the tautness in his features wasn't. "I know this is more of a social get-together, but I did want to suggest a few potential contributions. If you agree they're worthwhile, I'd be happy to swing by later today and pick up any checks you might want to write."

Exactly the sort of offer Colin had suspected he'd make.

Any lingering doubts she'd had about his guilt evaporated.

"I'll tell you what." It was a struggle to maintain a pleasant tone. "Why don't you send me the recommendations by email and I'll review them over the weekend?"

A muscle twitched in his jaw. "Some of the needs are rather urgent."

Like his own?

She swallowed past the bitter taste on her tongue.

"In that case, I'll review them this afternoon. In the meantime, though . . ." She opened her purse and pulled out the envelope containing the checks she'd already prepared. "I do have a few other contributions I'd like to make. Could you handle them for me, as usual?" She held out the envelope.

An emotion that looked a lot like relief softened the hard edge in his eyes. "I'd be happy to." He took the checks and slid them into the inside pocket of his sport coat. "I'll send you the other recommendations later today."

"Great." She slung her purse over her shoulder and stood.

Parker rose too. "I'll walk you to your car."

"That's not necessary." She wanted this meeting over as fast as possible.

"My mother taught me to be a gentleman."

Trish tried not to gag.

Keep it together. You'll be away from him in less than three minutes. You can maintain a friendly pretense that long.

Looping that mantra through her mind, she managed to hold on to her smile even after he took her arm as they walked toward the door.

But she almost lost it—and her breakfast—once they arrived at her car and he not only pulled her into a hug but brushed his lips across her forehead.

Despite herself, she stiffened.

Backing off, he studied her. "Are you sure you're okay? You seem on edge today."

"I'm fine." She fumbled with the car door and swung it open. "I just have a lot to do to get ready for next week's class. With everything that's happened, I'm behind schedule."

"I hear you." He eased back as she slid behind the wheel. "Be safe down at that school."

"I will." She closed the door, started the engine—and tried to control the tremors in her hands as she pulled out of the lot.

Safety *was* on her mind at the moment.

But after all the cues Parker had sent during their coffee date that confirmed Colin's suspicions, she'd feel far safer in the questionable neighborhood around her school than she would in the presence of the man she'd left behind in the parking lot.

At least her part in this was over. All she had to do now was sit back and let Colin and his cohorts do their job.

There was no more risk to her.

. . . . .

"He followed our predicted script to the letter." Colin flipped off the audio feed from Trish's mike and watched Parker pull out of the Starbucks parking lot.

"Yeah." Mac leaned forward, posture intent.

"I see it." Colin tracked a black Kia as it fell in behind Parker. It stayed with him until both cars disappeared. "And it's not Phoenix."

The PIs were too professional to be that obvious. They'd be tailing Parker too—but more discreetly.

"My money is on our Russian friends—and it doesn't appear they care whether he knows they're following him."

"Could be an intimidation tactic." Colin pulled out his phone. "They might be trying to rattle him, hoping he lets something slip that confirms his identity."

"Let's hope we beat them to that."

Colin's phone began to vibrate. "Trish." He put it to his ear. "I was about to call you. You did great."

"Thanks—but it was harder the longer we were together. Beyond the fact he recommended some donations requiring checks, I picked up lots of signals suggesting he had more on his mind than helping legitimate causes."

"Mac's with me. I'm going to put you on speaker and you can give us your impressions." He changed the setting and laid the cell on the dash. "We're set. Go ahead."

He listened while she recounted her observations, exchanging a look with Mac as she described Parker's subtle but telling behavior after she made a move to leave before he had an assurance of getting checks in hand.

"I think you guys are right about him," she concluded. "This isn't the Matt I knew. The whole exchange creeped me out. What's next?"

"We wait—but not for long." Colin watched one of their undercover operatives saunter out of the Starbucks, sipping her iced coffee. No one would ever suspect there was a Sig Sauer in her fanny pack. "Given the presence of the Mafia, I expect he'll act fast. If he overnights the checks, we could get an alert from the bank as early as Monday. Once we have that, we'll expedite a search warrant. If there's anything to be found on his property, we'll find it."

"And if there isn't?"

"We'll still get him on embezzlement—and keep digging for more."

"Now that Parker has what he needs from me, is there any reason I can't resume my normal activities?"

Frowning, he tapped his finger against the wheel. "I'd rather you lay low until we wrap this up."

"Not a problem for the weekend, but my art class starts Monday, and I'm scheduled to meet Kristin for dinner that night."

"By Monday, this should be winding down—or over. I don't think the activities you have planned for then will be a problem." He glanced at Mac, who concurred with a dip of his head and tapped his watch.

Oh yeah. His colleague had a noon meeting at headquarters.

Colin twisted the key in the ignition. Assuming this wrapped up soon, as he expected, he'd like nothing better than to set up a tentative date with Trish for next weekend—but his colleague was already too tuned in to the budding relationship. He'd have to keep this parting simple and hold the invitation for later.

"I'll touch base with you Sunday. In the meantime, let me know if you hear any more from the Phoenix guys."

"I will. Be careful, Colin."

"You too. Talk to you soon."

Mac fastened his seat belt as the call ended. "With this winding down, I'm surprised you didn't ask her to hold next Saturday night open for you."

Colin concentrated on backing out of the parking space and merging with the busy traffic on Lindbergh. "The case isn't over yet."

"Close enough to pencil in a date."

"I'm not having this discussion."

Mac chuckled. "Fine. But if I was a betting man, I'd put money on you and Trish for next weekend."

"You might lose."

"Nope." He dug out his cell and began to scroll through messages. "The evidence is all there."

Silence fell in the car as Colin steered it toward the highway entrance ramp—and he didn't try to fill it.

Because Mac was right.

If all went well over the next few days, he didn't intend to spend next Saturday evening alone.

*　*　*　*　*

"I have a new piece of information that may prove useful."

Dmitri waved off a tall blonde approaching him with a drink in her hand and turned his back on the tiresome cocktail party, cell against his ear as he spoke to Oleg. "Tell me."

"There is a woman in the picture."

"In addition to the dead one? The manicurist?"

"This one is very much alive. She and Parker met for coffee earlier today."

"You have done some research?"

"Yes."

Dmitri wove through the Friday evening crowd toward the

bar, signaling to the bartender for a refill of his vodka as he listened without interrupting until Oleg finished briefing him.

"So she is a client."

"Perhaps more, based on their affectionate parting."

"Dig deeper." Already the gears were spinning in his brain, searching for a way to turn this new information into a tactical advantage.

"As you wish."

"Do you have the people you need for the next step we discussed in our last conversation?"

"They are arriving. We will be ready to proceed by Sunday."

"It will be instructive to see his reaction."

"Da. Especially if we find what we expect."

"I will look forward to hearing your next report."

He ended the call and slipped the cell into the pocket of his suit jacket, scanning the noisy crowd with disinterest. Putting in an appearance at these sorts of parties might be necessary to court influentials, but events like this were a total bore.

His gaze settled on the tall blonde, who continued to eye him. Or *stalk* might be a better word. He was known to be a generous . . . friend.

Swirling the clear liquid in his glass, he considered her. Why not take advantage of her less-than-subtle interest? Elizaveta wouldn't miss him at home. The passion had long ago evaporated from their marriage. She had her life; he had his.

And tonight he was in the mood to be entertained.

He smiled at the blonde and lifted his glass slightly toward her.

Half a second later, she was weaving through the throng in his direction . . . as he'd expected.

Perhaps this Friday night would be pleasurable after all. The unfinished business of the day could wait until tomorrow.

Besides, now that they were closing in on Parker, he had much to celebrate—and how better to do that than with a beautiful woman?

Michael Parker would understand that sentiment—though he had chosen his playmate unwisely.

And if the man living in Matthew Parker's house was his brother, he would pay for that mistake.

Very soon.

24

Michael flipped on his blinker as he approached the gravel driveway that led to Matt's house, yanking off the tie he'd loosened as soon as he'd left church. What a waste that boring hour and a half had been—as usual.

But until he had the money from Trish's foundation, he couldn't raise any red flags. To the eyes of the world, he was Matt—and he needed to keep up the pretense for now.

Even if not everyone was buying his story 100 percent.

He scanned the empty road behind him for the tail that had never been far behind since Oleg and his goon had visited.

Why wasn't the Kia there today?

Was Dmitri's lieutenant finally convinced he was Matt?

As he rolled up the drive, tires crunching on the loose rock, he rotated the kinks out of his shoulders. Getting the Russian Mafia off his back would be a huge relief—but even if they were gone, he was bowing out of here tomorrow. The instant he confirmed the checks he'd overnighted yesterday were deposited at Providence House Ministries, he'd funnel the funds to the secondary pseudo charity accounts, and from there transfer them offshore with a few keystrokes. Then, new ID in hand, he'd disappear to Mexico until he could make some discreet travel arrangements to the new home he'd establish in the Cayman Islands or Panama.

All he had to do was hang in for another eighteen hours and—

He jammed the brake to the floor, uttering a profanity as the car skidded on the loose gravel.

Oleg's Cadillac was parked near the detached garage, along with a Suburban and the Kia.

His stomach knotted.

No one from the Mafia had been following him because they were all here.

Why?

And how many thugs were waiting on his doorstep?

He sat unmoving for a full minute, fingers gripping the wheel, every instinct in his body screaming *Run!*

But he couldn't do that.

The papers he needed for his new identity were stashed in the house. His computer was inside too. Not that there was much chance Dmitri's people would be able to get into his hack-proof, encrypted documents . . . but why take the risk?

Plus, running away would undermine all the groundwork he'd laid to convince them he was Matt.

Only guilty people ran.

He sucked in a lungful of air as the left side of his brain began to hum. He needed to do what his brother would do in this situation—act outraged by the continued invasion of his privacy . . . and hope Oleg bought the act rather than resort to the kinds of interrogation techniques he was rumored to use.

Psyching himself up for the encounter and tamping down his fear as best he could, he continued toward the house.

Rather than pull into the garage, he stopped beside the Cadillac, set the brake, and slid out of the car.

The engine on the luxury car was idling, but the dark windows hid the occupants.

Was it possible Dmitri himself might have come to call?

No.

Dealing directly with a potential traitor would be beneath him. That dirty work was delegated to underlings.

It was Oleg.

Seconds later, his conclusion was confirmed. The familiar bodyguard slid out from behind the wheel, stood, and grasped the handle on the back door. After a quick sweep of the surroundings, he swung it open.

Oleg stepped out. Today the man was dressed in more casual—but no less expensive—attire. Dolce & Gabbana jeans, Gucci loafers, Armani shirt. Some of the brands he himself had favored in his more flush days.

Why had Oleg ditched his customary suit and tie?

"Good afternoon, Mr. Parker. I trust your trip to church was edifying?"

So someone had been watching him after all.

Matt, however, would be taken aback to discover he'd been tailed.

"How do you know where I was?"

"We have eyes everywhere."

Michael lifted his chin and pretended to bristle. "Why are you harassing me? And who are all these people?" He swept a hand over the other two empty vehicles.

"They are . . . associates."

"Where are they?"

"Exploring your property. They like the outdoors, and you have a very secluded place here."

Oleg's men were traipsing around Matt's land?

That was bad news.

The graves were well disguised, but he'd expected Mother

Nature to apply the finishing touches of camouflage long before anyone might think to search for them. It was possible there were markers, if someone was searching for them.

"This is trespassing."

"Yes, it is. Perhaps you would like to call the police?"

Checkmate.

And Oleg knew it, based on his smug expression.

But he needed to keep up the indignant charade.

"If you leave, I won't have to resort to that and create problems for you."

"I do not think it is our problems that concern you."

Had they already found something—or was the man bluffing? Was Oleg hoping he'd crack and save them the effort of further searching?

Not going to happen.

He straightened up, maintaining his irate demeanor. "I have no idea what you're talking about. I'll give you fifteen minutes to vacate my property."

Without waiting for the man to respond, he spun on his heel and stalked to the door.

Once inside, however, his angry façade evaporated and he slumped against the wall.

Oleg wasn't going to leave.

The idle threat he'd issued to the Russian had been no more than an exit line, and the man no doubt knew that.

He didn't want the police invading his property any more than he wanted Oleg's goons poking around.

But maybe, if he was lucky, the Russians scouring his property wouldn't find anything.

Yet as Michael pushed off from the wall and raked shaky fingers through his hair, he doubted that was how this was going to play out.

Luck wasn't in his corner these days.

All he could do was be prepared with a credible story if Oleg knocked on his door with news of a grisly discovery.

■ ■ ■ ■ ■

Painting scenery was *not* his forte.

Nor was it how he wanted to spend a sunny Sunday afternoon better suited to a brisk run or a long swim or a game of one-on-one basketball.

Sighing, Colin dipped his brush back into the can of gray paint. He shouldn't have let Rick guilt him into volunteering yesterday at breakfast.

But with Kristin's show three weeks away, half the scenery crew on vacation, and nothing urgent on his Sunday afternoon schedule, how could he say no?

He aimed a disgusted look at his so-called buddy, who was instructing another new recruit on the fine points of adding texture to a tree trunk.

As if sensing his scrutiny, Rick glanced toward him, said a few more words to the hapless volunteer who seemed as lost as Colin felt, and walked across the church hall to join him. "How's it going?"

"How do you think it's going?" Colin gave the simulated stones he was painting on the castle wall a disgusted perusal. "This is not my shtick."

"Yeah. I can see that." Rick withdrew a few paces to examine the expanse. "But from the audience, it'll read as stone. Sort of. If they use their imagination."

"Why don't you let me work on that plain wall instead?" He waved toward a guy who was slapping a coat of yellow paint on a large flat.

"He's less talented than you are at this kind of stuff."

"Not possible."

"Very possible. Remember that weeping willow on the back-drop last year?"

"You mean the weird-shaped tree that would have been better suited to a horror movie? Yeah."

"He painted it."

"Oh."

"Stick with the stone wall, okay?"

"I'm not making any promises. You may have to have some-one touch it . . ." His phone began to vibrate, and he pulled it off his belt. Trish. "I need to take this."

"Go for it. You're not on the clock here." Rick moved on to assess the progress of another piece of scenery.

"Hi." Colin set his brush down and angled away from the assembled group. "What's up?"

"I heard from Phoenix. Cal says Parker has visitors again. Three carloads full."

Colin frowned. Not the kind of news he wanted to hear.

"Can he see what's going on?"

"No. He did call in reinforcements, and they're moving in as close as they can get on public land. But there are quite a few people there, and they've spread out over Matt's place, which is heavily wooded."

Doing the same thing he and Mac wanted to do, he suspected. Combing the property for bodies.

Not only was the Russian Mafia on a parallel track with County, they were one step ahead—because they didn't have to wait for a warrant.

Best case, tomorrow afternoon was the earliest he'd get legal access to the land.

He blew out a frustrated breath. "Let me know if Cal calls back with anything else."

"I will."

After confirming over his shoulder that no one was close,

he lowered his voice. "Listen . . . assuming this case wraps up in the next few days, I was wondering if you might like to have dinner with me next Saturday."

"Yes."

At her instant assent, one side of his mouth quirked up. "I like a decisive woman."

"I'll keep that in mind."

He grinned. Getting to know Trish Bailey was going to be a lot of fun.

"Why don't I come by for you at six? And dress up. We're going to launch this new chapter together in style." Some banging started up behind him, and he cupped his hand around the phone. "Sorry about that."

"You sound like you're in a construction zone."

"Close. I got roped into helping with the sets for Kristin's show."

"If Kristin and I hit it off tomorrow, maybe I'll pitch in too."

"She'll be your friend forever if you do. In the meantime, I'll be counting the days until Saturday." The banging got louder. "That's my cue to hang up. Keep me in the loop with Phoenix."

"Will do. Have fun with the sets."

"Right." Still smiling, he pocketed the phone and pivoted back toward the room.

Rick was standing six feet away.

"Why are you anxious for Saturday to get here?"

"Were you eavesdropping?"

"Nope. I came over to help with the castle"—he waved a paintbrush at the flat—"and found you'd abandoned your post. That was Trish, wasn't it?"

"Let's paint." Colin brushed past him.

"*Now* you want to paint." Rick trailed behind him. "Must mean that was her. You finally set up a date?"

"You know I don't mix work and play."

"The work will end one of these days." He dipped his brush into a can of paint. "If I know you . . . and I do . . . you made a date for Saturday. Where are you taking her?"

Colin kept painting.

"First dates are important." Rick stroked some paint on the backdrop, continuing as if he hadn't noticed his friend's lack of response. "Dinner is always appropriate—but pick an upscale place. Not over the top, but impressive. Quiet is also a must. You want to be able to talk to each other without raising your voices."

"Since when have you become an expert on how to woo a woman?" Colin slapped on a streak of dark gray to simulate a weathered stone. Or so the theory went.

"Hey. I've been to my share of chick flicks. And when do I get to meet her? Kristin said the two of them are having dinner Monday. Do I have to ask her out for a meal myself to get an introduction?"

Colin gave him a narrow-eyed glower. No way did he want Rick anywhere near Trish until he had at least a first date under his belt. His buddy had the looks to turn a woman's head—and he was too available.

"I'll invite her to one of our Saturday breakfasts soon."

"You mean after you've staked your claim."

"This isn't the gold rush."

"A good woman is worth her weight in gold." Rick dipped his brush in a can of paint. "But women can also mess with a man's head."

"She's not messing with my head. She's messing with my heart. But whatever happens between us, you and Kristin will always be family."

"Glad to hear it." Rick kept painting. "I'll email you a few restaurant suggestions for that date you made."

"Thanks." Might as well ditch the evasion tactics. His friends already knew Trish had gotten under his skin, that he was determined to get to know her better.

And if all went as he expected, come Saturday night he'd make that official.

．．．．．

The fifteen-minute warning he'd given Oleg had expired an hour ago.

Yet the man was still here—along with his minions.

Michael eased the front blinds a scant half inch further from the window and inspected the front yard. No sign of anyone from the other vehicles. Oleg was ensconced in the air-conditioned comfort of the Cadillac while his bodyguard stood watch by the door, arms folded, feet planted wide.

He let the blinds drop and moved to the sliding glass doors in the kitchen that offered a panoramic view of the backyard and surrounding woods.

Again, no sign of anyone.

But Oleg's men were out there, combing through the woods. And if they were thorough . . . if they poked into every corner and examined every area that showed any sign of disturbance . . . they were going to . . .

A sharp rap sounded on the front door, and Michael's pulse lost its rhythm.

Stay calm. The story you cobbled together over the past hour is ready. You can pull this off.

He forced his stiff legs to carry him toward the summons, trying not to hyperventilate as he grasped the knob and twisted it.

Oleg stood on the other side.

"I told you to leave." The knob was slippery beneath his sweaty palm.

"And I told you to call the police. But you did not do that.

301

Now I understand why. One of my men has made an interesting find. Shall we take a walk to see it . . . or is that necessary?"

Michael's gut clenched.

Was the man bluffing? Hoping the mere suggestion of a discovery would elicit a confession?

Or had they actually found a body?

No way to know.

Keep playing dumb, Parker.

"What are you talking about?"

Oleg gave him the kind of chiding look usually reserved for small, misbehaving children. "Must this game continue?"

Yes . . . it must. He had to make certain they weren't trying to fake him out—even if walking into a dense, isolated woodland with Russian Mafia members all around wasn't how he'd expected to spend this Sunday afternoon.

Instead of responding, he exited the house, locked the door behind him, and waited.

"So . . . you insist on this hike?"

Again, he remained silent.

"Very well." Oleg brushed an imaginary speck off his slacks. "Clothes are replaceable—and worth the sacrifice for a just cause." He signaled to his bodyguard, who fell in behind them as Oleg led the way around the house.

At the edge of the woods, across the overgrown backyard, another burly man with aloof eyes waited.

No words were exchanged once they reached him. The man simply swiveled around and guided them into the underbrush.

Toward Matt's shallow grave.

When they arrived in the small clearing, two other men were waiting, both of them holding shovels.

The roiling in Michael's stomach intensified.

Oleg examined the spot their guide indicated. For anyone

looking for signs of disturbance, it was clear the ground had been excavated in the not-too-distant past.

"Excellent work." The Russian honcho bestowed the accolade on the assembled men with an all-encompassing glance, then turned to him. "Others continue to search the rest of the property. Perhaps this is not the only noteworthy piece of ground we will find."

Michael remained silent.

"As you can see, these men are prepared to dig. However, it is a warm day, and I believe we both know what they will find. Shall we save them the exertion?"

There was no doubt in his mind Oleg would follow through and have his people unearth the remains. Better to admit defeat—on this front.

"Yes—but I have an explanation."

"I am sure it is fascinating. Please proceed."

"I'd prefer not to have an audience."

"Ah. A confidential tale." He motioned the bodyguard forward. "You will agree to let him search you, yes? Security is always a concern in this troubled world of ours."

"I don't mind."

After giving him a thorough frisking, the muscleman backed off.

"You will wait at the edge of the woods. All of you." Oleg waved off the men gathered around him.

They melted into the shadows of the trees rimming the clearing, close enough to act as sentries but far away enough to allow for a private conversation.

"Whenever you are ready." Oleg's posture was relaxed, but his eyes were sharp. Searing. Probing.

A bead of sweat popped out on Michael's forehead. It was warm for June . . . but not that warm. Oleg wasn't sweating.

He needed to control his responses—and his behavior. He could give this man no grounds on which to doubt his story.

"Do you mind if we move under a tree?" He pulled out his handkerchief and mopped his brow, hoping Oleg would attribute the sweat to the sun.

"Wherever you wish."

Michael crossed to a shady patch. It *was* cooler here. That should help him get the sweating under control.

Taking a deep breath, he plunged into the story he'd spent the past hour finessing.

"If you dig in that spot"—he indicated the disturbed ground—"you'll find the body of my brother, Michael Parker." He closed his eyes and called up a grimace, as if it pained him to say the words. "It was an accident."

A few beats ticked by.

"You are telling me you killed your brother?"

"Yes—but I didn't intend to. One night while he was here, he borrowed my car, went to a bar, and brought a woman back with him. I was working in the yard and didn't realize she was in the house until I came in at dusk. The two of them were having a fight, and the next thing I knew, the woman grabbed a knife out of the block on the counter and lunged at Michael. They struggled . . . and she ended up on the floor. Dead."

"That is very tragic." Oleg's expression didn't change.

"I wanted to call the police, but Michael said she didn't have any family and would never be missed. He wanted to bury her on the property. I said no. We argued about it. I went for the phone, he picked up the knife . . . and I could see in his eyes he intended to kill me."

"I assume you won that fight."

"Yes . . . with a few scars as souvenirs." He touched the line on his forehead. "I buried the bodies on the property and told people I'd been in a car accident. I knew no one would miss Michael, since I assumed he was on the run from some kind of mess, and I believed him about the woman. He always did gravitate toward loners."

"Why did you not call the police and explain all this?"

"I've built a new life here, far from the troubles in Boston, and I didn't want it tainted with a sensational story like this. In hindsight, it wasn't the best choice. Going back now, though, would be difficult."

"Yet the police have visited you anyway."

"They know Michael's been here—but they have no reason to doubt me . . . just as you don't. You can check my background. I've never done anything illegal. I'm a churchgoing, law-abiding citizen."

"Yes. We are familiar with Matthew's history."

Matthew's history.

Not *your* history.

Oleg either wasn't buying his story, or he wasn't certain about it and was trying to provoke him into a revelation.

But that wouldn't happen.

He was done talking.

As the silence stretched between them, a squirrel scuttled over a branch in the oak tree above them. A dog barked in the distance. The faint drone of a passing plane echoed high overhead.

Michael held his ground, his gaze never wavering under Oleg's assessing stare.

At last the man spoke. "You tell an intriguing story."

"It's the truth."

"So you say. But we shall see." He turned on his heel and strode out of the small clearing, motioning for the others to accompany him.

The sound of them crashing through the underbrush faded as they disappeared into the trees. Only after it ceased did Michael follow.

Based on his retreat, there had been sufficient doubt in Oleg's mind to stop him from carrying out the justice Dmitri wanted. If he had been convinced the man living in Matt's house was his target, the execution would have taken place today. In the woods.

Instead, Michael Parker was walking out alive.

That was a small victory.

But it might be short-lived.

Oleg would speak with his boss, get further instructions. It was possible Dmitri would tell him to proceed with the Mafia's version of justice despite any doubt that remained about identities. The big man in Miami wouldn't lose any sleep over a potential mistake, especially if he thought the odds of a correct call were in his favor.

However . . . there wasn't likely to be any more action today—and by tomorrow morning, the money from the foundation would be in his shell charities, ready to transfer to his offshore account.

As long as there weren't any glitches.

There shouldn't be—but in case a problem arose, he needed to stick here until he had the money in hand.

Then he could take off and be free of Dmitri and his ilk.

And this time, he *would* be free. This escape would be clean—as the one to St. Louis should have been. *Would* have been if Natalie hadn't put him on the cops' radar. How Dmitri had picked up on that was a mystery . . . but there would be no slipups on this go-round. He would talk to no one until he was safely out of the country, his old identity left behind.

The Russians might be sticking close, but eluding them once he was ready to disappear would be a cinch. Vanish into the mall crowd at the Galleria, alter his clothing and appearance in the men's room, leave by a different exit as a different person. Hike a mile to the Sheraton, take a cab to the airport, pick up a rental car under his new name, and flee. He had sufficient cash on hand to fund his escape, and a new credit card was waiting for its first transaction.

The instant he got confirmation the funds had transferred, he was ready to roll.

He emerged from the woods and circled around the house.

All the vehicles were gone.

Excellent.

And in less than eighteen hours, if all went smoothly, Michael Parker would vanish off the face of the earth.

This time forever.

25

"Yes!" Colin pressed the end button, vaulted to his feet, and pumped his fist in the air. "We've got him."

"I take it you were talking to the bank that handles the foundation money?" Mac stopped beside his desk and held out a cup of coffee.

"Bingo. Grounds for a warrant is great news on a Monday morning." Colin took the venti dose of caffeine he no longer needed. "I'll alert Sarge."

"I'll call my contacts with the cadaver dogs and put them on standby. What's your best estimate on timing?" The other detective took a sip of his java and sat on the corner of his desk.

"Depends on how hard Sarge pushes the warrant. But Phoenix has Parker in their sights, so he's not going anywhere without us knowing about it. I'm thinking mid to late afternoon."

"I'll pencil it in. You planning to let Trish know this is going down?"

"I'll leave a message. Her summer art class started today, and she told me she keeps her phone on mute while she's teaching."

He nodded toward the window. In the distance, gray clouds were banking on the horizon. "Let's hope this rain holds off until tomorrow."

"Mud won't stop the dogs."

"Makes for messy searching outside, though." He took another gulp of coffee and moved toward the door. "As soon as I have the warrant in hand—or a go from Sarge—I'll let you know."

"My afternoon is yours. I'll be glad to get this one off my plate."

"You and me both."

"You set up that date yet with Trish?"

Sheesh. Everyone must have romance on the mind these days.

"Yes." He kept walking.

"That's what I figured."

Mac's chuckle followed him out the door . . . but he was past trying to hide his interest in the lovely art teacher.

In fact, if this wrapped up today, he might even take her out for ice cream long before their official Saturday date.

. . . . .

The meeting was running long—and the incoming call from Oleg gave him the perfect excuse to cut out for a few minutes.

"Excuse me, gentlemen." Dmitri rose and lifted the phone. "An urgent matter requires my attention. Please continue. I will rejoin you as soon as I can."

Without waiting for a reply, he put the phone to his ear, issued a curt "hold," and crossed the plush carpet at the private club that was part of his empire. A profitable venture, thanks to the B-girls in his employ, who could pick out a susceptible male customer from five hundred yards.

He smiled. A skimpy dress, some heavy-duty flirting—and the next morning the guy would wake up to find the girl gone and a five-thousand-dollar bottle of champagne on his credit card. It was the perfect con. If the mark went to the police, it would be a major embarrassment for him—and if any of them complained about the charge, the threat of violence always shut them up and put the matter to rest.

A simple scam with a tidy wrap-up.

Clean finishes were always best.

A rule he intended to apply to the Parker matter today.

"I am now free to talk. The arrangements we discussed after your discovery yesterday are in motion?"

"Yes. The matter will be finished by tonight. We will return tomorrow."

"Excellent. Do you foresee any complications?"

"No. We have canvassed the location. It is quiet, with little activity. But we have an emergency exit strategy in place, should it be needed. It is a shame about the girl, though."

Dmitri shook his head. Oleg had always had a soft spot for the innocent. His one flaw.

"It is necessary. I want additional assurance we are punishing the correct brother. Based on our dealings with the man we knew as Elliott and the research you provided on Matthew Parker, I believe our test will prove which brother is still living. On the slight chance it is Matthew, you know what to do. If it is Michael—I want an admission of guilt. And I want him begging for mercy. You will document everything. That will add credence to the story we will circulate of our relentless—and successful—pursuit, despite his clever deception."

"I understand."

"You will have no trouble getting away?"

"No. It is arranged."

"You are not being watched?"

"I have seen no indication of it."

"Good. You will report back tonight, and I will see you here tomorrow. A small token of my appreciation will be waiting for you."

"I am grateful for your kindness."

"Skill—and loyalty—should be rewarded. I will talk with you soon." Dmitri ended the call, a satisfied smile lifting the corners of his lips.

At last this unpleasant episode was coming to an end.

And once punishment was meted out, word would spread that no one . . . no one . . . escaped Dmitri Kozlov's wrath. He would see to that.

There would be no more traitors in his organization.

· · · · ·

The money wasn't there.

Frowning, Michael clicked through the Providence House Ministries account again.

Zip.

The washed checks hadn't yet been cashed.

He slammed a fist against the table.

This made no sense.

The test check he'd overnighted soon after he'd slipped into the role of Matt—the one Trish had legitimately written to Providence House—had cleared by ten o'clock central the next morning in New York.

That hadn't happened today.

He'd been monitoring the accounts since eight thirty, and it was now after noon.

This delay was out of pattern.

And it didn't feel right.

He rose from the laptop at the kitchen table and began to pace. He was ready to go; his new ID and important papers were in the computer bag in the bedroom, along with a change of clothes, glasses, baseball cap, hair gel, and other items that would alter his appearance. All he needed to do was confirm the money was in the account and transfer it offshore via the sham charities supported by Providence House.

But he couldn't leave until it showed up and he moved the funds . . . just in case there was a glitch.

Meaning he had to stay in Matt's skin for now—no matter how dangerous that role-play was becoming.

Tension thrumming through his nerve endings, he veered back toward the computer to click through the account again . . . but came to an abrupt halt at the sound of crunching gravel from outside.

A car was coming up the driveway.

The cops—or the Mafia?

Neither visitor was on his wish list . . . but at this point he'd take the detectives over Oleg and his crew.

At least they wouldn't kill him.

He darted into the living room and cracked the blinds.

A panel van with his internet provider's logo on the side swung around on the gravel pad near the garage and stopped by the walk that led to the front door, facing toward the road.

Huh.

As far as he could tell, his satellite connection was working fine.

So why was a repair guy here?

A dark-haired man emerged from the driver's side, clipboard in hand, a small box tucked under his arm, and circled around the van toward the front door of the house.

He looked legit.

But it couldn't hurt to stash the computer bag and slip the new ID documents back into their hiding place under the laundry hamper.

By the time he'd secreted the items, the doorbell was ringing.

Ignoring the summons was an option—but if there was an

issue that could affect his internet access, it might mess with his plans. He needed to keep monitoring the account.

Better talk to the guy.

He crossed to the door and pulled it open. "Yes?"

"Sorry to arrive without notice, but I was in the area and decided to see if I could catch you at home. You were on our call list for tomorrow. There's been a recall on your modem. I have a new one with me I can install." He indicated the box.

"I haven't had any trouble."

"Well, your model has some major bugs. We've had a lot of complaints about interrupted service."

Great.

With his luck, the thing would pick today to die.

"Fine." He reached for the box. "I can hook it up myself."

The man shifted it away. "I'm sorry, sir. This is leased equipment and has to be installed by an authorized technician. It won't take long."

He hesitated. If he told the guy to come back another day and his internet gave out, he'd have to go searching for Wi-Fi. That could delay his escape.

Not in his plans.

Pulling the door wide, he stepped back. "Make it fast."

The man entered.

"The modem's in the back." He motioned for the guy to follow him and led the way to the rear of the house. At the door to Matt's office, he turned. "How long do you—"

His breath jammed in his windpipe.

A pistol was pointing at the middle of his chest.

This wasn't about modems.

This was about murder.

Even though the man had no trace of a Russian accent, wore a uniform shirt, and was driving what appeared to be a legitimate satellite service van, he was one of Oleg's men.

And they were done biding their time.

But why had they resorted to this elaborate ruse if they were planning to take him out? Why not haul him out to his own woods and put a bullet in his brain?

"What's going on?" His words came out tight. Strained.

"We're going to take a trip."

"Where?"

"You will walk out the back door, circle the house, and enter the van from the rear. Move."

With a gun aimed at his heart, what choice did he have except to comply?

Exiting the house, he saw the logic behind the location of the van. On the off chance someone might be watching the house through the trees from the main road, the vehicle was positioned to block their view as he walked toward it.

At the back of the van, the thug with the gun spoke. "Knock twice on the door."

He did as instructed.

It swung open.

As the gun pressed against his back, urging him in, he inventoried the passengers.

Oleg.

The bodyguard.

The guy with the indifferent eyes who'd led them to Matt's grave.

And the real driver of the van—bound with duct tape, blindfolded, and gagged, dumped among the boxes of satellite parts. Blood was seeping out of a large bump on his head . . . and he wasn't moving.

"Get in." Another jab in the back.

Before he could respond, Oleg's guard grasped his arm, hauled him through the door, and shoved him down against the inside panel.

The guy without the accent kept his pistol trained on him during that maneuver while Oleg watched the proceedings in silence, then slammed the back door closed. A few seconds later he took his place behind the wheel, put the van in gear, and retraced his route down the gravel drive.

What was going on?

Hard as Michael tried to fathom Oleg's plan, he could make no sense of it.

If Dmitri's people were sure enough of his identity to resort to abduction at gunpoint, why not just kill him and be done with it?

"Does anyone want to tell me what this is about?"

No one responded.

"This is kidnapping, you know." The words sounded hollow even to his ears.

Oleg, dressed again in jeans, folded his arms and watched him in silence.

Was his casual attire an indication of more dirty work to come?

Pulse pounding, Michael wrapped his arms around his bent knees and gripped his wrist. He had no idea what Oleg had planned for him in the hours to come, but as the van swung onto the road and began to accelerate, he did know one thing.

This trip was not going to end well.

■ ■ ■ ■ ■

Tote bag slung over one shoulder and juggling an armful of art supplies, Trish pushed through the back door of the house, deactivated the security system, and dumped everything on the kitchen table.

Whew.

Busy didn't begin to describe this day. It might be only four forty-five, but after dealing with back-to-back sessions of boisterous fourth and fifth graders, she was ready for a nap. And the half-hour delay in her departure while she waited with one of her students for his ride had lengthened an already long day.

But the messages she'd found waiting for her from Colin, plus the anticipation of a pleasant get-acquainted dinner with Kristin, perked her up. According to Colin's second message, the warrant had gone through. They should already be at Parker's place, wrapping this up.

It couldn't happen too soon for her.

After detouring to the fridge for a soda, she dashed down the hall. As late as she was running, she should have gone straight to the restaurant where she was meeting Kristin—but a swing by the house to freshen up had been too tempting to resist. If she hurried, she could be out of here in ten minutes and . . .

Ding dong.

Drat.

Trish set her soda on the bathroom vanity and blew out a breath. She didn't have time to deal with whoever was on her doorstep.

Except . . . it might be Stan Hawkins. He'd promised her some homemade ice cream from his next batch, and the way he kept tabs on the comings and goings in the neighborhood, he might have been watching for her.

Exiting into the hall, she picked up her pace. Stan would understand if she told him she was running late for a dinner date and couldn't chat.

But when she peeked through the peephole, it wasn't her friendly neighbor on the other side of the door. It was some guy with a clipboard, wearing what looked like a repairman uniform.

Edging to the sidelight, she peeked at the driveway. A satellite-service utility van was parked there.

Odd.

Everyone she knew in the neighborhood had cable.

Maybe the guy was lost . . . or had been given some incorrect information by his dispatcher.

She ought to be able to dispense with this fast.

Grasping the handle, she pulled the door open. "May I help you?"

"Yes." After transferring the clipboard to his left hand, he reached into his pants pocket, angled toward the door . . . and pulled out a gun. "Say one word, I pull the trigger. Move back inside."

Trish gaped at the deadly weapon aimed at her chest.

Was this for real?

"Move!"

Yeah.

It was for real.

She stumbled back, gaze locked on the gun.

He followed her in, shut the door, and motioned toward the rear of the house with the weapon. "Go to the back door."

Despite the sudden rubber in her legs, she managed to walk down the hall.

This wasn't some random robbery. Too coincidental. It had to be related to everything else that had been happening,

But how?

"Unlock the door. Then sit there." The man waved the gun toward one of the kitchen chairs.

She did as he instructed.

Keeping the gun trained on her, he set the clipboard on the kitchen table and pulled out a cell. "I'm in." He returned the phone to his pocket, withdrew a piece of black cloth with strings attached to it, and tossed it to her. "Put that over your head."

She fumbled to catch the . . . what was it?

Panic choked her as she realized it was a drawstring bag.

"I . . . I won't be able to breathe."

"It's porous. Do it now."

She wadded the fabric in her fingers. If she put this over her head, she'd be blind—and helpless.

A wave of nausea rolled through her, and the room tilted. Hard fingers gripped her shoulder. "Do as I say. Now."

She stared at the gun hovering inches away from her face. Should she lunge for it?

Maybe.

This guy was a lot stronger than she was, but the self-defense moves she'd learned had worked on that mugger.

The man's grip tightened. "Don't try anything foolish."

She tensed, muscles coiling in preparation. Her plan might be foolish—but this could be her only chance to—

All at once, the gun veered away . . . then swung back and connected with her temple.

Hard.

Pain ricocheted through her skull, and she groaned as black spots muddied her vision.

Before she could recover, the bag was jerked from her grasp. The man yanked it down over her head and pulled the drawstring tight around her neck.

She tried to claw at it, but he grabbed her arm and twisted it behind her back.

Moaning again, she doubled over, trying to relieve the pressure.

It didn't help.

Somewhere in the distance, beyond the haze of pain and fear, she heard the back door open . . . and a voice spoke in a language that sounded like Russian.

Seconds later, the pressure on her arm eased and she was able to straighten up—but instantly rough hands slapped her wrists together and secured them with a tight cord in front of her.

"Why did you bring me here?"

Matt's voice.

No.

It wasn't Matt.

It was Michael.

The man who'd killed her mother, his brother, and probably that unfortunate manicurist who'd crossed his path.

But why was he here instead of at his house, where Colin and his men expected him to be? Hadn't Phoenix alerted them that Parker had left?

Or . . . perhaps they had. Colin might at this very minute be approaching her house, charging to the rescue.

Yet even as that hopeful thought flitted through her mind, she dismissed it.

Stuff like that only happened in fairy tales—and her life had been no fairy tale of late.

The truth was, these guys had somehow managed to spirit Parker away from the house undetected—for purposes known to them alone.

"It is much easier to come here than risk a kidnapping." The same Russian voice spoke again, this time in accented English.

"But what does Trish have to do with any of this?"

No one answered Parker's question, but a scuffling noise suggested someone was sitting down.

"I passed on the story you told me yesterday to the person who sent me here." The Russian's tone was conversational. "He agreed it was quite inventive."

"It was the truth." A slight tremor underscored Parker's words.

"We would like to believe you—but it is difficult. You are friends with this woman?"

"Yes."

"Close friends?"

"We've known each other a while."

"You socialize?"

A slight hesitation, as if he didn't know where these questions were leading.

That made two of them.

"Mr. Parker?"

"We've had a couple of dates."

"That is what we determined. And that is why she is important to us this afternoon. Now, here is the deal we will make you, Mr. Parker. You may live . . . or she may live. It is your choice."

Dear God!

She'd become a bargaining chip for the Russian Mafia!

Trish began to shake.

"What do you mean?" Parker's tone was wary.

"It is very simple. A life must be sacrificed for the treachery and disloyalty of Michael Parker. It has been decided one of you must die to satisfy this debt of honor. You may choose who lives."

"But that's . . . this is crazy!"

"Nevertheless, that is your choice."

"What if I refuse to decide?"

"Then you will both die. I will give you five minutes to choose."

A tomblike silence settled over the room.

Inside the blackness of the hood, Trish squeezed her eyes shut.

Five minutes.

That was all the time she had left to live.

Because a man who had killed three people in cold blood wouldn't hesitate to sacrifice someone else to save his own skin.

As the desperateness of her situation sank in, Trish choked back a sob and turned to the only source of comfort—and help—available to her.

Please, God, stay with me through this ordeal. Give me strength and courage and hope . . . because I know that bleak as this situation seems, nothing is impossible with you.

Yet as she finished the prayer, a wave of despair swept over her. She believed in miracles. She did.

But miracles had been in short supply during the past two years.

And it would take nothing less than divine intervention to save her life today.

26

Now that was peculiar.

As thunder rumbled in the distance, Stan Hawkins snipped off a Double Delight rose from the bush near his front porch and watched the white service van roll around to the back of Trish's house.

The blossom's sweet scent wafted up to his nose, and he inhaled. The missus was right. This one smelled like heaven.

But whatever was going on across the street didn't.

First of all, nobody around here had a satellite, as far as he knew.

Second, service vehicles usually parked on the street or by the walk that led from the driveway to the front door. They didn't go around back.

Third, why had the truck sat there for a few minutes before it disappeared to the rear? And who had moved it, anyway? The guy who'd gone to the front door had never come back out.

No sir.

This didn't smell good.

And that little lady didn't deserve one more speck of trouble.

But what to do?

He repositioned the flower in his hand to avoid the prickly thorns as he considered the matter. Back in the day, he'd have hustled over there, knocked on the door, and scoped out the situation himself.

That, however, was a long time ago.

Sad to say, he wasn't a strong, strapping weightlifter anymore. If things got rough, he'd be no match for the big guy inside Trish's house. That bruiser would squash him like a pesky mosquito.

This was a job for a younger man.

And he knew just the man—that fine young detective Trish had taken a fancy to. The one with the Irish name. Colin . . . Colin . . . Flynn. Yes, that was it.

Why not give the County police a call and ask them to patch him through to the detective? And if they wouldn't do that, he could tell his story to whoever answered the phone and ask them to send a patrol car by.

Another ornery thorn stabbed him, and a drop of blood beaded on his fingertip. Some kind of warning, perhaps? A reminder that sticking his nose into other people's business could be as thorny as the rose in his hand?

Possible.

Hadn't the missus accused him only yesterday of becoming an old busybody?

But there was a difference between being nosy and being concerned—and he'd rather live with egg on his face than let fear of embarrassment stop him from assisting a neighbor who might need help.

Holding the rose gingerly to avoid any more damage, he turned around and marched into his house.

．．．．．

"I don't get this." Colin leaned forward and gave Parker's doorbell a third jab. "If his car's in the garage, why isn't he answering the door?"

"He has to be here. The Phoenix guys didn't say he'd left when you called to alert them we were on the way and tell them Trish had authorized you to cancel surveillance." A bark sounded, and Mac glanced toward the volunteers with their cadaver dogs, waiting in the driveway with two police officers. "He could be in the woods out back."

"Possible. Why don't you get the dogs started while I walk the perimeter of the house?"

"You got it."

As Mac headed toward the dogs and their handlers, Colin began checking windows and doors. They'd break in if they had to . . . but he'd prefer easier access—and despite daily stories in the news about robberies, it was amazing how many people were lax about home security.

It didn't take him long to discover that the sliding door in the back was open.

Too bad other parts of the case hadn't been this simple to crack.

As he slid the door open, Mac ascended the deck stairs two at a time and joined him. "Dogs are dispatched."

"Let's see what we can find inside." Colin snapped on a pair of latex gloves and entered the kitchen. A quick sweep didn't reveal anything out of the ordinary—but he homed in on the plugged-in laptop sitting on the table. "I bet that will yield some incriminating evidence once our people get past whatever encryption he's rigged."

"Yeah." Mac pulled on some gloves too. "I've got the officers walking the woods to see if they can locate Parker while the dogs nose around. In the meantime, let's see what else we can find that might be useful. Why don't you go right and I'll go left." He indicated the hall off the kitchen.

"Works for me." As Colin moved forward, Mac pulled his phone off his belt.

"Hang on a sec. It's one of the handlers." His colleague put the device to his ear. "McGregor . . . Okay . . . got it. We're on our way." He slid the phone back into its holster. "Our bodies-buried-on-the-property theory just got legs. One of the dogs already has a hit."

"Seriously?" He'd expected the search to take hours.

"Yep. One of the officers spotted some disturbed ground, and the dog instantly alerted. The area around it has also been trampled—by multiple types of footwear, based on a few prints they found."

"I have a feeling the Mafia found the spot first."

"That doesn't bode well for Parker."

"Not if they decided he's Michael."

"Why don't you touch base with the officers scouting around for him, find out if they've seen any evidence he might be out there? I'm going to give Cal at Phoenix a call. I'm getting some unsettling vibes."

"Me too."

While Mac went out to the deck to call both officers, Colin punched in the number for his former County colleague.

Cal answered on the first ring. "What's up?"

"We haven't located Parker yet. Officers are searching the woods, but so far nothing. You certain he's on site?"

"He drove in yesterday after church and hasn't left since."

"Any other activity?"

"One visitor today in a satellite-service van. I ran the plates. The vehicle was legit."

"What time?"

A rustle came over the line. "According to the surveillance log, it pulled in at 12:52 and pulled out at 1:10."

"Give me what you have on the vehicle in case we need it."

Colin pulled out a notebook and jotted down the information as the other man spoke. "Got it. We'll keep looking around the property. Thanks."

As he ended the call, Mac returned. "I talked to both officers. They're covering ground fast and haven't seen any sign of Parker. He's also not responding to shout-outs. What did your guy at Phoenix say?"

Colin filled him in. "If we don't find Parker somewhere on the property, I want to track down that van."

"Agreed. I also called the ME's office. They're sending someone out to excavate."

"Let's get some additional backup out here now that we're pretty certain we have at least one body. We also need more eyes in the woods. It's possible Parker got scared and took off, but without the money in hand, I don't think he . . ." His phone began to vibrate and he pulled it out again. Frowned. Dispatch never called him directly.

He pressed the talk button. "Flynn."

"Detective Flynn, I have a caller on hold who insists on speaking with you. A Stan Hawkins. He says it's urgent. Do you want me to put him through or send him to your voicemail?"

If Trish's neighbor had made the effort to track him down, there had to be a good reason.

"I'll talk to him."

"Sir, Detective Flynn is on the line." The dispatcher exited the call.

"What can I do for you, Mr. Hawkins?" Colin fisted his free hand on his hip.

"Well . . . I don't mean to bother you, young man, but it seems to me there might be a problem over at Trish Bailey's house."

Colin's pulse picked up. "Tell me."

He listened as the man passed on his observations.

As soon as he mentioned the utility van, Colin's gut twisted.

Hard as he'd tried to keep Trish out of this, it appeared she was smack dab in the middle of whatever was going down between Parker and the Mafia.

"Okay. We're on it. Stay in the house and let us handle this."

"I intend to. That's why I called you. My days of diving into the fray are long gone."

Colin punched the end button.

"What's going on?"

Before he could answer Mac's question, his phone began to vibrate again.

Kristin.

Dread congealed in the pit of his stomach as he put the phone to his ear. "Trish didn't show for dinner, did she?"

"Hi to you too. And no, she didn't. I tried to call her, but there was no answer. I knew this case of hers was heating up, and since I didn't have a warm and fuzzy feeling about her being AWOL, I wanted to let you know. What's going on?"

"We don't know yet—but we're getting ready to find out."

"Good luck . . . and Godspeed."

"Thanks."

And as he ended the call, he had a feeling he'd need both God and speed to bring this case to an end without anyone else getting hurt.

■ ■ ■ ■ ■

"Your five minutes are up. What is your decision?"

As the Russian's words echoed in the room, Trish's heart stuttered.

This was it.

Despite Parker's attempt to do some fast talking, the Russian had silenced him each time with the same admonition.

"This is not open to discussion. You have five minutes. Be ready with your answer."

And now the moment of truth had come.

"You're asking me to play God! I can't do that."

"Then I will—and both of you will die."

There was the sound of movement—of weight shifting . . . or rising from a chair.

Trish tensed.

"No! Wait! How do I even know that's her, with the hood covering her face?"

If Parker's stall tactic was obvious to her, it had to be transparent to the Russians.

"Speak to him." The Russian gave the order, and a gun poked her between the shoulder blades.

"You know it's me . . . Matt . . . or Michael . . . or whoever you are."

"Ah. The lady herself is not convinced you are who you say you are. You have ten seconds to give me your decision."

Cold metal pressed against her temple.

Trish stopped breathing.

"Get that gun away from me!" A touch of hysteria hiked up the pitch of Parker's voice. Apparently he was feeling the pressure of a gun barrel too. "Okay. Fine. It doesn't make sense for both of us to die."

"You are choosing her?" The Russian again.

"Yes."

"Very well. Take her in the next room. I want no blood on my clothing." The Russian's tone was nonchalant. As if he was discussing the weather.

Bile rose in Trish's throat as she was pulled to her feet and propelled away from the scum that had invaded her home.

She stumbled down the hall, legs wobbling as the guy held her arm with a viselike grip and pulled her along beside him.

As suffocating panic locked her lungs, she tried to jerk free—but his grip was like iron.

Struggle was useless.

When the man stopped and pushed her to her knees on the floor, she knew she had no more than a few heartbeats to live.

God, please hold me close!

She braced . . . but all at once the drawstring was loosened and the bag was pulled off.

It took her a moment to orient herself in the sudden brightness. She was in the study that had become her bedroom after she'd returned home two years ago. A practical choice, allowing her to be close at night in case her mother needed anything. A small haven of privacy in the home where she had spent her childhood feeling loved and secure and safe.

Now it was the place where she was going to die.

The man masquerading as a satellite company employee leaned down, a strip of cloth in his hand.

Was he going to strangle her instead of using the gun?

But no. He whipped the strip around her head, forced it between her teeth, and secured it in the back.

He wanted her mute.

There would be no chance to plead for her life.

Or scream.

Tears pricked her eyes as she gazed up at him, but his black irises were as cold and merciless as a frigid winter night.

He shoved her back to sit on her heels . . . pulled the bag down over her head . . . tugged the drawstring tight . . . and barked out a loud word in Russian.

Muffled voices spoke. There was the sound of bodies shifting around.

"Say your good-byes, Parker." Spoken by the Russian who had pronounced her death sentence. "Unless you are having second thoughts?"

"No. It's . . . there's no other way. I'm sorry, Trish."

The Russian issued a command in his native language. There

were more shuffling sounds, as if people were changing position. Hard metal pressed against her temple, the cold seeping through the fabric and into her skin.

It was over.

She squeezed her eyelids shut.

Held her breath.

And prepared to meet God.

. . . . .

They'd killed Trish.

Despite the silencer, Michael flinched when the shot ripped through the air behind him as he retraced his steps down the hall to the kitchen.

This was a nightmare.

Oleg and his men cared nothing for innocent life. Retribution and vengeance were their priority. The Mafia's odd brand of honor and justice demanded that someone pay for traitorous acts, and it didn't matter who got hurt along the way.

But at least it hadn't been him.

And now that Dmitri had his pound of flesh, there was a chance he could still walk away in one piece. Claim the money that had to be in the accounts by now and disappear.

Maybe . . . just maybe . . . he'd survive this.

"We are finished here." As they entered the kitchen, Oleg's words boosted his hopes.

The man's bodyguard retreated to the back door, stepped out to look around, and gave a silent nod.

Oleg slipped outside and disappeared.

Trish's executioner came back in, gun drawn. "Get back in the van. One word, I pull the trigger."

His hopes of deliverance dimmed.

This wasn't over yet, after all.

He could balk at the order—but three against one didn't offer favorable odds . . . especially when all three were armed. Oleg might not have displayed a weapon, but he had one.

And the Russian lieutenant would be even less hesitant about using it than the guy who'd put the bullet in Trish's brain.

Michael did as the man instructed.

Once back inside the stuffy van, he retook his place against the wall, knees drawn up. The real driver was still there, emitting muffled groans through the gag.

"Shut up." The bodyguard kicked him.

He fell silent.

"I thought you said you were going to let me go?" Michael directed the question to Oleg.

The man ignored him as he scrolled through messages on his cell.

No sense asking again. His captor would answer when—or if—he chose.

Two silent minutes later, the front door opened. The guy who'd killed Trish slid behind the wheel, started the engine, and rolled down the driveway.

No one spoke again as they left the high-end subdivision behind and zoomed onto the highway entrance ramp.

Heading away from the city.

And as the miles rolled by, Michael had a sinking feeling that whatever Oleg's plans were for this day, the climax hadn't yet played out.

27

As Colin sped through the Monday rush-hour traffic, the Taurus's lights flashing, the siren screaming, his cell began to vibrate.

One hand locked on the wheel, he maneuvered around a car that had pulled off the highway barely enough to accommodate an emergency vehicle, yanked the phone from his belt, and held it out to Mac. "Answer this."

It wasn't much of a conversation on Mac's end, but Colin heard enough to get the gist.

"I take it the casual patrol drive-by we asked for was a bust."

"Yeah." Mac tapped the end button. "No utility van was visible from the front, like the neighbor said . . . but he's circling around to the street behind Trish's. He thinks he might be able to see the back of her place better from there."

"Her neighbor would have called if the van left."

"Unless he got distracted . . . or nature called."

That was possible. Patrol officers were watching the exit of the subdivision—now. But the van could have left before they arrived.

"Let's get a BOLO alert issued to cover all the bases."

While Mac took care of that piece of business, Colin moved over to the exit lane. In less than five minutes, he'd be able to scout out the situation himself.

But the drive into town from Matt's place had eaten up valuable time. Should he have had County street cops knock on the door?

No.

If this setup involved the Russian Mafia, as he suspected, they'd be way out of their league and might ramp up an already volatile situation.

The best option to avoid bloodshed was to go in quietly and take whoever was there by surprise. If that didn't seem feasible once they got on site, he'd bring in the SWAT team and let them storm the door.

The latter was a very real option.

That's why Sarge had the team on standby.

As Mac completed his call, Colin roared down the exit ramp and barreled toward Clayton Road. "Let's drive past the house first, see if we can spot any activity."

"Sounds reasonable. If everything seems . . ." He picked up the phone again and put it to his ear. "Okay . . . No, but stick close. Our ETA is less than five minutes." He ended the call. "The officer was able to get a clear view of Trish's garage and driveway from the backyard of the house behind. No van."

Colin squeezed the wheel.

Either they'd taken Trish with them, or their business here was finished.

He didn't like either option.

"If they're gone, there's not as much need for caution."

"The officer did say there's excellent access to the house from behind."

"That helps. I'll still do the drive-by, but if everything appears to be normal, I'll park on the other street and we'll go in from the back. Let's not assume Trish's house is empty."

"Trust me, I'm not."

Half a mile from the entrance to her subdivision, Colin cut the lights and siren, eased back on the accelerator, and entered the development like any normal visitor.

A slow drive past her house confirmed all was quiet. There was no sign of activity.

He looped around the maze of streets and parked behind the patrol car. The officer was standing by his door, shifting from foot to foot as he waited for them.

Colin beat Mac out of the Taurus and flashed his creds at the young, antsy cop who had *rookie* stamped across his forehead. "Any new activity since you talked to us?"

"No."

"Anyone home here?" He motioned toward the two-story Georgian house that backed up to Trish's.

"I don't think so. No one answered the doorbell."

"Okay. We're gonna take a look. If you see anything suspicious while we're in there, call us—and call for backup. Don't wait. Got it?"

"Yes."

"Let's do this." Colin tossed the comment to Mac over his shoulder and jogged across the manicured front lawn of the house behind Trish's.

At the end of the backyard, screened from Trish's house by bushy shrubs, he parted the boughs and peeked through. Mac did the same a few feet down.

After thirty quiet seconds ticked by, he glanced at his colleague. "I say we go in."

"Agreed."

"I'll take the lead." He pulled out his Sig.

Mac did the same.

They stayed in the shadows as long as they could, then sprinted to the house and flattened themselves against the brick walls.

Colin had no qualms about breaking down a door to get in. Trish wasn't likely to complain even if this was a false alarm.

But it wasn't.

He knew that deep in his gut.

Fortunately, he tested the back door before applying heel to wood—because the door opened with a quiet twist of the knob.

Bad news.

After all the warnings he'd given Trish about being cautious and keeping the house secure while she was inside, an open door was a major red flag.

Coupled with a visit from the same van Phoenix had spotted at Parker's place, this spelled trouble.

He motioned Mac to follow him inside.

Once in the kitchen, he paused. Listened.

Deathlike quiet seeped into his pores.

Whoever had been here was gone. He was 99 percent certain of that.

But much as he trusted his instincts, it was better to proceed with caution.

After bypassing the two chairs pulled out from the kitchen table, he motioned Mac toward the living room and dining room on the left of the foyer and crept down the hall on the right.

The sunroom was empty.

So was the bathroom—though the can of soda on the vanity seemed out of place. From what he'd observed, Trish didn't leave messes in her wake.

He edged around the door of her mother's room.

Empty.

That left Trish's room.

The only one with a closed door.

A tingle of apprehension skittered along his nerve endings, and he gripped his Sig tighter.

Bad vibes were wafting his way.

For an infinitesimal second he hesitated . . . but then he forced himself to walk forward. Putting off bad stuff didn't make it go away. He'd tried that after Neal died—and it had done nothing but delay the inevitable. In the end, he'd had to face the truth that his brother was dead and he was at least partly to blame.

He wouldn't stick his head in the sand this time—even if his faulty assumption that the Mafia would have no interest in Trish had led to dire consequences. Even if guilt would gnaw at his soul forever.

But please, God, don't put me through that kind of pain again.

The prayer came unbidden . . . and from deep within the recesses of his heart.

Sucking air into his balking lungs, he grasped the knob.

Swallowed.

Just do it, Flynn.

Gritting his teeth, he twisted the handle and pushed the door open.

. . . . .

They'd left the highway fifteen minutes ago. Now the van made a wide turn, throwing Michael against the utilitarian metal walls. As it bumped over uneven pavement, every jounce ricocheted through him.

From his position on the floor, the windowless sides of the vehicle rising up around him like the walls of a high-security prison, he didn't have a clue where they were.

But as the vehicle slowed . . . then stopped . . . it was clear they'd arrived at their destination.

The driver shut off the engine, and a few moments later the doors at the back swung open.

Once again, the man pointed his gun at him.

The same one he'd used to kill Trish.

"Get out."

Michael unkinked his stiff legs and scooted to the back of the van. Stood.

"Move a few feet that direction." The man motioned toward a small, abandoned warehouse.

As he complied, he assessed the location. Several similar structures in various stages of decay lined the pothole-littered road. It was clearly an area that had seen better days.

He had no idea where they were.

But the isolated location spooked him.

Big time.

As did the soot-gray Dodge Dart with dark-tinted windows parked nearby.

Oleg and his bodyguard got out of the van, and muscleman shut the door behind them.

"After you, Mr. Parker." Oleg swept a hand toward the closest structure and peeled off the latex gloves he'd been wearing since the first trip in the van. The other two guys did the same, tucking them in their pockets.

"If you want to talk, let's do it here." The notion of going into that dilapidated structure sent a chill through him—as did the black skies and ominous growl of distant thunder.

"You know . . . you are beginning to try my patience. We will talk inside. Either you will come on your own, or my associates will help you."

The two thugs edged in closer.

"Fine."

He walked past Oleg, fear congealing in his belly. Dmitri's deputy hadn't brought him here to have a casual chat. But they had their sacrificial lamb. This private tête-à-tête had to be about a different matter—and he'd do everything he could to use it to his advantage.

The inside of the building was dim, but the holes in the roof provided sufficient illumination to see the place was empty save for some piles of trash and a rodent that scurried for cover at the human intrusion.

"Move about twenty feet in . . . Michael. Or should I say Craig?"

His lungs froze, and his step faltered.

Oleg had figured out his identity.

But . . . that was impossible. There was no proof.

Keep up the pretense, Parker.

He rotated slowly. The Russian and the two sentinels flanking him were backlit in the open doorway, their faces in shadows.

"I told you I'm Matt."

"Yes, you did. And it was a lie—as was everything else."

"That's not true."

"Still playing games, Michael?" Oleg shook his head. "You have become tiresome. It is time to end this matter." He pulled out a compact pistol.

"Wait! I'm not Michael! Why do you think I am?" Panic choked his words.

"You did not pass the test."

The man's words were clear; his meaning wasn't.

"What are you talking about? What test?"

"We studied Matthew Parker. He was a good man. A selfless man. A man who believed in protecting and helping the innocent, no matter the cost to himself. Even if he was not guilty, given a choice between saving his own life or the life of someone he cared about, he would have chosen to sacrifice himself. That is how we knew you were not him . . . Michael."

They had him.

He could argue to his last breath, but Oleg wasn't going to budge. The Russian had the proof he needed.

And in truth, it was irrefutable.

Boy Scout that he'd been, Matt would have done exactly what Oleg had suggested.

But there had to be *some* way out of this.

At a nod from Oleg, the guy who'd driven the van moved off to the side, slid his gun into his concealed holster, and took out his phone. The bodyguard approached Michael.

No!

It couldn't end like this!

He backed farther into the crumbling structure.

"Look . . . I'll admit it. I'm Michael. And I made a mistake in Florida. I shouldn't have skimmed off the money. But I can repay it . . . with interest. I've transferred a sizeable amount of cash from Trish's charitable foundation to my own accounts. I can repay what I owe. In fact, I'll double or triple it."

"So now we are bargaining." Oleg sounded amused.

"I'm willing to work with you to make this right."

"This is not about the money."

Oleg signaled to the guard.

The man circled around behind him.

Michael watched him warily . . . but when he remained several feet away, he refocused on Oleg. "Dmitri would be happy to have the kind of money I can deliver." Not how he'd expected to use the foundation funds, but it was money well spent if it saved his life. "Why don't you ask him?"

From behind him, the guard grasped his arms and secured his wrists with a zip tie so fast he had no chance to resist. The next thing he knew, he'd been shoved to his knees.

"He is not interested in your bargains, Michael. By the way, I hope you enjoyed your shoes. You are paying a very high price for them."

At the non sequitur, he tried to switch gears.

Shoes?

The man was talking about *shoes*?

What did that have to do with . . .

He sucked in a gasp of air.

Natalie.

The bimbo had loved shoes. She'd mentioned once that friends bought her footwear. And she'd seen Elliott's credit card the night she'd come to visit. Since he hadn't offered to buy her any, she must have taken it upon herself to purchase some on his "friend's" behalf. She *had* called his attention to a new pair of shoes the night he'd picked her up for their dinner date.

That had to be what had happened.

And now he was going to die because of that tramp.

This wasn't fair!

"Listen . . . I'm sorry, okay? I'll do anything you want if you let me go. Why don't you . . . just tell Dmitri I got away. I can make you a rich man if you do."

"Loyalty does not have a price." Disgust mottled Oleg's voice, and he turned his attention to the guy who'd driven the car. "You are getting all this?"

"Yes."

Michael looked toward him. He was holding up his cell—and it was aimed toward him.

The man was recording this whole drama.

His confession . . . and execution . . . were being documented.

A slash of lightning zigzagged across the sky behind Oleg through the open doorway, followed by a crack of thunder that rattled the ground beneath him.

And as the bodyguard loomed in his peripheral vision and lifted the gun toward his head, Michael knew he'd finally run out of second chances.

28

"Mac! In here!"

As Colin barked out the hoarse words, he did a quick sweep of Trish's bedroom.

It was empty except for the woman lying on her side on the carpet, her back to him, her bound wrists and ankles zip-tied taut to the posts on the footboard of the bed. A drawstring bag was pulled over her head.

But he didn't need to see her face to know it was Trish.

And she wasn't moving.

No blood was visible—from the back, anyway—but there was no mistaking the bullet hole in the end of the mattress, above where she lay.

Behind him, Mac's footsteps pounded down the hall from the far side of the house.

"Call 911!" Colin shouted the command over his shoulder.

And as he knelt beside the woman who was fast becoming the center of his world, he prayed it wasn't too late for the paramedics.

* * * * *

Was that Colin's voice?

Trish tried to rouse herself from the pit of pain where she'd spent the past . . . who knew how many hours? Time had stopped ages ago—not long after the sharp pain in her temple had morphed into a constant, throbbing ache and she'd lost feeling in her hands and feet.

All at once the string around her throat loosened, and a moment later someone gently lifted her shoulders, eased off the black bag, and pressed cold fingers against her neck.

She blinked her eyes open and squinted at the fuzzy form above her.

It *was* Colin!

As he came into focus, she searched his eyes. They looked moist.

Or was that a mirage induced by her blurry vision?

His whispered "Thank God!", however, came through loud and clear.

He leaned closer and untied the gag, easing it gently from her mouth.

"Get her feet." Colin threw the taut order over his shoulder.

She couldn't see who he was talking to, but a few seconds later someone was cutting the restraints around her ankles while Colin worked on her wrists.

Only after she was free and he'd rolled her onto her back did he stroke an unsteady finger down her cheek and speak to her.

"Tell me where you're hurt—besides your face." His words came out raspy.

She tried to respond, but only a croak emerged from her parched mouth.

"Mac, would you get—"

"On my way."

The tall, dark-haired detective who'd visited her with Colin not long after her mom died stood and disappeared out the door.

In silence, Colin took her hand and held on tight. Less than half a minute later, the muted sound of running water drifted down the hall. Then Mac was back with a glass.

With Colin supporting her, she was able to sit up far enough to take several long drinks, the cool water a balm on her dry throat.

"Thank you." The words came out raspy, but they were intelligible.

"Now tell me where you're hurt." Colin's expression was somber as he gave her a thorough scrutiny.

"I'm not—except for this"—she held up her wrists and pointed to her ankles—"and my forehead." In the distance, the faint wail of a siren seeped through the exterior walls. "Would you help me sit up all the way?"

"It might be better if you lay back down until the paramedics check you out."

"I'm okay, Colin." When she tried to struggle up on her own, he gave her the assist she needed, settling her against the footboard. Feeling was returning to her fingers and toes, prickly and painful—but proof she was alive.

"Can you tell me what happened?" Colin stayed down at her level, resting on the balls of his feet beside her.

While Mac went to usher in the arrivals, she told him her story. As she neared the end, the other detective and two paramedics entered the room.

"You two can take over in a minute. I need to hear the rest of this." Colin waved them all in, never breaking eye contact with her. "Go on."

"After Parker and the others left, the guy who stayed with me took the gun away from my head and fired it. Then he tied me to the footboard. He said I was lucky to be alive, and that I should stay still until they left the house. I heard the door close behind him, and after a while I kind of drifted. The next thing

I knew, I heard your voice." Even as she recounted the tale, she couldn't make sense of it. "Why didn't they kill me? They said they were going to."

"I have no idea. Those types aren't known for mercy—and they usually have no qualms about collateral damage. But based on what you've told me, it sounds like they intended to keep you alive from the beginning. Otherwise, there would have been no need for a hood. Maybe the person in charge has some remnant of a conscience." Colin exhaled. "All I know is, it's a miracle you're still with us. One I'll give thanks for every day for the rest of my life."

He moved aside to let the paramedics take over, hovering within touching distance, his haggard face telling her she wasn't the only one who had gone through hell today.

But in the end, by the grace of God, heaven had prevailed.

. . . . .

She was going to be fine.

Colin leaned back against the wall in the ER hallway and drew in a long, slow breath. Trish's wrist and ankle abrasions would heal, and despite the purple bump on her temple, she didn't have a concussion. The doctor had signed off on her release and she was getting dressed.

Thank you, God!

Pushing himself upright, he exited into the warm twilight air to check messages again.

Mac had texted twice in the past thirty minutes.

Van spotted. Call me.

He moved on to the second message, left three minutes ago.

On site. Call me.

He punched in his colleague's number. Mac answered at once. "How's Trish?"

"No serious damage. I'm about to drive her home. What

have you got?" He could hear the sound of police radios in the background.

"Some underage kids—who I suspect were looking for an off-the-grid place to drink—stumbled across the van. They heard noise inside, and found the driver tied up in the back."

"He's alive?"

"Yeah. Another surprise. Anyway, that's not all they found. While they were waiting for the police to arrive, they wandered into an abandoned warehouse. Parker was there."

"*Not* alive, I assume."

"No. It was a typical execution-style shooting. The kids are pretty green around the gills."

"Any sign of our Russian friends?"

"Nothing apparent. I could use your eyes on this if you can get out here."

"I'll be there as soon as I take Trish home. Give me the location." He fished out a notebook and jotted down the information. Poking through a murder scene wasn't how he'd like to spend his evening—but this was his case. "Is the driver of any help?"

"No. They hit him from behind, and he was in and out of consciousness. He does remember hearing two voices, but neither had a Russian accent. Did Trish offer anything else that might help us ID these guys?"

"She gave me a description of the fake serviceman who came to the door, but he's the only one she saw. I expect he's a lesser minion who isn't on anyone's radar. That's probably why they picked him for that job. She also heard one voice with a Russian accent, but that's not going to help us much. Hank is at her house now. Maybe her visitors left behind some useful evidence."

"My money says they didn't. They came here to take care of a specific piece of business, covered their tracks, and left."

Mac was likely right. These guys were pros.

"Let's hope you lose that bet. I'll be there in less than an hour."

Ending the call, he returned to the examining room where Trish was dressed and waiting.

"Ready to ditch this place?" He took her hand and forced up the corners of his mouth.

"More than."

He led her to the car, aimed it toward her house, and filled her in on everything that had happened over the course of the day.

By the time he finished his update and made a quick detour through a drive-through Panera, he was pulling into her driveway.

"It's hard to believe all this actually happened—but those make it very real." She motioned to the two patrol cars and a CSU vehicle parked in front of the house.

"At least the worst is over. All that's left is the cleanup." He set the brake and angled toward her. "I'd stay for a while if I could."

"I know—and I appreciate the thought. But that cleanup you mentioned needs your attention more than I do tonight. I'll be fine."

He wasn't certain of that . . . but much as he wanted to stay, duty required his presence elsewhere.

"I spoke with the CSU tech. They'll be concentrating on the first floor, so you're free to wander around upstairs. They should be out of your hair in a few hours."

"To be honest, I don't mind the company. I think I'll do better for a while if there are people around."

"For the record, this person intends to be one of those people."

"That's what I was hoping."

He squeezed her fingers. "Sit tight. I'll get your door."

As he circled behind the car, Stan waved at him and hurried across the street. He was huffing as he drew close.

"Everything okay? I asked the officer at the door, but he wouldn't tell me a thing." He peered into the Taurus.

"Yes—thanks in large part to your call. Trish is hurt, but her injuries aren't serious. Hang on a sec." He continued to her door and helped her out, relieving her of the Panera bag and soft drink. "Your neighbor's asking about you."

When she stood and faced him, the older man's complexion lost a few shades of color.

"Oh my word!" He hurried forward and took both her hands in his. "Are you sure you're all right?"

"Yes. It looks worse than it is. Nothing some of your home-made ice cream wouldn't help fix."

"I'll churn a batch first thing tomorrow and deliver plenty for two."

Colin grinned. "I claim the second portion."

"I hoped you would. Expect me before noon." Stan gave Trish a gentle hug and retreated down the driveway.

"Nice man." Colin took her arm again and urged her toward the house.

"I can think of a nicer one."

"I might need some proof of that."

"I might give it."

"Hold that thought."

He signed the scene log a patrol officer at the door handed him, let Hank know they were on site, then followed her up the stairs to the second floor.

On the landing, he set the Panera bag and drink on a small table and turned her toward him, resting his hands on her waist.

"Now, about that proof . . ."

"What did you have in mind?" She looped her arms around his neck and smiled.

Despite the purple-hued lump on her forehead and the lines of weariness etched in her features, she was the most beautiful woman he'd ever met. How she was managing that flirty tone after all she'd been through, however, was beyond him.

Unfortunately, what he had in mind wasn't going to happen tonight. She was hurting and exhausted and suffering the aftereffects of her traumatic ordeal. What she needed to do was soak in a hot tub, eat the take-out food he'd insisted they stop for on the way here, and get some sleep.

"Let's try this for starters." He dipped his head for what he intended to be a simple, gentle first kiss.

But it turned into more.

Much more.

When he at last backed off, he was breathing as hard as if he'd just run a five-hundred-meter race.

So was she.

"Whew." She rested the uninjured side of her forehead against the curve of his neck. "If that's starters, I may need to rest up for whatever comes next."

Rest.

Right.

He needed to let her get some rest.

Summoning up every ounce of his willpower, he quashed the urge to kiss her again. "I'll give you until tomorrow at six. And dress up. I'm bumping up our official first date. But I'll call in the morning to confirm you're up for it."

"I'll be up for it."

"And I'll be counting the hours." He leaned down and brushed his lips over hers before descending the steps.

At the bottom, he looked back up at the woman he'd come so close to losing.

And as he smiled at her and turned to go, he gave thanks for all his tomorrows that would be brighter because of her.

EPILOGUE

It was a perfect October day.

The light was golden . . . the air was crisp . . . the leaves were strutting their autumn finery . . . and Colin Flynn was coming up her front walk.

Life didn't get any better than this.

Trish pulled the door wide as he approached. "Good morning."

He gave her the familiar heart-melting smile that told her even before he spoke how much he'd missed her during the hours they'd been apart.

"I'm early."

"I know."

"You were watching for me anyway?"

"Always."

He slipped inside, closed the door, and gave her a proper welcome.

"Now my day can start." He rested his forehead against hers. "Mmm . . . you smell good."

"New shampoo."

"Nope. It's all you. My favorite perfume."

"Very smooth."

"Very true." He draped an arm around her shoulders. "I see the realtor put the sign on the lawn. You're positive you want to sell the house?"

"Yes." She'd talked it through with him, sought his advice, but in the end he'd left the decision to her. "I want to start fresh. I'll always treasure my happy childhood here . . . but everyone I made those memories with is gone. Now the quiet, empty rooms just remind me of all I've lost."

"There could be laughter in these rooms again one day."

"I'll let a new family fill them with joy. I want to find my laughter somewhere else."

He squeezed her shoulder but didn't press.

That's how Colin was. He listened. He played the devil's advocate if asked. He posed smart questions. But he never pushed. Only when it came to joint decisions did he present persuasive arguments for his position.

And they were usually sound.

"You want to sit for a minute before we leave?" He motioned toward the living room.

She studied him. In the months they'd been dating, she'd learned to judge his moods from tiny nuances only a woman in love would notice—barely detectable changes in facial expression . . . subtle variations in inflection . . . slight alterations in body language.

Something was up today.

"What's going on?"

One side of his mouth hitched up. "We could use your intuitive skills during interrogations if you ever want to change careers."

"No thanks. The kids I teach are all the challenge I need." She nudged him with her elbow. "Stop evading my question."

"I have some news."

"Did you by chance find some evidence to incriminate the Russians who paid us a visit last summer?"

"No." His features tightened. "We're still trying, though."

But it wasn't going to happen. If there'd been any way to pin Michael's murder or her own trauma on them, this man and his colleagues would have found it by now.

She suspected Colin knew that as well—and that it would remain a thorn in his side. This was not a man who liked to admit defeat.

At some point, however, they were both going to have to make their peace with the frustrating reality and move on.

"Then what's the news?"

He took her hand and led her toward the sofa in the living room. Once they were seated, he pulled out a single sheet of paper.

"During our investigation, we had some conversations with Matt Parker's attorney. Once we were able to verify through DNA that both Parker brothers were dead, he executed Matt's will. This letter from him was with his papers. His attorney gave us a copy, and I thought you'd like to read it."

She took the single typed sheet he handed her and skimmed the contents.

The first section detailed the problems in Boston, which she already knew about.

But the last paragraph was news.

Based on our history and my brother's avarice, I wouldn't put it past him to come forward and try to claim my estate if anything should happen to me. For the reasons listed above, I want to be clear that he is not to get one penny of my assets. Every dime that remains after my estate is settled is to be donated to Habitat for Humanity. My father dedicated his life to building quality homes for people and giving them fair value for their money. I wish to continue his legacy by providing homes for people who might not otherwise be able to afford one.

Trish's throat tightened. "This sounds like Matt. He might not have been the man for me, but he was very kind and generous."

"The evidence certainly supports that. I thought you'd want to know that at least one positive result came out of the whole ordeal."

"Thanks for sharing this."

He took the letter, folded it, and slipped it back in his pocket. "Now let's put all this behind us for the rest of the day."

"I agree—but aren't Kristin and Rick going to be mad at you for skipping the every-other-Saturday Treehouse Gang breakfast so we can go on a picnic?"

"No. They love you almost as much as I do."

Love.

He'd begun tossing that word out casually in the past month, though he hadn't yet strung together all *three* magic words. But that was coming.

She hoped.

"Well, tell them I'll make it up to them. In fact, I'll invite them for homemade lasagna one night next week."

"Am I included?"

"What do you think?"

"I'll take that as a yes." He rose and held out his hand. "Let's go."

She let him pull her to her feet. "What's the rush? It's only ten o'clock. Isn't this kind of early for a picnic?"

"No." He tugged her toward the door.

"Okay, okay. I get the message you're in a hurry. Are you certain you don't want me to provide some of the food? I baked brownies last night."

"Save them for later. This one's on me."

A sudden buzz of excitement zipped through the air, and she studied him out of the corner of her eye.

Colin was the steadiest guy she'd ever met—solid in the face of danger, a rock in turbulent seas.

But he seemed unsettled . . . jittery . . . nervous . . . today.

She could think of only one thing that might unnerve her handsome detective.

And as she joined him at the door, activated the security system, and returned Stan's thumbs-up with a wave, a delicious trill of anticipation raced through her.

Maybe the day she had hoped would arrive sometime in the months ahead was going to come early.

. . . . .

The moment had arrived.

Colin crumpled the butcher paper his sandwich had been wrapped in, leaned back on his palms, and tried to rein in his galloping pulse.

No dice.

Despite the fact he'd been sitting on this blanket for more than half an hour, his heart was beating as hard as it did after an intense game of one-on-one basketball.

How nuts was that?

He carried a gun to work, for crying out loud. Put his life on the line day in and day out. Willingly walked into volatile situations that could—

"This is a beautiful spot."

He looked over at Trish sitting beside him on their hillside perch. She was drinking in the view of the colorful trees, lips curved up. Contentment softened the planes of her face, and the golden highlights in her light brown hair glinted in the noonday sun.

"I agree. The scenery here is beautiful."

She turned toward him, and he winked at her.

"Are you flirting with me?" Amusement twinkled in her eyes.

"Yep."

"I bet you do that with all the girls."

"Just the pretty ones—and you're at the top of that list. That's why you got lunch too." He nodded toward the wicker picnic basket.

"And what a lunch it was. Cheese plate, spinach-artichoke dip, crackers, chicken salad sandwiches, strawberries. You can take me on a picnic anytime."

"I'll keep that in mind."

"So what's for dessert?"

His pulse picked up again. No matter how certain a guy might be about the signals a lady was sending, when he was getting ready to pop the question, it was best not to take too much for granted. After all, he *was* sort of rushing this. Four months of dating wasn't all that long.

But at thirty-five, he knew what he was looking for in a woman.

And since Trish was it, why waste time?

He opened the basket, pulled out two gourmet chocolate cupcakes—each in its own plastic-domed container—and handed her one.

"Wow." Her eyes lit up at the confection decorated with shaved white and dark chocolate curls. "You definitely know the way to this lady's heart."

He hoped that was true.

"Before we eat these, I wanted to . . ."

All at once, the sun vanished, a rumble of thunder intruded on the bucolic tranquility, and a raindrop plopped onto his nose.

What the . . . ?

He checked out the sky behind him.

Dark clouds had encroached while they enjoyed their lunch . . . and unless he missed his guess, they were in for a serious deluge.

"When did *that* happen?" Trish assessed the heavens too. "I didn't think it was supposed to rain today."

"It wasn't—according to all those meteorologists who get paid the big bucks."

Another raindrop splashed onto his forehead.

This was so not how he'd planned this moment.

"We better gather up all this stuff and relocate to my friend's porch." He went into action as he talked, stuffing everything on the blanket back into the picnic basket with Trish's help.

By the time they had it all stowed, the sky had blackened even more and the rain was beginning to fall in earnest.

"Let's go." He picked up the basket, grabbed her hand, and sprinted toward the cabin.

They reached the covered porch mere seconds before the skies opened.

"You know . . . we could be stuck here for a while." Trish surveyed the downpour from under the sheltering eaves, then motioned toward the porch swing. "But that's a fine spot to sit. Very cozy. And those cupcakes will taste wonderful wherever we eat them."

"I like how you make lemonade out of lemons."

"Better than going around with your face all puckered up." She contorted her features into a sourpuss expression and nudged him with her shoulder.

The corners of his mouth flexed at her comic antics. Trish's ability to roll with the punches was one of the things he loved about her—and an ideal attribute in a future mate.

Time to get to the main item on today's agenda—rain or no rain.

"Why don't we swing for a few minutes before we dive into dessert?"

"You're going to make me wait for my chocolate?" She pretended to pout.

"There are other ways to satisfy your sweet tooth." He waggled his eyebrows.

"Hmm." She pretended to consider that. "Okay. You're on." She crossed to the porch swing and sat.

Colin glanced again at the steady rain. Maybe he wouldn't have the blue skies and beautiful panorama he'd envisioned as a backdrop for his proposal . . . but after working up his courage for the past two days, changing the program wasn't an option.

He fingered the small box in his pocket, joined her on the seat, and set the swing in motion with his toe.

"Don't worry about the rain." She scooted closer to him. "The sun is always shining in my heart when I'm with you."

"You stole my line."

"I'm glad we're on the same page."

"As a matter of fact . . ." His voice hoarsened, and he cleared his throat. "I'm hoping we're also in the same book."

She tipped her head, faint creases denting her brow. "What do you mean?"

"Stories are found in the pages of a book—and I'd like our stories to merge in the next chapter." He pulled out the small jeweler's box.

Her gaze dropped to it . . . and she went absolutely still.

"I know we only met a few months ago, but we're not twenty years old." He twined his fingers with hers and held on tight. "We're mature adults who have our priorities in reasonable order and enough experience to be clear about what we like and don't like. I knew almost from the day we met you were the kind of woman who comes along once in a lifetime—if a man is lucky."

He flipped up the lid with his thumb to reveal the budget-straining oval diamond the sales clerk had assured him any woman would love.

Based on Trish's gasp, the man's advice had been sound.

"So here's the bottom line. I could have waited a few more weeks—or months—to ask you this question . . . but I'm tired of going to bed every night wishing you were by my side and tired of waking up every morning alone. I want my days to start and end with you—the sooner the better." He took a deep breath . . . and spoke the words he'd been saving all his life for the special woman he'd hoped someday to find. "I love you, Trish Bailey . . . and I'd be honored if you would be my wife."

Her eyes began to shimmer, and when she spoke, a quiver rippled through her voice. "I love you too—and I can't think of any role I'd rather play." She held up her left hand.

It took him two tries to get the ring out of the box, and he fumbled it as he slipped the band on her finger.

But once it was securely in place, he rose and pulled her to her feet. "This calls for a kiss."

"We could have done that on the swing."

"Not like this." He wrapped his arms around her and pulled her close.

Very close.

"I see what you mean." She looped her arms around his neck and smiled up at him. "Ready whenever you are."

"On the count of three. One . . . two . . ."

Suddenly the sun peeked out from behind the dark clouds, bathing the rain-refreshed landscape in dazzling light.

"Perfect timing. *This* is the kind of ambiance I wanted for this moment."

"It must have been a passing storm." She locked her hands behind his neck like she never wanted to let go. "But I can weather *any* storm if you're by my side."

"Count on that . . . forever. Now—where were we?"

"Two."

"You sure you don't want to eat those chocolate cupcakes before I say the magic number?" He grinned. "We might be a little too distracted to eat after this."

"Chocolate has its charm . . . but it doesn't hold a candle to you, Detective Flynn. You can be my dessert any day. And I'll prove it. Three!"

She stood on tiptoes and tugged his head down.

"A lady who takes the lead." He could feel the whisper-warmth of her breath against his chin as he spoke.

"A lady who knows what she wants."

"I like that."

"Good. Because I'm done talking."

With that, she pressed her lips against his.

And as the mood shifted from teasing to tender . . . as the skies changed to blue and the sun shone warm and bright . . . as birds chirped a joyous chorus overhead . . . Colin gave thanks.

For unexpected blessings.

For a future brimming with promise.

And for this special woman who would fill his world with love and laughter and hope all the days of his life.

READ ON FOR A SNEAK PEEK AT IRENE'S NEWEST *Hope Harbor Novel*

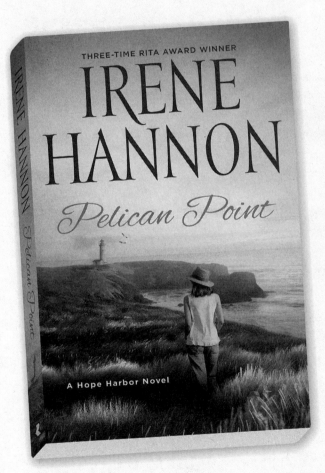

He'd inherited a *lighthouse*?

Ben Garrison stared at the dark-haired attorney, inhaled a lungful of the tangy, salt-laced air drifting in through the open window, and wiped a hand down his face.

No way.

Skip wouldn't do that to him.

It must be jet lag playing tricks on him. After all the flights he'd taken through multiple time zones to reach the Oregon coast, he was definitely in zombie land. And frequent changes in air pressure could mess with a person's ears, distort words.

At least he hoped that was the explanation.

Otherwise, this say-good-bye-and-take-some-time-to-decompress trip was going to turn into one gigantic headache.

Gripping his mug of coffee, he gave the view from the window a sweep. Usually the peaceful scene of bobbing boats in Hope Harbor's protected marina had a calming effect.

Not today.

Bracing, he refocused on the man across from him. "Tell me you didn't say lighthouse."

"Sorry." Eric Nash folded his hands on the round conference table and gave him a commiserating grimace. "I wish I could."

He closed his eyes and stifled a groan.

"I take it you weren't aware of this . . . unique . . . asset in your grandfather's estate."

"No." Ben took a long slug of his coffee, willing the caffeine to kick in.

Nada.

Too bad this brew wasn't as potent as the stuff they chugged in the forward operating base hospitals where he'd spent his days for the past seven years. He could have used a high-octane boost about now.

"It's the one on Pelican Point." The man motioned toward the north. "You might remember it from your visits. Your grandfather said the two of you used to walk up there in the evening."

An image of the fifty-foot-high weather-beaten lighthouse dating back to 1872 flashed through his mind—and despite the ache beginning to pulse in his temples, the corners of his lips rose.

Yeah, he remembered those walks. They'd been a nightly ritual during the summer visits of his youth. Fair skies or foul, they'd trekked from Skip's small house in town up the winding, rocky path to the lighthouse after dinner. The view was amazing, and the stories Skip had told about shipwrecks and danger and the steady beacon of light that guided frightened sailors home on stormy nights had stirred his youthful imagination.

But his grandfather hadn't owned the place.

And in the almost two decades since his last summer-break stay at age sixteen, Ben couldn't recall Skip ever mentioning it. Nor had the subject come up during any of his whirlwind visits through the years.

So what was going on?

"I have clear memories of the lighthouse—but how did he end up owning it?" Ben held tight to the ceramic mug, letting the warmth seep into his fingers.

"After it was deactivated and decommissioned by the Coast Guard three years ago, the government offered it to Hope Harbor. But the cost of restoring and maintaining the property was too high and the town declined. In the end, it was put up for auction."

Ben knew where this was heading. Skip had loved that lighthouse—and all it symbolized. Light in the darkness. Guidance through turbulent waters. Salvation for the floundering. Hope for lost souls.

"I'm assuming my grandfather offered the highest bid."

"He offered the *only* bid. It's been his baby for the past two years. The price was reasonable—as lighthouses go—and from what I gathered, restoring it was a labor of love. However, it was also a money suck. I'm afraid there isn't much of an estate left, other than his house and personal possessions."

"I didn't expect a lot, even without the lighthouse expenses." No one who spent his life mining the sea for Dungeness crabs got rich—except the big operators. And if the cost of restoring and maintaining the structure was too high for a *town*, it was amazing Skip had anything left at all.

Other than the lighthouse.

An albatross that now belonged to him.

The throbbing in his temples intensified, giving the pounding bass beat of a rock concert serious competition.

What in tarnation was he supposed to do with the thing?

"I'm afraid the lighthouse isn't in the best shape, either—despite your grandfather's efforts to restore it. Since his knee issues began, he hasn't been able to do much physical labor, and contractors charge a lot for that kind of work. Some people in town lent a hand on occasion, but progress was slow."

Tucking away the bad news that the lighthouse might be crumbling, Ben homed in on the other piece of information the man had shared. "What knee issues?"

The attorney cocked his head. "You didn't know?"

"No. In his emails, he always said everything was fine. We didn't often talk by phone, but whenever we did, he was upbeat."

"Maybe he didn't want you to worry, given the demands of your job."

Yeah. That sounded like Skip. His grandfather knew army surgeons working near the front lines had a high-stress, high-adrenaline, fast-paced lifestyle. They'd discussed it often. And Ned Garrison had never been the type to burden other people with his problems.

But Ben wasn't other people.

He was family.

And he owed Skip. Big time. Without those summer visits to look forward to after the acrimonious divorce that had rocked his childhood, who knew how he'd have ended up?

There was nothing he wouldn't have done for the man who'd been his lifeline.

Ben took another sip of the cooling coffee, buying himself a few moments to rein in his wobbling emotions. "Tell me about the knee issues."

"Your grandfather wasn't one to dwell on unpleasant subjects, but I understand he had bad arthritis and opted for a knee replacement not long after he acquired the lighthouse. An infection set in, requiring revision surgery. When that didn't work, a third surgery was done to insert a metal rod—which left him with a permanent limp and hampered his physical activities. He couldn't do much on the lighthouse anymore, so four months ago he decided to sell."

"Who was his surgeon?" Ben's jaw tightened. If someone had botched this job, they were going to be held accountable.

And why hadn't Skip taken advantage of his expertise? No, he hadn't done a lot of battlefield knee replacements—but he was an orthopedic surgeon, for crying out loud. He could have consulted on the case, vetted the specialist his grandfather had chosen.

Eric riffled through the papers in front of him and extracted a sheet. "Jonathan Allen in Coos Bay. I don't see a primary care doctor listed for your grandfather. He must have done what a lot of the locals do and simply visited the urgent care clinic in town for everyday medical needs. They may have recommended Dr. Allen."

"Thanks." Ben jotted down the man's name. Before he left Oregon, he intended to pay the doctor a visit and review his grandfather's medical records.

But it wasn't likely the knee procedure had anything to do with the massive heart attack that had felled him.

Swallowing past the lump in his throat, he shifted gears. "If my grandfather put the lighthouse on the open market, I'm assuming the town still doesn't have any interest in buying it."

"Correct. A few residents tried to stir up some interest, but the effort petered out. Even if the structure was in pristine condition, Oregon has a lot of lighthouses already—many much more impressive than ours—so it's not as if it would draw tourists who might contribute to the local economy."

Hard to argue with that logic—or fault the town for passing on the purchase.

"So a private buyer is the answer."

"If you can find one." The attorney didn't sound any more confident than Ben felt. "Your grandfather listed it with an agent, but I don't believe there have been any inquiries."

Of course not.

That would be too easy.

"I'll go up and look it over after I arrange the memorial service for my grandfather. Is there anyone in town who might be able to do a structural assessment?"

"My wife's an architect and runs a local construction firm." Eric rose, crossed to his desk, and pulled a business card from a drawer. "She went out before your grandfather bought it to give him her thoughts. She won't mind running up there again to reevaluate it." He returned to his seat at the table and handed over the card.

"Thanks." Eric pocketed it. "Is there anything else we need to discuss?"

"No. Your grandfather's estate was in order. Transitioning the assets will be simple. You have the keys to his house and car, and the paperwork's been signed. You're set." Eric pushed an envelope across the table. "This is the key to the lighthouse."

For a fraction of a second, Ben hesitated.

But there was no avoiding the truth.

He owned a lighthouse.

One apparently no one wanted.

Including him.

Heaving a resigned sigh, he picked up the envelope and rose.

Eric stood too and extended his hand. "My condolences again on your loss. Your grandfather was a wonderful man—and an asset to this town."

"Thanks." He returned the attorney's firm clasp.

"If I can be of any other assistance while you're here, don't hesitate to let me know."

"I appreciate that. But I don't plan to stay long." Or he hadn't, until he'd inherited a lighthouse. "Thank you for delaying our meeting a few hours."

"No problem. I know how hard it can be to maintain a schedule on travel days. With all the ground you've covered, you must be operating on fumes."

"I am." Hard to believe he'd been in the Middle East thirty-six sleepless hours ago. "I'm going to crash at my grandfather's house for a while until I feel more human."

"Sounds like a plan. The Myrtle Café is open if you want to grab an early dinner first. Or you could swing by Charley's on the wharf. You might have gone there with your grandfather as a kid."

"I did. Often." His mouth watered just thinking about the savory fish tacos the man concocted. A visit to Charley's was on his Hope Harbor must-do list—but not until he got some z's. He needed sleep more than food.

The attorney walked him to the door, and Ben exited into a steady drizzle typical of the Oregon coast in mid-April—or any month.

Tucking the paperwork the man had given him under his jacket, he hit the remote and jogged toward his rental car.

Fifteen seconds later, he put the key in the ignition. Hesitated.

Should he drive up to Pelican Point and pay Skip's folly a quick visit, or save that disagreeable task for later?

No contest.

Later.

He was fading fast—and the lighthouse wasn't going anywhere.

Unfortunately.

After checking for traffic, he pulled onto Dockside Drive. Maybe, as with the prophets of old, a solution to his dilemma would come to him in a dream.

And if it didn't?

He was going to be beating the bushes to find a buyer for his unexpected—and unwanted—legacy.

. . . . .

At the sudden peal of her doorbell, Marci Weber's fingers tightened on the tube of toothpaste, sending a minty-striped squirt arcing toward the mirror over her bathroom sink.

Who could be on her front porch at this hour of the night? No one in Hope Harbor came calling after eight o'clock, let alone ten fifteen.

Pulse accelerating, she dropped the tube onto the vanity, ignoring the sinuous line of goo draped over her faucet and coiled in her sink.

Rubbing her palms down her sleep shirt, she crept into the

hall, sidled up to the window in her dark bedroom, and peered down into the night.

Drat.

The tiny arched roof over her small front porch hid the caller from her sight, despite the dusk-to-dawn lights flanking the front door.

And the notion of going downstairs to get a better view from one of the front windows goosed the speed of the blender in her stomach from stir to puree.

No surprise there, given her history.

The bell pealed again, jolting her into action. She scurried over to the nightstand, snatched her pepper gel out of the drawer, and yanked her cell from the charger. Finger poised to tap in 911, she tiptoed back to the window, heart banging against her ribs.

Breathe, Marci. This is Hope Harbor. Bad stuff rarely happens here. They caught that teenage vandal who was getting his jollies destroying other people's property, and there haven't been any serious incidents since. You're overreacting.

True.

Nevertheless, she kept a tight grip on the phone while she waited for her visitor to vacate the porch and walk away.

But if he or she didn't leave . . . if her uninvited caller *did* have malice in mind . . . she had a first-rate alarm system that was already armed for the night, the Hope Harbor police would be here in minutes, and a faceful of pepper gel would stop anyone in their tracks.

She'd be fine.

Still . . . why couldn't Great Aunt Edith have chosen to live in the middle of town rather than on the fringes? The Pelican Point cottage might be charming, but the old saying was true.

There was safety in numbers.

AUTHOR'S NOTE

Launching a brand-new series is always exciting. I love introducing readers to a whole new cast of characters—in this case, three childhood friends whose bond has been strengthened by time . . . and danger.

I'd like to offer my deepest thanks to the following people who assisted me during the writing and production of this book:

Tom Larkin, former Commander of the St. Louis County Police Department's Bureau of Crimes Against Persons, who answered my many law-enforcement questions with promptness, thoroughness, and seasoned expertise. When it comes to expert sources, Tom is top-tier, and his input has always been invaluable.

The polished professionals at my publishing house, Revell, who are a joy to work with. Special thanks to Kristin Kornoelje, Jennifer Leep, Michele Misiak, Karen Steele, and Cheryl Van Andel.

My husband, Tom, who keeps our life running smoothly while I'm lost in my fictional worlds.

James and Dorothy Hannon, my mom and dad . . . and the world's best parents. Even though I lost my mom very suddenly a year ago, she is always in my heart.

And all the loyal readers who let me live my dream.

I hope you'll return for book 2 in the series, coming in October 2018. I guarantee Kristin's story will keep you up late at night! And next April, please return with me to my charming Oregon seaside town of Hope Harbor—where hearts heal . . . and love blooms. *Pelican Point* features an endangered lighthouse, Charley's famous fish tacos, and a memorable love story (or two!).

Irene Hannon is the bestselling, award-winning author of more than fifty contemporary romance and romantic suspense novels. She is also a seven-time finalist and three-time winner of the RITA award—the "Oscar" of romance fiction—from Romance Writers of America, and is a member of that organization's elite Hall of Fame.

Her many other awards include National Readers' Choice, Daphne du Maurier, Retailers' Choice, Booksellers' Best, Carol, and Reviewers' Choice from *RT Book Reviews* magazine, which also honored her with a Career Achievement award for her entire body of work. In addition, she is a two-time Christy award finalist.

Irene, who holds a BA in psychology and an MA in journalism, juggled two careers for many years until she gave up her executive corporate communications position with a Fortune 500 company to write full-time. She is happy to say she has no regrets.

A trained vocalist, Irene has sung the leading role in numerous community theater productions and is also a soloist at her church. She and her husband enjoy traveling, long hikes, Saturday mornings at their favorite coffee shop, and spending time with family. They make their home in Missouri.

To learn more about Irene and her books, visit www.irene hannon.com. She is also active on Facebook and Twitter.

"Hannon's novel promises to be a bestseller and classic. It's easy to see why people are falling in love with the characters of *Hope Harbor*."
—CBA Retailers + Resources

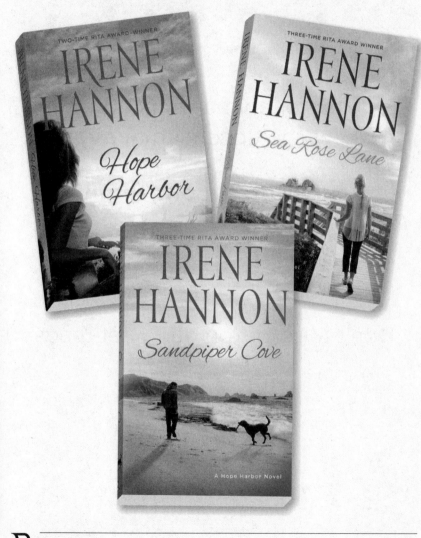